THE LOST AND FOUND GIRL

Also by Catherine King

Women of Iron
Silk and Steel
Without a Mother's Love
A Mother's Sacrifice
The Orphan Child

THE LOST AND FOUND GIRL

Catherine King

sphere

SPHERE

First published in Great Britain in 2011 by Sphere

A CIP catalogue record for this book
is available from the British Library.

ISBN 978-1-84744-387-8

Typeset in Bembo by Palimpsest Book Production Limited,
Falkirk, Stirlingshire
Printed and bound in Great Britain by Clays Ltd, St Ives plc

Papers used by Sphere are from well-managed forests
and other responsible sources.

MIX
Paper from
responsible sources
FSC
www.fsc.org   FSC® C104740

Sphere
An imprint of
Little, Brown Book Group
100 Victoria Embankment
London EC4Y 0DY

An Hachette UK Company
www.hachette.co.uk

www.littlebrown.co.uk

To the memories of Lester Dale Piper and Albert
Robin Piper

Acknowledgements

I should like to thank Betty Davies, secretary of the Friends of Rotherham Archives, for telling me about an old myth concerning twins, also Jean Grantham from Fareham Writers Group who is a qualified midwife and who verified the facts for me. My thanks are also due to Dennis Ramsbottom for introducing me to the wilder aspects of the Yorkshire Dales, and to his son Andrew who told me about the South Craven Geological fault.

This book would not be finished without the encouragement and support of my agent Judith Murdoch and the wonderful hardworking team at Little Brown, especially Caroline Hogg, Hannah Hargrave and Manpreet Grewal; my grateful thanks to all of you.

Catherine King

PART ONE

PART ONE

Chapter 1

February 1829

Beth dropped her bundle of belongings to the stone floor and shivered as she stood in the draughty church porch wearing her best bonnet and gown. She hugged her old winter cloak closely to her body. 'Is he here, sir?' she asked.

'Be patient, child.'

She hadn't been a child for years, she thought irritably. Thankfully, no one would dare to call her that after today. 'May I go inside?' she suggested.

The principal of Blackstone School scowled at her. 'You must wait here until he arrives.'

'But I am very cold, sir.'

'You'll do well to get used to it. It's a wild place you're going to.'

Beth did not mind the windswept landscape, but her journey to the Dales in an open trap had been long and tedious, and she was hungry. It can't be as bad as Blackstone, she thought. She had suffered the frugalities of poverty in that dreadful place for as long as she could remember and had prayed, four years ago when she'd reached fourteen, that the school would find her a position away from it. Instead she had been employed as a servant in the principal's home to 'learn to housekeep', he had told her. She had been considered fortunate by other girls in the school who had been sent to work as house- or nurse-maids in the homes of shopkeepers or tenant farmers. So Beth had not complained about the long days of servility with little time for reading or recreation.

At first she had been excited at the prospect of leaving the harshness of school life, although she missed the company of her friends. One had been special to Beth and they had corresponded regularly until she had received a note from her which read: *My mistress does not think it fitting for domestic servants to be writing letters. I am so sorry.*

Beth's life in the principal's house had been lonely and miserable, for Mr Barden was strict and believed in the strap for discipline. His wife and daughters were lazy and she had been at their beck and call from six in the morning until ten at night. Over the years they had taught her very little apart from how to cook, clean and mend. But they had given her one of their out-grown gowns to wear today. Although it was plain with long sleeves and buttoned to her neck, it had not needed to be repaired and it was, by far, the nicest gown she had ever worn. The plain grey did nothing to enhance her fair colouring but it was well cut and made her look like a lady's maid rather than a more lowly servant. She had fashioned a new collar and matching cuffs edged with her own drawn thread work and looked forward to removing her cloak for the ceremony.

However, in spite of the dreary routine she had left behind,

4

her new-found excitement had turned to nervousness as Mr Barden's trap had rattled along the rutted track, climbing away from the only life she had known, and across the moor until she reached this small stone church on the edge of the Yorkshire Dales. The bleak expanse of scrubland and rock did nothing to quell her anxiety.

She heard horses' hooves on the track and the churnings in her stomach started again. 'Is – is this him?' she asked. Her voice wavered. Would he be as cold and strict as Mr Barden? Or would he be pompous and overbearing like the school benefactors? She knew little about him except that he was nine and twenty and came from a sheep farm high on the fell. She straightened her chilled back and hoped that she would please him.

A clatter of a carriage following shortly afterwards caused Beth's heart to beat faster. It was really happening to her. In a short while she would be the wife of Edgar Collins and go with him to live at High Fell Farm. She heard the church-yard gate creak and moments later two people entered the gloomy doorway.

She recognised the woman as Edgar's mother who had visited Mr Barden to inspect her and ask about her demeanour and habits. Beth thought at the time that Mrs Collins had put on airs and seemed grand for the mother of a sheep farmer. But, although she had looked down her nose at Beth, she appeared to approve of her as a bride for her son.

However Beth soon realised that this initial condescension had not gone away. Mrs Collins wore black from her velvet cape to her full silk skirts and her dark eyes glittered as they travelled over Beth's cloak and bonnet. She did not smile. She turned her attention to Mr Barden and asked, 'Do you have the gold?'

'After the ceremony, madam,' he replied stiffly.

'I want sight of it before the vows.'

'Very well. Wait here for me, child.' He went outside with Mrs Collins, leaving Beth alone with her future husband.

Beth looked at him with a tentative smile on her lips. She had thrown back the hood of her cloak to reveal her cheap straw bonnet that she had decorated with evergreen leaves and grey ribbons. Tendrils of fair hair escaped around her pale face. They trembled in the draught and caught on her lips as she hovered in the chilly church porch. But her blue eyes were bright and she had a wide smile that showed off good cheekbones, even if it was too late to pinch them for a rosy glow.

He was taller than she, with the outdoor swarthiness of a country man, and he was dressed as gentry in old-fashioned breeches. His long jacket was cutaway to reveal a richly embroidered waistcoat. His tall hat stayed firmly on his head and he clipped his riding crop against high leather boots in a gesture that Beth took to be impatience. Beth's initial confidence in her appearance drained away as she realised that her dress did not match his in status. However she rallied when he murmured, more to himself than to her, 'Well, she's pretty enough.' But his eyes did not meet hers and, although he sounded satisfied, his face was grim and his mouth turned down at the corners. 'Come on, then. Let's get on with it,' he added and disappeared into the church.

As she listened to his boots ringing on the stone flags of the empty church, Beth did not know whether to follow him or wait for Mr Barden. For as long as she could remember she had been obedient to the orders of Mr Barden, his teachers and latterly his wife and daughters. Agreeing to this marriage had been the first time he had consulted her for an opinion of any kind, though it was made quite clear to her at the time that her answer would be 'yes' even without sight of her future husband. It was a good offer. He was a farmer and she was a nobody, a ward in chancery, a bastard child; but one with a settlement.

Beth had no illusions about this match. It was her dowry that enabled her to be married and she silently thanked her unknown benefactor for his generosity. There was no point in asking who he was for even the London lawyer did not know. He had provided a weekly amount for her education and lodging until she was eighteen and then a significant sum for a dowry. After today she would be off his hands for ever. At least, Beth thought, marriage would be better than life as a servant.

While she was deciding what to do, Mrs Collins swept through the entrance porch, past her and into the church. Over her shoulder she said, 'Bring the girl.' Mr Barden followed, took hold of Beth's elbow and propelled her through the door.

Beth walked purposefully down the aisle with Mr Barden by her side. She must not show her fear. She rehearsed the vows she had practised using her prayer book and the task took her mind off the anxiety bubbling in her stomach. There were no flowers, not even a winter arrangement, and the air smelled dank indicating the church was little used. The clergyman was talking to her future husband in a relaxed manner, as though they were acquainted. They were, Beth judged, of a similar age and they lapsed into silence as she took her place in front of him with Edgar Collins by her side and looked directly ahead. In the periphery of her vision she was aware that Mrs Collins watched keenly when they exchanged vows and Edgar slid a thin gold band onto her finger.

She gazed at it in awe, bright yellow and shiny against her pale skin. It was the first time she had been given jewellery of any kind and its symbolism overwhelmed her. She was no longer Elizabeth Smith. She was Mrs Edgar Collins. She was someone's wife and a part of his family. She had his name, a home, a position and the respect that went with it. Of course she was aware that she had new duties and responsibilities, but Blackstone had prepared her well to do her husband's bidding as mistress of his house. She would, with the help of his servants, keep his home clean and sweet smelling, wash and mend his clothes, provide wholesome meals and, of course, tend to all his husbandly needs. She wasn't very sure about the latter in spite of asking Mrs Barden, who had brushed away any discussion of the more intimate of her wifely duties.

Mr Barden was impatient to leave and said, 'She's all yours now, sir,' before turning to walk back down the aisle. Beth glanced sideways at her husband. He looked pleased and his mother too had a self-satisfied look on her sallow lined face. Relief flooded over Beth. They were happy with the match and she resolved to be a good wife. She put her hand on his arm, expecting him to escort her back down the aisle and out of the church to his waiting carriage.

He shook her off. 'Go with Mama. I am in need of refreshment.'

Well so am I, she thought. It had been a long time since her breakfast porridge.

Her husband smirked at the vicar. 'Come, Milo, we shall celebrate and look forward to the Lady Day shoot.'

The clergyman replied, 'This is only the beginning, Edgar. It pleases me to help a friend secure his future.'

'I have you to thank for everything: the girl, the ceremony

and the loan of your carriage for Mama. How shall I repay you?'

'There will be time enough for that when you are installed in the Abbey. All I ask is the living there. It has the finest rectory in the South Riding.'

They walked off towards the vestry without a backward glance at Beth and she wondered about the Abbey. Blackstone was on the edge of the South Riding and the only Abbey she had heard of was Redfern, for its coalfields spread across the Riding. Mrs Collins was already on her way out and Beth hurried after her. She watched Mr Barden carry a small box from his trap to Mrs Collins, who instructed her driver to secure it inside the carriage beside her feet. Beth's bundle of belongings, she noticed, had been stowed outside under the driver's seat. 'Goodbye, Mr Barden,' she said, and thought, Goodbye Blackstone. She heard, and then saw, a pair of hunters gallop away carrying the vicar and her husband, their travelling cloaks flapping as they rode.

Finally, Mrs Collins climbed into the carriage and settled her full black skirts across the plush. In the gloomy daylight Beth noticed that the silk was old and discoloured in patches. The lace too was worn and fragile. 'Hurry up, girl,' she ordered and Beth scrambled after her as the older woman rapped on the coach roof.

The carriage jolted forward and she waited for Mrs Collins to open their conversation. After several minutes of silence she asked, 'How shall I address you, ma'am?'

Mrs Collins's thin lips barely moved. 'Did Blackstone not teach you to be silent until your betters speak to you?'

'I beg your pardon, ma'am.'

They rode on without further exchange. Through the carriage window Beth realised they were climbing. The Yorkshire Dales

9

were considered beautiful by visitors. But that was in the sun of summer. In failing daylight they were brutish and threatening, the fells exposed to wild weather. The sight of deserted cottages with missing roofs and tumble-down walls was testament to the harshness of daily life. She guessed the former occupants had been driven out by poverty and the fierce winters of the hills to seek better wages in the towns. She supposed that's why the church no longer had a congregation or, it seemed, a vicar of its own.

Beth gripped her seat as the horses pulled the carriage up a rutted track. Mrs Collins sipped occasionally from a dull metal flask but did not offer any of the contents to Beth. A tot of spirit would have been welcome to relieve the cold. Finally, the older woman spoke.

'Your silence does you credit. Barden assured me you are well disciplined and I expect obedience without question. Do you understand?'

'Yes, ma'am, I have promised to obey my husband and I shall.'

Mrs Collins's nostrils flared and her mouth pinched. 'You will obey *me*, girl. I am the mistress of High Fell Farm.'

Beth's eyes widened and the turmoil in her stomach increased. Before today she had fretted only about becoming the wife of a farmer she had never met and feared he would be as hard a taskmaster as Mr Barden. Now she worried that she had to deal with this severe woman too. She said, 'I believe my first duty is to my husband, ma'am.'

Mrs Collins glared at her. 'And my son's duty is to me. I warn you, girl, do not presume to argue with me. My son does my bidding and so will you.'

Beth clamped her mouth shut. From her brief interaction with Edgar he had not seemed subservient to his mother.

10

But she supposed Mrs Collins indulged him his failures as mothers tend to do their sons. She wondered how much time to learn her new responsibilities Mrs Collins would give her. Not much, she concluded with a heavy heart.

Beth still had everything to learn about being a farmer's wife and the house at High Fell would surely be bigger and grander than any she had known. She supposed Mrs Collins would not trust her to take over the household affairs just yet. Perhaps Edgar would be her champion in times ahead and meanwhile she might need Mrs Collins's help and so she replied, 'Very well, ma'am.'

Her feet and hands were frozen by the time she reached her new home. Dusk was falling and the grey stone walls of the farmhouse looked austere and forbidding in the failing light. It was bigger than Mr Barden's house, though not as large as she'd imagined. Mrs Collins supervised the unloading of her strongbox. 'Take that straight up to my bedchamber, Roberts, and tell your wife to see to the girl. I shall rest for an hour and then take dinner.' She swept past her driver and through the iron-studded front door.

Beth picked up her bundle and followed her into a large entrance hall with a high vaulted ceiling and a wide wooden staircase leading to a galleried landing. Mrs Collins had already climbed the stairs and she didn't look back as she disappeared along the dark landing. At one end of the hall, an ornate marble mantle surrounded a paltry fire burning in the grate. A table was set for dinner before it. Beth was so enthralled by her new home that she did not notice where the driver had gone and found herself alone. Hungry and thirsty, she walked across the stone-flagged floor and took an apple from a pile on a metal plate and bit into it with relish.

'*Don't let the mistress see you do that.*'

Surprised, Beth swung round to see an older woman carrying a lighted lamp and wearing an apron over her gown. 'Whyever not?'

The woman frowned, lifted her chin, looked down her nose and answered, 'Dessert is eaten from a plate with a fruit knife.'

'Oh.' This must be Mrs Roberts. Beth recognised the woman's disdainful tone as one used by Edgar's mother and, she presumed, learned from her. 'Are you my housekeeper?' she asked.

The woman's neck stiffened. 'I am Mrs Collins's housekeeper.'

'I am Mrs Collins,' she explained patiently.

'You are not my mistress.'

Beth decided to ignore her disrespectful attitude and speak to her husband about her later. Until yesterday she had been a housekeeper herself and would have been soundly chastised for such a response. However, she considered that charm was the better part of valour and managed a smile. 'This must have been a busy day for you.' She stretched out the hand that held her bundle. 'Will you show me to my chamber?'

Mrs Roberts did not take the bundle; nor did she return Beth's smile. 'It's at the east end of the landing, overlooking the backyard. You'll find hot water in the kitchen. As soon as you've washed I need you to help with dinner.'

This was too much and Beth hoped she did not show her mounting anger. Perhaps she should speak to her husband now? It was not that she minded the work, even on her wedding day. Mr Collins was a farmer and she expected to be involved in domestic tasks. But this woman's insolence needed checking. He had left church on horseback so he ought to be home. 'Where is my husband?' she demanded. 'I should like to see him now.'

'Don't ask me. Dinner is on the hour. I'll need help before then, or we'll keep the mistress waiting.' Mrs Roberts turned her back and walked away. Her footsteps echoed in the cavernous hall.

Astounded afresh by the housekeeper's rudeness, Beth watched her disappear through a door. After a few seconds, she gave an exasperated sigh and followed her. The kitchen was low-ceilinged and three times the size of the one she had worked in before. It was warm. A cooking range of blackened hotplates, bake ovens and water boiler took up one wall and a dark wood dresser stood opposite. A large deal table took up the centre space. She was in time to see her housekeeper go outside and close the outer door behind her. Beth finished her apple slowly wondering why, apparently, no one had told Mrs Roberts about her. She drew a jug of hot water from the brass tap in the boiler next to the fire grate and struggled with it and her bundle up the stairs.

There was only one east chamber but it couldn't possibly be hers as it was far too small for the mistress of the house and sparsely furnished. She dropped her bundle on the narrow bed and went back to the main landing but all other doors were locked. Puzzled, she returned to the small chamber, sat in a wide chair by the empty fireplace and determined to make the best of it. She had many questions for her husband when he arrived and undaunted she took off her cloak and prepared to wash.

Sitting in front of a small spotty looking-glass to tidy her hair, Beth reflected that Edgar had said she was pretty. Well, 'pretty enough' were his actual words. Pretty enough to marry she supposed, even though she was aware he would have wed her if she had not been pretty. She smoothed back her thick fair hair and thought she would buy combs and

13

ribbons so that she could be more adventurous in the way she pinned it up. She wondered what clothing allowance he would give her and where she might go to spend it.

The market town of Settle was not far away, though the road was rocky and steep and the carriage had had to negotiate a narrow stone bridge with great care. A carriage went from Settle to Skipton and the post from there could take her to Leeds. She dreamed for a moment of visiting drapers' shops she had only heard of. Until she had a new Sunday gown, the one she was wearing would have to be kept in the cupboard for best and her old housekeeper's gown used for everyday. However, she resolved to strive to always look as pretty as today for Edgar and pinched her cheeks to raise a little colour.

The sound of horses' hooves on the farmyard cobbles sent Beth scurrying to the window. A rider appeared in the twilight and his dark cloak flapped as he reined in his horse. Steam streamed from the horse's nostrils and there were flecks of white in its sweating flanks. Edgar, she guessed. Neither he nor his mother had made any effort to welcome her so far. A shiver of apprehension ran down her spine. She was his wife now and nothing could change that so she had to make the best of it. Surely life at High Fell Farm could not be any worse than at Blackstone? Could it?

'Roberts!' her husband yelled as he slid from his horse and left the reins trailing. Roberts came hurrying into the yard to stable the horse. Edgar was home and this really was the beginning of her new life as a wife. She took one last glance at her appearance, turned down the lamp and went out onto the landing to wait for him at the top of the stairs. She stepped forward from the shadows as he reached the top step.

'Good God, girl, you gave me the fright of my life!' He raised the lamp he was carrying to light up her face. 'What the blazes are you doing lurking up here? Shouldn't you be helping Mrs Roberts?'

As he moved closer she could smell strong drink on his breath. Of course he needed spirits to keep warm when he rode out on the fell. She bent one knee and bowed her head deferentially, then gave him her widest smile 'I – I was waiting to – to greet you, sir.'

'You were?'

Clearly he was taken aback. He looked from her to one of the wide wooden doors on the landing and back to her with raised eyebrows and his mouth widened into a lascivious grin.

'I had not expected a Blackstone girl to be so eager for the bedchamber.'

As she realised what he was thinking a blush rose in her face and neck and she protested, 'Oh no, sir! I mean, sir, I mean I—'

'That comes after dinner,' he interrupted with a smirk. He moved the lamp closer until she could feel the heat on her flushed skin and then he trailed the flexible tip of his riding crop over the bodice of her gown, tracing the curves of her breasts and waist. She tried to maintain her smile but could not. 'At least you're something to return home for.' His eyes glittered harshly in the same way as his mother's and another shiver of apprehension trickled down her back. Then suddenly he gave her bottom a quick swipe with his crop. 'Off you go to the kitchen, then,' he ordered and, rattling a key, disappeared into his chamber.

15

Chapter 2

He hadn't hurt her, but he had shaken her already jittery nerves. She was aware of how little she knew about a gentleman's needs and how unsure she was of her household responsibilities. It was several minutes before she was composed enough to go downstairs and into the kitchen. She welcomed the opportunity to learn her household's routines and resolved not to upset Mrs Roberts further by introducing her own ways too soon. In any case, she had to be sure to meet Edgar's expectations of how his home must be managed.

He did appear to be devoted to his mother and probably wanted her to run his household in the same way that she had. Also, this was a gentleman farmer's household and different from Mrs Barden's aspiring but frugal ways. Beth was uncertain what the future held for her, but optimistic that she would be able to adjust. She resolved to watch and learn to fit in as best she could. When she was more settled in her role she might suggest changes, although even as she thought of this she realised that Mrs Collins was not likely to be a woman who considered change easily.

As she walked down the old wooden staircase to the cavernous hall she saw Mrs Collins sitting at the head of the dining table with a place set, presumably, for Edgar on her right and one for Beth on the left. She hurried past her, bobbing a curtsey as she did, and went into the kitchen, not quite knowing what to expect.

Mr Roberts was sitting at the table drinking from a metal tankard and his wife was slicing at the cooked and drained leg of mutton and piling the chunks of steaming meat onto a large oval platter.

'Not before time,' she muttered without looking up. 'Take the meat in and come back for the potatoes and turnips. Offer them to the mistress first and then Master Edgar.'

She was to wait at table! She had done this at Blackstone when the Board of Governors had visited and knew how to present the food so that those at table may help themselves. Edgar had joined his mother at the table. Beth, grateful at least to be doing something that pleased surly Mrs Collins, stood patiently, holding hot dishes while her mouth watered. She placed the serving dishes on a sideboard to fill her own plate later. After her third journey with a sauce boat of thick onion gravy, Edgar emptied the stoneware ewer of ale into his metal tankard and brandished the heavy jug at her.

'Re-fill this before you sit down,' he ordered.

She made a final trip to the barrel in the scullery. There was no sign of a scullery maid and Roberts and his wife were already sitting at the kitchen table eating their dinner as she hurried past them carrying the full ewer. When she sat down at the third place set at the table Beth was so

17

hungry she would have eaten boiled rat if it had been set in front of her. She had taken liberal helpings of food not caring if they thought her greedy and filled her own metal tankard to the brim.

Neither her husband nor his mother noticed; or if they did, they did not comment. Edgar was too busy with his own food. He ate well as she would expect of a country gentleman who spent his time outdoors. His mother took less and finished before either of them. Beth thought Mrs Collins might take the opportunity to open a conversation but she merely watched her son without expression. Eventually he dropped his cutlery with a clatter and pushed his plate away.

'When will you be ready to leave, Mama?'

'The horses should rest. We shall set off the day after tomorrow.'

Edgar looked cross. 'They do not need a whole day. My hunter thrives on a good gallop and Milo's carriage horse is strong.'

'But I am not,' his mother argued.

Edgar looked as though he did not believe her. Neither did Beth for, in spite of her advancing years, Mrs Collins seemed physically strong. Beth guessed than she had not led her ladylike life for all her years.

'Besides, Milo is kicking his heels in Settle waiting for me.'

'And is he more important to you than I?'

'Of course he is not, Mama. But we owe him, both of us. After all, he told us about the girl's dowry.'

Beth considered briefly how Milo knew about her. Mr Barden had consulted the vicar at Blackstone about her future and she supposed Milo, as a fellow clergyman, was acquainted with him. Certainly, this match had happened quickly after Mr Barden had informed her that she must marry or be sent out to find paid work.

Edgar continued. 'You have Milo's carriage at your disposal. Roberts will drive you and bring you back.'

'Will you not need his carriage for your journey to Leeds?'

'We prefer horseback. It's quicker.'

'Shall I accompany Mrs Collins to Settle, Edgar?' Beth asked. If she were to ride in a carriage she ought to have a more presentable cloak and a market town would surely have a draper or gown-maker.

Mother and son turned to stare at her with similar looks of surprise. Edgar picked up his empty plate, handed it across the table to her and said, 'Your work is here. Clear these pots and bring in the pudding.'

She took his plate automatically and wished she hadn't. He was effectively dismissing her from the table and the conversation. She stacked it on her own plate in front of her and Mrs Collins added, 'Did they teach you nothing in the Barden household? Do that on the sideboard.'

Her son responded. 'A manservant would know better how to behave. He would be of greater use to me, Mama.'

Beth pressed her lips together to prevent a retaliation. They were not so grand that they could afford a footman to wait at table. Silently she cleared the table of dirty pots and carried them out on a heavy wooden tray that she deposited thankfully on the kitchen table.

Roberts was already eating his pudding. His wife took one look at the laden tray and snapped, 'Take those straight into the scullery.'

She stacked them in the shallow stone sink and returned to collect the pudding. She felt Edgar's eyes on her the whole time she unloaded the tray onto the sideboard. She served the pie as she had done the meat, holding the heavy dish in front of them while Mrs Collins and then Edgar helped themselves. She had placed a jug of cream on the table but when she came to pour it on hers, the jug was empty. She sighed and rose to her feet to fetch more, only to be stopped by Edgar's mother.

'For heaven's sake, girl, be still,' Mrs Collins said irritably.

Beth looked down and tried to quell her anger. She was not a girl. She was Edgar's wife and deserved to be addressed with the dignity that her position deserved. She took courage from that and said, 'My name is Elizabeth, Mrs Collins.'

Mrs Collins pursed her lips and flared her nostrils but did not answer. Edgar glared at her and said, 'Be quiet.'

Beth glared back. 'I shall not. I am not a servant, I am your wife.'

'And you will do well to remember that,' Mrs Collins snapped. 'You have my son's name and his home for shelter. It is more than you deserve as an orphan of questionable breeding.'

Beth was hurt by this. She did not know who her mother and father were but they had provided for her education and she protested, 'One of my parents must have had a family with means.'

'And neither of them wished to own you!'

The hurt turned to insult, but curiosity for knowledge of her family overcame her emotion and she asked, 'Were you acquainted with them, madam?'

'That is enough! You at least should be aware that girls like you are best considered as orphans.'

Beth stifled a sigh. They didn't know any more than she, or indeed Mr Barden. She wondered what Mrs Collins might do to her if she ignored her demands. Take her back to Blackstone? She hardly thought so for Mr Barden would want the dowry back and how would she pay for Edgar's manservant then?

Beth did not begrudge them her dowry for it would never have been hers to spend anyway and the farmhouse obviously needed an indoor servant to fetch and carry. Edgar had not answered her when she had asked him about their forthcoming journey. But there would be time enough to speak with him about her wardrobe when they were alone tonight. Beth felt the colour rise in her cheeks at this thought and she began to feel nervous again. She wanted to get it over with so she would know what Edgar expected of her.

Edgar noticed her discomfort. 'See, Mama, she has humility.' He continued to look at her, his eyes darting back and forth as he took in her appearance and added, 'I think I'll go straight to my chamber after dinner.'

'But Edgar, I want you to read to me tonight.'

'It is my wedding night, Mama.'

'My dear boy, your marriage is a necessary inconvenience. You do not have to treat her as your wife.'

'Milo says I must lie with the girl for the marriage to be lawful.'

Beth expected Mrs Collins to admonish her son for such conversation at the dinner table. Instead she turned down the corners of her mouth and said, 'But no one will question her and we have the dowry. Surely there is no need?'

Beth looked from mother to son astounded by this exchange. Neither even glanced in her direction, and continued speaking as though she were not present.

Edgar sounded impatient. 'This is a legal necessity, Mama. I do not take pleasure in going against your wishes but I shall do my duty no matter how distasteful.'

Beth could not stay silent any longer and gasped, 'Sir, you offend me!'

Edgar scowled at her. 'And your interruptions offend me. If you cannot be quiet, I shall be obliged to beat you.'

Beth was horrified. She had done nothing to deserve such chastisement and she responded firmly. 'I am not a servant, sir. I am your *wife*.'

'You are a nobody,' he said. 'Be satisfied with your situation here. I have my duty and it is to take my rightful place in society. That does not include you.'

'Indeed it cannot,' Mrs Collins added. 'She has no breeding so we must find reasons to keep her hidden.'

'I shall need to tell his lordship about her at some point, Mama.'

His lordship? Beth hid her surprise and lapsed into silence to listen.

'Not unless he asks and he has not even met you yet. The lawyers' letters have secured an invitation for the shooting only. Make sure that his lordship notices your excellence in the field.'

'They have told him who I am. He will surely wish to speak with me.'

Mrs Collins appeared doubtful. 'He has stubbornly refused to acknowledge me, and my mother was his sister. You must be sure to note carefully where he places you at the dinner table. It will indicate his thinking. Speak only of the day's sport.'

Beth kept her eyes on the table. Mrs Collins was the niece of a lord? No wonder she had so many airs about her. 'Surely there will be ladies present?' Beth queried lightly. 'They may have little experience of sport.' Her intended irony was lost and rewarded only by impatient glances. She was not deterred and went on, 'A wife's presence is desirable on such occasions.'

'Don't be ridiculous! You would be an embarrassment to my son. You do not have the accomplishments of a gentlewoman.'

Then why, she thought, did Edgar not choose a different bride? Sadly, Beth realised, a gentlewoman with such capabilities, from a family with status and means, would never have considered a match with a Dales sheep farmer.

'I have been schooled to be a dutiful wife, ma'am. I should not disgrace him.'

'Your mother's behaviour brought disgrace to her family. I shall not risk you bringing the same to mine.'

At the mention of her mother, Beth forgot her growing dislike of Edgar and became anxious. 'Then you do know who my mother was, ma'am?' she asked.

'Of course I do not! Nor should I wish to. One of your parents may or may not have been well-born. I *know* that *my* grandfather was a lord and one day my son – my son will—'

'Mama! Not in front of the girl.'

Mrs Collins tried to compose herself. 'No – no, of course not. Perhaps she should take her meals in the kitchen.'

Beth blinked as she absorbed this knowledge of Edgar's family and addressed him. 'Is this true, sir? Your great-grandfather was a lord?'

Mrs Collins was unable to conceal her agitation. But, Beth realised, it was not wholly because of her presence. The older woman's eyes were glassy and a fleck of spittle had gathered in the corner of her mouth. It was Mrs Collins's own kin who were causing her such distress as she muttered, 'If it were not for my mother's foolishness I should be moving in the highest circles in society. My son will not suffer as I do.'

Beth wondered who their aristocratic ancestor was. She considered that if Edgar was truly related by birth, the fact that he had little money ought not to make a difference to his being accepted by them, unless the family rift ran deep. Beth became curious about his errant grandmother's behaviour.

Edgar ignored her question about his ancestor. Mrs Collins stood up and said, 'I am tired. It has been a long day and I have to prepare for Settle.' She appeared to be talking to the air above Edgar's head and added, 'While you are away, the girl will eat in the kitchen with Roberts and his wife. They will show her everything she needs to know to fill her days on the farm.'

Beth rose to her feet and picked up her pudding plate to place on the sideboard. She cleared the other pots and waited by Edgar's chair for him to drain his tankard. As she took it from him, he leaned towards her and she felt the palm of his hand run up the back of her leg under the edge of her drawers until it found the naked skin of her thigh above her stocking and garter. He pinched the flesh making her jump and she almost dropped the tankard.

'Finish your chores and go to bed. Wait for me in my chamber,' he murmured.

Beth padded along the landing to Edgar's bedchamber in her felt slippers, wearing her new nightgown and robe. She had made them all herself from grey flannel but had had no lace and very little time to spend on adornments. Inside, she wandered around with her candle gazing at the wood-panelled walls, commodious cupboards and chests of drawers.

There was easily room enough for both of them and she resolved to tell Edgar so in the morning. She crossed to the leaded window that overlooked the approach to the farmhouse and fingered the heavy curtains made from the same woven tapestry as the drapes hanging from the bedposts. There was a small fire in the grate. She hoisted herself onto the bed and wondered whether to climb inside.

She decided not. Earlier, Edgar had made a wrong assumption that she was eager for this aspect of her marriage. If the truth be told she was as anxious of what was to come as she had been standing in the draughty church porch waiting for her first sight of him. Hastily, she jumped down and sat on the upholstered couch at the end of the bed. If only she knew more of what to expect. She yawned and pulled at several pins holding the coils of her abundant fair hair, letting it fall in waves over her shoulders. Her head drooped. It had been a long day and she, too, was tired.

The door opened, banged against the wall and a cold draught rushed into the room. Beth twisted around swiftly to see Edgar sway against the jamb. She shivered and pulled the edges of her robe together. She welcomed its warmth and serviceability but realised it did nothing to enhance her appearance.

Edgar sat down heavily on the bed, flopped backwards and stuck out one of his feet. 'Well, girl, come over here and take off my boots.'

When she did so without question he sat up and watched her, slowly unbuttoning his jacket and waistcoat. Her hands shook as she placed his riding boots in the hearth and heard him say, 'You've not done this before, have you?'

'Of course not, sir!' She was shocked he even considered such a wicked thought of her.

25

'Of course not, sir,' he mimicked her innocent tones and warned, 'I hope you are truthful as well as a maid.'

Nervous, she replied hastily, 'I am, sir!'

He found this amusing and stood up to remove his clothes. 'Take off that nun's habit and get into bed.'

She supposed he meant her dressing robe because she agreed with his description of it and obeyed him as swiftly as she could, hiding her voluminously swathed body under the bedding. Her heart thumped in her breast as she waited. He had his back to her as he pulled on his nightshirt and she gazed in fascination at his male form, broad and muscular with lean buttocks that were smaller than she would have imagined – if her thoughts had ever strayed in that way. She began to tremble slightly, but it was from fear rather than excitement. She hoped he would be kinder in this aspect of their marriage than his manner towards her so far had indicated.

'Every night when I am home, when I tell you to go to your chamber,' he said as he climbed in beside her, 'you will wait for me here, like this, in my bed.'

He half crouched over her, breathing heavily. She could smell brandy on his breath and waited for him to kiss her but he didn't and a mixture of other aromas crowded her senses: sweat and wet wool from his body, stale food and tobacco on his breath. His chin had produced stubble since the morning and some parts of his unclothed body were covered with dark hair.

He pushed her nightgown up around her waist, did the same with his own nightshirt, and straddled her body on his knees. He seemed to tower above her for a few seconds before it happened. Then suddenly he was lying on top of her, her face was muffled by the coarse hair on his chest and his weight forced the breath out of her body. One of his knees pushed her thighs wide apart and he was prodding and poking her private area with his – not his fingers, for his hands were moving underneath her back to lift her towards him as this hard – hard *thing* – jabbed and poked at her softness. Instinctively she shrivelled away from him trying to shrink into the soft feather mattress. But he would not let her. She was held against him by one of his arms while his other hand descended to her private area to push aside her flesh and guide himself into her. It wouldn't go in. Why wouldn't it go in? She had seen animals do this in the fields and it should be easy. Something must be wrong. She tensed against him hoping he would stop. But he did not. He pressed her body against his and rammed into her until she yelped with pain and he was inside her.

He had really hurt her and she suppressed a cry in her throat. He was such a heavy weight on top of her and this – this hard thing inside her was rough and large. The hurting continued. Surely this is not how it is meant to be? She stared wild-eyed at the darkness. It felt as though he was tearing her flesh apart as he pushed and shoved at her. His rutting became more frantic, increasing her soreness. He began to grunt like a pig until he let out a strangled groan and arched away, putting a strain on her back as he did. She yelped again and realised that this was far too painful to continue. She must insist that he stop. But she did not need to. He let her go and flopped forward smothering her face with his sweaty hairy chest.

He was still inside her and she felt a pulsing sensation. The hardness melted away but her flesh was stinging. He lay motionless on top of her for quite a few minutes before she heard a snore, and then another as he drifted into sleep.

She was trapped beneath his heavy body, hardly able to breath with a hurting back and a sore private area that she wanted to wash and dress with salve.

As she considered what she should do next she understood why Mrs Barden had not been willing to talk of this particular wifely duty. It was surely the most dreadful part of marriage and there was no wonder she wished to ignore it. Dear Lord, if any woman knew beforehand what she would have to endure she would never willingly agree to any marriage! Although this bed was large and soft, Beth thought fondly of her narrow mattress in the small chamber overlooking the farmyard and wondered anxiously how often Edgar would be at home, meaning she must do this.

He snorted loudly and shifted so she tried to move from under him but he was too heavy. When finally her face was free she wiped the sweat off her face, closed her eyes and, exhausted, fell asleep herself. The next thing she was aware of was his knee between hers and his weight bearing down on her again. Bleary-eyed and hardly aware of what was happening, she made an attempt to push him off and roll away, protesting, 'Not again, Edgar. Please allow me to sleep.'

He grasped her shoulder painfully and said, 'Stay where you are, girl.'

Angered by his rudeness she breathed hoarsely, 'Do not address me in that manner. I am your wife.'

'Then behave like one,' he answered, shoving both his knees between her legs and pushing them apart.

His hardness was obvious to her and she groaned. He was a big man and already she ached and was sore from his attentions. He invaded her roughly, not caring that she was in pain and whimpering. She bit back her cries, aware that her duty as his wife was to satisfy his needs in this respect.

But there was need and there was greed, she thought as she turned her face away from him and stared wide-eyed past his shoulder to the dark wood panelling of the walls. He seemed in such a hurry that she thought it would be over quickly but he rutted and sweated for what seemed like an age until she grew hot underneath him. How much longer must she endure this suffering, she begged silently?

However she did not know whether to be thankful or horrified when the bedchamber door opened suddenly. Beth's eyes swivelled towards it. Surely a servant would knock first? But it was not a servant. Mrs Collins walked in, fully dressed and carrying a lighted lamp. Beth's eyelids closed with embarrassment. Had she no concept of what her son might be doing on his wedding night? What on earth could she want of him at such a late hour?

'That is enough, Edgar,' Mrs Collins said.

He stopped his fruitless thrusting and twisted his head sideways and groaned.

'I said that is enough. I heard you with her earlier and once is sufficient.'

Beth saw his flushed angry face in the lamplight. 'Go away, Mama,' he growled.

'Remember to whom you are speaking!' she snapped and marched across the chamber. 'Remember also that you are a gentleman and she is nothing. Already, she seeks to rob you of your strength.'

It is not I who rob him, Beth thought. I know it is my duty to serve my husband's needs, but surely he must have a care for my comfort in return! If anyone was robbed in this bed, it was her. She felt he had taken her against her will in a most cruel and callous manner without the slightest regard for her sensibilities. He had not treated her as his wife; rather, she felt as though she were nothing more to him than a common street woman, paid to relieve his urges. She realised, with increasing unease, that his past life must have included such activity.

But Beth's feelings were not the concern of either mother or son. Mrs Collins threw back the covers exposing their naked bodies and legs. To her surprise, Edgar obeyed his mother and rolled away from her. Cold air rushed into the fetid space between them and riffled over Beth's naked skin. She felt a blush rise to her cheeks as she struggled to push down the folds of her nightgown. In the lamplight she noticed smudges of blood on the white cotton and more on the linen bed-sheets. Her embarrassment turned to anger as Mrs Collins stared at her dishevelled appearance with an expression of pure disgust. Beth clenched her jaw and demanded, 'Am I not allowed my privacy, madam?'

Her answer was a cold accusing glare as though the whole of this incident were her fault. 'You, girl, go back to your chamber now.'

Beth considered disobeying her and held her eyes for as long as she dare. What kind of mother was she to invade her son's bedchamber on his wedding night and then insult his wife?

Edgar sat on the edge of the bed and pushed his feet into carpet shoes. 'Go on, then. Do as Mama says,' he muttered, taking the robe his mother handed to him. He added, as though making an excuse, 'I'm tired.'

Mrs Collins's face grew even sourer. 'Do not develop a taste for fornication with servant girls until your position with his lordship is secured.'

Beth was astounded. She was not a servant girl and as far as she was concerned, Edgar already had a taste for excess.

'The girl will not be with you,' Mrs Collins continued, 'and your behaviour must be impeccable at all times.'

He responded to his mother with a nod and half turned. 'Do as Mama says.'

This time Beth was thankful to obey and escape to her small, sparsely furnished chamber.

Chapter 3

The sound of someone raking a fire roused her the following morning. Her chamber was over the kitchen and she lay awake in the darkness thinking that this used to be her task at the Bardens'. She washed in cold water, applied salve to her sore areas and dressed quickly, knotting a woollen shawl firmly around her shoulders. Her candle had burned down so she pulled on a cap as best she could and went downstairs. A fire was already drawing in the cavernous hall and a lamp glowed through the open door to the kitchen.

'Good morning, Mrs Roberts.'

'At last. Put the porridge on and set a skillet to heat then see if there are any eggs.'

Beth obeyed silently and escaped to find the hen coop as soon as she found a bowl. Dark grey streaks were lightening the eastern sky and contrasting starkly with the menacing dark outcrops of rock. She searched everywhere but it was too early in the year for hens to be laying, she thought as she fastened the latch to the nesting boxes.

'Here, take these indoors.'

'Oh, Mr Roberts! You startled me.'

He placed a couple of eggs in her empty bowl. 'Wild duck,' he said. 'They'll do for the Yorkshires this dinner time.'

'Thank you.'

'Have you ever milked a cow?'

She shook her head.

'I'll show you after breakfast. The dairy will be your job from now.'

Beth's eyes widened. She didn't know the first thing about dairy work! But she supposed she could learn and at least she would be out of the house and away from Mrs Collins. And Edgar, she thought with mixed feelings. She did not like her husband. He was inconsiderate and brutish. His mother seemed to control him in some ways yet indulge him in others.

'We've only the one cow and she's getting on in years, but we keep a couple of milking ewes to eke out.'

'Do you look after the sheep as well, Mr Roberts?'

'That's Abel's job. He's taken them out on the fell now the snows have gone. He prefers it out there, he does. I tend the pony and keep the trap looking nice, and I look after Master Edgar's hunter when he's home.'

'We have a trap? I shall be able to go to market. Is Settle the nearest?'

'You'll be kept busy here, my lass. Anyway, Master Edgar is off again today.'

'Today? I thought it was tomorrow.'

'We're short on flour. I'll drive them as far as Settle in the vicar's carriage with our pony in tow and bring him back, packhorse style.'

So this is how it is to be, she thought: her husband away shooting and ingratiating himself with his estranged aristocratic kin while she is left behind with the servants to run the farm.

'Is the vicar's parish local?'

'He's not from round here but Master Edgar has known him since schooldays.'

The sky was a lighter grey already and Beth's mood lifted. Mrs Collins, too, would be absent for several days giving her a chance to become familiar with her new routine. She was overwhelmed by a feeling of reprieve that she would not be subjected to another brutal invasion of her body tonight. Indeed, Edgar might not be back for weeks, giving her torn flesh time to heal.

In contrast to Blackstone, food was plentiful at High Fell Farm. Roberts tended a small garden and a pigsty as well as the stable and she had noticed a leaden trough in the scullery for curing the flitches and hams. In the kitchen, Mrs Roberts gave Beth more orders and stood back to watch but after a few minutes left her to pour hot water into waiting ewers to be carried upstairs. Her husband brought in kindling and peat for the fires and Beth followed him to the dining hall to lay the table.

She took the porridge in when she heard Mrs Collins come downstairs and later, when Edgar joined her, she carried through a covered dish of aromatic sizzling bacon to join them for her own breakfast. She heard Edgar raise his voice and slowed, hovering in the shadows.

'I want more money than this, Mama. I need outfits for shooting and balls, a new gun and a respectable manservant. Milo has agreed to ride with me to Leeds. He has been a good friend to me of late and I must repay his generosity, too.'

'He has a living, does he not?'

'Yes, but he's not a rector, Mama. He's only a vicar with a stipend. You know how much it costs to keep a carriage and a hunter.'

'Well, you must have the best for the Abbey.' Mrs Collins slid several bags of coins across the table.

Edgar opened one and took out a few sovereigns. 'So must you, Mama. Why not order a new gown from the drapers in Settle?'

Beth heard the chink of coins. 'I shall,' his mother replied. 'Make sure you go to the best outfitter in Leeds for your clothes and purchase a portmanteau for your onward journey to the South Riding. The manservant you engage will carry it on the post and you must pay him too. He will be your valet at the Abbey. A gentleman does not travel without his valet.'

'His lordship will be aware that I am a farmer, Mama.'

'You are a *gentleman* farmer. Make sure you behave as one. But it might be a good idea to choose a man who will double as your loader at the shoot.'

Edgar's face brightened at this thought. 'What an excellent notion. I've always wanted my own loader. I shall purchase a second shotgun to make best use of him.'

'Of course, dear; that is what the gold is for. Two guns will impress his lordship.'

Beth's boots clacked on the stone-flagged floor when she walked across to the sideboard with her tray as Mrs Roberts had directed. 'Good morning, Mrs Collins. Good morning, Edgar,' she said and filled a bowl with porridge for herself.

Neither greeted her in return. Mrs Collins slid the remaining coins across the polished wooden surface into her hand and returned them to her strongbox. She closed and locked it before placing it carefully on the floor.

'Ah the bacon's here at last,' Edgar said. 'Will you take some, Mama?'

Beth sat down at the table. When Edgar joined her with two plates of bacon she said, 'Roberts tells me you are leaving today, Edgar.'

'Cut me some bread,' was his response.

She ignored his rudeness and went on, 'I am in need of another gown and new cloak, sir.' She turned to Mrs Collins. 'May I accompany you to Settle to order them? I should welcome your guidance on local gown-makers, ma'am.'

Mrs Collins glared at her so intensely that she faltered and added, 'Or perhaps the best draper for fabric to sew myself.'

Neither her husband nor his mother replied, but she noticed they exchanged impatient glances. She put down her spoon and turned to Edgar. 'Which is it to be, husband? I do not wish my appearance to be disrespectful to your position.'

He looked uncomfortable and muttered, 'What do you say, Mama?'

'If Roberts is driving the carriage, the girl must remain here to look after the farmyard.'

'I do have a name, ma'am,' Beth protested and turned to Edgar. 'I need another gown and cloak for church, sir.'

Mrs Collins did not even look in her direction. 'It is best for her to stay here. The farm will take up too much of her time for church. It is a long walk, anyway.'

To his credit, Edgar appeared mildly embarrassed and shrugged, 'Speak to Mrs Roberts about your attire.'

Beth did not argue further but resolved when the time was right to speak firmly with Edgar. He had lived too long under the domination of his mother. Surely he was master of the house? Now he had taken a wife he must see that his mother should behave differently. She wondered briefly why, if Mrs Collins regarded her only as a servant, she allowed her son to be married to her in the first place. But the answer was obvious. It was her dowry that had attracted both of them.

Beth frowned. She had expected Mrs Collins to respect her as Edgar's wife and not encourage the servants to treat her as some insignificant hired help. She was tempted to ask Roberts and his wife to call her Beth but thought better of it. In spite of her mother-in-law, she was their mistress.

Mr Roberts seemed her sole ally and she excused herself as soon as she could to find him. He was smoking a pipe by the kitchen fire and Beth took a chair and sat beside him.

'Where is Mrs Roberts?' she asked.

He jerked his head. 'She's in the pantry, seeing what else we need from Settle.'

'Mr Collins seems to leave all the farm tasks to you,' she commented.

'Well, 'tis not his, is it? 'Tis his ma's.'

'Mrs Collins owns the farm?'

'Oh aye. Old Jacob had got nobody else to leave it to, see.'

'Is she a good farmer?'

He made a noise in his throat. 'She's run it into the ground and if it weren't for having such a hard-working shepherd as Abel, the bank would have foreclosed on her years ago.'

The mention of a bank and foreclosure rang alarm bells for Beth. Wouldn't her dowry have been better spent in paying off the mortgage?

Mr Roberts continued. 'All she borrowed went for master Edgar's schooling so he could lord it with the sons of gentry that he met there. I tell you—'

'You shut your mouth, Mr Roberts. You've said too much,' Mrs Roberts called from the pantry.

'Well, the girl ought to know what she's come to. Nowt here 'as ever been good enough for her precious son. Her mother was well-born you see, but she was cut off without a penny when she ran off with a travelling man.'

Beth absorbed this without changing her expression and Mr Roberts continued, 'It i'n't no secret. Just before the old lady passed on she made the mistake of telling her daughter the titled family she came from and the mistress hasn't been the same since.'

Beth looked over her shoulder at Mrs Roberts. 'Who was Mrs Collins's mother, then?' she asked.

'That's enough, Mr Roberts,' his wife snapped.

'Aye maybe. That's what comes of having no one to talk to except Mrs Roberts, week in week out.' He got to his feet awkwardly and began coughing. 'Come on, girl,' he wheezed, 'I'll show you the milking, then it'll be your job from this afternoon. We only have one milker and she's drying, but she'll make a racket if you don't see to her.'

'What about Abel's provisions?' Mrs Roberts demanded.

'The girl'll have to take 'em while I'm down in Settle. She'll be there and back in a day.'

'Yes, I'll do that,' Beth volunteered eagerly, grasping the chance of seeing less of Mrs Roberts and more of the farm. 'Do I use the trap?'

'Dear Lord, no, lass. The track's too rocky, even for a pony. We have a donkey for that. I'll load 'er fer you before I leave and you can set off after breakfast tomorrow.'

'Where do I go?'

'There's only one track up the fell. It goes round by yon scar then drops into a dip where it's sheltered from the

38

northerlies. You'll see Abel's hut, you can't miss it. There's nowt else up there.'

The light was better as Beth crossed the untidy farmyard. As well as barns, a substantial stone outbuilding with an outside flight of steps stood at the other side. The animals were housed on the ground floor and she followed Mr Roberts inside.

The cow was restless and Beth was nervous of being kicked. But Mr Roberts held her head and spoke soothingly to her as Beth developed the gentle squeeze and stroke necessary to produce a small jet of milk. It was hardly worth the time for the amount of milk she produced for it wasn't nearly enough to make cheese, let alone skim for butter. She was just getting into the rhythm when the cow began to low fretfully.

'Don't understand her,' Mr Roberts frowned. 'She's as docile as they come as a rule.'

'Perhaps she doesn't like strangers,' Beth suggested.

'Maybe.'

The donkey in the next stall suddenly let out a lengthy bray, spooking them all.

'What's that?' Alarmed, Beth leapt to her feet knocking over the milking stool and only just retrieved the pail of milk from the cow's shifting hooves. There was a low distant rumbling and Beth distinctly felt the stall wall trembling as she held onto it.

'The roof's coming in!' she squealed.

'Steady now,' Mr Roberts soothed as he held tight on the cow's halter. 'Don't jump about like that, girl, you'll frighten the beasts.'

It was over so quickly that Beth wondered if she had imagined it. 'Did you hear that thunder?'

'No need to worry, lass. It's a long way away.'

'But you felt the barn shake, didn't you?'

'Well, there's no wonder. You've got the horses going now,' Mr Roberts complained as they whinnied and shied in their stalls.

'It was more than that, I'm sure,' she demanded.

'Nay, lass. They're not used to you, that's all.'

Beth didn't agree. 'There must be a storm brewing. The cow was restless. Surely that's a sign?'

'She's settled now. Don't you fret yoursenn. It's over.'

'I – I don't want to set off up the fell if there's a storm brewing.'

'You'll have to get used to it up here. Besides, it'll have blown over by tomorrow, I expect.'

Beth accepted this and took the milk pail indoors to scald it over the fire. She heard the carriage leave as she scrubbed the pail and pan in the scullery. She dashed out with reddened wet hands to watch it receding down the fell. Edgar had not been to find her to say goodbye, which gave her a clear indication of how unimportant she was to him. She went back to her washing up. It was no different here from being pushed around by Mr and Mrs Barden and their daughters at Blackstone.

Mrs Roberts continued to be offhand and rude. Beth guessed she didn't know how else to behave, having learned her ways from Mrs Collins. But she acknowledged Beth's need for suitable clothing for farm life and found her patterns and fabrics for sewing.

'You'll be needing these an' all, for leading the donkey,' Mrs Roberts announced, handing her a pair of riding gloves.

They were close fitting and made from soft kid, clearly too small for Mrs Collins, and Beth was grateful for the protection they would give her. She set off for her day out with the loaded beast, well wrapped against the weather and inhaling the fresh Dales air. A bitter wind whipped around her ears and clouds raced across the sky giving infrequent glimpses of weak sunshine. But they were not storm clouds and she climbed the track with confidence.

A few sheep stopped their grazing to watch her progress but she did not see a living soul or habitable dwelling on her journey. The track was rocky and difficult to negotiate in parts but she pressed on, glad of her thick woollen shawl knotted firmly under her cloak.

When she found the stone and slate dwelling it was deserted. She unloaded some of the donkey's burden, tethered it in the lee of the wind and sat in the sun with her back against the wall to wait for the shepherd. Her eyelids drooped and she let them close. She had milked a cow, fed some hens and a herded a noisy flock of geese away from the stable before breakfast this morning and felt tired.

The next thing she was aware of was the donkey braying and she opened her eyes quickly. He was tugging at the halter in some kind of panic and – and – the wall behind her was moving! She heard distant thunder but the sky was as bright as ever. It was the ground, the ground was shaking, stones rattled down the sloping fell; a slate slid off the roof above her and landed, edge on in the grass, missing her by inches.

The hut was falling down! Disoriented she scrambled to her feet, untied the donkey, holding on to its halter as best she could, and dragged the screeching recalcitrant animal away from the hut. Then suddenly it was over. Everything stopped and the fell was quiet again, until a different kind of rumbling alerted her attention. She watched with alarm as a section of the crag above the hut a few hundred yards distant broke away, crumbling and tumbling down the slope and across the track winding down to the farm.

Dear Lord preserve her! Was the devil himself escaping from Hades before her eyes? The donkey bucked and heaved and eventually broke loose from her grip to follow the sheep scattering in all directions across the fell. Shaking with fright, she dropped to her knees, pulled her hood over her face and huddled in a heap on the ground until the rumbling slowed and finally stopped. Everything stayed silent for a long time before she peeped out. The rocks were still. There was a gap in the rocky outcrop that had not been there before and a heap of boulders trailing down to the track and across it to the lower slope beyond. She noticed more broken slates on the grass and the door to the hut was swinging open. Cautiously she got up and looked inside.

It was small and sparsely furnished with a fireplace, bed, table and chair. A few cooking utensils were scattered in the hearth in front of the fire. A tin bowl and jug had fallen from the table. She picked up the scattered pots that had not broken and pushed the shattered shards of others together with her boots. If she had been wearing an old gown and an apron she would have cleaned up with a broom. But she supposed she ought to behave more like Edgar's wife than his housemaid to his farm workers.

She was, she recognised, very nervous of this alien fell and hoped the shepherd would return soon. Daylight shone though the roof where the slates had been and one of the stone walls showed a jagged crack in the lime wash. The relentless wind whistled in through cracks in the window panes. Then her alert ears became aware of another sound: sharper, more penetrating and intermittent.

She went outside as the occasional piercing whistle grew closer and saw the flock of sheep first, pushing and shoving through a gap in a long stone wall. A black-and-white dog scurried close to the ground then dropped on its belly as the shepherd followed his flock and lifted a wooden hurdle across the gap. He waved when he saw her and headed towards the hut followed by his dog.

'Are you Abel?' she called as he approached.

'I am, madam. You must be from the farmhouse,' he replied.

'Yes. I've brought your supplies.'

'You came back with Master Edgar's party?'

'I beg your pardon.'

'You came back with Master Edgar. He has got himself wed at last.' The shepherd seemed to find it amusing. His black straggly beard hid most of his face and his hair was wild. He wore a grubby thick calico smock over his clothes. She felt uncomfortable with his disrespectful attitude towards her husband and didn't answer.

'I should return to the farm straight away,' she said. 'Have you seen my donkey? He ran off.'

'He'll be back. There's no need to look so frightened.'

'I – I haven't seen a landslide before.'

'We've had tremors before on the fell. But nothing like this in a long time, I can tell you.' He bent down to inspect his supplies and winced.

'Are you hurt, sir?'

'I caught a falling rock on my shoulder. What about you?'

'I was frightened, that's all.'

'So were my sheep. I hope I haven't lost any. Sally will find them for me, though, dead or alive.'

His dog pricked up her ears at the sound of her name.

Beth scanned the track that had disappeared beneath a

pile of boulder and rock. 'Is there another way back to the farm?'

He shook his head. 'I'll see what I can do about clearing a track through for you as soon as I've found all my ewes. They're in lamb, you see.'

'Will it take you long?'

'I'll be a day or so if I'm lucky.'

'But I have to get back before nightfall.'

'You won't be going before tomorrow; maybe the day after. The mistress will have to manage without you.'

Chapter 4

Beth hesitated, picking up a definitely ironic quality in his last remark. He didn't know that Mrs Collins wouldn't miss her at all as she had taken herself off to Settle in her borrowed carriage. Nonetheless, Beth did not wish to stay out here longer than necessary. Nor was she easy in the company of this shepherd. 'Can I help you search?' she asked.

'It's too dangerous. The fell is full of potholes and underground streams that escape through cracks in the rock. Stay here in the hut.'

'Oh. It's a bit of a mess in there.'

He raised his eyebrows and she noticed he had blue eyes like hers. 'You've nothing else to do,' he commented. 'There's peat for the fire and water in the butt.'

She frowned. She didn't think he ought to speak to his employer's wife like that. And then it dawned on her. He didn't realise who she really was. He thought she was a maid that Edgar's new wife had brought with her. She had better avoid further embarrassment and explain. 'Ah,' she began, 'I think you've made a—'

In the distance his dog began to yap insistently. 'Sorry, lass. Sally has found something,' he interrupted and sprinted off in the direction of his barking dog.

I'll put him straight when he returns, she thought with a shrug. She unbuttoned her cuffs and rolled up her sleeves.

He was away for several hours. Once she had got over making her only good gown, the one that had been her wedding gown, as dusty and grubby as his shepherd's smock, she enjoyed putting the hut to rights. It was work she was used to. She was confident as a housekeeper, but realised with misgiving that Mrs Collins didn't even think she was fit for that role at High Fell. Her donkey came back looking for water and food and Beth attended to him then left him to roam. Peat smoke puffed out of the stove and stung her eyes but she had water heating and a pot of broth simmering when Abel returned. The front of his smock was turned up enclosing something in his arms.

'Make space by the stove and bring a blanket from the bed,' he demanded.

She stared as he unrolled the blood- and slime-smeared calico to reveal a newborn lamb.

'Make haste, lass. I think I can save him.'

She jumped up and prepared a cocoon of warmth for the small creature.

'His mother was injured and slipped her lamb,' he explained. 'But this little fellow is a fighter. Did you bring cow's milk in the supplies?'

'Yes.'

'Heat some on the stove.'

When it was warmed he poured it into a stone bottle

and then stretched an India rubber teat over the neck. He knelt by the stove, supported the lamb's head and offered the milk. The tiny lamb began to suckle, weakly at first and then more vigorously. Beth watched, fascinated that a large strong man had such a gentle way with him. Eventually she asked, 'May I?'

'Do you want to?'

She nodded, knelt beside him in front of the stove and took the soggy smelly animal in her arms as she would an infant.

He gave her an approving smile. 'You're a natural. I'd expect an indoor maid to run a mile from this.'

Now was the time to tell him. She had taken off her gloves to clean and held up her left hand to show him her wedding band. 'I'm not a maid. I am Mrs Edgar Collins.'

He looked astounded. 'You? You can't be!'

'Why not?'

'He – he – Roberts said Edgar was marrying for money. You – you –' His voice trailed away.

She blushed. She was not the well-born lady they had expected. She did not look like one and would not pass for one. He scrambled to his feet, looking shocked. 'Madam, why did you not say?'

'You did not give me an opportunity until now.'

'But what is Master Edgar thinking of by allowing you out on the fell alone?'

'He's gone to Leeds for new clothes and then to a shooting party in the South Riding.'

'He has left without you?'

She was silent for a moment. Edgar didn't want her. Even though she did not like him, his behaviour hurt her deeply. His mother made things worse by belittling her at every opportunity. But Beth was Edgar's wife and that was that.

47

High Fell Farm might well be a pleasant place to live when mother and son were away. She said, 'I am learning how to run Edgar's household. I have not managed a home as large as his farmhouse before.'

'You're not one of his South Riding cousins then?'

She shook her head. She wondered how much she could trust him. It seemed disloyal to question Abel about her husband, but how else was she to find out? She asked, 'What do you know about Edgar's well-connected relations, Abel?'

'I don't think it's my place to say.'

'Please. No one else will,' she replied.

'I only know what the drovers tell me. Some take sheep down to the South Riding towns.'

'Is it true that Edgar's grandmother was gentry?'

'Daughter of a lord, they say, and sister of the present incumbent. He's a younger son, I believe. Edgar's grandmother was much older than he was. She ran away with a horse trader who used to roam the Ridings so she was disowned by her family.'

'Edgar's grandmother really did marry a travelling man?' This echoed what Mr Roberts had told her.

'Aye, and he promised his daughter to Jacob Collins in exchange for a piece of land to use for his wagon and horses over the winter.'

Beth gave an astonished laugh. 'Are you saying that Mrs Collins with all her airs and graces is truly the daughter of a gypsy?'

'That's right. Soon after the mistress was wed to Jacob her mother got a fever and stayed over winter with them in the farmhouse. The gypsy said he couldn't live in a house and slept in his wagon in the field. But one night in early spring he upped and left with his horses and they never saw him again. They say that Jacob was the only one who was happy with the arrangement. He'd got his land back, two women to keep house for him and, later on, there was Edgar to work the farm for him.'

The lamb's eager suckling slowed and Beth laid the tiny creature by the stove. 'Will this little one have a foster mother?'

'Doubtful. I don't want to find any more slipping their lambs this early.' Abel finished trimming the wick of an oil lamp. He strapped a cartridge belt around his waist and picked up a shotgun from the corner of the hut. 'I'm off to deal with his mother before a fox gets her. Then I'll make a start on clearing the track.'

'But it's already getting dark!'

'I'll take a storm lantern. I have to get you back to the farm as soon as possible.' He stared at her for a moment and added, 'Please accept my apologies for any offence I caused earlier.' He bowed his head formally and left.

Beth was disappointed. She had enjoyed caring for the lamb and would have liked their conversation to continue. She saw a notebook on the only table in the hut and opened it idly. It was a record of his livestock: numbers of rams and breeding ewes, lambs produced and fattened stock sold. He even noted weather conditions and she wondered what he would write about the land tremor and rock fall.

It reinforced her opinion that Abel was no illiterate peasant. She felt more cheerful about her future life at this isolated farm if there was someone intelligent to converse with and wondered how often he came down from the fell. The hut seemed empty without him. He had finished the broth while she nursed the lamb and there was little to do except make porridge for the morning. She looked forward to taking it out to him.

The small bed was clean and she stretched out on it fully clothed, covered herself with a blanket and went to sleep. But she awoke with a start. The bed was shaking and Abel was tugging at her arm.

'You must get out of here.'

'What the—' She clutched at the blanket. Something crashed to the ground raising dust.

'Hurry! It's an after tremor,' he urged. 'Come on.' He put one arm around her shoulder and shoved the other under the blanket and under her knees then dragged her from her bed and carried her into the night.

'Where's the lamb!' she cried.

'Under the table.'

A slate slithered down the roof slope and broke in two as it hit an exposed rock. Sally was cowering by the gate as Abel whisked her through and away from the hut walls. Terrified, Beth clutched at his neck and buried her head in his chest. He set her down on some cold, damp and scratchy pasture.

'I think it best if you stay out here for the rest of the night.'

'But I'll freeze to death!'

He pulled the blanket around her. 'I'll fetch my oiled cape for a ground sheet.'

She grasped his hand. 'No, don't go back in there. It's dangerous.'

He remained quite still for a minute. Her eyes became used to the moonlight. He was looking down at her whitened knuckle as her fingers clung to his. She bit her lip. She did not want anything to happen to him and her grip tightened. 'Don't,' she repeated.

'Let me go, Mrs Collins,' he said. But he did not pull his

50

hand away. He waited until she realised he meant it and she had released her hold.

He returned with his cloak and more blankets and she cocooned herself in her makeshift bed in the open air. Abel wasn't far away and his presence dominated her restless sleep. He was so different from Edgar, so very, very different.

She had to clean the hut again before warming up the porridge, which they both ate hungrily. More rocks and loose shale had blocked the track. She would be foolish to try to climb over the rubble and Abel reckoned he had several days' labouring to clear it. She took a piece of salt pork and a sack of vegetables from his supplies and put them to boil over the fire.

Abel kept himself away from her and very busy during daylight hours which he spent repairing his hut and clearing a way through the rock fall as well as tending his ewes. Beth tended to the lamb and was acutely disappointed when another ewe gave birth and became his foster mother. She cleaned up the hut again, kept the fire and cooked. But when they ate and talked together in the evenings it was difficult for Beth not to be aware of Abel as a man rather than one of her husband's farmworkers.

For his part, he maintained a physical distance between them always, even apologising if he accidently brushed by her. During the night he disappeared to sleep she knew not where. But she was at ease in his company. He did not threaten her in any way and she respected him for that. He addressed her as 'Mrs Collins' or 'madam' and only once did their conversation approach the personal. He was tired and cold and had taken a tot of brandy in his tea. She had talked at length of her former school friends and favourite teachers.

'You have been an education for me, Mrs Collins,' he said. 'You have reminded me what I am working towards.'

'And what is that, sir?'

'I wish for my own home in which to raise my own family.'

'You must seek a wife then,' Beth smiled.

'Indeed I must,' he mused. 'I shall search for one like you. Edgar is a lucky man.'

Beth was flattered and she blushed in the lamplight. But Abel apologised for his comment immediately and picked up his bedroll. She wanted to protest that he had not embarrassed her unduly and he need not leave, but he bid her goodnight and went out into the night. She was aware of his reasons. He was a bachelor and she was a married woman. He took the lantern with him leaving her the candles, but she felt as though the light had gone out of the evening. If only, she reflected, her husband was a man like Abel.

Early next morning he clambered through the remaining rocks on the track and walked round the scar to where there was a view down to the farm. When he came back his face was grim. 'There is no smoke from the farmhouse chimney.'

'But Mr Roberts ought to be back from Settle by now.'

'I fear not.'

'Then I must make haste to return.'

'I'll try to clear the path before noon.'

He seemed anxious for her to leave as soon as possible and she guessed that she should. A familiarity was developing between them and it would not do.

'Thank you, sir,' she replied formally and prepared for her journey.

Chapter 5

'It's a chill, Mrs Roberts. I'll mix you a remedy.'

Beth was concerned about the older woman's fever. She had found the farmyard in a chaotic state. The hens were out and a barn wall had collapsed on top of the trap. But the sturdy stone buildings were standing. She had tethered the donkey and hurried past the swinging door of the stable holding her hand over her nose to avoid the putrid smell. There were no horses left on the farm and the goats were running free so she guessed it must be the cow.

Mrs Roberts had fallen, banged her head on the kitchen floor and lain there until she came round. Beth made her comfortable on a couch that she dragged in from the dining hall and lit the fire. Where was Mr Roberts with the supplies? She hoped nothing had happened to him but guessed that others would have suffered in the tremors. The older woman's condition worsened. Beth did all she could, making her mixtures from recipes she had used at Blackstone. After five days the fever had not broken and there was still no sign of Mr Roberts. Beth decided to go to Settle and fetch a medical man for Mrs Roberts.

She followed the track until it came to the stream. She heard the rushing water long before she could see it. Surely it had not been so wide and turbulent on her journey up the fell. As she neared the narrow bridge she realised that only half of it was standing. One of the stone supporting arches had gone.

The area, she knew, was riddled with potholes, underground caves and streams. The earth tremor must have widened a crack in the crag and sent water and boulders gushing downstream, taking the bridge with it. There was no way across until the water subsided. She stared at the bleak expanse of fell on the other side hoping to catch sight of a walker or rider. But it was futile. Every able-bodied man would be dealing with his own disaster from the tremor. Even when the water subsided, there would be no way a trap could cross the river until a new bridge had been built. Nonetheless, Beth waited for sight of someone, anyone, who could relay a message to the doctor. As she did, her anxiety increased. Any one of the party that had left High Fell Farm might also be injured.

She searched the bank for a crossing point but the current was too strong and she gazed up at the high fell wondering just how much water it held in its catacombs. Reluctantly, when the light faded, she re-traced her steps back to the farm and prayed that Mrs Roberts's fever had broken. I shall have to ask Abel for help, she thought. The notion had crossed her mind several times and she had dismissed it, uneasy with her feelings for him. But this was an emergency and she needed him. It could be weeks before Mr Roberts, or indeed anyone, would get through. A frisson of apprehension made her shiver as she realised she had no other choice.

There was a lamp glowing through the kitchen window and a dog barked as she approached the back door. Within seconds it was open. 'Who's there?'

'Mrs Collins. Is that you, Abel?' She felt faint with relief to hear his voice. 'I was coming to get you in the morning. The bridge has been swept away and we are cut off.'

'Dear Lord, no. It will take weeks to repair. Could we get the donkey across?'

'Not until the water goes down.' Beth stepped inside. The fire was going well and a kettle was bubbling on the plate. 'How is Mrs Roberts?'

'She will live. Her fever is bad but she isn't delirious. She told me you had left her to die.'

'I went for a doctor.'

'You are safer in here. This is a fortress of a farmhouse.'

'The farmyard has not fared so well.'

'So I see. I'll stay and get it cleaned up.'

'What about your sheep?'

'I've moved them down the fell to this side of the rock fall.'

'Heavens! Don't bring them any closer. There's a putrid cow in the stable.'

'I know. I'll deal with her tomorrow.'

'Thank you.' Beth was exhausted. 'Have you somewhere to sleep?'

'I shall be comfortable outside.'

She wondered where. The upstairs of the stable, over a rotting corpse, was not habitable. She wanted to invite him indoors, yet dared not for fear of her reputation. He must be aware of that. She looked at his face, directly into those intense blue eyes, and thought, I believe he knows how I feel and he understands. She said, 'Thank you, Abel.'

He nodded briefly. 'I shall have no reason to come into the farmhouse at all.'

How could she feel relieved by this and irritated at the same time? He picked up his lantern and said goodnight, leaving her alone to ponder on her disappointment. He was an honourable man, perhaps a little too proud, she thought, but considerate and hardworking. As the days turned into weeks Beth often found herself staring at him through the farmhouse windows. He noticed. He stopped whatever he was doing and gazed back until she lowered her eyes and moved away.

Mrs Roberts recovered and returned to her former self, blaming Beth for her prolonged fever and calling her a witch. Abel created order out of chaos in the farmyard and returned to tend his lambing ewes leaving Beth with two milking nannies and the hens. Only Mrs Roberts complained about eating oatcakes instead of bread. February turned to March and still no one had attempted to contact them.

However, as soon as all his lambs were born, Abel loaded the donkey with rope and timber and set off to construct a temporary crossing over the stream. The days lengthened and the weather improved. Beth wished she could enjoy it more but feared she was sickening for something. She felt unwell. When she looked at her reflection she was pale and resolved to take regular walks in the bracing Dales air. The stream subsided and Abel had managed to cross it with the donkey and his temporary raft. He went on to Settle for news and their much-needed supplies. It was a full three months after the tremor before Beth noticed a small procession winding up the track towards the farmhouse.

Edgar led the way on his hunter, leading the pony with

Mrs Collins perched regally on its back. Abel followed with a burdened donkey. Beth broke into a run then checked her eagerness and waited patiently by the track wrapped in her cloak. She noticed Abel took the donkey straight round to the farmyard without a word. She guessed he did not like Edgar and his mother any more than she did. But Edgar was her husband and she greeted him loyally.

'You are well, sir?' She did not expect a reply and went on, 'I must speak with you urgently.'

'Don't bother me now. Help Mama down.'

Beth held out her hands for support. Mrs Collins leaned heavily on her shoulder as she slid off the pony and went into the house without a word.

'Where is Mr Roberts?' she asked. But Edgar was already leading the pony away and she followed him to the stable. Abel was unloading the donkey at the back door but there was a commotion indoors, a cry and then – was that weeping?

'Where is Mr Roberts?' she repeated.

'He died.'

'Dear Lord, no. What happened?'

'God knows. I've been in the South Riding.'

'Was your visit a success?'

She noticed a grimace and guessed it had not been.

'Not your affair,' he shrugged.

Perhaps not, she thought, but my news is *your* affair.

'Please Edgar.' She was not going to let him dismiss her as he had in the past. Not now. 'I have something important to say.'

'Nothing at High Fell is important to me any more,' he replied and concentrated on unbuckling his saddle.

'Edgar, will you stop doing that. I must speak with you. I have news.'

'You have news? What news can you possibly have?'

'I am with child,' she smiled. She was pleased. It was what marriage was for and it made the horrid experience of her wedding night worthwhile.

He was genuinely astounded. 'You're what?'

'I am carrying your child, Edgar.'

'Good God, are you sure?'

She hadn't been at first, but she was now. 'I am. I wanted you to be the first to know.'

He appeared to forget what he was doing. 'So soon,' he murmured. 'This will make a difference.' He dropped the tack on the floor and led his horse into its stall, securing the door thoughtfully 'I must speak with Mama immediately.' He left her standing in the stable and went straight into the house.

Beth caught up with him in front of the marble fireplace in the hall. Mrs Collins was warming her hands and both mother and son turned to look at her. She opened her cloak and smoothed the front of her skirt to show her small but noticeable swelling.

'It cannot be yours, Edgar? Look at her. Barden assured me she was a maid but –' Mrs Collins shivered, 'she is showing already.'

'How dare you accuse me so!' Beth protested. 'Of course my child is Edgar's.'

But Mrs Collins continued to fret. 'I should have had a physician look at her. You never know with orphans. She could have lain with any number of passing tradesmen.'

'Madam, you insult me! Ask your son. He knows I was a maid when he brought me here as his bride. Edgar?' Beth turned to her husband to support her and to her surprise he did.

'Calm yourself, Mama. The girl speaks the truth. I can

58

swear she was a maid on her wedding night.' Beth tried not to show her distaste as she wondered how many maids he had lain with before her. He went on, 'The child is mine and, oh don't you see, Mama, if the child is a boy he will secure the Redfern line. This will work in my favour. His lordship must receive me now.'

Redfern? Lord Redfern? So it *was* Redfern Abbey they had been referring to. It was the biggest and wealthiest estate in the South Riding with a reputation for having a hundred servants. However, she realised from Edgar's comment that his recent visit, despite the advantage provided by her dowry, had not had the intended outcome. The family rift had not been healed.

Mrs Collins's eyes gleamed for a second. 'A son, certainly, will be welcome for the succession. But Lord Redfern will wish to see the child and, heaven forbid, its mother. She is not a lady and his lordship may not approve of her.'

'He will not involve himself. His lawyers tell me he is firm in his views. He has tried to disinherit me and cannot because Grandmama's marriage was legal and so was yours. I am the heir and Milo has ensured the legal people have the documents to prove it.'

Beth noticed Mrs Collins's eyes glaze over and her mouth began to work at unspoken words. The woman was obsessed by her quest to restore her son to Redfern, and she, Beth, had become a pawn in her plan. 'They will want to see the birth,' Edgar's mother said. 'What shall we do?'

Edgar began to speak soothingly to his mother. 'I shall tell him she is too delicate for the journey. They will understand that I do not wish to take any risks with a possible heir to Redfern Abbey. You are tired from your journey, Mama. Why don't I take you to your chamber for a rest?'

Edgar had forgotten she was there as he reassured his mother and they moved away wrapped up in their own thoughts. Beth smoothed her hands over her swelling. She might be carrying the heir to Lord Redfern! She could hardly believe it. Edgar was the current heir. Yet in spite of an invitation to a shooting party, he had not been received by the present lord so his grandmother's behaviour was not forgiven. But, Beth realised, her child would make a difference to her status at High Fell Farm. She smiled to herself and stroked her small stomach again.

When Edgar ordered her to his bedchamber after dinner that evening she echoed his own words and responded, 'It is not wise, sir. I do not want us to take any risks with our unborn infant.' And, oh joy, he accepted her reasoning. Moreover, he left on horseback the following morning to convey his news to Lord Redfern's lawyers and wait around hoping for a thawing of relations. Beth watched him ride away and thought that married life at High Fell would not be so bad, after all.

Beth liked being with child. She felt it had gained her status in the household and, somehow, made her more comfortable in Abel's presence. She could accept his offers of help to carry a pail of milk or climb over a stile without uneasiness or guilt. She had her child to think of now and the safety of her child must come first.

Abel went down to Settle again for men and materials to repair the bridge. A letter came for Mrs Collins from Edgar to inform her he was staying in the South Riding for the summer. She was angry and snapped and snarled for a while. Beth realised how irrational she could be in her behaviour and stayed out of her way, pleased to have the farmyard to occupy her. She enjoyed the outdoor life at High Fell and looked forward to her gardening and dairy work while she could. In June, Abel brought his sheep down for shearing and went with the carter to take the fleece to market. The summer was kind and the fells became her friends as she walked the paths and tracks. Her happiness was complete when Edgar sent word to his mother that he would not return to High Fell until Michaelmas, by which time Beth's size was really slowing her down.

Beth felt her awkwardness most when she was milking the nannies in the morning. The milking stool was so low. One day she heard a sound in the quiet stillness of the stable.

'Is that you, Mrs Roberts?' she called.

It was a dark morning. The clouds were low, enveloping the farm in a dampening drizzle. Then she heard the sheep baa-ing. Surely they had not wandered this close to the farm? But the fells were strange mystical places in the mist and sounds were known to travel across valleys. In spite of her knotted shawl, Beth's back was chilled and she wished she had donned her cloak to do the milking. Beth's stomach was so huge she could hardly reach round it for the udder. She grasped a knotted rope on the side of the stall to heave herself to her feet and as she did so felt a twinge in her back. She would have to have help with the farm once the baby was born.

She grimaced as she bent to pick up the pail of milk, suddenly alert as she heard a shrill whistle and the distant bark of a dog, then the sheep again. They were nearby. She hurried outside and strained her eyes through the mist. Sure enough, the flock was pouring across the lower fell and into one of the fields enclosed by dry-stone walling on the slope behind the farmhouse. She put down her pail and walked in that direction until she saw Abel burdened by a large

61

backpack, holding open the gate as the sheep streamed through.

Her heart lifted and she waved. 'Good morning, Abel.'

He glanced in her direction and raised his hand. She waited patiently until Sally had herded the flock into the pasture and he had secured the gate.

'It will be a fine day when the mists lift,' he called as he walked across to the farmyard.

'I hope so,' she responded. Beth loved the fell and escaped to it as often as she could.

She was excessively pleased to see Abel and felt cheerful as she waddled towards him. He was the only person on the farm worthy of a conversation and she wanted to throw her arms around his neck to welcome him. His face, she thought, registered a little pleasure, but he always retained the stiff formality that he had assumed when he had first discovered her identity.

'Are you keeping well, madam?' He held out his elbow. 'Here, take my arm.'

She did and felt the hard sinewy muscles as she gripped. 'Thank you.' She was breathless from her exertion. 'I can't wait for it all to be over. I am so huge, it must be a boy.'

'Maybe,' Abel replied, looking straight ahead.

He was a man of few words, Beth knew, unless he had something to say, and she was content for them to walk in silence because it did not feel wrong for him to be here, by her side, supporting her. She had not met many men in her short life but she thought that Abel was by far the kindest. He was gentle and strong at the same time, with all the qualities any woman could want in a husband. If only . . . She allowed her fantasies to wander until they reached the abandoned pail of milk. Beth let go of his arm and bent to pick it up, bringing on another of her back twinges. 'Oooh,' she uttered and immediately straightened.

'I'll take that,' he said. 'Surely you should be resting, madam.'

'There's no one else to see to the farmyard.'

'You mean that, while I have spent the summer on the fell with my sheep, Mrs Collins hasn't taken on anyone to do Roberts's work? Who looks after the pony?'

'I shall see to him after breakfast.'

'I shall do it,' he stated.

'Will you?' She was hugely grateful to him. 'Oh thank you, Abel.'

He gave a silent nod in response. She was used to his grave expression now and went on, 'Why have you brought down the sheep this early in the autumn?'

'I lost too many of them last year, what with last winter's snow and then the rock fall. It's more sheltered here and I can move the lambing ewes to the barn.'

Beth was impressed by his husbandry. 'Mrs Collins is lucky to have you.'

His mouth gave a small wry twist. 'If you say so, madam.'

They approached the back door leading to the kitchen. 'Will you be staying in the farmhouse with us?'

'I'll sleep over the stable where Roberts used to live.' He deposited the milk pail just inside the kitchen door. 'Would you tell your mother-in-law I shall be in to see her after breakfast?'

'Of course.' On impulse she added, 'You do not have to behave quite so formally towards me, Abel.'

He did not answer her. He gave her a stiff bow, muttered, 'Excuse me, ma'am,' and went off in the direction of the barn.

As she washed up the breakfast pots in the scullery, Beth pondered over his choice of words for the message to

Mrs Collins. She couldn't imagine anyone 'telling' Mrs Collins anything. Rather, she thought it would be the other way around. She finished her chores quickly and went into the kitchen drying her hands.

Mrs Roberts looked up from weighing out bread flour. 'Abel said to tell you he'll be seeing to the farmyard from tomorrow morning.'

'Really? Oh that is a relief. I can barely look after myself now, let alone the livestock.'

'You've got young legs,' Mrs Roberts muttered. 'I've already told the mistress to expect him.'

Beth collected her cleaning box and a broom to sweep and tidy the dining hall. She did this cheerfully as she no longer thought of herself as Mrs Collins's servant. High Fell's farmhouse was a beautiful home and it contained a few pieces of fine, if old-fashioned, furniture. She enjoyed caring for it. Nonetheless, she looked forward to resting her back for half an hour before emptying the chamber pots. Abel was standing by Mrs Collins as she sat at the table. He seemed to tower over her and she looked angry and uncomfortable. As soon as Beth appeared she left her chair and went upstairs.

'Is Mrs Collins quite well?' Beth asked.

Abel gave a rare wry smile. 'I need medications for my sheep and the farm needs supplies so I'm taking the pony and trap down to Settle.'

'I don't see why Mrs Collins would be so angry.'

'Does she need a reason?'

'Well no, but if there are things I should know . . .' Her voice trailed away. It was Abel's business and not hers.

'It is no secret. I have arranged for her to recompense me for taking over Roberts's duties. She does not care to part with any of her money to me.'

Oh, money again. It was all that Mrs Collins thought about apart from her precious son and his inheritance. But Beth did not dwell on it. She had other things on her mind, most of all her lack of confidence in either Mrs Collins or Mrs Roberts to deal with her approaching confinement. Edgar ought to be here making sure she had everything she needed for the birth of his first-born. She said, 'Would you take a letter to the post for me? It's for Edgar. He wrote to his mother to tell her he has been staying at Fellwick Hall these past few weeks.'

'Very well, madam. Have it ready by morning.'

Chapter 6

Edgar returned to High Fell shortly after Michaelmas Day, full of news for his mother of invitations he had received as the acknowledged heir to Redfern. But not, Beth realised as she listened to their conversations in silence, any request to visit the Abbey.

'Lord Redfern may not receive me but there are others who do.'

'And the money has all gone,' Mrs Collins replied sourly.

'I am the heir to Lord Redfern, Mama. I have access to means. Just write and ask for what you need.'

'Will you not live here, Edgar?'

'High Fell is too isolated. Milo has his living just outside Leeds. I shall stay with him until I find suitable lodgings. Why don't you move to Settle, Mama? The Golden Lion is very comfortable.'

Mrs Collins's eyes became alert at this idea. 'His lordship

will surely change his mind about you when you have a son. I believe there is a Dower House on the estate.'

'It will be yours, Mama.'

Beth saw the obsession take over Mrs Collins's eyes as she receded into her dream.

'If I have a son,' Edgar continued, 'we shall both be installed in Redfern Abbey. Everything rests on a son.' He glanced in Beth's direction. 'The girl is well? Mama! I asked you about the girl.'

'I can speak for myself, Edgar, if you take the trouble to ask me.'

He raised his eyebrows. 'Barden was not totally honest about you. You are wilful. I should not wish to present you to Lord Redfern. However, I shall not need you once the infant is born.'

Will not need her when her child is born? What was he thinking of doing with her? Banishing her to a convent or worse?

'Unless my child is a girl,' Beth said. Even as she said it she wished she hadn't. She would rather be in a nunnery than be forced to share Edgar's bed again. In fact the harsh Blackstone regime would be more welcome to her than any more of Edgar's assaults on her body.

Edgar shrugged. 'You have proved yourself fertile and in robust health. You will give me a son eventually.' He walked over to her, tweaked her nose between his knuckles and bent close to whisper in her ear, 'The bedchamber will be my consolation.'

Beth felt a blush rise in her cheeks and wondered if she could put him off until after the birth. 'How long will you be staying at High Fell,' she asked.

'I shall be here for the birth,' he replied. 'His lordship has expressed a wish that he witness the birth.'

Beth's eyes widened. 'His lordship will journey here?'

Mrs Collins, too, recovered and expressed surprise. 'Surely he will not visit!'

Edgar addressed his mother. 'He has insisted that a trusted servant attend the girl. Where the bloodline is concerned he will not leave things to chance. The birth will be observed.'

Beth had ceased to be shocked by the ways of the gentry, but that did not stop her protesting. 'I will not have some stranger at my confinement!'

'You will be quiet and do as you are told.'

'I shall not, sir, not when you speak so of my well-being! You would do well to remember that my child will need a mother.'

'Dear God, she is impudent as well as wilful.'

Mrs Collins advised her son, 'You must take the strap to her after the child is born. I shall do the same.'

To Beth's horror, he appeared to consider this. He stroked his mouth with his fingers and nodded thoughtfully.

She responded, 'You would be wise to take great care of me, sir. Even if my child is a girl, you will need me to remain in good health.' But these words made Beth realise that she was as anxious as he for her child to be a boy. Heaven forbid that she would have to lie with him for years until she produced the necessary heir.

'His lordship is sending his own surgeon, a loyal and trusted gentleman who has served the family all his life. He is advanced in years but his lordship is insisting that he sees the mother and delivers the child himself.'

Beth felt a sense of relief that the servant would be a medical man, but Mrs Collins seemed affronted by this

68

explanation. 'I do not see the need. Does he not acknowledge that you are the child's father?'

'He does. Milo presented the evidence to his lawyers and clergy,' Edgar shrugged. 'However, his lordship believes that if the child is a girl I shall swap her for a boy born to some local family. Milo tells me it has been known to happen where fortunes are concerned.'

And there is a considerable fortune at stake here, Beth thought. She remembered from her marriage ceremony that Milo wanted the Redfern living and she wondered what other favours Edgar had promised him.

'Dear God, Mama, she had better give me a son. It will secure me an income, for his lordship will consider it his duty to settle a trust on the boy that I shall control as the boy's father.'

If her dowry had gone, Beth wondered where his money was coming from at present.

Beth's favourite spot for her afternoon rest was a window seat on the landing that faced west. Not only was it sheltered from the cold easterly winds but it also had a view of the track down to the stream. While Mrs Collins slept, she curled up and watched for the surgeon's trap to appear, constantly worried that he had not led it safely over the bridge.

She had eaten as well as she dared for any excess gave her lingering heartburn and she hoisted her feet onto the ledge and covered them with a warm woollen blanket while she allowed her food to digest. Dusk came early as the days shortened towards winter and she had to peer through the gloom but, yes, two riders were approaching. As they neared she saw that it was Edgar and Milo. Milo's carriage was following at a distance behind.

When they swept into the farmhouse yard below her she heard Edgar say, 'Leave the horses, Milo. Shipton has taken over from Roberts and he will see to them.' She remembered that Milo was the clergyman who had married them and a long-standing friend of her husband. The draught from the door rushed up the stairs and riffled her skirts as they entered. She heard their boots echo on the floorboards and then the sound of sparks flying as he added logs to the fire. They were almost beneath her and she could hear their voices clearly.

'Sorry about taking the carriage back, Edgar old chap, but you know how these things work. I shall need to impress the ladies.' He laughed. 'I should have kept Elizabeth Smith for myself.'

'You're a vicar with a good stipend. You'll find an heiress, surely?'

'I am the son of a brewer and my parish is on the edge of a middle-class town.' Milo sounded doubtful. 'Were it Redfern Abbey with its fine rectory and prosperous village, I might be able to tempt some minor aristocrat.'

'The Abbey living will be yours just as soon as his lordship dies, I promise you.'

'That could be years away. He is old but I am reliably informed he has a sound constitution. My vocation requires me to take a wife and I have put it off for too long already. Like you, I have no family trust to draw on so I must marry into money.'

'What about one of the daughters from Fellwick Hall?'

'I'm afraid they are too coarse and tweedy for my parish. They like their country pursuits too much to settle in a town.'

'Then you must look to the towns for your bride. Redfern coal mines have been feeding manufactories all over the South Riding. Many fortunes have been made already.'

'Indeed. Commercial and trades men like my father have prospered as a result. A successful merchant would pay well to see his daughter married to a respectable clergyman.'

'I believe you're right. Have you anyone in mind?'

'Not yet. But I shall have invitations over the festive season. The town matrons hold *soirées* in town – musicians and singers, card tables and suppers. I am a presentable bachelor and with my own carriage I am sure I shall be popular with the well-off daughters in my parish. I plan to be wed within the year.'

'Let's sit by the fire and drink to that.'

Beth returned to her chamber and heaved her bloated body onto the high bed. It was November and there was a good fire. She had been moved to a large bedchamber next to Edgar's in readiness for the birth. Although he never stayed more than a couple of nights at High Fell, she was relieved that he had not insisted on his marital rights in deference to the child. But did all women grow so large? Dear heaven, her child must be ready now, and surely only a male child would grow so big. Mrs Roberts had to wait on her and she did so most ungraciously but nonetheless competently. The housekeeper came in and set down an armful of linen on the chest.

'Leave my undergarments out,' Beth said. 'We have a visitor and I should like to dress and come downstairs for dinner.'

'The mistress won't have it, you being such a sight. I'll bring you a tray.'

Probably with poison in it, Beth thought. Mrs Roberts blamed Beth for everything that went wrong with her life including being too ill to see her husband buried as though it were Beth's fault the bridge had collapsed.

Beth did not argue and kept calm for the sake of her

unborn baby. The days passed, and every day she willed him to appear. He squirmed and kicked so frequently she thought he must have eight legs. But she loved him already and knew he was sure to be a blessing for all of them. She looked forward to and welcomed motherhood. Her marriage was not happy but an infant would give her the fulfilment she needed to survive her life at High Fell Farm. The months of waiting would soon be over and she allowed her excitement to bubble as she listed the names she might choose for her child.

She heard the distant sound of shotguns on the fell. Edgar was staying at Fellwick Hall with other visiting gentry, to stalk deer. He would be back soon though for the birth if not for her sake. Knowing how much he needed an heir gave her the confidence to ignore the rudeness of the other women she lived with. Motherhood was her future and she grew excited at the prospect. Beth acknowledged that she would never be able to love her husband, not even as the father of her child. She had no respect for him so it was impossible. She realised, though, that she did not care because she would have her children. Yes, children. She would have more. A few minutes of Edgar's brutishness could give her a lifetime of love from a child. Do hurry up, she whispered to the mound under the bedclothes in front of her.

A few days later, she watched through the bedchamber window as Edgar arrived with Milo and the Redfern surgeon, Dr Melville, in Milo's carriage. Edgar brought the medical man into her bedchamber. He was elderly and dressed in old-fashioned breeches and powdered wig. He had a serious face and brisk manner.

'Good afternoon, ma'am.' He bowed his head briefly and turned to her husband. 'Forgive my intrusion, sir, but when labour starts I should like a day bed put up in this room so I may be with your wife at all times. I trust you do have your own bedchamber?'

'I do.'

'Excellent. You may continue relations as normal before the birth.'

There was a pause of a few seconds while Edgar realised what the doctor meant.

'But I have not lain with her for months. She said it was for the baby's safety.'

'There is no need for that, sir. You will not harm the child. Indeed you may bring on his birth and by the size of her it is time.'

'Is that so? It will hurry him along?'

Dr Melville nodded seriously. 'I advise it, sir. It is a tried and tested method.'

Beth despaired of this advice. 'Is there no other way, sir?'

The doctor's offended expression told her he was not used to his wisdom being questioned.

Edgar glowered at her and she glared back. He grimaced as though the idea was as distasteful to him as it was to her. 'We'll do it after dinner,' he said and opened the door to leave, adding, 'Be ready for me.'

When he had closed the door behind him she pleaded with the doctor. 'Surely such activity must harm my unborn child?'

'I sincerely hope you are not going to be a difficult mother. You are under my orders now and I know what is best. Now, call your maid so I may examine you.'

Beth threw back her bedcovers and attempted to swing her legs out of bed. 'I do not have a maid but I am not an invalid. I'll fetch Mrs Roberts.'

The doctor looked about the chamber. 'No maid and no bell. I shall speak to your husband. Stay where you are.' He went out leaving Beth to contemplate nervously how he would examine her. She would have preferred a village midwife, a mature woman who had borne children herself and understood how she felt. But, she supposed she should be grateful that his lordship's lawyers had seen fit to send his personal surgeon for her benefit.

She was relieved that he didn't return before dinner. Through the door she heard voices and laughter from the hall below and guessed Dr Melville was dining with Edgar and Milo. Mrs Roberts brought her some soup which she placed on a side table without a word. Beth called a 'thank you' but clearly the housekeeper was far too harassed by visitors to acknowledge her. She lay awake listening to the deep tones of the gentlemen's voices below, then boots on the stairs and landing until, finally, Edgar entered the chamber.

She was prepared for him. 'Surely you can't want to do this, Edgar. See how large I am? I cannot seem at all pretty for you.'

He turned down the corners of his mouth and frowned. 'You've not even tried. Look at you! Your hair is tied off your face and not curled, and that nightgown—'

'It is the only one large enough, dearest. Why not wait until after the birth?'

'Because Lord Redfern's surgeon has advised me otherwise and he knows what is best. It is time my son was born.'

'My baby will come when he is ready. I – I –' Her voice dropped for she knew she would be disobeying her husband. 'Truly, Edgar, I should prefer you to wait.'

'Oh would you? Why should I listen to you?'

'Because I don't want you to do it,' she replied quietly.

'How dare you insult me? You are my wife. It is your duty to want what I want and do as I wish.'

'Please understand, Edgar. My body is uncomfortable and I am weary. You are – well, a large gentleman and too heavy.'

'Oh, cease your whining and untie your hair.'

He was already taking off his boots and trousers. He stood at the side of the bed in his shirt with a distasteful expression on his face. Her hopes rallied. Perhaps she was too ugly for him and he did not want her. He whipped back the covers. 'Lift your nightgown.'

She gathered the material until it bunched around her bosom to fully expose the curve of blue-veined belly. Surely he would change his mind when he saw her? 'See how large I have become.'

He grimaced. 'Good God, you're grotesque. How would any man want to – well, you'll have to get me going somehow. Give us a smile and start playing.'

Playing? Her eyes widened but she pasted an artificial grin on her face until he grabbed at her hands and shoved them under his shirt. 'Go on, then.'

Beth had no idea what to do with this squashy collection of male parts that landed in her palms. The feel of his cold saggy skin made her shrivel inside and her hands jumped away. 'Useless,' he rebuked, looking around. 'Where's the fly swat.'

Beth had no idea and, alarmed that he might beat her with it, offered no suggestions. But he produced it from a cupboard by the hearth, pushed it into her hands and ordered, 'Use this.' He took off the rest of his clothes and lay face down on the bed. 'Don't you know anything? On my back-side,' he seethed into the pillow. 'Good God, I suppose I should be grateful that this shows you were never a whore.'

But she felt like one, like a woman used for someone else's pleasure. When her uncertainty had receded she realised what she had to do and she relished it. She whipped his bare backside with the swat making him yelp and whine with pain. She whipped him as hard as she was able from her position reclining on pillows, and she hurt him, half expecting him to return the beating. Instead, he muttered something and she tilted her head to hear. 'I'm sorry, Mama, I'm sorry,' he whimpered.

Dear heaven! What went on inside her husband's head?

Suddenly he reared up and grabbed the swat from her, flinging it across the room.

'Turn over,' he snapped.

'I beg your pardon?'

'*Turn over*,' he repeated.

Her eyes widened but she obeyed awkwardly, uneasy about his intentions. Was she now to suffer as he had? She lay on her side so as not to squash her stomach.

'On your front, girl,' he persisted. 'Hurry up.'

'I can't, it hurts my back.'

He pushed her from behind. 'You've seen the tupping, haven't you? Get yourself on your hands and knees. I'll take you from behind.'

She had little option other than to obey him but she felt no better than one of his breeding ewes as she crouched there with her forehead on her hands and waited. She heard a growling chuckle and winced as he slapped each of her buttocks in turn. The weight of her bulge dragged on her spine making it difficult to keep her back straight and tears welled in her eyes. She felt his roughened hands caress her exposed buttocks and then his fingers pushed apart her flesh and probed her private area. The room was silent except for his noisy breathing – a sort of rasping pant that developed into a hoarse growl as he invaded her. Her back hurt and saliva gathered in her mouth. He went on and on, sweating and grunting, and she grew tired of holding herself in the same position. If her back sagged he yelled an obscenity, shoved one of his arms under her belly and heaved her up again. She lifted her head and braced herself against the wooden bed head as he thrust inside her. She felt so utterly degraded by his lack of thought for her comfort at this critical time.

She had no more worth in this house than one of the farmyard animals and wondered, children notwithstanding, how she was going to survive a lifetime of such humiliation. She wondered if she could – somehow – get away. When her child was born, find a way out of this place and somehow disappear from Edgar's life! If her child was a girl he wouldn't mind if she went. She felt she would have to go rather than face another attack on her body by her husband.

He had her dowry; was that not enough? With a sickening realisation she knew it was not; not now Edgar had been accepted as heir to Redfern Abbey. If she had a boy and ran away with him, they would hunt her down for him and she could not give up her child. Whatever happened she was trapped. It seemed that her baby, whom she so looked forward to cherishing, had trapped her in a life with Edgar for ever.

Her head cracked against the solid wooden headboard as he reared up, cried out like a stuck pig and fell against her. Thank heaven, he had finished. The bed creaked and shuddered as he flopped on his back lying diagonally across the mattress. She held onto the headboard and glanced at him under her arm. His hair was awry and his face was an angry red. The clean white shirt was crumpled in a heap on the bed. She watched him pick up a section of fabric and wipe around his flaccid private parts. The way she felt at the moment, if she had had a knife to hand she would have cut them off. She wanted to vomit and had to swallow the saliva collecting in her mouth. His eyes closed and within minutes he was snoring.

Awkwardly in the small space he had left her, she turned herself to sitting on the pillows with her back against the headboard. Her feet touched his still body. He grunted and shoved her legs away roughly, settling back quickly into his slumber. She had never hated him as much as now. And she hated his mother just the same. She even hated Mrs Roberts. The only decent person at High Fell Farm was Abel, the shepherd, and he stayed well away from the farmhouse and any contact with her.

Her baby started kicking again and in spite of her discomfort she smiled. Soon she would have someone she could love without reservation and her optimism revived. Perhaps too, when her child was born and she was nursing him at her breast, her husband and his mother would treat her with more respect.

Chapter 7

Dr Melville examined Beth in her bedchamber after luncheon the following day with Mrs Collins in attendance. He listened to and felt around her swollen stomach and examined her in the most intimate and embarrassing way.

Surrounded by pillows and lace, Beth listened with interest as they conversed above her head.

'Well?' demanded Mrs Collins.

'She is close to confinement, ma'am.' He frowned and glanced around the room. 'Where is the day bed? And the crib? See to it immediately.'

Beth had never seen anyone speak to Mrs Collins like that in her own home. But she seemed to accept it and said, 'Very well.'

The surgeon looked affronted and replied, 'Immediately.' Mrs Collins left the chamber and Beth heard her call for Mrs Roberts from the landing.

Beth enjoyed the exchange. She turned back her bed covers. 'I should like to sit by the window.'

The surgeon glared at her. 'You will do exactly as I say and stay where you are. Save your strength. The birth will be long and difficult.'

'Is something amiss, sir?'

'You must do exactly as I say, madam, and leave everything to me.'

Beth shrank back into the feather mattress as Dr Melville imprisoned her in between covers tucked in so tightly she could barely move.

Glowing lamps were gathered around the foot of her bed as she writhed and yelled in the middle of the night. But the pains and the pushing, the sweating and the slime counted for nothing when her firstborn slid from her to the waiting hands of the doctor. 'A boy, my lady,' he said. Beth heard him cry and she thanked the Lord for answering her prayers; a boy, an heir, she had done her duty well and wished there was someone – anyone – who loved her enough to share her joy.

'Let me hold him.'

'I shall take him to his father first.'

She wanted to hold him herself but her baby was carried away by Mrs Roberts to be cleaned and wrapped.

'Is it over? Dear Lord, it doesn't feel like it.' Beth gazed down at her still-bulging belly. 'Why am I so swollen?'

The doctor took his ear trumpet to listen to her belly, probed gently around her swelling with his fingers and murmured, 'Very high, as I thought. You have not run to fat, madam. I only ever saw a belly this big when—' He hesitated. 'You have another babe in there.'

Beth laughed. It had not occurred to her that she was so big because she was carrying two babies. But her second infant, it seemed, was in no hurry to be born and she became anxious, even more so when she noticed the surgeon frowning.

'Why isn't he coming? Has he died?'

'His heart beats but he — or she — is — is not ready yet.'

'Why not? He is a twin. Why isn't he coming? Something must be wrong!'

The surgeon did not respond to her anxiety. 'Your husband needs to hear of this immediately. I'll send in Mrs Roberts to clean you up.'

'But my other baby may start coming.'

'Pray that he does, ma'am, for everyone's sake.'

'What do you mean?' she cried. 'Is he going to die?' But she was calling to an empty room and a closed door.

She calmed after a while and reflected on the reason why she had grown so large. Two babies in one go! She had heard of such a thing, of course, and had once seen two sisters as like as two peas in a pod. Edgar and even sour old Mrs Collins would surely be pleased that she had produced two heirs in one go! Two babies at once! Dear heaven, she hoped her second child would be healthy.

She smoothed her hands over her bump and said softly, 'Hurry up my little one. It's time to follow your tiny brother.'

But as she lay there basking in her happiness, preparing herself for more pains, intrusive dark thoughts flitted through her mind taking away her euphoria. Why was this baby not moving? Had he died in her womb? Her heart thumped in fear. She heard the sounds of voices and laughter and celebration from beneath her. Her firstborn was something to celebrate but were they being hasty in toasting a second child?

Yet, even as she contemplated her worst fear, she knew it was not true. Her second baby was alive. She would have known if he had died inside her. He simply was not ready for the world and, as though to reassure her that he thrived, she felt him stir. Her hand darted to where she felt the kick. It was high in her belly and she held her breath waiting for another movement. Sure enough, he obliged and the thumping in her heart receded.

She inhaled deeply and lay back contentedly. 'Take your time, my little one. There is no hurry.'

Mrs Roberts seemed unusually smug when she brought in hot water and cleared away the soiled linen. She kept glancing at Beth and at one point Beth was sure she had sneered. Was she envious of Beth? The Redfern succession was secured within a year of their marriage. Even Mrs Collins would be obliged to recognise that she had done her duty. Beth nestled in the pillows and closed her eyes. The next sound she heard was the clock on the landing chiming the hour. Six o'clock and her second child had not moved. How much longer, she sighed. Dawn was breaking and her chamber was empty except for the surgeon who had returned and fallen asleep in the day bed. She clambered out of her bed to use the chamber pot in the commode and was grateful to climb back to the comfort of the pillows.

The surgeon grunted and stirred, then roused himself quickly and looked at his pocket watch. 'Any pains, ma'am?'

She shook her head.

He frowned. 'It is too long already.' He placed his ear trumpet over the mound of her stomach. 'But he lives.'

His worried expression seemed permanent and Beth asked anxiously, 'Then why does he not move?'

He went back to his chair looking distinctly dissatisfied.

'May I have my son?' she asked. 'Will you fetch him to me? He will be hungry.' When the surgeon did not reply she added, 'Please. My breasts are painful.'

'If you suckle, madam, you will stop the pains of your second child and he has delayed too long already. A wet nurse is here. I arranged for her to follow me from Settle.'

'But I don't want her! He is my child and I want him at my breast!'

'Calm yourself. It is normal for ladies of the aristocracy to engage wet nurses.'

'But I am his mother. I want to nurse him.'

'His father is heir to Redfern, ma'am,' he pointed out.

'But you must let me hold him!' Beth protested.

Dr Melville did not smile. 'He is healthy, madam. You have my word on that.'

Fear gripped Beth's heart. 'Where is he? I want to see him now.'

'Do not be difficult, ma'am. You have another child to consider.'

Beth saw the sense in this advice and tried to quell her fears. As soon as her second infant was born she would be able to hold them both. She considered asking for a potion to hurry along the birth but feared Dr Melville might suggest Edgar as a remedy and she was unable to face that. Besides, as the next day passed without any birth pangs the grimace on Dr Melville's face became a set expression. However, he continued to reassure her that her second child had not died in her womb.

From time to time, she heard her son cry and climbed out of bed to search for him. But either the surgeon or Mrs Roberts were prepared to physically restrain her from leaving the chamber and she feared a struggle might harm her unborn baby. More worryingly, after her third attempt, they locked the door when they left her alone. Neither Edgar nor his mother visited her.

After five long days of frowning and grimacing, Dr Melville appeared to lose interest too and stopped attending her. She was left to the ministrations of Mrs Roberts whose smugness became more pronounced as Beth grew increasingly anxious about her unborn child.

'Why is he taking so long?'

Mrs Roberts busied herself tidying the bedchamber.

'Is something is wrong. Will you ask Dr Melville to speak with me?'

'The babe'll come when he's ready.' Mrs Roberts shook her head as though in despair.

'Have – have you known of twin babies born separately before?'

'I have heard tell of it – and why it happens.' The smug satisfaction was in her voice. 'Got found out, haven't you?'

'What are you talking of? You must tell me, Mrs Roberts! Will my baby live?'

'Best if he doesn't, ma'am, for your sake.'

Oh dear Lord, no. To go through all this and then to bear an infant who was – was what, a cripple or an imbecile? It was all too much. Perhaps that is why they were keeping her healthy son from her, so he would not be tainted by association. The phrase insinuated into her consciousness – was her second child a freak of nature? She began to feel ill in her mind as well as her body. Why didn't the surgeon come to see her? She fretted about both her babies and their future in her travesty of a marriage. She was willing to be a good wife. She had tried so hard yet it seemed she was to be blamed for bearing a freak of nature.

A whole week after her son was born her waters broke for the second time and Beth struggled with her birthing pains all over again. At least this time she knew what to expect. So did Mrs Roberts who, in spite of their differences, behaved in a competent manner. But Beth realised something was dreadfully wrong and was quite frantic with worry by now.

It was daylight and when Mrs Roberts placed her child – a girl, a delightful girl – in her arms she could see her rosebud lips, tiny nose and blue eyes as well as every detail of her fingers and toes. 'But she's perfect,' Beth breathed in questioning surprise. 'Edgar will surely adore her?'

Mrs Roberts half laughed. 'Don't be foolish, madam. He doesn't want to see this one.'

'Whyever not? Is it because she's a girl?'

Her temporary midwife did not reply and busied herself with collecting soiled linen for the laundry.

'She is well, is she not?' Beth queried, but still received no reply. 'What is so wrong with her that my husband will shun her?' she persisted. 'Tell me. I insist that you tell me.'

'Surely you know, ma'am. After all, you had both infants.'

'What am I supposed to know?'

Mrs Roberts grunted. 'Your innocent airs may have deceived others but not me. Babies made together are born together and – well – I've seen the firstborn and he's got the Redfern brow from Master Edgar, so this one must be the bastard.'

Beth did not believe that she had heard correctly. 'What did you say?'

'Two infants born days apart like this have different fathers. I learned that at my mother's knee. I thought they'd have taught you that at that school for bastards you've come from.'

Beth's mouth dropped open in astonishment. 'It's not true!' she protested.

'I was there when Dr Melville was talking to Master Edgar and the mistress. It stands to reason, if there's two like yours born separate, then they're bound to have separate fathers. You should be ashamed of yourself. Master Edgar swore you were a maid when you came here and there weren't many you could have gone with at the time. I told 'em, I told 'em straight, it weren't my Mr Roberts even though he were right friendly with you. It couldn't 'ave been him because he couldn't do it, he hadn't done it for years.' Beth gazed at the smug contempt on Mrs Roberts's face as she finished, 'I bet your mother was a whore.'

'Get out,' Beth breathed, 'and take your filthy accusations with you.'

Mrs Roberts picked up a bundle of linen. 'You ought to be nice to me. You are going to need my help with two bairns to look after.'

Beth found her heart was thumping with suppressed rage and her baby whimpered. She inhaled deeply to quell her anger. 'Hush my sweet,' she murmured. 'You are a pretty little flower, aren't you? What shall I call you? Daisy, I think. I like Daisy, do you?'

Daisy snuffled against her breast. Beth wondered about her son's name. She wanted Albert after the Prince Consort but he wasn't popular with everyone so she couldn't decide; maybe Thomas or William or – or George, perhaps. She must speak with Edgar and stop this cruel gossip. Dear heaven, he was the only gentleman who had known her in that way and he was aware that she did not have a coy or playful nature. He would believe her. Propped up by pillows she dozed with Daisy in her arms until the bedchamber door opened again and Mrs Collins advanced to the foot of the bed.

Beth pushed back Daisy's wrappings to show her face. Mrs Collins did not seem pleased so Beth lifted Daisy and said, 'Your granddaughter Daisy, madam.'

'Don't you bring that – that bastard anywhere near me! Don't think you can lie to me either. You will answer me and tell me who the father is.'

Oh no, thought Beth. She kept as calm as she could for Daisy's sake. But her tone was firm. 'She is Edgar's child.'

'It will be better for you to speak the truth and show remorse if you wish to see your son.'

'I have done nothing wrong, madam.'

'You are an adulterer and a liar, girl. If it were not for the boy I should have the marriage annulled and send you back to Blackstone.'

Beth thought that an angry exchange was not in the best interests of her child and stayed silent until Mrs Collins barked, 'Well, answer me, girl. Who did you lie with when we were away – as if I cannot guess?'

Beth replied quietly, 'I should like to speak to Edgar, ma'am.'

'You wish to throw yourself on his mercy and hope he'll want more heirs from you? He'll see you in a nunnery first.'

'He would send me to a convent?'

'Rather that than have his lineage in question. You are a disgrace.'

'I am Edgar's wife,' she retaliated, 'and I have been faithful to my vows.'

Beth saw Edgar hovering in the open doorway. Mrs Roberts pushed past him with an armful of clean linen and a familiar smug smile. 'They all say that, madam.'

'Edgar! She is your child, I swear it.' But he grimaced and answered, 'Mrs Roberts has told us.'

The housekeeper seemed to be enjoying her chance to speak. 'We know it was that Abel when you went up on the fell to take supplies. She was up there with him for nigh on a week of nights, madam.'

'There was a rock fall! I had no choice. The track was blocked and neither of us could get through.'

'Aye. Just a week after Master Edgar brought you here as his bride.'

'But Abel did not touch me! As soon as he realised who I was he insisted on sleeping outdoors in the freezing cold.'

Mrs Collins's face was as grey and still as stone. 'Fetch him at once. I shall have the truth.'

Chapter 8

Mrs Roberts hurried away followed by Mrs Collins who hovered outside the open door and spoke to Edgar in a low voice. Beth was losing her patience. Of course Abel was not responsible for her second child! She was insulted that they should even consider the possibility. Dear heaven, he was going to be furious for he was an honourable man! She heard the thumping of his boots on the stairs. Even so, she was surprised to see him push past Edgar and Mrs Collins, and stand on the threshold to her bedchamber. He was dressed for riding and carried his crop in one hand and his hat in the other.

He bowed his head to Beth. 'Forgive my intrusion, madam, but I shall not be slandered in this way. I insist that you tell them the truth.'

Mrs Collins's shrill voice carried past him. 'You forget your position in this household, sir. You will wait in the kitchen.'

He did not budge except to turn his head and reply over

his shoulder, 'No, madam, you forget yours. This farm does not survive without me.'

Beth watched Mrs Collins's dark and angry face behind him. 'Get out of here and take your coarse impudent ways with you! Not only have you coveted ownership of this farm since you arrived, but your festering jealousy of my son has pushed you to the lowest imaginable depths!'

Abel whirled on her. 'He did not need my help, madam. He was assisted well enough by you. As for the farm, my interest is solely to prevent its further decay into ruin.'

Beth was shocked by Abel's response. She had thought him a mild-mannered considerate man. Indeed he was but he was also observant and astute and, she would have guessed, not given to jealousy. He had seemed content with his lot as a shepherd, but his venomous tone indicated to Beth a hitherto suppressed hatred of Mrs Collins, a hatred that she shared.

Mrs Collins raised her right arm and brought the flat of her hand across his cheek with such force that it was she who reeled and had to clutch the door jamb to prevent herself from falling over. She was shaken but not deeply enough to stop her seething, 'How dare you cuckold my son.'

Clearly surprised, Abel rubbed his cheek and directed his flinty gaze to Beth. 'You must tell them, madam, that I have not touched you, nor would I, not ever.'

Of course he would not, Beth thought. He was a principled man and she was a married woman, so he would be deeply offended by such an immoral suggestion. But in spite of the emotional turmoil she was suffering, Beth felt another, different, stab of disappointment; a real hurt that drove through her as she registered his words. *Nor would I, not ever.*

These were words she did not care to hear from his lips for, she realised, with a sinking despair, that although she dreaded the prospect of her husband touching her, she knew she would welcome such an advance from Abel. If anyone harboured wicked thoughts it was Beth. Her instincts were telling her that he would treat her kindly, that he would love her in a selfless, considerate way; that he would love her as a husband ought to love his wife. Her wide-open eyes became shiny with unshed tears as she realised that she wished she had been married to Abel for her dowry. She stared at the pleading that flooded his face and her heart began to crumble.

'I – I have told them the truth,' she choked. 'They do not believe me.'

Mrs Collins was not going to be persuaded, Beth was sure of that. She had made up her mind about her wilful daughter-in-law of dubious background. Perhaps Beth's generous dowry had merely reinforced her view that it was the only way to secure a marriage for one who is handicapped by birth. Mrs Collins had treated her no better than she would a servant so why should that change now? Abel suffered a similar prejudice, Beth realised, as Mrs Collins's attention and anger were focused on him.

'I shall not tolerate such deviance from servants on my land. You will leave my farm today.'

'Dear Lord no, Mrs Collins,' Beth protested. 'You cannot take away his livelihood!'

Strangely Abel did not appear as concerned as he ought to have and his response intrigued her. 'Your land? Your farm? The bank owns half of it and without my sheep it will soon have all of it. You are in no position to end our agreement.'

Mrs Collins was shaking with anger. 'My son is heir to Lord Redfern. This farm is nothing compared to his future wealth. Now remove your possessions from my stable and yourself from my sight.'

Beth was alarmed. This was financial suicide for the farm. Experienced shepherds were hard to come by and surely the sheep must be their main source of income? Although Beth realised that Mrs Collins never took any notice of her, she could not keep quiet. 'But who will look after the sheep, Mrs Collins?' Beth protested. 'Surely you will lose them without a shepherd?'

Mrs Collins did ignore her, but Abel did not. He turned to her and explained, 'The sheep belong to me, madam. I lease the fields from Mrs Collins.' He turned his attention to the older woman and added, 'It is my rent that keeps your farmhouse going, is it not, madam?'

'Then surely you have an agreement, sir?' Beth asked.

'Indeed I have. But I shall not stay where folk think so ill of me. My sheep will be on the move tomorrow.'

Again Beth felt a hurt shoot through her and she wanted to shout out, 'Take me with you,' an act that would simply confirm his guilt in Mrs Collins's eyes. But when Abel looked at Beth she saw sorrow in his eyes and uneasiness on his face. Perhaps he wished to say something to her as well, but knew better than to compromise her position further. He seemed undecided and, sensibly, Beth thought, said nothing. He simply gave a curt bow of his head to Beth and murmured, 'Your servant, ma'am.'

'*Take your bastard infant with you.*' Mrs Collins's imperious tone echoed through the chamber.

Horrified, Beth clutched her child closely to her breast. She had already given up her son to a wet nurse until her daughter was born. What was Mrs Collins thinking of? The woman was a monster! She gazed wide-eyed at Abel and for a moment she believed he actually considered the wicked offer.

Abel kept his voice level and low. 'If the child were truly mine, madam, I should welcome her as a gift from God. Sadly, she is not mine and even if she were, I should not contemplate separating a newborn infant from her mother.'

Beth wanted to scramble out of bed and hug him for those words. The feeling was strong, as though he had tied a thread to her and was pulling her towards him.

'*Get out.*' The venom in her mother-in-law's voice made Beth shudder.

She wanted to shout, 'Don't go, I need you', but she didn't and he left. His riding boots thudded on the landing and stairs, gradually lessening in their vibration until she could hear them no longer. Where would he go and what would he do? He was her only friend on this godforsaken farm and without him her life would be austere.

Beth sank back into her pillows dejected. He had been her only ally and confidante and now he was gone. But she had her daughter; Abel had known how much she would need her child, for who else was there to cherish in this hellhole?

Where was Edgar, she demanded silently? In all this exchange he had remained outside the open door, leaving everything for his mother to deal with. Beth would have thought more of him if he had swung a punch at Abel as he left. Surely any supposed cuckold had an obligation to do that? Beth mused on what Abel's retaliation would have been. He might have punched him back but perhaps not. Abel would have ignored the challenge as beneath his dignity and walked on. Abel was a proud man and she – dear heaven, the words formed in her head – she loved him for it.

Beth inhaled with a shudder. She was Edgar's wife and could not reverse that. Her marriage was not happy but she had borne two infants, including a much sought-after heir. She must be strong about this. Soon she would be able to see her son and her life would be whole again. She cared not for Mrs Collins or her weak-willed son. She had her own two children to cherish.

Life was more comfortable here than Blackstone, in spite of her servant status. The work was nothing compared to her previous situation, although with two infants someone else would have to help. The farmhouse was old and large and she had, despite its occupants, grown to like its ancient timbers. But, she acknowledged, she would have lived for ever in a shepherd's hut to be with the man she loved. Beth sighed. It was not to be for her. From now on, her children were her life.

Mrs Roberts fetched and carried willingly enough but Beth guessed she was Mrs Collins's spy. The following day Beth asked her to bring her son, and she noted Mrs Roberts's enjoyment in her reply.

'The mistress has given strict orders to keep her grandson away from the harlot and her bastard.'

Beth had heard his cries and the crib had been taken from her chamber days ago. Daisy slept in an emptied drawer from the chest by her bed.

'Get my robe and slippers,' she demanded, climbing carefully out of bed. 'And give me your arm.'

'Oh I can't do that.'

'Just help me to the door. I'll manage from there.' But Mrs Roberts refused. Beth was weak and her head felt dizzy. Gratefully, she sat on a chair on the landing. She had no idea where the wet nurse was caring for her son, but Edgar, surely, must tell her. Eventually Mrs Roberts went downstairs and came back with Mrs Collins.

'Get back into bed,' the older woman ordered, 'and I shall tell you what you can do.' She waited impatiently while Beth did as she asked.

'If you wish to see your son then you must give up the bastard.'

'Do not speak of my daughter in such terms!'

'Edgar is your husband and I cannot change that but the boy is his. Edgar will let you see him when you have sent the other infant away.'

'I don't understand. Send her where – and f-for how long?'

'For ever. You cannot keep her. Her existence will not be communicated to the Abbey. Lord Redfern is interested only in Edgar's son.'

'But I can't give up my daughter!'

'*It is not your choice.*' Mrs Collins hated to be challenged about her decisions. 'If you are difficult, Edgar will have you taken to a nunnery and you will not see your son either.'

'No! He cannot do that to me.'

'He can. He is your husband.'

'And he does as you tell him,' she sighed.

'And so should you if you had any sense of duty,' she shrilled. 'It is all arranged. The clergy will place your bastard with a family that will ensure she does not grow into a harlot like her mother.'

Beth wished she had the strength to hit her. Mrs Roberts already had Daisy in her clutches. Beth struggled out of bed. 'You can't take her. You can't.'

But they were out of the room before she was near enough to stop them. Beth heard the key turn and Daisy begin to cry. She thumped on the door with her fists calling for Edgar

95

to let her out, to give Daisy back to her, until she crumpled into a heap on the floor. Eventually there were footsteps on the landing and Edgar called through the door. 'Do as Mama says or it will be the worse for you.'

'How can it be worse? You have taken my daughter from me.' She thought she had cried out all her tears but more were coursing down her face.

'Do not fight me on this, girl, or it'll be the asylum for you.'

The threat shocked her into silence and she staggered back to bed. She had to regain her strength and get out of this prison of a bedchamber. There was cold food and drink on a tray. She had no appetite but she must eat for the milk to feed her son. If she had lost her daughter, at least her son would be hers, wet nurse or not.

Exhausted by her own emotions Beth slept and felt better when she woke. It was afternoon by the sun rays and she heard the sound of horses and a carriage in front of the house. She went to the window and saw Edgar and his vicar friend loading boxes. The surgeon was there too. She pressed her face to the glass panes hoping for a glimpse of Daisy.

Her only consolation was that Milo was a clergyman and she hoped he would place Daisy with kindly people. When he visited again she could ask where he had taken her child. But her knowledge of Milo did not give her hope. Clergyman or not, his actions, she believed, were motivated by self-interest. He and Edgar were two of a kind with ambitions only to increase their own wealth and status, regardless of others.

Depressed by this notion she washed at the marble wash-stand and searched without success for her chemise and gown. The sound of the carriage alerted her again and she rushed to the window. It was leaving, driven by Milo. She saw the surgeon lean out to look back. Edgar was driving his old pony and trap piled high with boxes and the hunters tethered and trotting behind. Was Daisy with them? Beth called out her name but no one heard. She spread her fingers on the glass. 'I'll come and find you my little one,' she cried. 'I promise.'

Chapter 9

Her head was swimming and she held on to the window sill to prevent herself keeling over. The house was quiet and Beth had another child to occupy her thoughts. She looked forward to sending away the wet nurse and reclaiming her son. Reluctantly she returned to the bed and waited, straining her ears for his cry. For the second time she contemplated running away with her infant. But it was a foolish notion for without money or friends, where would she go? She did not doubt that Edgar would hunt her down like an animal for his heir.

Mrs Roberts brought her day clothes and a medicine left by the surgeon.

'What is it?' she asked.

'It's a tincture to calm your nerves.'

'Well, I shan't take it. It will come through my milk.'

'You won't be doing no feeding.'

'You can't stop me. Where is my son? I want to hold him.'

'He's gone.'

'No, it is my daughter who has been taken away. Edgar promised me my son.'

'Well, not until he brings him home again. He's gone with the surgeon to show him to Lord Redfern himself.'

'But he'll be away for days! My milk will dry.' Beth's anxiety seemed to close her chest and she could barely breathe. 'Help me dress, Mrs Roberts, I will go after him. My baby needs me!'

'Master Edgar will bring him back. He'll have to because Lord Redfern won't have him or the mistress at the Abbey. So you can stop your weeping and wailing.' Mrs Roberts grimaced at her. 'That surgeon said you'd be a handful.' She went to the bedside table and poured a wineglassful of water, and added a few drops of the tincture. 'Here, drink this, it'll give you strength.' She stretched out her hand. 'Go on. It'll do you good.'

Beth took the glass and sipped the potion. 'It's very bitter.'

'It's medicine. Get it down you.'

Beth tried again. 'What is it?'

'It's a tonic for your nerves. That surgeon said you could take it in wine if it was too bitter for you. Master Edgar agreed that I could give you wine.'

'He did?' Then he must really understand her despair. It had overwhelmed her and she needed her strength for her son. But she determined to be firm about her position in this household. She was mother to a future lord and would be respected as such. She sat down and drank her medicine.

A calming warmth suffused her mind and body. It gave her contentment and the strength to go on. She took it every day and it made her feel better. High Fell wasn't such a bad place after all. Even Mrs Roberts became more acceptable as Beth recovered her composure and took up her domestic chores once more while she waited for her son to come home.

Beth scanned the lower fell every day listening for a carriage or trap. When her despair became too much to bear she took a small glass of wine with a few drops of her tincture and her burden became tolerable again.

One day a cart arrived from Settle with supplies including brandy and a box of sweetmeats that Mrs Roberts said were for her and not Beth. She had a length of good fabric, too, and lace for a new gown. There was wine and bottles of tincture for Beth but Mrs Roberts took them and locked them in the pantry.

'Is there a letter?' Beth asked anxiously. But there was never one for her and after two months Beth realised that Edgar was not coming home with her son. At these times her medicine was a great comfort to her although she always had to ask for it. Mrs Roberts was in control of affairs at High Fell and, Beth guessed, being well rewarded for the privilege.

So Beth took to walking the fells when her work for the day was done. They were her friends. She felt at home with their cold, wet and hostile bleakness. She trudged to the shepherd's hut, sat inside its derelict walls and searched her mind for happier times. But all she found was a desolate despair and she returned to the farmhouse for its warming comfort. At these times her draught was waiting for her on the kitchen table. It was her medicine and she depended on it.

Milo felt confident his life had taken a turn for the better and his future would be comfortable. He was pleased to have

100

his carriage back. The birth of Edgar's son ensured more favour with Lord Redfern and Edgar needed that, for Lord Redfern's lawyers kept him well away from the Abbey. However neither he nor Edgar troubled Mrs Collins with trivial detail. Milo drove Edgar's mother to Settle and deposited her safely at the Golden Lion before continuing with Dr Melville and his wet nurse for the infants. Dr Melville had already stated his sole interest was in Edgar's son and heir as far as Lord Redfern was concerned and the wet nurse was being well paid to keep her mouth shut. Edgar had left the trap to be returned to High Fell and ridden horseback for the remainder of the journey.

It was a pity about the Blackstone girl and her bastard, Milo thought. He promised Edgar that he would take care of the child so that no one need ever know of her existence. He knew how to make an unwanted bastard disappear and serve the needs of his parish at the same time. A God-fearing childless couple in his parish had already taken a lad from him as their own under similar circumstances. The couple were getting on in years and needed children to look after them when they were too old to fend for themselves. The boy was the bastard son of one of his church congregation, a wealthy town merchant, and a housemaid. The merchant's wife had no knowledge of their liaison and the maid had been dismissed. But Milo offered help for which he was well rewarded. He bought himself a carriage and pair, and the couple had a son to keep them off parish relief when they were older.

His reward for placing the girl would come later when he had the living at Redfern Abbey. As soon as he had delivered his valuable passengers to their destinations he whipped up the horse and headed for the far side of the Riding. The infant began to whimper when he hoisted her

101

in a laundry basket from under the carriage seat. 'Be quiet! Mrs Higgins does not want a whining child to help her in the house. It is bad enough that your mother is a whore and you are fit only for the workhouse. But why should any parish have to pay for your keep when you can earn it well enough as you grow?'

Daisy's cries strengthened as he carried her towards a tiny farm labourer's cottage on the edge of a growing industrial town. It was evening and if Mr Higgins was home he would be in his workshop repairing anything that needed his attention while his wife occupied herself in the hovel they called a home. They were well-suited as a couple, Milo thought, pious to a fault and sanctimonious about others; they would bring up their family to be the same and expect them to work all the hours that God sent.

Mr and Mrs Higgins had married late in life and after ten years had given up hope of having children of their own. They were destined in their dotage to be a burden on the parish. But they believed that God had chosen them to suffer in this way and they did so in self-righteous silence until Milo had brought them baby Boyd three years ago.

'As soon as he is grown,' Milo had explained, 'he will provide Mr Higgins with a pair of hands for his workshop. He is the Lord's reward for your forbearance.'

He placed Daisy's basket on the stone threshold and raised the rusting iron doorknocker and then picked her up, wrappings and all. For a few moments she quietened and Mrs Higgins opened the door. She was a plain woman with greying hair, now past forty years, and wore a large apron and had floury hands. She looked at the bundle in Milo's arms and said, before any sort of greeting, 'Not another one, vicar. I don't want any more under my feet all day.'

'The Lord has sent her here, Mrs Higgins. I prayed for direction and he sent me to your door. Would you reject the hand of Lord?'

'You'd better come in then.'

'Bring in the basket,' Milo responded.

The cottage was damp and chilly even though a fire burned in the grate. A small child was sitting on the stone-flagged floor with a sullen expression on his face. He had a leather strap around his middle that was fastened to the leg of the kitchen table. Milo looked down at him briefly and the boy's eyes lit up with interest. Daisy started her crying again and the child stood up, straining at his strap to see where the noise was coming from.

'How is young Boyd?' Milo asked.

'He's into everything. I'll be glad when he's grown up.'

'Well, this one's a girl,' Milo said. He placed Daisy in her basket in front of the fire. 'When you've two grown men to feed at the end of the day and your legs are a few years older, you'll be glad of a housemaid.'

'Aye, you might be right about that.' Mrs Higgins looked at Daisy's wailing reddened face. 'She's got a good voice on her, I'll say that, and my legs don't get any younger. Is she hungry?'

'Have you hot water to hand for warming some mother's milk? It's in a feeding bottle at the bottom of the basket.'

'She has a feeding bottle? Who bought that for her then?'

'You know better than to ask, Mrs Higgins.'

Mrs Higgins wiped her hands and busied herself warming the milk. 'I've not seen you out and about round these parts recently.'

'Most of my parish work is in town. It's expanding all the time.'

'Aye, it's all them mills and factories. I thought you'd been tekken poorly.'

'Church business keeps me very busy.' The kitchen table legs grated on the floor as it moved slightly. 'Look at young Boyd. He's certainly growing strong. He wants to see what's going on.'

'He's too much for me, vicar. I don't really see how I can take on another bairn at my age.'

'Why don't you ask Mr Higgins to have Boyd in his workshop with him? Now he can walk, he could take him out on the cart delivering.'

'That's an idea. Start learning the lad now. Well, he'll have to if I keep this one. Mr Higgins is such stickler, you see. He can't be doing with things not being just the way he likes.'

'Then you need a girl to help you, Mrs Higgins.'

Mrs Higgins picked up Daisy to give her the milk. 'Does she have a name?'

'Her mother called her Daisy.'

'That's pretty. Was her ma pretty? She won't be much use to me if she grows up to catch the fellas' eyes and gets wed.'

'You'll just have to make sure she knows where her duty lies. I'm sure Mr Higgins can keep her in line.'

'Oh aye. He's not above taking his belt to me if he thinks I've been straying from my duty. Her mother wasn't a – a – you know?'

'You have my word that she's from good stock. This one has a real aristocrat's blood in her veins.'

Mrs Higgins's eyebrows shot up. 'She's not from round here is she?'

'No, of course not; she's from miles away, but you know I can't say where. You'll keep her then?'

'As long as she grows up a grafter – and Mr Higgins will see that she does – she'll do me.'

Milo stood up, satisfied that his work here was finished. 'I shall say a special prayer for you in church.'

Chapter 10

Early in the New Year, Abel lifted a heavy brass knocker and let it fall twice. Within minutes a young girl in a brown dress, white apron and cap opened the door.

'Abel Shipton.'

The maid stepped back. 'Come in, sir. Mr Stacey is expecting you.'

As he followed her to a back room, he glanced around. Mr Stacey had done well for himself as a drover. He stood up as Abel entered.

'Sit yourself down, Abel. Will you drink a dish of tea with me?'

'Thank you, I will.'

The maid left the room and the two men sank into comfortable chairs before a good fire.

'I heard there was trouble up at High Fell.'

'I moved out before Christmas. I was ready to leave anyway. There was nothing for me up there and too many years of isolation are not good for any man.'

'So you've decided to look for a wife and apply for your drovers' licence at last? It's high time you did, if I may say so, Abel Shipton.'

Abel looked around at the polished furniture and comfortable seating. 'It's certainly a good living. But I wouldn't set up against you. Besides I'd need to afford the wife and home first for my licence. I was thinking there might be more of a future as an agent for the stock.'

'Not in Settle. Most of my dealings are direct with the farmers and we have the market for selling. Skipton might offer you better options. It's more of a centre for commerce than around here.'

'I was thinking of establishing myself in one of the South Riding towns. They're growing so fast the farmers and butchers can barely keep pace.'

'That's true. I hear that mutton prices are shooting up.'

'I'm interested in cattle and pigs as well as sheep, especially these new breeds that have more leg and loin. They fetch good money on the hoof.'

'Yes, I've been reading about them. It'll take you a year or two to get established though.'

'I've got a fair few head to sell to tide me over.'

'It's a good idea but it's a long trail from here to the South Riding.'

Abel didn't waste any more time. 'I have a proposition for you. I want you to drive my flock to the industrial towns around the Don navigation. I'll come with you on the trail to keep down your costs. My plan is to sell the whole lot, fat stock, breeding ewes, my rams and all and use the profits to set up a livestock broker's office.'

The maid came in with the tea and Mr Stacey got up to fetch his decanter. 'You'll have a drop of brandy in it for this cold weather?'

'I don't mind if I do.'

'Try one of these savoury biscuits with it. My good lady has them sent over from Leeds.'

Abel helped himself and waited for Mr Stacey's response.

'That's a long haul. I'd have to turn down shorter trails, so it would be a dear do.'

'You'll have me and Sal to help speed things up,' Abel volunteered. He was beginning to feel anxious. He had to get himself and his flock to where he could make the most money.

'And you want me to quote you a lower price?'

'I've put a fair bit of work your way for the last few years, Mr Stacey.'

'Aye I know, and not just from your own flocks neither.'

'As I say, I think I can make a good living as a decent broker.'

'I agree with you. You're an honest man and folk who know you trust you so I'll cut a deal with you. I'll do it for a percentage.'

'You want a percentage of my livestock profits?'

'Yes but I don't want cash. I want a share of your brokerage business.'

'You mean you want a partnership?'

'More like an investor. That way you can put all you make into the new venture and it'll be on a sound footing from the off.'

Abel saw the sense of this. He wouldn't be beholden to any bank either if he had a partner. But he was wary. 'That's very generous, sir. You risk losing your investment if I am not successful.'

'There is a condition. Once you're set up, I'd like you to take on my youngest boy. He's got an eye for livestock and that's all he interested in.'

'He's his father's son, is that one,' Abel commented.

'Aye. Do we have a deal?'

'Very well,' Abel agreed. He held out his hand and said, 'We have a new partnership for the New Year.'

They shook hands on it and Mr Stacey asked, 'Where are you keeping your flock now?'

Abel told him where he had leased another field. 'I have lodgings in the farmhouse.'

Mr Stacey seemed satisfied. 'You can have my youngest to help at lambing time for nowt.'

'Thank you, sir.'

'You'll be doing me a favour. He's restless with his book learning.'

Abel finished his brandy-laced tea and stood up. 'I'll get back to my flock then.'

'There's just one more thing. You didn't say why you left High Fell and I've heard rumours about you and Edgar Collins's young wife. Was the bastard child yours?'

It hurt. Abel tried to hide it and his brow furrowed only slightly. It wasn't the gossip. He was five and twenty and tough enough to ignore the scandalmongers. It was – it was that he truly wished Beth's daughter had been his. He answered, 'You know me better than to believe that.'

'Aye, I do. That's all I wanted to hear. I'll put my good lady straight and we'll say no more about it.'

'Thank you, sir. I'll get partnership papers drawn up right away.'

As he went outside, Abel thought that it was just as well he was moving away from the Dales for he must put Beth Collins right out of his mind. But he grieved for her in the knowledge that she had lost any hope of a happy marriage through prejudice and malice. He wondered what would happen to her daughter and almost wished he had followed his desires during those nights on the fell. She had felt the passion too, he was sure. He would have had a claim on the child. At least Beth was accepted as mother to Edgar's heir and that was a kind of compensation for her. She would need something to help her through a future as Edgar Collins's wife.

After the Spring lambing Abel considered riding up to High Fell to find out how Beth was. He was a stockman. He had good reason to be out on the fell but he knew how contrived it would look if he was seen by any of the local folk. He guessed as soon as her son was older and Beth's scandal was overtaken by someone else's, she would come down to Settle in the trap for market day. But by then he would be long gone to his new life in the South Riding.

Even if Beth removed to Redfern Abbey when Edgar inherited, their paths were not likely to cross. Beth's future was as Lady Redfern, however much she was disgraced now, and his — his? He did not know what the future held for him, only that he regretted not being able to share it with the woman he had grown to love.

As he thought of her he felt a stirring in his loins and it was not the first time this had occurred when she was in his mind. No woman had affected him like this before. Good God, the fact that he was thinking of her in this way shocked him. She was another man's wife, a lady destined for greater things than being a simple country wife. He must put Beth

110

Collins out of his head and ensure he kept a great distance between them.

Perhaps Mr Stacey was right. It was time he took a wife. He had seen what he wanted in Beth Collins, a pretty woman to be sure, but straightforward, practical, one who was strong in spirit, a wife who would be his friend as well as his lover. But first he must be well set up and solvent, for children would follow. A goodly number of them, he hoped.

Eight years later

'This is a respectable house, sir. I do not tolerate lewd or drunken behaviour. Payment is due on Saturday night for the following week. Your washing is extra but my charges include mending and pressing. My late husband was a clerk to the law court and you will find that my standards are high.'

Mrs Carter, Abel's prospective landlady, sat primly on a low chair in her front parlour. Her back was ramrod straight, her gown was fashioned from plain fabric but was prettily adorned with ribbon. She wore a lace cap over her fair hair.

'You are a widow, ma'am?'

'These three years, sir.' She looked sad for a moment then her features returned to seriousness. 'I have a brother living but a few doors away. He works for the town constable.'

'I see.' Abel glanced around the neat, well-furnished chamber with polished wooden floorboards and heavy drapes at the window. It was a house similar to Mr Stacey's home in Settle and one that Abel aspired to for himself and – and – he put a stop to his wandering thoughts. It was too early to think about a future family. 'Are your children at their labours?' he asked.

111

'My children are full grown and wed, sir. You will find my house is quiet and very suited to a professional gentleman.'

She must be older than she looks, he thought. But clearly a woman who had taken care of herself and had never had to milk a goat on a frosty morning. He guessed she had a housemaid to light her kitchen range at first light.

'May I enquire the nature of your profession, sir?' she prompted.

'Livestock, ma'am,' he replied. 'I am a livestock dealer from the Dales and looking for premises near the market place.'

'Oh, you are in trade.' She looked disappointed.

'It is a very necessary trade if I may say so, ma'am. We all have to eat. Perhaps I should explain that my vocation is more that of a broker or agent. I shall need offices not sheep pens.'

This information seemed to impress her. 'You are from the Dales, you say?'

'Indeed I am. Your home is very comfortable, ma'am. I should like to take the large chamber at the front.'

Her eyes lit up briefly. They were a fine clear blue and now that he looked more closely, he noticed that some of the fair hair curling from under her lace cap was more white than yellow. Nonetheless, she rose to her feet in one smooth movement and went to open a small bureau where she completed the formalities. 'Very well, sir. When will your luggage arrive?'

Abel had left his travelling bag outside the front door, but he believed in honesty and responded with all the charm he could muster. 'I have it with me, ma'am, but I should be most obliged if you would direct me to the best gentleman's outfitters in town.'

It worked and she summoned her maid to bring in his

few possessions and take them upstairs. His lodgings were near enough to town to avoid the expense of a horse. He had gold in his pocket from his stock dealings but he was a newcomer to this town and he needed central premises and new clothes to impress existing traders. He had had a good start as Mr Stacey had given him letters of introduction to established businesses. His new life was taking shape and he walked towards the market place with a spring in his step.

Abel was successful in his new life. He quickly found premises near the beast market of this thriving industrial town. Mr Stacey was an enthusiastic partner and had plans for their office in Skipton as soon as Abel had installed a clerk to run things in the South Riding. They corresponded regularly, but for the present Abel had no reason to return to the Dales and he did not. Mrs Stacey urged her comfortably off husband to take her to the cities of Leeds and Sheffield where the shops and stores occupied her and her daughters and gave the gentlemen time for their business meetings.

But Abel did not forget the ill will that Edgar Collins had wished on him at High Fell Farm and with his accumulating wealth purchased the mortgages Mrs Collins had taken out with the Dales bank. The bank wished to offload them as the return of the capital borrowed was long overdue and her son was borrowing more on the strength of his future inheritance to pay the interest.

At first it was revenge on the Collinses but later when Abel discovered quite by chance from Mrs Stacey that Beth had remained at High Fell and not removed to Redfern Abbey, he did it for her. Of course he could never admit that to anyone, and there were times when he even denied it to himself. She was a married woman and had to be part of his past whether he wished it or not. The widow who was his landlady, he reflected, might be part of his future for she possessed many good qualities of the kind that would serve him well as a wife.

He realised that he was starved of female attention. His daytime dealings were with men, his club dinners were men only and he kept long office hours to foster trade connections. He was not established as a man of means, nor was he well-versed in social conversation. Invitations to meet the wives and daughters of his business colleagues were not forthcoming.

He lacked social intercourse. He lacked the other kind of intercourse as well. He was three and thirty and he felt the frustrations of this enforced celibacy. He was aware that this state of affairs was not good for him, though he had not, so far, been tempted by the whorehouse despite the encouragement of some of his more unsavoury associates. Marriage, he reflected, was the only solution for him.

Abel considered his landlady, who went out of her way to please him and he was aware of her growing affection for him. She was older than he and wise, a quality that attracted him. But he did not love her and wondered if he ever could. He knew the answer for he could never love another woman with the desperate longing that he loved Beth. His face crumpled at her memory and he covered his eyes with his hands.

It did not matter where he went or what he did, Beth was always there to haunt him, to provide a comparison for any woman he met. He could not have her but in the short time he had known her his feelings for her had been strong. He longed to know such love again. But would he ever find another woman to match Beth? Was he to be forever in this purgatory?

If his love for Beth could not be equalled with another he must reconcile himself to less. There was regard, respect and admiration. Surely a man who felt these for his wife would be happy? He must find a dear sweet girl who would be a good wife to him and mother to his children. In return he would make sure he was a devoted husband and father.

But not a lover, for even as he thought of it he knew he would not deceive a woman so. His vows before God would be a sham and this conclusion caused him anguish as he reconciled himself to continuing his life of celibacy and hard work. It was time to move on and he did not wish to dwell on his decision.

'I have decided to give up my chamber here,' he said.

'Oh no, please don't leave.' The widow sounded genuinely upset.

'I have arranged to view a horse today and I shall look for new lodgings at the same time,' he explained. 'I shall, of course, pay you one month's rent in lieu of notice.'

A clean break, he thought. He walked past her and up the stairs where he packed all of his belongings into his new travelling valise and carried it down to the front door. He left it in the porch and placed his key carefully on the hall table. She lingered, watching him with reddened eyes. He was not unmoved by her tears but if he stayed her affections for him might grow and, as he was unable to return them, it would be unfair on her. 'I'll send a man for my belongings,' he said.

She nodded wordlessly.

As he walked into town he felt a huge sense of relief at his decision, as though a burden had been lifted from his shoulders. He booked in at the Crown where the landlord knew better than to enquire into his changed circumstances.

Later, he bought the horse he'd viewed and arranged livery, then ate dinner at the Red Lion where the cooks were better than those at the Crown. By morning he had decided to upgrade his assistant to manager and spend a few months at his office in Barnsley. But a letter later in the week caused another change of plan.

His partner Mr Stacey took ill and died with a few weeks, leaving only his son in charge of their Skipton office. The Dales trade was busy and Abel removed himself to Skipton instead of Barnsley. Mr Stacey's son was disappointed not to take over from his father but Abel judged he was not ready. So Abel set him up in a small office in Settle for him to learn more about his responsibilities and be nearer to his widowed mother at the same time. Abel stayed in Skipton, visiting Settle from time to time on market day. He had friends and colleagues all over that part of the Dales and renewing his old business acquaintances filled his time adequately. He often thought of High Fell but he did not go there.

Chapter 11

Two years later

'Come on, girl, get yoursenn outta bed, there's work to be done.'

Beth kept her eyes closed. Another day to get through, another day of hell on this godforsaken fell. What was the point? She may as well be dead. 'Where's my medicine? You're supposed to give me my medicine.'

'Not until you get yourself off your back, otherwise I'd get no work from you ever.'

Beth couldn't get through her day without the medicine. 'Witch,' she seethed.

'Whore.'

'Chance would be a fine thing,' she snapped. No one visited except the quarterly supply cart that brought their flour, oil, candles and other essentials including her medicine.

'If you don't curb that temper of yours you'll get none of your poppy juice until tonight.' Mrs Roberts rattled the keys in her hand. She must keep them under her pillow at night, Beth thought. She had searched everywhere else for them.

Beth was immediately contrite. 'I'm sorry, Mrs Roberts.'

'That's better.'

'When can I have it?'

'I'll think about it when you've milked the nanny.'

'Evil witch,' Beth said under her breath as the older woman left her chamber. Mrs Roberts had become hard of hearing lately, which was a blessing for Beth, who hated her with a vengeance yet fawned on her pathetically for her medicine. She picked up a damp flannel from the washstand and wiped it over her face, peering into the long cheval glass that graced her chamber.

Her drawers, chemise and stockings were wrinkled and crumpled but it was her face that shocked her. Who was that woman, the one with wild knotted hair and sunken shadowy eyes in a ghostly face? Oh, her? She was the mad woman who lived on the fell; the woman whose children had been taken away because she was a whore. She was the woman whose husband had left her; the woman no one wanted.

The hurt would not go away. It travelled through her, all over her body, inflaming every nerve ending. Only her medicine soothed it, lifting her out of her torment and laying her gently on a cloud; calm, free of all hurt and placid. 'I want my medicine,' she yelled, and picked up a stray boot to throw at her image. The glass shuddered but did not break and she shivered. She mustn't upset Mrs Roberts, not until she had her medicine. Everything would be all right then. As long as she did as she was told, Mrs Roberts would unlock the larder and take out the bottle. There were several bottles in there, all neatly labelled 'Laudanum' and lined up in the corner, enough to last until the next quarterly delivery.

118

She'd tried to get past her once and reach for the medicine herself but Mrs Roberts had her orders and had been angry. For an older woman she was surprisingly strong and she had pushed her to the floor and had made her wait a whole nerve-jangling frantic day before letting her have a single drop.

Beth struggled into her stained rank gown and boots, rammed a cap over her hair and staggered down the stairs. Mrs Roberts was tending the fire in the range. Beth knotted a wool shawl about her shoulders, took a clean pail from the scullery and went outside to the nanny. Her hands shook as she placed a milking stool in the stall. She forced a long suppressed growl out of her throat and the nanny shied as she shoved the pail under her teats. Spooked, the goat kicked away the pail and reared, tugging at her halter. The ring tethering her to the wall, already loose, fell out.

Beth grabbed the trailing rope and screamed, 'You stupid, stupid animal!' The frightened nanny butted her sending her off-balance and she stumbled against the wooden stall. Her feet tangled in the legs of the upturned stool. Desperately she retrieved the pail and pushed it over the goat's head, scrambled for the stall door and escaped. She must have her medicine. She couldn't do anything without her medicine. Why didn't Mrs Roberts understand that? She must make her understand. She must.

Every nerve-ending screamed as she stumbled through the kitchen door. Mrs Roberts was stirring porridge over the fire. The table was laid with bowls and plates. A half loaf of bread stood on a board, the large kitchen knife beside it, ready to cut.

Beth picked up the knife, brandished it in the air and cried, 'You give me my medicine now or I'll kill you!' She crossed the muddy flags and raised her arm high.

119

Mrs Roberts turned and saw her approaching. For a fleeting moment Beth glimpsed naked terror in her eyes as she backed away. The older woman's hands fumbled in her pocket and dragged out her keys. She threw them on the floor. 'Have it,' she squealed. 'Have all of it. It'll kill you anyway.'

Beth saw the keys lying on the flagstones and let the knife fall from her fingers, clattering to the floor. The keys! They were her salvation. She bent quickly to retrieve them, feverishly sorting through for the one to the larder. Which one? *Which one?* She crossed the kitchen to the larder door, frantically trying each key in turn, forcing it into the lock, straining her fingers to turn it. At last, the door opened! There! There in the corner. Two bottles waiting for her, all for her. Her fingers shook as she removed the stopper from the nearest and tipped it to her lips. The bitterness made her shudder and she gagged, splashing the precious liquid on her skin. The empty bottle slipped from her grasp and smashed on the stone floor. She wiped her grubby fingers over her face, sucking off the bitter fluid. Slowly she sank to the cold hard granite. She heard the kitchen door slam shut. Everything was so much quieter now, so much calmer. Her nerves began to soothe and soon she would be floating on her cloud, her own private cloud . . .

Mrs Roberts paused only to collect her shawl from behind the scullery door. She had had more than enough of this madwoman and was not staying a moment longer. High Fell Farm had been her home since she had been sent there by the parish as a ten-year-old when old Jacob was alive, but the workhouse was preferable to being murdered in her bed and Mrs high-and-mighty-Collins could like or lump it. Her anger kept her going but by the time she had crossed the stream she was exhausted and had to sit for a while. Fear of the cold made her push on and she sidetracked to a small farmstead. If they didn't have a pony and trap, perhaps they had someone who could take a message to Mrs Collins to send for the asylum cart. One thing for sure, she was never going back to the farm again, not while that madwoman lived there.

She left the farmstead the following morning on a crowded cart taking the whole family and a ewe to the market in Settle, having entertained them the night before with lurid stories of goings-on at High Fell Farm. Oh, and did Mrs Roberts have some tales to tell! Only when she arrived in Settle did she begin to worry about where she would sleep that night. Perhaps now was the time to call in a few favours from the tradesmen who had delivered to High Fell Farm in the past.

She knew Mrs Collins had taken rooms in the Golden Lion and ate her dinner there on most days. The inn was crowded by 11 a.m. when most of the stock sales had finished. The farmstead family went off to visit kin in Upper Settle and Mrs Roberts set herself up in a corner by the fire ready to tell anyone a story for pie and a jar of porter. She sent word by way of the landlord that she wished to speak with his distinguished resident. The landlord returned to show Mrs Roberts to Mrs Collins's rooms.

'If it's more money you want I'm sure that can be arranged. My son sends money every quarter.'

'I wouldn't go back while that madwoman is there for all the tea in China. She took a kitchen knife and tried to murder me. She needs locking up.'

'Yes, I am sure you are right. I shall write to my son immediately. He will know where to send her.'

'What about me? That farm was my home. Where do I go in the meantime?'

121

'Find lodgings in Settle.'

'Who will pay for them, madam?'

'My son will, of course. Tell whoever you lodge with that my son will take care of your bill. Everyone in town knows that he is heir to a fortune.'

'Aye, and that his wife is mad.'

'Well, if they didn't, they most certainly will now. Did you have to be so lurid and public in your complaints?'

'She tried to murder me, madam,' Mrs Roberts repeated. 'Folk need to know just how loony she is.'

'Very well.' Mrs Collins undid a small purse and drew out a coin. 'You acted in my son's best interests. Take this for your trouble. But no more tale-telling, do you hear?'

'Ma'am.' Mrs Roberts's fingers closed over the gold coin, she bobbed a curtsey and retreated to the fireside downstairs. The dining room and saloon were even more crowded and she pushed her way to the door until a heavy hand fell on her shoulder.

'A moment of your time, Mrs Roberts.'

She twisted her head. 'Oh, it's you. I'd heard you were back. Doing very well for yourself, they say, now you're a fancy stock dealer.' She turned round to get a good look at him. 'Aye, it looks like you've found a bit of prosperity.'

Abel Shipton glowered at her. 'Are these stories about Edgar's wife true?'

'Depends what you've heard.'

'I'll give you a guinea for the truth. But it has to be the truth, mind. I'll find you if it isn't.'

Her head dipped slightly as she considered the offer. 'Aye, then. You know the history.'

'Not here. I have an office in the Shambles.'

'Is there a fire?'

He nodded. 'And some good brandy.'

She disappeared out of the door with Abel close on her heels. She was impressed by his office. He had certainly made a shilling or two and already employed a clerk who knew the Dales as well as he did, one of the drover's lads if she wasn't mistaken. Abel sent the clerk away for his dinner and threw a log on the fire. Mrs Roberts sipped her brandy and told him what had happened since he had been forced to leave.

'Are you telling me she has never left the farm since she went there as a bride?'

'Well, there's no farm to speak of now. Mrs Collins let the land go and moved down here.'

'Is that what she told you?'

'It's the truth, isn't it? She needed the money for her son's hobnobbing with the gentry. But she held on to the farm-house and yard. The girl had to have somewhere to live.'

Abel gave a harsh laugh. 'The girl? The *girl's* son will be heir to a fortune one day.'

His tone made Mrs Roberts glance at his face. He was angry. She blinked. There was suppressed rage in his troubled eyes. Well, he had been sent away in disgrace as the father of the bastard child. Perhaps he had really been fond of the mad whore. He seemed to notice her staring at him and relaxed his features.

'Who is with her now?' he asked.

'With her? Nobody. Nobody in their right mind would stay.'

'But she must have someone to look after her!'

'She can take care of herself. She was a housekeeper before she wed and she has the keys to the stores . . .'

'You have left her there alone?'

123

'She came at me with a knife! I wouldn't be much use to her dead, would I? At least she'll be dealt with now.'

'Dealt with? How do you mean?'

'Mrs Collins says her son'll send her to the asylum. Best place for her if you ask me.'

Abel threw his hands up in despair. 'But you have just told me they took *both* her children away from her and then fed her laudanum to keep her quiet. Whose mind would not be turned in those circumstances?'

Mrs Roberts shrugged. 'It doesn't make no difference what causes it. She's still a loony.'

He stood up, towering over her and for a moment she felt threatened by the tautness in his curling fists. She added, 'And it ain't my fault either. I'm just telling you like it is, so don't go throwing your weight around me.'

'I am indeed in a fury, but not with you, Mrs Roberts. You've been very helpful. Now if you don't mind, my clerk is back from his dinner and I have affairs to deal with.'

She got up and pulled her cloak around her. 'Oh don't mind me. But don't ask me to go up to High Fell while she's there.'

When Mrs Roberts had gone, Abel had a conversation with his clerk and went off in search of a young physician who had recently bought into the local medical practice. He had met him as a business acquaintance through the late Mr Stacey's colleagues and they had become friends. The physician had trained in Scotland and his innovative approach to treatment was not going down well with the traditional views of Dales residents. Abel, blessed with sound health, had not had reason to consult with him yet. But now he needed his medical advice.

Dr Simon Brady could not leave before nightfall. Already Beth Collins had been alone for two whole days and Abel feared that she would have come to some harm. Abel's impatience got the better of him as he waited in his front room for him to finish his market day appointments. Dr Brady's patients appeared to be a sorry collection of farm labourer's wives and their offspring.

'Dear God, Simon, cannot the apothecary see to these people?'

'He asks for payment.'

'Don't you?'

'Not all at once. It's a system I've brought with me. I have a book for my patients. If they give me a small amount each week, they can call on me with whatever ails them and be treated.'

'So you only see poor people?'

'No. But there are many more of them and I have a regular income until I am trusted by the local gentry.'

'Aren't you worried you might catch something from these people?'

'My dear Abel, I am a physician. I care for the sick.'

'Well, I hope you have a good horse.'

'Of course I do. As I said, I am a physician and I shall forgive your ignorance about my calling because I can see that you are, indeed, worried about this woman on the fell. Now let us waste no more time.'

Their horses were packed and ready for mounting and they galloped off into the darkness. They made good progress until the river and dismounted to cross the bridge. The track became more rocky and unpredictable and, although there was a moon, it frequently disappeared behind clouds.

'Keep close behind me, Simon. I know the fell like the back of my own hand.'

'That will be useful if my patient has wandered out.'

'Dear Lord, I pray not. The nights are cold up here.'

He guided his horse around strewn boulders; rocks that would have been removed by himself or Mr Roberts in the old days. How much more had been neglected since he had left? A sense of urgency crept over him and he felt his heart beating faster making his hands shake as he gripped the bridle. The moon reappeared, lighting up a dark silhouette of farm buildings ahead.

'There! Do you see it, Simon? That is where we are going.'

He could no longer contain his impatience and re-mounted, spurring his horse once more into a gallop, fearing that the dark and the quiet that lay ahead of him meant the worst. Dear Lord, please keep her safe, he prayed.

He tethered his horse by the front door and tried to open it. It was firmly locked and barred so he hurried round to the back, noticing briefly that Simon was approaching at a more sensible canter. Everything was in darkness but the kitchen door was ajar.

'Mrs Collins,' he called, then stood stock still to listen. Not a sound. Dear God, no. He raised his voice. 'Mrs Collins!' As his eyes became more used to the interior he found a candle and lit it with a lucifer from his pocket. The kitchen was cold and empty but the larder door was open. He crossed the flagged floor to peer inside and saw the empty laudanum bottle on the floor next to its stopper and – and – a staining of vomit on the cold stone. She was sick! Dear heaven, where was she? 'Mrs Collins! Beth! Where are you? Answer me! God in heaven, Beth, it's me, Abel Shipton!'

He held his breath and strained his ears in the silence. Yes! A noise. Boots! He heard the crunch of boots – boots on the hard ground outside as Simon had followed the sound of his voice. 'Be quiet, man,' he snapped.

126

Simon picked up another candle and lit it from Abel's. 'There's a smell of vomit.'

'Yes, in here, on the floor.'

Simon lowered his candle. 'More than that and it's worse in the kitchen. Didn't you notice?'

They re-examined the kitchen with their candles. 'The scullery. It's coming from the scullery door.'

Sure enough, there she was, lying at full stretch on the freezing floor, her arm outstretched and a horn beaker falling from her fingers. Her head was turned to one side and another patch of dried vomit stained the flags.

'Beth!' Abel darted forward and sank to his knees, stroking her tangled hair and rolling her onto her back to cradle her head in the crook of his arm. 'Beth? Wake up, Beth.' Her flaccid head rolled and lolled. 'What's wrong with her? Do something, Simon, for God's sake.'

'I will if you will be kind enough to allow me access to my patient.'

Abel heard his friend's words but did not heed them. He could not leave her. Dear Lord, what if she were to die? He had wasted all those years when he could have been with her!

'Did you hear me, Abel? *Get out of my way and leave her to me.*'

'I can't. I can't let her go.'

'Be a good fellow and light lamps and candles for me. I shall need hot water, too.'

Abel stared helplessly at Beth's still, white face until Simon added, 'Look to it, my friend.'

'Yes, yes, of course.' His hands were shaking as he lowered her head gently to the floor. He stood up and allowed Simon to kneel beside her. 'She is alive, isn't she?'

'I believe so, but I fear we may be too late.' Simon uncurled the fingers of Beth's hand that had been concealed by her skirts to reveal a second phial of laudanum without a stopper. He glanced at the water pump over the stone sink. 'First, fetch a jug, draw me fresh water and bring the salt box.'

Abel felt better when he was occupied and Simon seemed to realise this, giving him directions as he tended his patient. He lit the kitchen range and took a lamp outside to find more fuel. He dragged a couch from the dining hall, set it before the warmth of the fire and then gently lifted her limp cold body from the hard stone floor. She groaned as he settled her on the cushions and wrapped her in his riding cloak.

'She's coming round,' Abel whispered urgently.

'I doubt it, for this bottle is empty. Sit her up,' Simon ordered, 'and find a pail. We must make her vomit again.' He stood at the kitchen table surrounded by candles and mixed a powder in warm water. 'We have to get this down her as soon as possible. Hold her shoulders for me.'

Abel followed Simon's instructions but she would not swallow and the fluid bubbled out of her mouth and down her chin. Abel stroked her throat, a technique he had used with sheep, but to no avail. 'Why doesn't she swallow?' he asked desperately.

'All her functions have been depressed by the laudanum. I'll try a tube. It will make her gag so you must hold her steady.' Simon took a long piece of India-rubber tubing from his bag and fed it slowly into her mouth.

'Dear God, man, you'll choke her!'

'I've done this before. I learned it in Edinburgh when I treated poisonings. Keep her still, will you!'

Abel obeyed. Beth gagged and coughed but Simon persevered until Beth made a gurgling, choking noise and in the lamplight he saw her throat move as she swallowed. She groaned and her hands clawed at her mouth. Abel took a firm grip on her arms and Simon moved quickly. He raised the tube and poured his mixture through a small funnel fitted into the end. When the liquid had drained into her stomach, he withdrew the tube and Beth gagged again. Abel's frown deepened into a grimace and he felt her pain as though it was his own.

His thoughts were in turmoil. He must save her. He hated what Simon was doing to her but he couldn't let her die. Not his Beth, his dear sweet Beth. What was he thinking of? She wasn't his. She was Mrs Edgar Collins in spite of the fact that her husband had all but deserted her because he thought her daughter was Abel's child. Dear God, he wished it had been! If this is what Edgar had done to his darling Beth it would have been as well to have given him good reason. Dear heaven, why had he left her alone for so long? If she should die, how could he forgive himself? She was more precious to him than his own life. He must save her. He must.

'Lay her on her side,' Simon urged. 'No, not like that, keep her head high and put the pail underneath.'

Abel did as he was told. 'What now?' he asked.

'We wait. I don't know how much laudanum she has taken, nor how long ago, but if she vomits up any of it, her chances of recovery will improve.'

The only sounds were the hissing of wet peat in the fire-place and the thumping of Abel's heart as he waited. Simon gathered his tubing contraption together and picked up the kettle from the hob.

'Don't leave her,' Abel begged.

'I shall be in the scullery.'

Simon's mixture worked and the contents of Beth's stomach came retching out of her mouth and into the waiting pail.

Abel held her head over the pail, taking a cloth from Simon's hands to wipe her chin as her vomiting eased. She groaned and lolled as he laid her back on the couch and for a brief second her eyes opened. But they were rolling, unseeing eyes, Abel realised, and his heart clenched in his breast.

Simon was sitting at the kitchen table, watching him as he tended her as gently as any newborn lamb. 'What is she to you?' he asked.

'She's – she's – she's a friend.'

'She's more than that, my good fellow.'

'She is another man's wife – a powerful man's wife. She can never be more than a friend.'

'If you say so.' He stood up. 'She needs someone with her at all times. We'll take turns. I'll do the first stretch until dawn. Get some rest, Abel. She is going to want all your strength and more to pull through this.'

He slept in a chair by the kitchen range until an hour past dawn, when the sound of the water pump in the scullery roused him. A cold grey light filtered through the window. He focused his eyes on Beth's still form, her stained and grubby gown, tangled hair and pale, pale face. Dear God, it was the face of a corpse, surely? He started to his feet and picked up her cold hand from where it rested on his cloak. Why was she so cold? The kitchen was warm, the log basket and peat box filled and a simmering kettle sitting on the hob.

Simon came in from the scullery wiping his face and neck with a cloth. 'There's food in the pantry and ale in the barrel. Let us take breakfast and I shall explain what you must do to help her recovery. I hope you understand that it will not be pleasant – either for her or for you.'

Abel yawned and stretched. 'I'll do whatever it takes to get her well.'

'Yes, I believe you will. But you do not know how testing it will be. I can stay only until market day but I shall leave some laudanum with you just in case . . .'

Abel waited for him to continue, and when he did not, said, 'Speak plainly, Simon.'

'She may not wish to continue living without it and you will have to watch her carefully. We must talk seriously, my friend.'

Chapter 12

Beth was shivering with cold, yet her head was burning hot and the demons were coming for her again; small black figures with wild red eyes that crawled over her body and invaded her head. Her arms flailed in the air as she tried to fight them; her nails clawed at her skin as she scraped them off her breasts and stomach. But they were still there, flying above her, darting through her eyes and ears, into her head. She screamed and cowered, covering her head with her arms as they overran her. 'Get away from me! Leave me alone!' But it did not stop them coming for her, devouring her body and eating into her soul. She had to run to where they could not find her and she tried to clamber from the couch. But they held her down and she screamed and fought until they left her an exhausted heap of jittery nerves and mindless despair that only her medicine could alleviate.

She wanted her medicine, where was her medicine, why

had they taken it away from her? 'Give me my medicine!' she yelled. But he wouldn't, he was as bad as Mrs Roberts. Mrs Roberts? Where was Mrs Roberts? Had she taken her medicine away? 'Give me my medicine!' she yelled again, punching with her fists and kicking with her feet.

Through the red oblivion she saw a face, a distant face from the past, a strong face full of pain, a masculine face with tears in his eyes and on his cheeks. A man's face; a man she knew; a man who wept. He brought her warm gruel and held a pail under her head when she vomited. He held her hand as she flopped exhausted on the couch pushing away his offers of fresh water or a damp cloth.

She wanted to die. Death was preferable to this tortured hell and she kicked and shouted again to tell him so. He was cruel to her. When she was thirsty he forced her to drink a warm concoction of bitter herbs, tipping the fluid into her mouth and pinching her nose so she had to swallow. But the brew calmed her demons to allow her a brief respite of sleep and when she awoke he was there. He was always there, sitting in a kitchen chair, watching her.

Abel was astonished by her strength when he was forced to restrain her. He never knew when her pale thin form would turn into that of a tigress or where that energy came from, for she could lift a chair and throw it at him if he was not vigilant. He rubbed a bruise on his shoulder which was evidence of his neglect. But a week after Simon Brady left, Beth was taking light broth and keeping it down.

The sun, though weak and without much heat, graced a cloudy Dales sky on the day that Beth remembered his name. 'Abel Shipton, isn't it?'

'Yes, madam,' he replied.

She rubbed her hands up and down the sides of her head.

'Oh don't you "madam" me. It hurts. Everywhere hurts. Are you my prison guard?'

'Is that how you see me?'

'Mrs Roberts ran away from me so they have sent you instead.' She rubbed her arms where he had gripped them. 'You are most certainly stronger.'

'No one sent me and I am sorry if I have hurt you.'

'What have you done with my medicine?'

'It is the medicine that has made you ill. You took too much of it.'

'*I needed it!* And I need it now.'

'Dr Brady advises that you do not.'

'Who is he to tell me what I need? Of course I need it! Where is it? Give it to me.'

He shook his head, frowning. 'I cannot. I do not have any.'

'You lie! You all lie to me. Give it to me!' She reared her body off the couch and staggered. 'I'll get it myself. Where have you hidden it?' She crashed around the kitchen and scullery, pulling away pots and jars, leaving them where they smashed to the floor scattering their contents over the flag-stones. She heaved against the latch of the locked larder door. Yes, Mrs Roberts kept it in there and the key on a chain around her waist. She ran against him, thumping his chest with her fists and yelled, 'Give me the key!'

'It will be of no use to you. There isn't any medicine, as you call it, in there,' he replied calmly. Simon had prepared him for the worst and she was no contest for his strength. But he must be gentle with her for in spite of her ferocious bouts of anger, she was fragile.

'Why should I believe you?' she yelled. 'You are the same as all the others, scheming against me for your own ends!'

He did not resist her flying fists and eventually she stopped beating him.

Her eyes darkened. When she had first met him she had thought that he was a servant rather than a tenant and had been wrong. Had he not wanted her then? Once upon a time, he had desired her as a woman, at least until he had discovered she was Edgar's wife. He would have wooed her all those years ago if she had been the ladies' maid he thought she was. He had truly desired her.

'Why are you here?' she asked.

'Would you prefer me to leave?'

She reached up to dust off and straighten his lapels with her hands. 'Your jacket is very smart for a shepherd. Have you turned yourself into a gentleman, Abel?'

For a moment his eyes widened and then narrowed again just as quickly. 'I have means,' he answered evenly.

She smiled and allowed her fingers to trace the edges of his lapels until her knuckles brushed his jawbone and he flinched. She was standing too close to him for his comfort. 'Do you have a wife as well?' she murmured, nudging at his knee with hers.

'Not yet.'

Her knuckles continued along his chin. She turned her hands and traced her forefingers around his cheeks and then – and then very gently across his lips.

'Once upon a time, you wanted me as your wife,' she said softly and felt his body stiffen. His lips parted a fraction and nibbled at her fingers as she held his gaze with her own. She knew from Edgar what men wanted from women and how urgent that need might be. Then she remembered how horrendous the act was and for a second she wavered. But he would fall asleep afterwards and then she could search his clothes for the key. Her desperation for the key surmounted all her fears. She only had to communicate to him her willingness to partake but in that she had no experience for with Edgar she had not been willing.

Abel closed his eyes as he nibbled her fingers and his breathing quickened. But no, his eyes were not quite shut for she detected a tiny glitter between the thick dark fringes of his lashes. He was different from Edgar but she supposed the act would be the same. The couch was not big enough for them both and the kitchen floor was cold and hard. Her bedroom too would be cold, not to say unkempt, but the bed was large and soft for Abel to slumber afterwards as Edgar had.

She would have the key and be down to the larder and back before he woke for another bout. And with her medicine it would not matter what he did to her and how many times, for she would have no feeling and that is how she wanted to be. When she was floating on her cloud of oblivion Edgar could behave as cruelly as he wished towards her; as indeed could his mother or Mrs Roberts. And now Abel Shipton. No one could hurt her when she was shrouded in her fog for she felt nothing.

She inhaled Abel's masculine aroma, remembered Edgar's demands on her and hesitated. But she must go on for she needed her medicine, her medicine . . . Saliva gathered in her mouth and she recalled Edgar's boorish brutish invasion of her virtue. The hurt and pain had assaulted her feelings as well as her body and he had been indifferent to her protests. He had not loved her, not even cared for her. He would have realised how much she hated him if he had. Edgar's affections were for himself and she supposed all men were the same in the bedchamber.

136

Edgar had fallen asleep afterwards. If Abel slept she could take his key and find her medicine. She needed her medicine. She would do anything for her medicine . . .

She swallowed the saliva gathering in her mouth and pulled at the neckline of her gown until she had exposed the swell of her breasts. She reached inside with one of her hands, cupping the soft flesh and pushing it upwards, until she revealed the nipple . . .

Edgar had growled at her like an impatient hungry dog. Abel – Abel did not growl. He was – was, well, different, she thought briefly, but he was a man and all men were the same, Mrs Roberts had told her, when it came to taking their pleasure. Pleasure? For Beth it was no pleasure, only an endurance and she hesitated. But she wanted her medicine and this was the only way . . .

She heard the muted rumble of a suppressed groan and sidled closer, using her other hand to reveal a second nipple as she attempted to squirm against him. But Abel did not bend his head to bite her flesh, nor use his hands to knead and squash her breasts together as Edgar had. His eyes opened wide and the lump in his throat rose and fell as he stared at her and swallowed.

'My God,' he whispered, 'what has Edgar done to you?' Then his hands did move to her breasts. His firm fingers pushed them back into her gown. 'Do you truly believe you can persuade me with your body?' He pulled up her neckline and snatched her woollen shawl from a chair. 'Cover yourself,' he snapped. 'And get your cloak. We are going outside.'

'I won't!' she shrilled. 'Not before I have had my medicine!'

'There is no medicine!' he shouted. 'Stop calling it that. It's laudanum. It's poison. The same poison that is smoked

137

in the opium dens of Liverpool and London. You have to stop taking it.' He lowered his voice. 'And I am here to make sure that you do.'

'But I must have it. I must.' Her voice cracked and she slumped on the chair. 'I can't go on without it.'

'Yes, you can.' His voice was firm but softer. 'You have to. It's the only way. Come with me.'

He took her cloak from its hook on the door and wrapped it around her, fiddling with the fastenings. He spoke as though to himself. 'Had I known how he would treat you I would have taken you with me. But you were – are – his wife, destined to share his title and his wealth. How wrong can a man be? Dear God, I should have realised then. It was a mistake to leave you with those who did not believe you were telling the truth.'

She wasn't listening to him but a few of his words lingered in her muddled brain. He had reminded her that she was Edgar's wife. She had so much wanted to be someone's wife until she realised what it really meant. She was merely a possession to be used and discarded as her husband saw fit, not even allowed to keep her own daughter or see her son. She swayed a little as she stood and allowed herself to be wrapped against the bitter weather. The fell was hidden in mist but for a second the blur in her brain cleared and desperately she tried to hold on to her thoughts.

'Where are my children?' she asked in a small voice. 'I have two children. Do you know where they are?'

He stopped in the process of pulling on his long hunting coat. He hardly knew how to reply for fear of distressing her further. Simon had warned him of his physical task in helping her, but not how to care for her broken mind. Make her face each symptom, he had said. Do not pretend it is not happening. At least, Abel reasoned, she had stopped pleading for her laudanum for a minute.

'Your son is well,' he answered, adding, 'to the best of my knowledge.' Abel knew that it was in Edgar's interests to ensure his son's well-being.

'My poor baby,' she murmured. 'I must see him.' She frowned. 'I have a daughter, too. They took her away from me. They said she was a b – b – they said she was yours. They lied. Everyone lied.'

'I didn't.'

'Why did they take my daughter too?' she pleaded.

Abel chose his words carefully. 'The – the laudanum would have affected your ability to look after her.'

'Don't you understand, you stupid man?' she wailed. 'It was because they took my children that I had to have it. I should have gone mad without it.' Her eyes were flashing and she was panting. 'Perhaps I have gone mad. But I know for certain I should not be if Edgar had allowed me to keep my daughter. Where is she?' Beth demanded.

Until then Abel had thought she had kept her daughter and the child had been removed to another place for safety, sensibly in the circumstances. What had happened to Beth's daughter? He tried to hide the concern in his eyes and in his voice. 'When did they take her?'

Beth knew she wasn't mad. She couldn't be or she would not remember any of that day. The day she had been so distressed that she could not see or even think straight. She remembered how Mrs Roberts had given her the medicine to calm her, and how it had worked, taking away the pain of her loss, the pain of her heart, the pain of everything. There was no wonder that she was a sorry shell of a woman now. Her life had been empty for so long. And now Abel

139

had returned and he reminded her of joy as well as pain. She reached out to grab his hand. 'You were there when they took her away. Where did they go?'

'When did they leave with her?' he asked.

'After you had quarrelled with Mrs Collins they left in the carriage and trap. They took her then and Mrs Roberts said Edgar would return with my son. I waited and I watched but he – he—' She choked on a sob. 'He didn't come back. Not ever. Where are my babies? Will you take me to them?'

Anger simmered through Abel. Dear Lord, surely Edgar was not that cruel? But, he realised with misgiving, that even Edgar would not have a choice when faced with the power of Lord Redfern and his lawyers. He had no idea where Beth's daughter was – or – or if the child was still alive. What should he say? Empty promises were no solution. He dared not raise her hopes only to dash them later. At this stage of her recovery she would be devastated.

Beth was so distraught that she was gulping back small sobs. 'They said she wasn't Edgar's child and I could not keep her. They said if I let my daughter go I would be able to keep my son. How can a mother choose between her children? I could not so they chose for me. Mrs Roberts said it was for the best and they were being kind by taking my daughter from me and not sending me to the asylum.' Suddenly the bleakness welled in her heart. Where was her medicine to take away the memories? 'They lied to me,' she choked. 'They all lied.' The wild desperation returned to her eyes. 'I want my children. I'm their mother! Why can't I see them?'

Abel held her hand tightly and responded hastily, too hastily he realised as he said, 'You will! I promise. I shall find them for you.' He had to do this for her, no matter how long it took him. He was confident he could find the boy, although less sure that he would be allowed to see his mother. He was even more uncertain that he would be able to locate Beth's daughter for he had no idea who had taken her away or where they had placed her, if she had survived. He pushed the latter thought away. Only a handful of people had knowledge of the girl twin. Abel determined to squeeze the information out of one of them, if he could find them. He corrected himself, *when* he found them.

His determined tone raised Beth's spirits. 'You will?' she said. 'You'll bring them here to me? When will you bring them?'

'You must get yourself well first.' He picked up her other hand. 'Come, walk with me in the fresh air.'

She shook off his helping hands. 'I can't. I can't do anything without my medicine. Give it to me. I can't go without it.' He had the key, she recalled. She must get the key from him.

Her lucid moment had gone, Abel realised, and sighed. Her obsession for more laudanum had taken over. He must not let her retreat into the comfort of oblivion again. It would be tough on her and he hated himself for the pain he must inflict on her. He had known from the beginning it was the only way and Simon's instructions had confirmed his fears and raised his anger at those who had reduced her to this pathetic soul.

'The medicine was Edgar's solution,' he growled at her. 'It is not medicine, it is laudanum. Do you hear me? Laudanum. You know what it is and I know it will kill you. What use will you be to your children if you are dead?'

'But I have to have it,' she whined.

'No, you do not.' He snatched up her hand again and half dragged her outside, pulling her behind him as he walked around the yard. 'You need to start living again. You once told me how much you loved the fell and it was the only thing that was good about your life.'

Beth was clearly distressed by his actions. She pulled against him and shouted. He heard his horse whinny in the stable. He had neglected to exercise the poor creature in his concern for Beth. The horse was lonely, too, now that Simon had departed with his mount, as High Fell Farm no longer kept a pony and trap. He recalled Beth's instincts for the well-being of animals and hauled her into the stable.

'Now calm down while you are in here or you'll spook my horse,' he ordered.

She fell against the stall, panting and sweating then crumpled into a heap on a pile of straw. He felt desperately sorry for her, but knew he must not weaken. He took the opportunity to have a closer look at the tack and an idea germinated in his mind. After a few minutes Beth seemed calmer.

'Come and make friends with him,' he suggested. When she did not move, he added, 'You can help take care of him.'

'I've not seen to horses since before . . .'

'Well, you'll just have to learn. If you are not well enough to look after a horse how will you manage in charge of a child?'

This time he thought he noticed a vestige of his message getting through to her and he realised that it was her need for her children that would motivate her to get better. This was the brightest glimmer of hope for him so far. She was in a dreadful state as a human being but she was above all else a mother and that was rooted deep within her. She might do his bidding for her children. He fervently hoped that she would. He hated himself for being the cause of so much pain, and he guessed that she despised him as much.

Would she ever forgive him, he wondered? It was hard enough to know she could never be his true love, but he hoped they might resurrect their friendship. Simon had not prepared him for this personal despair that had descended over him.

However, she did not snatch her hand from his when he took it for a second time and allowed herself to be led out of the stable. He lifted her bodily and sat her on a mounting stone outside the stable and reckoned that if she did make a run for it, she wouldn't get far before he caught up with her. He led his horse outside to saddle him. She watched but made no comment and he wondered where her thoughts were. Laudanum, he guessed.

Abel had come across the sidesaddle when he had tidied the tack room before Simon left. It was very old but had been well oiled in the past and was serviceable. He tightened the buckles and mounted, settling himself on the horse blanket behind the saddle and walked his horse towards her. She was watching him.

'When did you last climb the fell?' he asked.

Her eyes were blank. He leaned down towards her. 'I can't hear you. What did you say?'

She looked about her. 'I want to get down.'

The stone wasn't very high but he said, 'Don't jump. You're too weak and you'll hurt yourself.' He offered his hand for support. 'Come for a ride on the fell with me.'

She shook her head. 'I want my medicine first.'

'This is medicine. Stand up.'

'Where is it?' she demanded but she took his hand and scrambled to her feet on the mounting stone. 'Where is it?' she repeated.

'It's out on the fell. Will you come with me?'

143

He saw the alarm in her eyes and kept a firm grip on her hand. 'Don't be frightened.'

'I – I can't ride.'

'I'll be with you,' he replied.

'I don't want to.' She pulled at his hand but he held tight.

'I'll teach you. Turn around and I'll lift you onto the saddle. You want your new medicine, don't you?'

'You'll take me to it?' she asked, turning and backing into his waiting hands.

'I'll show you it,' he answered, hoisting her over the saddle.

She yelped as the pommel dug into her thigh, but quickly sank into position. 'I don't like it,' she protested.

'You will,' he answered and took up the reins from behind her.

Her hands gripped his forearms and he could feel the rigidity in her body. 'Relax. You are quite safe. You can't possibly fall off while my hands have the reins. Hold onto them if you wish.'

He walked his horse slowly around the farmyard before he felt her body soften and relax. The sun had broken through the mist and the fells rose majestically in front of them. He headed his horse towards the fields behind the farm and spurred him to a canter.

She shrieked and his arms tightened around her.

'Move with me. Gently does it. Feel the horse's rhythm.'

'Stop him!' she yelled. 'I want to get down!'

'Don't shout. You'll frighten him. Keep your back straight.'

'I can't!'

'You can.' He continued with the canter.

'Slow down, I'll fall off!'

'No you won't. I've got you. Don't resist him. You're riding, not fighting.'

'I want to go back.'

'Not yet. My horse needs his exercise.' He pressed his heels gently into the horse's flanks and increased the canter, heading him around the field then across from corner to corner and side to side. The sun's rays stroked his face.

'Please take me back,' Beth said every time they neared the gap in the wall where the gate used to be.

'One last effort,' he answered. 'Hold on tight.' He flicked the reins and increased the canter to a gallop.

'No!' she protested.

He tightened his arms around her, so that his elbows dug into her body. They rose and fell as one on the horse's back. He could hear her panting with exhaustion and wondered briefly if he had taken her too far too soon. Simon had advised that a physical challenge would help her to fight. He doubted it himself as she was so weak but the physician insisted and Abel respected his advice. Eventually, he slowed his horse to a canter and turned his head towards the gateway and the farmyard. Beth had ceased her protestations and gone quiet. Her shoulders were sagging with fatigue and he hoped he had not over-exerted her in this first outing.

He slid from the horse and just caught her as she slumped towards him and her body draped limply over his shoulder. He lowered her feet carefully to the firm ground. Her head lolled and as he lessened his grip on her, her knees buckled.

'Hold up, Beth. You're down now. Stand straight.'

Her eyes focused briefly. 'I can't,' she mumbled and crumpled in his arms.

Dear God, she had fainted. He had gone too far. He had reckoned without her ten years of lethargy under the influence of the laudanum. He should have known she had no reserves of energy, she was as light as a feather anyway and although she ate some of the food he prepared for her, her appetite was not good. But as he carried her to the kitchen couch he noticed a delicate pink glow in her pallid cheeks and he was reminded of the healthy young girl she used to be. His heart swelled with hope that it was not too late to make her well again.

She was as mud-spattered as he was from where the horse had kicked up turf. He laid her on the couch and fetched the smelling salts from the kitchen cupboard. To his great relief they revived her and she opened her eyes. He offered her water, which she took.

Beth sat up with a groan, drank the water then wiped the back of her hand across her mouth.

'Feeling better?' he queried.

'No,' she replied. Every aspect of her body was hurting and she needed her medicine. 'Why did you do that to me?'

'Dr Brady advised physical effort in the open air.'

'He's a monster. Did Edgar send him? Oh yes, I see now that Edgar will never come back to me. I am a burden to him and he wished to be free.' Suddenly she was overcome by a genuine fear that she was right and Edgar wanted rid of her from his life and that he was prepared to leave her to rot, away from his aristocratic family. How long had she lived here, roaming the fell and slowly fading? Seven years? Ten? She had at times overheard the carrier telling Mrs Roberts Edgar had visited Settle to see his mother but came no further. 'Does Edgar want me dead?' she cried. 'Has he sent you to do the deed? He's going to kill me!' She pulled the rug around her and squeezed up against the back of the couch. 'You are a monster, too!' she yelled. 'You want me dead, don't you? Edgar has sent you to kill me.'

Abel didn't reply at first. She lashed out with her arms

but he caught them and held them tight in his grasp until she grew tired of the struggle and weakened in his arms. Then he whispered, 'I want you well again. I shall not give up the fight until you are, and neither must you. You owe that to your children.'

'My babies,' she whined. 'Where are my babies?' But she felt calmer and her voice was tiny again. 'I – I don't know if I can do it. I don't have your strength.'

'I have strength for both of us and you must keep trying! You are through the worst!'

She fell back on the couch and closed her eyes. 'It hurts,' she wailed. 'My head and body hurt and I am so, so tired . . .'

She was exhausted and he hoped she would sleep. He covered her with a warm blanket and went to draw water from the scullery. For the middle part of her ride he had believed she had enjoyed the fresh air on the fell. He remembered how she used to love the fells and as he did it stirred his passion for her. He was determined to take her out there again. But he acknowledged that, in his haste, he may have pushed her too far. No matter, he would make it up to her and prepare her for another ride tomorrow.

Chapter 13

In Beth's brief interludes of clarity she was determined to get well. But she did not seem able to sustain the effort. She needed help. She needed her medicine, just a little of it to see her through and she begged him to give her some. He wouldn't and she hated him for that. Why wouldn't he give it to her? It was the only aspect of life worth living for and if that was taken away for ever, what was there left? And then she remembered her children and Abel's promise that he would find them for her. She believed him. She had to, for he was her only hope.

She woke from a sleep that had not been punctured by the demons and she surfaced slowly in the warm cocoon of a soft feather bed. She opened her eyes. It was daylight but gloomy and she was in Edgar's bedchamber. She had no idea how long she had occupied this bedchamber or how her dressing robe and felt slippers came to be warming on the fireside chair. She was dressed in her work-a-day calico petticoat and drawers. There was no sign of her gown or corset. Her head ached and when she tried to move her arms and legs, they screamed at her. She groaned. Everywhere hurt so much it was impossible to sit up.

A large fire burned in the grate, its flames licking the chimney back and lighting up dancing shadows on the walls. She swallowed. Oh Lord help her, it reminded her of a previous time, long ago, when she had been imprisoned on her back watching shadows over Edgar's shoulders. She heard heavy footsteps on the stairs. Please God, don't let it be Edgar! She couldn't bear for him to come back now unless – her heart leapt – unless he had brought her medicine with him to take away the pain. She groaned again as she moved her limbs. Her aches were similar to those she suffered after a day scrubbing laundry and beating carpets for Mrs Roberts. She was stiff and weary, and she remembered why. The footsteps stopped outside the door for a moment before it opened and she recognised Abel's tall figure carrying two buckets of peat. Not Edgar, but Abel. No humiliation but no laudanum either. Abel filled the fuel box wordlessly and went away. She lay there weakly and watched him.

He made the journey several times, bringing the tin bath from the scullery and then kettles and cans of hot water that he tipped into the bath. She watched the steam rising and once or twice he glanced in her direction. Finally he carried in a folding dressing screen from another bedchamber and set it around the bath.

'It's ready for you,' he said. 'I'll be on the landing.'

She stared at the steam rising in front of the flames, fascinated by the patterns in the air. She attempted to sit up and found it impossible. Pain tore through every muscle and her joints seemed to have ceased to move. She wanted her laudanum, but knew that asking for it would make Abel angry and she didn't want to do that because – because she wanted to please him. She turned back her bedcovers. 'Don't leave. I need your help. Truly, I can barely move.'

He hesitated with his hand on the door handle. This was his fault, she thought irritably. He should not have made her ride so far.

'Very well,' he said. 'I'll carry you to the bath.'

He approached the bed and hesitated again. 'You'll have to take those off.' He waved a hand ineffectually.

He meant her calico petticoat and drawers. They were so thick that they would absorb too much water and she would have none left to wash with. She nodded and lifted her arms. 'Help me to sit up.' He took her hands and swung her to a sitting position on the edge of the bed. But he did not turn his back and he watched as she fumbled with tapes. Then he took her hands so she could stand and let her undergarments fall to the floor. Her shoulders screamed at her as she pulled her chemise as far down as she could reach. 'Thank you, I'm ready,' she said and crossed her arms over her flimsily covered breasts.

She expected him to look away as he lifted her from the mattress. She remembered him as a respectful man in his behaviour towards women. But now she wasn't so sure and she anguished that he had lost his good opinion of her. His eyes travelled all over her and she was the one to look away in embarrassment. She blushed but she was being lowered through the steam into the warm water before she had taken in the strength of his arms and roughness of his jacket. The water was still quite hot and she twitched a little as it made her skin tingle. But she did not complain

150

and relished the heat seeping through her joints. She let out a long sigh and wallowed.

All she wanted was to hand: soap, jugs of clean warm rinsing water, drying clothes, even a comb and some dressing for her matted hair. She pulled out the remaining pins and worked up a soapy lather with her hands. She inhaled the heat and realised that there was something aromatic in the water and coming off in the steam. She inhaled again and lay back against the cloths draped over the metal edges of the bath, gently massaging the lather into her hair. Her chemise floated on the surface and she punched it down with her fingers, tracing patterns in the bubbles. After she had rinsed away the soap, combed her long hair and wrapped it in a cloth, she lay back again and drifted away in an aromatic haze. When she opened her eyes, another jug of hot water had appeared beside the bath alongside a night-gown and a pair of felt slippers. She groaned as she hoisted herself to her feet and tipped one last rinse over her shoulders.

'How are you feeling now?'

She jumped. Abel's voice was much closer than she'd expected.

'You said you'd wait on the landing.'

'I changed my mind. I was afraid you might slip as you climb out.'

'I have taken a bath before.'

'Not in this state you haven't. Sit by the fire until your hair has dried.' He had placed a small stool near the fender.

'I am easier, thank you. You can leave me now.'

He didn't answer and she did not hear him move, so she became apprehensive that he might appear suddenly. She knew he wouldn't but she half wanted him to and this confusion of feeling made her tense. He seemed so angry and strict with her yet behaved so gently in an intimate situation where a lesser man might have easily taken advantage of her; unless he had lost his desire for her because he had lost his respect for her. The notion jolted through her body as she stared at the smouldering fire. Was she destined to lose everything that was dear to her? She had no one to turn to. How could anyone expect her to go on without the support of her laudanum?

When she was in her nightgown and slippers with her hair just about dry, he spoke again from the other side of the screen. 'You ought to ride again soon.'

'Don't ever ask me to ride like that again,' she retaliated.

'It will help to ease your stiffness and you used to enjoy being out on the fell.'

She did, she admitted to herself, and riding was far more exciting than walking. But, oh, everywhere seemed to hurt when she moved.

'May I remove the screen?' he asked.

'If you wish.'

He folded it away and dragged a chair to the fireside. 'Sit there until your bed has warmed.'

He filled the empty jugs with her bath water and carried them onto the landing, dragged the tin bath through the door then sat with her in the flickering firelight.

'Dr Brady has advised that you take regular outdoor activity to make you well.' He thought for a moment before adding, 'I am sure your son would be very proud to know you when he visits and you can ride with him on the fell.'

'My son? My son will come here to see me? When will that be?'

'When you are well enough and you can ride. Let me teach you.'

Beth thought about this and imagined a warm sunny day with her children and a picnic high on the fell with their horses tethered nearby. 'I shall never be able to master your horse. He's too big for me.'

She noticed his eyes brighten in the firelight. His features lifted and instead of being cross with her all the time he seemed pleased. If her children were proud of her then she might regain Abel's respect as well. Abel's respect was as important to her as being reunited with her children. Her head was clear enough to be sure of that.

'I'll find you a pony,' he said.

'I have to get well, don't I, for the sake of my children.' She reached out to clutch a handful of his clothing. 'Promise me you will find them and bring them here to me.'

'I shall do my best to search for them. But I will not bring them to see a mother who cannot face the day without her laudanum.'

Beth's face puckered with pain. It was when she thought of her children that she needed it most. 'You don't know what it's like for me.'

He said, 'That's true. I and others can help but you and only you can overcome your craving. It is your war and you must win it. This is only the first battle.' He feared that he had been too hard on her.

She tugged at his clothing. 'You won't leave me, will you?'

'I promised Dr Brady I would stay with you until his nurse arrives.'

'I do not want a nurse. I am not confined to my bed.'

'Yet you have a constant need for something you call your medicine.'

'Will she bring my medicine?' Beth asked hopefully. She could see Abel's chest rise and fall as, again, he shook his head slowly and deliberately.

'She will look after you and I – I shall search for your children.'

'But you will visit me?' she asked anxiously.

'I cannot. It is not wise for me to be here alone with you now. You have a husband with a vindictive nature. I do not doubt that he would lock you away if he suspected a liaison.'

'Then you must write to me.'

'I dare not. It is so easy for a letter to fall into the wrong hands.'

'So you will desert me, just as Edgar did,' she sighed.

'I shall relate news of my searches to Dr Brady. Will you give him permission to report your progress to me?'

She nodded.

'Then we have a bargain. I shall find your children and you will stop taking the laudanum.'

The temptation to yell 'I can't!' was confronted by a dream of seeing her son and daughter and she swallowed her defiance. 'Very well,' she answered.

'Perhaps you can let go of my clothes now.'

She did, and straightened the fabric, smoothing it out with her fingers.

'I plan to leave as soon as your nurse arrives. She is travelling by the railways from Scotland and will arrive here in a pony and trap. The pony will need exercise. He will suit you well as a mount and you will enjoy riding him.'

Beth tried to shift her position and groaned. 'Or perish in the process.'

'May I try something that I have used on exhausted beasts to ease their suffering.'

Her hopes lifted. He had a potion of some sort for everything. 'Very well,' she agreed.

'Climb into bed.'

That sounded more than welcome to her aching limbs
and she obeyed, stopping only to remove the warming pan.
He took it from her and laid it in the hearth. She moaned
and groaned with every movement. As she rested her head
on the pillow she was aware again of a soothing aroma and
yawned.

'I beg your pardon,' she said automatically. How could she
be so tired? She had already slept for hours today.

'Don't fight your fatigue. Close your eyes.'

He peeled back the bedcovers leaving only the bed-sheet in
place. It was not a proper thing to do, he knew, but he was
sure it would help her and who was to know? Nonetheless,
Dr Brady had not suggested it. And – and he realised as her
breasts rose and fell under the sheet that this was a mistake.
He wanted her. He desired her as a woman and wanted to
love her as her husband ought. As he gazed at her form he
realised that he was too familiar with every inch of her
already. Was he doing this for Beth's recovery or to indulge
his own desires to be close to her?

Dear Lord, he should stop this minute. She was a married
woman. She belonged to another man, no matter that Abel
had no respect for him. She was sick and vulnerable and
needed his help. He ought not, would not take advantage of
her weakened condition. She needed the help of his strong
hands to ease her aching limbs. And he loved her. He must
be strong and fight his desires. But, he was so, so tempted
to remove his clothes, climb in beside her and show her that
love.

His voice was barely a croak. 'Turn onto your front.'

'Oh no, please don't make me. I ache too much.'

'Very well. I'll start with your feet. It will hurt you to begin with but I promise you it will ease your pain.' He began to massage her flesh between his thumb and fingers, working from her ankles towards her thighs.

She was alarmed at first. How dare he put his hands on her in this manner? She protested and tensed until he urged her to relax and not fight his fingers. She had to trust him and when he began to work on her other leg as if he were kneading bread, she did. He had not changed, she had. She had become the suspicious harridan that no one could love. She glanced at him from under her lashes. His face was grim as though he was concentrating on a distasteful task. Did he hate her so much? Surely if he did, he would not be helping her in this way? Perhaps he had a troubled conscience about – about what?

It didn't make sense. In fact nothing in Beth's turmoil of joy and sadness made any sense except – except that she did not want Abel to leave her. Not again. Not ever. Of course he would. He had to. He had a life of his own and – and she wanted him to find her children. That was the worst part about being aware of life again. She was aware of the joy of being with Abel once more and it could not last. How would she survive without him if she did not have her laudanum?

When he had finished his work on her limbs he said, 'You must turn over now,' and she obeyed. She checked her moaning and groaning, feeling proud of a new-found control and he soothed the muscles over her back until she drifted away into slumber.

The sound of the cock crowing woke her although it was still dark. The bath and its paraphernalia had gone, along with her grubby gown and stockings. She could not believe that she had slept so soundly all through the night. Miraculously, her body and limbs moved more easily and she searched for clean garments in the bedchamber.

Chapter 14

Two years later Abel Shipton spent an evening in the tap room of the Redfern Arms, where barrels were set up so that labouring men could slake their thirsts at the end of the working day. For the price of a few jars of ale he had learned that all was not well for Edgar Collins and his family. He was estranged from the estate and the current Lord Redfern had taken a ward as his heir.

He had not given Edgar's titled family much thought since he had been summarily and unjustly accused by the harridan of High Fell Farm. Indeed, it had proved to be the making of him as he followed the drovers' trails to sell his flock for a good price in the smoke-filled South Riding. His nose for negotiation ensured that his golden guineas mounted as his reputation grew.

However, his money had proved to be of little use in his searches for Beth's children. Lawyers did not answer his letters and why would they when his questions were none of his business. He could hardly say on whose behalf he acted. But he did not give up. Seeing Beth Collins at her worst and then her struggles to recover had rekindled a smoulder in his heart which had burst into a flame as she fought to regain her health and strength. Yet he dared not visit her or even write for he knew that to risk her reputation further would jeopardise her already precarious existence.

That night in his chamber at the Redfern Arms, he lay awake feeling an unholy pleasure in the continued estrangement of Lord Redfern's niece and great-nephew, who, he had believed until now, was his heir. Lord Redfern's ward, Abel found out, was being schooled to be the future master of the Redfern estate. The harridan, he knew, had stayed in Settle but her son, he heard, had a house somewhere in the Riding although noone, it seemed, had ever set eyes on his wife and children.

'Has his wife passed on?' he had enquired with a feigned innocence.

He was answered by a series of shrugs until he pressed for more.

''Tis said she is an invalid who had to live in the Dales for the air.'

'The Dales, you say?'

'He has a farm there.'

'Does he indeed?'

Well, Edgar Collins probably thought his bank still owned High Fell Farm and Abel had been particular for the bank not to disabuse him of that notion. But High Fell mortgages had been his first purchase from lenders willing to sell. As soon as he had enough gold he relieved the bank of the mortgages through an agent and leased out the land to Fellwick Hall. He arranged, also, for the Hall to send over a lad to work the farmyard and garden that was left. The only proviso was that his name was kept out of all negotiations.

Strangely, he did not care who knew any more. It had been an immature action but it had made him feel better at the time. He had expected, along with many of the regulars at the Redfern Arms, for Edgar to have inherited by now and his concern had been for Beth and her children. Tomorrow, he was riding towards Skipton for dinner with Dr Brady.

'Is Beth well?'

'Abel, will you allow me to remove my overcoat first?' Simon Brady shook off the rain and handed his riding coat to a waiting manservant.

The coaching inn was between Skipton and Bradford but it was worth the ride for the excellence of its dinners. The manservant showed them to a private dining room with a good fire and plenty of candles.

'Have you news of her children?' Simon asked as they sat down.

'I wish I had, but they seem to have disappeared.'

'Both of them?'

'I guessed the girl would be difficult to find, but not the boy. I have given up on lawyers and I'm following new leads myself. Now, how is Beth?'

Simon grimaced. 'Not good. She – we – had expected you to have at least found where her son was by now. She needs to have hope.'

Abel frowned. He was doing his best but replies to his letters took so long, if they arrived at all. 'Has she stayed away from the laudanum?'

'I gave her no choice and it has been a real struggle for her at times, especially in the early days. My nurse has seen her through the worst and Beth herself has made a huge effort. But for every two steps forward there is usually one step back.'

'Surely that is progress of a kind?' Abel asked.

'Slow progress I'm afraid. The two women ride together and have become friends. Beth has grown stronger in mind and body but she constantly asks about you and her children.'

'She hasn't given up hope for them, has she?'

'Interestingly, she has not. She believes you will find them and – and she has a very high regard for you, Abel. She seems sure you will keep your word so you must not let her down in this.'

'I shan't. Tell her I don't care how long it takes. I'll find out what happened to them.'

'Which is not quite the same as saying you will find them,' Simon cautioned. 'Have *you* given up hope on them?'

'No! I believe I am getting closer. Her son may be with his father but neither is living at the Abbey.'

'And her daughter?'

'I don't know. She could have been farmed out anywhere. Edgar disowned her but he may know where she went. He is the key to finding them, I'm sure.'

'Well, if there is anything I can do to help, you only have to ask.'

Abel considered this offer and lowered his voice. 'I – I should like to see Beth,' he said.

Simon shook his head. 'I shouldn't advise it until you have welcome news for her. Anything less might set her back for months.'

'Keep her safe for me,' Abel responded.

Later that night, Abel reflected on this conversation. He had to find Edgar to locate Beth's children. But Edgar was unlikely to allow any contact with him, and Edgar had learned from an expert how to exclude people. Who else might know what had happened to the children? Abel racked his brain for memories of the day Beth's daughter was born. He remembered a surgeon, a wet nurse and a vicar. It was then that he recalled Edgar's close friendship with the vicar, the one he called Milo. The clergy! Of course! It was then that Abel decided on another line of investigation.

PART TWO

Chapter 15

1847

'Boyd!' Daisy yelled at the top of her voice. 'Wait for me!'

'Go back home before Father catches you.' He climbed into the driver's seat of the wagon and took hold of the reins.

'He's gone shooting.' Daisy scrambled up to stand beside him clutching her basket in one hand and her bonnet ribbons in the other.

'Already?'

She nodded vigorously. 'Honest. While you were hitching the cart, I saw him take his gun and a meat pie.' She turned and beamed at her beloved brother. 'So he won't know, will he?'

But Boyd's response was a frown. 'Mother will. You should be helping her with dinner.'

'We're not having dinner until Father comes home at tea-time. She said I could take these eggs to sell.'

Boyd lifted the cloth covering the basket's contents. 'I sold some to the cooper's wife yesterday. She won't want any more.'

'Why didn't you say?' He didn't answer so Daisy went on, 'Does Mother know you took some eggs?'

'She didn't miss them, did she? The hens are laying well. Besides, you collect them for her.'

Realisation dawned on Daisy. 'You've kept the money!'

'Lower your voice. And sit down if you are coming with me.'

A troubled expression clouded Daisy's pretty eyes. 'I'd rather stand for a bit.'

'Don't be daft.'

'I'll get a better view.' Daisy noticed his frown and added, 'Please. I never go anywhere except to church.'

'Climb in the back then, and hold on to the side.'

Daisy secured her basket and clambered over the wooden struts. Boyd flicked the reins and their old carthorse lumbered forward. 'Why are you going to the cooper's again?' she asked.

'The brewery needs more barrels.'

'Oh well, I could go on to the brewery with you, then.'

'No, Daisy! You know you're not supposed to go any further than the cooper's workshop. You'll have to walk back from there.'

'What about my eggs?'

'I'll take them on to the brewery for you.'

'Oh, let me come with you, Boyd. Father won't even let me go to market because I have to clean the house.'

'I'll be gone all day and Mother will be furious with you.'

'I don't care.'

'You will if she clips you one round the head.'

Daisy chewed on her lips. The wheals from her last whipping had not yet healed, and she winced at the memory.

166

'She won't. I'm bigger than she is, she doesn't hit me anymore.'

'I should hope not. You're not a child anymore. You're seventeen and a grown woman.'

'She asks Father to beat me instead.'

'Father beats you? Dear heaven, Daisy, why didn't you tell me? What does he use?'

'His – his—' Her behind was still painful after a week. 'His cane.'

'No! Oh Daisy, that hurts. He used that on me before I threatened to wrench it from him. He's a brute. He's my own father and I hate him.'

'Me too.'

Even so, Daisy was shocked to hear him say it. She hated her sanctimonious mother as much as she did her father but she hardly dared say so. Honour thy father and mother, the Bible said. Suffer the little children too. Yes, the little children suffered in their house.

'Mother and Father are quite old, aren't they?' she said. 'Do you think they'll die soon?' Daisy wished they would. She knew it was wicked but she wanted them dead all the same.

'I hope not. I'm not old enough to take over the cottage tenancy yet and even if I were, where would I find a quarter's rent?'

'We could take things to market,' Daisy suggested hopefully. 'We could go together. It would be fun.'

'It wouldn't be enough to keep both of us.' He sounded disgruntled and Daisy wished she hadn't mentioned earning because it made him irritable. 'But it would if I worked for someone else,' Boyd went on, adding, 'At least I'd get a wage for my labours.'

His suppressed anger clutched at Daisy's heart. Father didn't give money to either of them for their efforts. Daisy didn't mind for herself but she knew that Boyd was angry. Father expected Boyd to labour from morning until night doing all the outside chores and the carrier work, while he went off shooting or fishing. Her father couldn't be very good at either, Daisy thought, because he hardly ever brought home anything for tea. Boyd said he sold his bag and drank it.

Anxiously Daisy asked, 'You wouldn't leave, would you?'

'I'm nineteen going on twenty,' he muttered. 'There are men my age down the pit earning enough for lodgings.'

Her heart began to thump in fear. Daisy's life was hard enough already without having to face it without him. 'Don't go, Boyd,' she pleaded. 'I'd hate it here with just those two.'

'Don't you fret yourself. I wouldn't leave you.' He twisted his neck to give her a smile and she felt better. But her anxiety didn't really go away for she knew he was as unhappy as she was.

'What will happen to us?' she asked.

'I don't know. But I promise I'll look after you. I won't let anyone treat you like they do.'

Daisy leaned forward and kissed the back of his head. His thick hair had stayed fair as he grew up and nowadays he had a good growth of beard to shave off for church on Sundays. Daisy's light-brown locks were darker than his but they became streaked with gold in the summer sun and the blue of her eyes intensified when her skin took on a little colour.

She did love her brother. But no matter how much she tried to do her duty, she found it very hard to love her mother and father. It was so difficult to warm to someone who never showed you any affection or even praised you. She was just a servant to her mother, doing all the dirty jobs in the cottage and forever at her bidding. The only time she had the total attention of her parents was when her father was punishing her while her mother watched. She was punished for the least little thing she had forgotten or not completed to her mother's satisfaction. She really did try to do better. But she would have run away before now if it hadn't been for her beloved Boyd.

Boyd always took her side even if it meant he got a beating too. But Father didn't beat him now he was full grown and more than capable of hitting back. Anyway Boyd had been turned out of their tiny house to live in the shed these past ten years and he didn't know what went on in the cottage after tea at night. Smaller, younger, weaker Daisy was the focus of her mother's righteousness and her father's discontent with his life.

Daisy didn't tell Boyd any more for she feared he would make matters worse. Whenever Boyd had stuck up for her in front of Father, Daisy had been given extra punishment, 'for engaging others in your wickedness', he told her between strokes. He may be an old man but he could still wield a cane with maximum effect. Well, Boyd knew about it now.

The cooper's yard and workshop came into view. 'You'd better go back from here,' Boyd said.

'But I don't want to,' she whined.

'You'll only suffer more. You know what Mother and Father are like about disobedience.'

'Can't you say one of the cart wheels came loose and we were held up?'

'How would I explain getting the barrels to the brewery? Father will be over here tomorrow for his money.'

'When Mother and Father die, we'll have that money,' Daisy pointed out.

'You don't really want them to die, do you?'

'Yes I do because then you and me can be married and live on our own in the cottage.'

'Don't start on that again. I've told you before. You can't marry me! I'm your brother. I thought you'd grown out of all that silliness.'

'But I want to.'

'Now stop it, Daisy. You're old enough to understand these things. When you grow up you meet someone from outside your family and fall in love with them, and then you marry that person.'

Daisy could not imagine meeting someone who would be as dear to her as Boyd and as she was reflecting on this he added, 'Well, if you're lucky, you marry her.'

He sounded sad and she glanced at him again. He was more grown up than she was. She suddenly realised the truth of what he was saying. He had met someone he did want to marry. Who was she?

Daisy stood up straight. Mother and Father let her go to church with Boyd so she was often with him. She thought hard. There was no one at church that he looked out for or spoke to. The only place he went alone was to deliver the new barrels to the brewery. It was someone there; someone at the brewery that he wanted to be with more than he wanted her. Who was she, this someone who was taking her darling brother away from her? Well, she certainly wasn't going to go back home now. She wanted to see who it was.

'I'm coming to the brewery with you,' she decided. 'I'll say I got down but climbed back when you weren't looking and hid in one of the barrels. Then none of it is your fault.'

Boyd pursed his mouth and frowned. 'You've got an answer for everything, you have. And you've put on your good gown. Oh, Daisy, why do you do these things?'

Daisy smoothed down her skirts. 'I like it and I'm only allowed to wear it on Sundays. It's not fair.'

'Well, it certainly won't be if you get it dirty or tear it. Go home to Mother.'

'No, I won't. She'll make me scrub all the floors – even the ones that don't need doing – while she reads the Bible at me. I can't spend my days doing that for ever. I only want a little fun. Is it too much to ask?'

'No, it isn't. It's just that I'm worried for you. More so now I know about the beatings. I'll make a detour and drop you in the village to sell your eggs.'

'But I want to go to the brewery,' she insisted.

Boyd gave an exasperated sigh and flicked the reins. 'Well, I don't want to waste my time going to the village just for the eggs.'

'Then don't.'

'Listen to me. When we get there, you're not to go off on your own. I mean it, Daisy. A young girl like you can get into a lot of trouble.'

'I can go with you, then?'

'I suppose so. I'll think of something to tell Mother and Father, but I'm not that good at lying.'

'I'll explain. You're not to say anything. It only makes it worse for me.'

'What do you mean?'

'Nothing.' Daisy dwelt briefly on the real possibility of a beating, pushed the notion to the back of her mind and commented, 'Father let you go with him to the brewery when you were only ten.'

'It's different for lads.'

Daisy didn't have an answer for this because she knew that it was. She'd had lessons at Sunday school until Mother

171

put a stop to it as she needed her home to cook the Sunday dinner. So although she could read and write well, apart from the few sermons she'd listened to, Daisy knew very little about the world around her except for what her parents told her.

The wagon with its valuable load of empty barrels bumped along the track until it left the woodland and joined the turnpike for town. The cooper's had made barrels since before the brewery came into existence. Boyd Higgins was welcomed as a more reliable carrier than his father had been. Daisy was serious about wishing her parents dead. As soon as he was one and twenty Boyd could set up as a carter in his own right. Daisy could keep house for him and even though they could not marry they could be together and look out for each other. Boyd couldn't argue with that. It's what brothers and sisters were for, wasn't it?

Daisy dreamed of that day. In her dream there were no parents, only the two of them, a horse and cart, the hens and – and some geese and a pig to see them through the winter.

'Do you think the cooper will always want to send barrels to the brewery?' Daisy asked.

'They will. The South Riding pits and furnaces produce thirsty workers as well as coal and iron. There's a tavern on every corner in the town. But they might not always want me to be their carrier, unless I do a good job. So you behave yourself, Daisy Higgins.'

Chapter 16

Boyd turned the horse's head into the brewery yard. Daisy inhaled the heady smells and her eyes darted backwards and forwards taking in the tall brick buildings and chimneys. Boyd carefully negotiated his wagon and several working men wandered outside to watch. One took the horse's bridle and Boyd tossed him the reins. 'Wait here, Daisy, while I'm in the office.'

'Let me take the eggs round to the kitchen. I want to see in the house,' Daisy said as she hitched up her skirt and clambered over the front of the cart to the driving seat.

'*Daisy, keep your legs covered! I can see your garters.*'

Boyd was too late to stop her. A ripple of comments and whistles from the brewery workers attracted more of their fellows outside and when she righted herself and straightened her bonnet she had a gathering audience. Boyd had covered his eyes with his hand and was shaking his head slowly.

'You're too old for those capers now, Daisy,' he whispered. 'You'll get a reputation.'

'I'm sorry.' She should have thought! She clutched the egg basket tightly and began counting them earnestly.

A voice called, 'What do you do for an encore, lass?'

Daisy blushed and looked at her feet. When she glanced at Boyd his face was like thunder.

'Haven't you got work to do,' he growled at the man.

At the same time the brewer appeared from his office building and strode across to the wagon. 'What's going on out here? Get back to work, all of you. I'll tell you when you can unload.' He looked angry too and Daisy concentrated on the contents of her basket.

'My sister Daisy, sir,' Boyd explained. 'She has some new-laid eggs from our hens.'

'Take them into the house, lass. The kitchen is round the back.'

The house was another high brick-built affair across the yard from the brewery. The brewer and his family lived there behind a large front door at the top of a flight of stone steps. The kitchen was underneath. Daisy followed a stone-flagged footpath round the side of the house and found a girl hanging out bedsheets on a network of washing lines in the yard. She was older than Daisy and quite plump. Her breasts pushed out her apron top. Daisy noticed these things on other girls and compared herself with them. She was thinner than this girl and her breasts were smaller.

The girl's hair was hidden by a plain cotton cap. 'Who are you?' she asked Daisy. She didn't sound like a servant.

'Daisy Higgins. I've brought these eggs.' She held out her basket.

The girl ignored the contents and asked, 'Is Boyd here with you?'

'He's unloading barrels in the yard.'

'Take the eggs in the kitchen.' The girl jerked her head in the direction of the house, smoothed down her apron and disappeared down the path to the front.

Alone, Daisy hesitated. The kitchen door stood ajar and she heard voices. Purposefully she walked towards them and stood on the threshold. It was a cavernous room with a big cooking range, cupboards and shelves of pots around the walls. Several women of different ages were sitting at a large deal table preparing vegetables and talking.

'Is that you standing in the light again, Mattie?' one of the older women called. 'In or out but don't dawdle.'

'It's not Mattie. It's me.'

'Who's me? Come over here where we can see you, then.'

One of the younger women recognised her. 'I know you. I've seen you in Sunday school. You're Boyd's little sister, aren't you?'

'I've brought these if – if you need any.'

One of the older women stood up and came to look in her basket.

'They're new-laid,' Daisy added. Then she remembered her manners, gave a curtsey and said, 'Madam.'

'Ee, you don't call me madam, me ducks. Madam is over there.' She took the basket from her.

The mistress smiled and rose to her feet and it was then that Daisy noticed her lace cap and clean neat gown half-hidden by a large white apron.

She curtseyed again. 'Sorry, madam.'

The brewer's wife smiled and said, 'Do you know my children?'

Daisy thought how lovely she looked. Her face was lined but her eyes and cheeks seemed to glow when she smiled. Her own mother hardly ever smiled and for a moment Daisy envied the brewer's children, not for their big house and thriving brewery, but for their cheerful, friendly kitchen that was so different from the one at home.

'Wait there, dear,' the mistress said and disappeared up a flight of stone steps in the corner of the kitchen.

There were three girls left at the table and one of them said, 'Come and sit down. Are they from your hens?'

'The hens belong to Father,' Daisy answered. Everything belonged to Father. He told them that regularly.

Another girl said, 'Shall we ask our father if we can keep hens?'

'Oh, don't do that,' Daisy responded. 'I want you to buy our eggs.'

They all looked at her and laughed. But it was in a good-natured kindly way and Daisy smiled nervously.

The older girl who knew her said, 'Of course you do.' She paused then added, 'I haven't seen you in Sunday school lately.'

'I have to cook the dinner for Mother.'

'I see. I expect Boyd brought you today. How old are you, now?'

Daisy told her and added Boyd's age for good measure.

'Our Mattie'll be seventeen next week!' one of the younger girls exclaimed.

The mistress returned with some coins that she handed to Daisy along with the empty basket. 'Thank you kindly, Daisy,' she said. 'Please give my good wishes to your mother. I shall be pleased to receive any eggs that she can spare.'

'Really?' Daisy's eyes shone. Her fingers curled tightly around the coins. If she told that to Mother when she got home she wouldn't be angry with her. Would she?

The older girl walked with her to the kitchen door and said goodbye. Daisy dodged her way though the flapping wet sheets and round to the front of the house where Boyd was unloading the brewery barrels alone, watched by the brewer. And by Mattie.

Daisy didn't notice her at first because she hovered on the corner of the house and shrank back out of sight when her father turned to say something to Boyd.

'Aren't you supposed to be here?' Daisy asked.

'Be quiet,' Mattie whispered.

'Why?'

'Why do you think?'

Daisy took a step sideways and stood in front of her as the brewer twisted his head and called out, 'Who's there?'

Boyd turned around and noticed her. 'It's only my sister, sir.'

'Come forward and show yourself, lass.'

Daisy edged out of the shadows.

'Who is that with you?'

'It's me, Father. I was showing Daisy the way out.' Mattie fell into step beside her and Daisy saw Boyd's face light up with a smile. She glanced at Mattie who was looking at the ground, biting her bottom lip.

'That's very civil of you, Mathilda.'

'Thank you, Father. Good morning, Master Higgins.'

Daisy watched her brother pull off his cap, bow his head formally and murmur, 'Good morning, Miss Mathilda.' Daisy frowned, turning down the corners of her mouth and remembering his words from earlier. *When you grow up you meet someone*

177

from outside your family and you fall for them and then you marry that person. Alarmed, Daisy realised that person was Mattie.

Mathilda was from outside of Boyd's family and Daisy reckoned he must have fallen for her because she had never seen him behave in this way towards a girl before. He'd fallen for her and by the look of it Mattie had fallen for him. Well, she couldn't have him. He was *her* brother and she wasn't going to let any Mattie take him away from her.

'Are we going home now, Boyd?' she asked, as he heaved down the last of the barrels. 'We have to hurry.'

'I just need a signature for the cooper's. Go and wait by the cart.'

He turned his attention to the brewery owner and the two girls walked away.

'You don't have to stay with me,' Daisy said.

'I don't mind. I like you,' Mattie replied.

Daisy didn't believe her and it must have shown on her face but Mattie persisted. 'Will you be my friend?' she asked.

Why would she want to be friends with her? Daisy's immediate reaction was, No! You want to take my brother from me! But Daisy did not have any friends. Their cottage was isolated and the only other children she had met were at Sunday school. The brewer's kitchen had been warm and friendly. Daisy would enjoy being a part of it as Mattie's friend.

This made her feel better, although she had a niggling doubt that she was being selfish. *If you're lucky, you marry her,* Boyd had said. Mattie wasn't interested in her. It was obvious to Daisy who Mattie was really interested in. Daisy didn't think the brewer would care for one of his daughters striking up a friendship with a carter's daughter, and definitely not a carter's son.

'I can't be your friend,' she answered. 'I have to look after the house.'

'Well, I could walk over to your cottage to – to collect our eggs then.'

And then I'd have no reason to go anywhere myself, Daisy thought. 'It's a long way,' she replied.

'Don't you want me to be your friend?'

'Yes. No. Oh, I don't know!'

'Mattie!' An adult voice called from behind them and Mattie's mother came along the a path carrying a calico-wrapped parcel and a corked stone bottle. 'I wondered where you were.'

Mattie swivelled round. 'I have been talking to Daisy. Mother, can I go and visit Daisy on Sunday afternoons? She wants me to be her friend.'

Daisy just stopped herself from saying, 'No I don't!'

The older woman looked thoughtful. 'It's too far to walk back alone, dear.'

'You could meet me halfway in the trap. Daisy and Boyd will wait with me.'

'Your father likes us all together on Sundays, dear.'

That means no, then, Daisy thought and was pleased. Mattie's mother offered Daisy her parcel. 'I've packed some bread and meat for your luncheon.'

Luncheon? Daisy had never heard of luncheon before. It was dinner or it was tea but no matter, Boyd was always hungry. Daisy took the bulky cloth with a thank you and a curtsey and found herself alone as Mattie was ushered away to finish her chores.

Daisy was hungry too when a sweaty thirsty Boyd clambered up to the driving seat beside her and flicked the reins to drive out through the brewery gates. He wiped his throat and chest on a grubby cloth and asked, 'What did Mattie have to say?'

'Nothing. Her mother came for her. Do you want a drink?'

'Is it ginger beer?'

'I don't know.' Daisy took the cork out of the stone bottle and sniffed its contents. 'Yes. Here.' She shoved it in his hand and watched him swallow. 'This is for our *luncheon*,' she said, unwrapping the calico. 'What *is* luncheon?'

'It's what the gentry have to keep them going until dinner because they have their dinner late on.'

'Can we go and eat it on Kimber Hill? You can see for miles up there.'

'Best not, Daisy. I want to get you back before Father's home from his shooting. We'll eat as we drive.'

'Look, there's a rabbit on the step. Father is home already!'

'But he was supposed to be out all day!' A shiver of fear went down Daisy's back. 'He'll be furious with me.'

'Don't go in alone. I'll come with you and give him your egg money. Wait for me to stable the horse.'

'What about the rest of this food?'

'I'll hide it in the shed. Let me do the talking, Daisy.'

'No, don't,' she cried, but he was halfway to the shed.

When they walked into the kitchen Mother was sitting at the table with her hands clasped and Father was standing in front of the fire with his hands behind his back.

'Where have you been?'

Boyd answered. 'To the cooper's and the brewery as you ordered, Father.'

'Don't lie to me. You should have been home hours ago.'

'I'm not lying to you, Father. I had to unload on my own. It took me ages.'

Mr Higgins clenched his fists by his side and grimaced. 'Tell me the truth!'

'It is the truth,' Daisy answered. 'I watched him.'

'Be quiet, Daisy,' Boyd hissed. But he was too late.

Father's face turned a dark red as he addressed Daisy. 'You went with him to the brewery, a place occupied by lewd men who drink and gawp at women?' Then his wrath focused on Boyd and he thundered, 'You allowed her to go with you, knowing your poor dear mother would be struggling alone at home?'

'She took eggs to sell,' Boyd replied. He held out the money. 'Look how much she has made for you, Father.' He placed the coins on the table.

'Mother said I could take the eggs, Father,' Daisy added. Her mother was sitting silently at the kitchen table. Her face was expressionless. 'Tell him, Mother,' Daisy pleaded.

But her mother looked fearful and replied, 'I didn't say you could go to the brewery. You are a wilful wicked child. Tell your father what you are.'

Daisy resigned herself to a beating and repeated, 'I am a wilful wicked child.' She had learned, sometimes painfully, that she must show remorse. If she did then her punishment was less severe. But her eyes were filled with dread. 'I am sorry, Father,' she added.

He brought his arms from behind his back and flicked his cane in his right hand. The tip sang in the air. Daisy swallowed. She wanted to rip it from his grasp, break it in two and put it on the fire. But any sort of retaliation would only make her punishment worse. She had learned to be docile and repentant to lessen the hurt.

'I should not have disobeyed Mother and I am sorry,' she said.

181

Her father smirked with satisfaction. 'You think that makes your sin less wicked? Well, it doesn't. A double sin deserves a double penalty.' He flicked his whip through the air again.

'No, Father,' Boyd protested. 'It was my fault and mine alone. I said she could come with me. If anyone deserves a beating it's me.'

'Be quiet and get yourself off to the shed where you belong!' He swayed and sneered. 'On second thoughts, I think you should stay. You're fond of your little sister aren't you? Well, I'll teach you to encourage her disobedience. You will observe her suffering so that you will not be so inclined to be a part of her wickedness in future. What did we do, Mother, for the Lord to punish us with such sinful children?'

'It is God's will, dearest husband, that we must suffer too.'

'Fetch the chair.'

Neither Daisy nor Boyd moved.

'I said fe—'

Daisy shot through to the front parlour and struggled back with the low-backed fireside chair that presented her at just the right angle for her father's whip. Boyd had already removed his waistcoat and was loosening his shirt from the waistband of his trousers. 'I'll take the beatings, Father,' he said. 'It is my fault. I'll take the punishment for both of us.'

'Silence! It is your sister who is in need of God's guidance. Bend over the chair and lift your skirts.'

'No, Father!' Boyd protested.

'I said silence.' The whip whistled through the air and caught Boyd on his face leaving a blood-spotted streak down his cheek. He yelped and clutched his wound with his hand.

'Mother!' he appealed. 'Stop him. She is no longer a child.'

For a moment Daisy hoped her mother would listen. But Mother remained motionless. Even her lips barely moved as

182

she said, 'Wilful, wayward girl, she must be taught a lesson. You will learn to obey.'

Silently, Daisy moved forward and bent over the chair pulling the back of her skirts over her head to expose her boots, stockinged legs and drawers.

'The drawers,' her father ordered.

Mortified, Daisy froze. At least her drawers offered some protection from his whip. She heard Boyd breathe in sharply. She knew if she could see him there would be fury in his eyes. She held her breath and suffered the humiliation of her father pulling down her drawers to expose her bare flesh, already criss-crossed with the scars and healing scabs of earlier chastisement. The backs of her thighs were the same. Her father had explained that it was to remind her of her wickedness every time she took a step or sat down.

'Good Lord,' Boyd breathed. 'Have you done this to her?'

'Be silent!' her father ordered.

She heard the cane whip through the air and a yelp from Boyd as he received another stinging blow. A chair scraped on the stone floor as he fell against it. Under the table Daisy stared at her mother's boots side by side as she sat impassively to watch. Daisy took a hunk of her skirt and shoved it between her teeth waiting for the first stinging blow.

She could not suppress the cry of pain as the cane seared through her skin like a knife. It escaped as a mix of screech and yell and a sob, quickly followed by another stroke making her cry escalate into a scream. And then – it was followed by what sounded to her like the roar of wounded ox. She jerked her head to the side to see Boyd flying at her father and wrenching the cane from his grasp, pushing him off balance. He grabbed her arm by the wrist, quickly pulled up her drawers and yanked her out of the door.

Chapter 17

'Run, Daisy. He can't catch us if we run.'

Daisy glanced behind her. Her father had toppled over and grasped the mantle shelf to stop himself falling into the fire. Her mother's face was a picture of horror. But she did not move. Boyd tugged at her hand and she stumbled after him.

'Where are we going?' she panted.

'I don't know, anywhere away from those two. Come *on*.'

He could run faster than she but he did not let go of her hand and when her legs began to buckle and her breathing was a series of hoarse rasps he slowed and eventually stopped. Daisy bent double to catch her breath.

They had gone deeper into the trees that stretched away from the village and well away from the paths and tracks she knew. The countryside went on for miles in this direction without a village in sight. It was known as the deer park and had once been part of a larger estate. No one in the village knew who owned it now but Boyd said it was a foreigner.

'You've only made it worse for us when we go back,' Daisy panted.

'We're not going back.'

'But we have to. Where else can we go?'

'I don't know but I'll find us somewhere. I can work. You can housekeep. We'll find somebody to take us in.'

'Father will find us, Boyd. He'll claim us back.'

'Claim us? Yes, that's what he would do, as though we belonged to him, his property, like the horse and cart to be worked to the bone as he sees fit. What sort of father is that, Daisy?'

'But Mother says—'

'Mother says? I don't care what Mother says. She sat there and watched you whipped like a dog. They treat us like their servants. They're not like other parents.'

'I don't know any others.'

'You know the brewer's family. Their children have to do chores too but they don't get humiliated and beaten regularly.'

She thought of the cosy happy kitchen and Mattie. Mattie's father was strict but her mother was kind and their children were happy. 'But they are gentry, Boyd. Mother says the gentry are different from us.'

'Well, they're not. I mean apart from their houses and things, underneath they are no different from us at all.'

'I wish Mattie's mother was my mother.'

'So do I.'

'Could we go to them?'

'No. They would give us straight back.'

'But what'll we do? Where will we sleep?'

'I'll find us a gamekeeper's hut for tonight.'

This sounded fun to Daisy. She felt safe with Boyd. He

was quick thinking and strong. No wonder Mattie had liked him. She wondered if Boyd would want to go back because of her and said, 'Are we going back in the morning?'

'We're never going back.'

'Not even for Mattie?'

'I've no future with Mattie. She's pretty and her father will marry her into proper gentry. It's just you and me now, Daisy. We can make our own way in the world. You're not frightened of that, are you?'

'Not when I'm with you. But I am thirsty.'

'Look for some fruit trees or bushes.'

'I'm hungry as well.'

'I shan't take you far tonight. I'll go back home after dark when Father is asleep and bring the food and my bedding from the shed.'

'Oh don't! Father has a gun. He'll kill you if he catches you.'

'Don't you worry about me. I'm too fast on my feet for him. Besides he's had a skinful of ale today so he'll be out cold.'

'Is it much further to the hut?'

'I don't think so. It's a long time since I've been this way.'

The hut was deserted. It had a fireplace and bench for sleeping but not much else. 'Shall I light a fire?' Daisy volunteered.

'Best not. Gamekeeper will notice the smoke.' Boyd made sure the door could be secured from the inside and then set off to collect as much as he could carry from the shed where he had slept for ten years or more. The cottage was in darkness and he did not approach it.

It was late when he returned to the hut. He had found a pheasant that had been overlooked by the dogs and judged that a fire in the middle of the night might not be noticed until they had moved on in the morning. Daisy had dozed while

186

he was away and set to energetically ripping out the feathers and guts in the moonlight. They ate the remains of their 'luncheon' and left the pheasant in an old iron pot sealed with clay to cook in the fire while they slept.

Daisy opened her eyes. Boyd was staring straight into them. It was only just light and for a second she wondered where she was and then yesterday's events came rushing back. His face was serious and the crossed lines of blood on his cheek had dried into a dark scab. The skin of her backside was stinging but she was snuggled against him, warm and comfortable under his blanket on the slatted wood bench. She squirmed to alter her position and murmured, 'Shall we stay here?'

Boyd chewed on his lip and shook his head silently. 'I'll find somewhere to take you in.'

'Will it be somewhere for both of us?' She sighed, sank deeper into the curving cocoon formed by his body.

Suddenly, he pushed her away and sprang to his feet. 'No. We can't be together like this. You're a grown-up and – and –' His brow furrowed deeply and his blue eyes became stormy. He looked away. 'And so am I.'

Puzzled, she frowned and pouted trying to understand. It seemed to make him worse. He seemed to be angry with her. Well, she supposed it was her fault they were in this situation.

'I'm going out,' he said abruptly.

'I'll come with you.' She sat up on the bench.

'No!' he shouted. 'Stay here. Do as I say.' Boyd never shouted at her normally. But now was not normal. They had run away from home, leaving their vengeful parents to fend for themselves.

'Don't leave me!' she called after him.

187

'I won't,' he barked over his shoulder and disappeared into the trees. 'Wait for me.'

Daisy didn't know what to do. She gazed at the embers in the fireplace and stirred them into life, adding fresh wood. The pheasant was cooked in its juices and she wrapped it carefully in the calico. She wondered how much egg money Boyd had saved and hoped it was enough to buy bread.

Daisy was starting to worry about Boyd when he came back. 'Where've you been?' she asked.

'Nowhere.'

'Well, what've you been doing nowhere?'

'I've been thinking.'

'Oh.' Boyd was good at thinking. He could surprise her with his thoughts. 'What about?' she pressed.

'We can't stay together like this.'

Fear clouded Daisy's eyes. Surely he wasn't going to go off without her? 'Why can't we?' she demanded.

'I – I – we have to find work and it'll be harder with two of us together.'

'But you're my big brother. You've always looked after me.' She was bewildered by this sudden change in his outlook.

'I shall!' he cried. 'I've said I'll find you somewhere, haven't I?'

'Don't shout at me.'

'I'm sorry but you have to realise how serious this is. We could starve and die living like this.'

'You've got your egg money.'

'I'm keeping it safe for an emergency.'

'Isn't this an emergency?'

'Not really. It's harvest time and there's plenty of labouring work in the fields for both of us.'

'But if we stay around here, Father will find us.'

'That's why we need to move on. There is a really big estate on the other side of the Riding. It goes on for miles and they say the mansion is the biggest in Yorkshire. Redfern Abbey, it's called. You've heard of it, haven't you?'

'Everybody has. They say it has a hundred servants.'

'I can't believe that. It's a long way but we're going there to see if they'll take you on as a farmhouse maid with lodgings. Will you mind being a maid?'

'That's all I am – was – at home. What will you do?'

'I'll find some farm labouring, carting, anything. I can handle horses, everybody says so.'

Daisy was aware of her stinging behind, which had stuck to her drawers in the night. 'How far is it?'

'It's too far for Father to come and find us. I'll cut a couple of stout poles for the walk. It'll take a few days but it'll be worth it.'

She had to walk for a few days! Daisy felt another trickle of blood where she pulled away her drawers and chewed on her lip. Better not to tell Boyd and worry him further. She didn't want to be a burden to him.

'Don't worry, Daisy, I'll carry you on my back if I have to.'

He would, too, Daisy thought and crossed the room to put her arms around his neck. 'Oh Boyd, I knew you'd think of something.'

Immediately, he took her arms from around his neck and pushed her away. 'Stop that, Daisy.' He seemed irritated with her and went on. 'Listen to me. You're a grown-up now and you might be doing outside work like me. You'll be fed and have a bed in the barn with other women. If we work hard and behave ourselves we might be kept on over the winter for the turnips.'

Daisy blew out her cheeks. Winter in the fields didn't

189

sound so pleasing. But anything was preferable to going back home. 'Will we be together?'

'I don't know. I'm looking for a position with proper wages. But I'll not be far away and wherever I end up I'll ask to go to church of a Sunday so we can see each other.'

'What if Father comes looking for us?'

'He won't cross the Riding to search. He's too lazy.'

'He'll have nobody to see to the horse and cart.'

'And Mother won't have you for the scrubbing. It'll serve her right.'

Daisy agreed with him, although she still wondered what would happen to them because they were getting on in years. 'What'll they do?'

'They'll get a couple of bairns from the workhouse to slave for them.'

'Oh. Poor things. They'll be younger than us. Do you remember what it was like for us? At least we're bigger now. Perhaps we ought to go back?'

'Never! And I don't want to hear you talk like that again.'

As they trekked Daisy felt the soreness on the flesh and from time to time a tiny hot trickle of blood from her wounds. But Boyd had fired her determination to push on as far as she could to get from her mother and father and their cruelty. They walked for two days, following the milestones and foraging for food and sleeping under hedgerows until they were confronted by a densely wooded forest.

Daisy glanced back along the track. 'I'm sure someone is following us.'

'Yes, I thought so too.'

'It isn't Father is it?'

'It could be.' Boyd took her arm. 'Don't worry. I'll knock him down before I'll let him take you back.'

'But he might have gone for a constable.'

'We'll cut through these trees. I think the Redfern estate is at the other side.'

'Do you think we ought to?'

'We've got to, Daisy. You're flagging.'

'I'm tired.'

'I know. It can't be much further.'

But they had not gone far before they were confronted by a large stocky man dressed in moleskin breeches and gaiters, and carrying a shotgun. He stepped out of the trees right in front of them.

'That's far enough, you two. State your business.'

'We're looking for harvest work, sir,' Boyd said.

He examined their appearance. 'Well, you look a strong enough fellow,' then he frowned. 'Are you travellers?'

Boyd replied quickly, 'We're not vagrants, sir. We – we have lost our home and don't want to go to the workhouse. Can you direct us to a farm?'

'I can direct you off this land. This is the Redfern estate and you're trespassing.'

'He said we were looking for work,' Daisy protested.

'Aye well, they might be able to use the pair of you for the harvest. Get yourselves on to the bridleway at yon side of this wood instead of skulking here in the trees.' He gesticulated with his gun. 'It'll take you to Redfern Village. Keep going and follow the estate wall past the Abbey until you get to Home Farm t'other side. If you look sharp you'll be there before nightfall.'

'Thank you, sir.'

He stood with his gun across his arm, watching them as they hurried on their way.

'Is she your wife, young fellow?' he called out after them.

'She's my sister, sir.'

'She'd do better at the Abbey, then. They need servants to look after servants in the Abbey.'

'Thank you, sir.'

Daisy eyes widened. 'Well, if they've got a hundred servants I'm not surprised.'

'I'd heard it was a big estate. We'll have more chance of work.' Boyd quickened his step.

Even Daisy, who was weakening by the hour, brightened. She'd rather do housework than stack corn stooks all day. But she was unable to keep up with him. 'I'm hungry, Boyd.'

'I'll buy bread in the village.'

Daisy's feet were hot and tired and she was bleeding. She could feel the warm trickle over her buttocks and thighs and the rub of her calico drawers against her sore flesh. She persuaded herself it didn't hurt much. It wasn't as bad as any of her previous beatings when she had been red raw for a week and had to sleep on her stomach. But all this walking had opened up old scabs as well as the fresh cuts. When she placed her hands on them her skin felt hot.

There was nothing she could do except perhaps find a stream in which to bathe. She could hardly expose her behind at a public horse trough and she was too embarrassed to mention it to Boyd. Besides she didn't want him to worry about her any more than he did already. Lately, he had been very proper about her behaviour when she was with him. He kept going on about her being a grown-up. Well, she was and he wanted her to behave like one, like Mattie Chandler she supposed. She pressed her lips together and tried to ignore the pain.

The village was larger than she expected with a provisions merchant, draper's shop and an apothecary that had large glass flasks of brightly coloured liquids displayed in the window. There was also a butcher's shop and an inn, a proper inn with stables and housing for coaches. Clearly, the wealth of the Redfern estate had a beneficial effect on the surrounding hamlets and villages. A hundred servants! They must have a huge family to need so many.

Boyd bought bread and cheese, and they both tore at it hungrily and then drank water at a horse trough. Boyd asked directions to Home Farm and Daisy's heart sank as she looked at the steep hill they had to climb next. She didn't want to complain to Boyd or hold him back so she gritted her teeth and persevered.

They set off towards the high brick walls capped with stone that surrounded Redfern Park. Daisy's legs ached and she felt sore and sticky. The wall went on for miles until they came to the fine park entrance and a pair of stone stags at bay surmounting two high stone pillars. She peered through the enormous ornate wrought-iron gates and saw a lodge, a miniature stone castle with turrets, set back in trees.

'That's a wide track. It's as big as the turnpike.'

'It's a driveway for carriages going to the Abbey.'

'Where is the Abbey?'

'Behind the trees, I suppose.'

'Who lives here, Boyd?'

'Lord Redfern. He owns everything around here and has a coal field under the ground. They say that's where his wealth comes from.'

'Is it much further to the farm?'

'I don't know, Daisy,' he replied irritably. 'I don't know the answers to everything.' He sighed. 'I'm sorry but I'm tired as well as you, and that gamekeeper said the farm was on the side furthest from the village. We'll have to go round the park.'

'I'm sorry too,' she muttered. 'Can we stop a while? I can't keep up with you.'

He gave her a sympathetic smile. 'Wait until we're out of sight of the gates.'

They had not progressed much further when the sound of a horse's hooves galloping up the hill caused Boyd to further quicken his step. 'Come on,' he urged.

But Daisy stopped and turned. 'Who is he, Boyd?' she asked.

'I don't know but he's gentry so come away!'

Daisy seemed rooted to the spot and continued to gaze. The rider reined in his mount at the gate and leaned forward to grasp a bell pull. Daisy heard the clang from inside the gates. As he waited for them to be opened he noticed her staring and cantered over.

She held her breath. Were they in trouble for loitering by the gates? He was young and fresh faced with dark hair and eyes, but dressed in gentleman's clothes with a tall hat, kid gloves and high boots. Everything about him signified wealth and position and Daisy's eyes, in spite of her misgivings, shone at his splendour. She had never seen anyone so handsome and could not take her eyes off him. Did he live at the Abbey, she wondered?

Her lips were slightly parted as she wavered between wanting a closer look or running for cover as Boyd suggested. She usually did as Boyd said because he was older and wiser than she but at that moment her legs would not move. The gentleman was going to speak to her! Where was Boyd? Had he disappeared into the trees? Remembering her manners, she closed her mouth, lowered her inquisitive eyes to the horse's hooves and dipped awkwardly into a curtsey.

Chapter 18

'Who are you?' the gentleman rider demanded.

He couldn't be as old as Boyd, she thought, yet he spoke to them as though he was their father and with such authority that Daisy shrank into silence.

Thankfully, Boyd retraced his steps and arrived breathless by her side. He gave a deferential bow. 'We are South Riding folk, sir,' Boyd replied.

'What is your business here?'

'We are on our way to join the harvesting at Home Farm. I have heard they need hands.'

The young gentleman seemed satisfied with Boyd's response. He looked at Daisy steadily for a moment or two so she felt compelled to repeat her curtsey and mutter, 'Sir.' Then they all heard the gates creak and whine open. He barked, 'Carry on,' turned his horse around and acknowledged a servant standing to attention. Then he spurred the horse to a gallop down the long rutted driveway. The servant secured the gates and returned to the lodge.

'Are we in trouble?' Daisy asked.

'I don't think so. But you never know with gentry. They make their own rules. Come on, the sooner we get there the sooner you can rest.'

Daisy pressed on, forcing one foot in front of the other until they came to a smaller entrance where the gates stood open. 'This must be the way to the farm.'

'Listen, there's a cart coming.'

Sure enough a farm cart trundled around the curve of the wall carrying cages of live fowl.

'Are you going to the Abbey, sir,' Boyd asked.

''Tis t'on'y place I know along here. Are you heading that way?'

'We are.'

'Hop aboard.' He leaned over and offered his grimy, calloused hand to Daisy. She swung up beside him and clenched her teeth against the pain as she sat down. Boyd settled beside her and they exchanged grateful smiles.

'Which part do you want, me ducks?' the driver asked Daisy.

Her eyebrows shot up. She had no idea.

'Never been there afore? It's a village in itself behind the Abbey. Have either of you got a letter?'

Daisy shook her head and Boyd answered, 'We'd heard they need housemaids.'

'Aye well, they'll not let you in the Abbey but one of the under-housekeepers might take you on in the servants' quarters. What about you, young man?'

'Harvest work, sir.'

'You're in luck. They want the corn in before the weather turns. I'll tek you over there.'

'Well, I'd like to see where my sister's going first.'

'I haven't time to hang about, lad. She'll not be sent away at this time of day. She'll be tekken care of fer t'night.'

The cart emerged from the trees and Daisy had her first glimpse of the rear of the Abbey in the distance. 'Go with him, Boyd,' Daisy urged. 'I'm a grown-up, I can look after myself.'

'She'll be with the women, lad,' the carter said. 'They're strict about that sort o' thing at the Abbey.'

'Try and get to church on Sunday,' Boyd said.

'That'll be the big 'un back there in the village,' the carter told them. 'You'll likely be off in time for evensong.'

'Send me a message if you can't get there,' Boyd added.

'I shall,' she replied emphatically. 'Go and find work on the farm.'

'I won't be far away,' Boyd reassured her.

The carter jolted through another gate in a smaller wall and pulled up outside a long low outbuilding. 'Go through that door and ask to see whoever's in charge. She'll find you summat, like as not.'

Boyd clambered down and gave her a quick hug as he lifted her off the cart. 'You look a bit flushed,' he commented.

'It's the sun,' Daisy explained, but she was feeling feverish. She put it down to fatigue and hunger.

'See you in church on Sunday.'

She nodded and waved him away, keeping a smile on her face until he had stopped looking back. She felt decidedly ill. Her drawers had stuck to her behind again and she dreaded walking as the movement would rip the calico from her skin and restart the bleeding. A collection of stone buildings and wooden barns arranged themselves neatly in rows and squares creating dark narrow alleys overshadowed by the rear façade of the stone Abbey. It was high and it was wide with three neat rows of sash windows rising to a parapet and slated roof. Daisy tipped back her head. There was another row of windows behind the parapet.

Cautiously she put one foot in front of the other. As she approached the door, several women of varying ages dressed in grey gowns covered in grubby white aprons spilled out of the door with their caps in their hands. Leaning against the rough stone walls of the low building, they looked as tired as she felt. Daisy took a deep breath and stood as straight as she could.

'Good – good evening to you,' she said. 'Is one of you in charge?'

They were taking off their aprons and undoing the top buttons of their high-necked gowns. One sat down on the step of a mounting stone to unlace her boots. They looked at her without much curiosity which made Daisy feel more confident.

'Not one of us. Try inside.'

Daisy swallowed and stepped over the threshold into a gloomy low-ceilinged room. It was a mess. The remains of a meal were scattered over a big wooden table and a few women had laid their heads down on its grainy surface, apparently asleep. One of them lifted her head and muttered, 'You've missed tea, but there's some ale in the jug.'

'Is anybody in charge?'

'You'll find the under-housekeeper in the office. It's through there.'

As her eyes became used to the gloom she noticed an open door at the other end of the room and purposefully walked across the room and through it. No one attempted to stop her. She found herself in a long dark passage lit only by

198

vestiges of light coming through glass partitions on one side. She peered into the first room. It was a scullery the size of a kitchen and a large kitchen at that. A door opposite opened and a woman walked out in front of her.

'Please, ma'am, are you the under-housekeeper?' Daisy asked.

The woman stopped in her tracks. She wore a dark grey gown with white collar and cuffs, and an attractive lace cap with a dark grey band on it. 'I am. I've not seen you before. Are you the new girl?'

'I suppose so,' Daisy answered. 'I – I haven't been taken on yet.'

'Nobody told me you were arriving tonight. Come into the office.'

The woman disappeared as quickly as she had emerged and Daisy followed her into a small sitting room with a fireplace, a table and chairs and some bookcases.

'What's your name?'

'Daisy Higgins, ma'am.'

The woman sat down at the table, turned up the oil lamp and shuffled through some papers. 'There isn't anything about you here. Show me your letter.'

'I haven't got one.'

'Well, where've you come from, then?'

'I've come with my brother. He's helping with the harvest at Home Farm.'

'I mean, where was your last position?'

Daisy looked alarmed and the woman gave an impatient shudder.

'I wanted to be with my brother,' she explained.

'You mean you've just turned up with him?'

'I asked for the person in charge and they sent me through here.'

The woman grimaced and clicked her teeth impatiently. 'And you say your brother is at Home Farm? Well, I can't do anything with you at this time of the day. We've had a houseful to feed for some politicking dinner and everybody's tired out. I'll find you a bed for the night and sort you out tomorrow.'

She went to her door and called out, 'Brown!' A few moments later a mature woman dressed in the same grey as the maids appeared, rolling down her sleeves and buttoning the cuffs. She was about the same age as Maltie's mother, Daisy thought, but she had a sterner countenance.

'This is Daisy Higgins,' the under-housekeeper said. 'Take her with you for tonight and bring her back here to my office first thing tomorrow.'

'Very well, madam,' Brown responded with a curtsey.

Daisy copied her and said, 'Thank you, madam.'

Outside in the cobbled courtyard Brown said, 'I'm Annie. Have you got your uniform?'

Daisy shook her head.

'Well, you can't start until your mother sends your uniform. If any of the housekeepers saw you, there'd be trouble.'

'Oh.' It didn't sound as though she could be a housemaid at Redfern Abbey after all. But Daisy felt so poorly that she was past caring. It was already getting dark and she was exhausted. She was hot and feverish. Her bottom hurt, her feet hurt, and now her head was beginning to hurt.

'Where are your things?'

'I – I – my brother took them with him.'

Annie was silent for a minute as they walked across the cobbles to another low stone building. 'I can lend you a nightgown,' she said finally. 'This is where we sleep.'

'I thought servants always slept in attics.'

'I don't know what folk have been telling you about here. But my brigade hardly ever go inside the Abbey. We look after the servants' quarters.' Annie opened the door into a dormitory of about a dozen beds in two rows with a fireplace at one end and three wash stands at the other. 'There's no one to fetch and carry for us.'

Daisy stared at the dormitory. Several candles burned on small cabinets that stood beside each bed. Two maids were already in their beds asleep and one was washing at the stand. A small group was sitting on the bed nearest the fireplace talking quietly with their heads close together.

Annie led her to a neatly made bed at the end nearest the wash stands. 'Don't put your feet on the bed with your boots on,' she said and went to rummage in a wooden box. She returned with a bundle of white cotton. 'That should fit you and there's a clean drying cloth, too. You'll find soap on the washstand and a chamber pot in the cabinet.'

'Thank you, Annie.'

'Get up as soon as you hear the bell.' Annie went and sat on the bed opposite her and began to unlace her boots.

Exhausted, Daisy did the same and then unbuttoned her gown and struggled out of it. She decided to wait until the end washstand in the darkest corner was free so that she could wash the sore skin on her bottom. Without a candle no one would see. She undid the tapes on her petticoat and stepped out of it.

When she straightened she found that Annie had appeared by her side.

'What happened to you?' Annie demanded. 'You've got blood on your drawers.'

'Oh – I – I – it must be my courses.'

'Not that much, dearie. I think you'd better tell me.'

Daisy shook her head in the gloom. 'I just want to have a wash.'

'Well, when did you last wash them drawers?'

Daisy was too tired to argue with her and Annie went on, 'Some o' that blood is fresh and I've only once seen a pair o' drawers like that in here before and the poor lass had miscarried wi'out telling anyone.'

'It's not that,' Daisy muttered wearily.

'I won't have whores in here, corrupting the others with their tales.'

Daisy was horrified. She had never been accused of being *that* before and whispered fiercely, 'I'm not a whore.' One or two of the other maids were looking in her direction with interest. 'Please, Annie, I just want to sleep. I'll be fine by the morning.'

'I'm not so sure. Summat's up wi' yer.'

'I'm – I'm sore, that's all.'

'You have been whoring!' Annie sounded shocked.

'No!' Daisy flopped on the edge of the bed with her head drooping. 'I'm just tired.'

Annie tipped up her chin with one hand and placed the other across her brow. 'You're burning up, do you know that?'

Daisy wished that was really true; then she'd be dead and all the pain and weariness would be gone.

'You can't stay here, lass, not until I know what's up with you. You might have summat catching. Get your gown on again.'

Annie sat on Daisy's bed to relace her boots and, half asleep, Daisy reluctantly did the same. When she was dressed again Annie led her back to the under-housekeeper's office and further down the corridor. It was quite dark now and the only light came from candle stubs burning in candleholders screwed to the partition walls. She knocked on two of the closed doors before getting a reply.

'Who's there?' It was a male voice.

'Annie Brown.'

'The housekeepers have gone to bed.'

'I've got one of the girls wi' me.'

The door opened and a footman in his shirtsleeves added, 'Can't it wait until morning?'

'No.'

The man sighed. 'It'll have to. There'll be hell to pay if I have to wake any of them after the day we've had.'

Daisy had closed her eyes and was lolling against the door jamb. Annie replied, 'Look at her. She's bleeding and I think it's serious.'

'It's not women's doings, is it? I don't want owt to do with that.'

'There must be somebody who can help her.'

'Can't you see to her fer tonight?'

'I've got the others to keep an eye on. Besides, she needs more tending than I can give her. Who do you go to when one of the upstairs maids gets sick?'

'The housekeeper, unless she doesn't want her to know, like.' He thought for a moment then reached for his livery jacket. 'The old nurse'll know what to do. She'll still be awake. She doesn't sleep much nowadays.'

'I thought she'd gone to an almshouse.'

'Naw, she grew up here and she'll die here.'

'Where is she?'

'In the attics. I'll show you.'

'Oh, I don't know that I should go up there.'

'You want the lass seen to, don't you?'

Daisy was only half aware of the conversation. Her head was muzzy with exhaustion and she felt hot all over. She felt her knees going and started to slither down the wall. Desperately she reached out and clutched at the man's jacket to stop herself collapsing. 'Help,' she croaked.

Annie jumped forward. 'Tek one of her arms. She's fair dead on her feet.'

'Who is she anyroad? I don't remember seeing her face afore.'

'She's new. Come on, lass. Brace yerself.'

She didn't know where she was going but hopefully to someone who was going to help her so she put one determined foot in front of the other as she was half carried through doors and down passages until she was standing at the foot of a narrow wooden staircase. It may as well have been a mountain as far as Daisy was concerned.

'You're nearly there, lass,' the footman encouraged and half dragged her up the stairs while Annie followed carrying a candle.

The climb went on, it seemed, for ever and several times Daisy stumbled on the steps but eventually she reached the very top of the staircase and a small landing. 'Do you know which door it is?' Annie whispered.

'Aye. I've been here before.' The footman rapped on a door.

'Who's there?' enquired a weak voice from within.

'I have a lass needs seeing to,' he answered.

'What's wrong with her?'

Annie Brown took over and said to the footman, 'Thank you. I'll explain.'

The footman, glad to be away, melted into the darkness of the stairway. Annie added, 'I am so sorry to disturb you, ma'am, but this is Higgins. She arrived today and she's – she's – well she 'as a fever.'

After a short silence a voice answered, 'Bring her inside, the door's not locked.'

The room was comfortably furnished as a sitting room with an upholstered couch and fireside chairs and a bed in the far corner. A small, very old woman was sitting at a table playing patience with a pack of cards by the light of an oil lamp. She was in her nightgown and a nightcap with a woollen shawl about her shoulders. She turned and peered at them over a pair of round spectacle lenses balanced on her nose.

'Sit her on the couch.'

But Daisy took one look at the bed and fell forwards, sprawling over the tapestry cover. Her skin burned and her head throbbed. She closed her eyes and prayed for oblivion. The last thing she was aware of was the old woman's thin reedy voice saying, 'You'll have to help me with her.'

She was vaguely aware of being undressed and aided as best she could. But her head seemed to be floating on the ceiling away from her body and she took the small draught that Annie offered to her without resistance. It made her drift away from the pain but she was aroused later by a stinging sensation on her behind and squealed. Somebody was applying a poultice to her, then pulling up her drawers and tying the tapes. 'Put her on the couch,' she heard. 'There's a blanket over the back.' Lying flat on her stomach, she sank into a slumber and the next thing she was aware of was a pale grey light in the chamber and dawn was breaking.

Chapter 19

Her head throbbed and felt heavy. She was hot and shivery at the same time. Her tongue was stuck to the roof of her mouth and she was thirsty. She moaned as she tried to move and it was not just due to the pain from her whipping, her limbs felt like lead and she was drained of all her energy. With difficulty she turned on her side and recalled how she'd got here. There was no sign of Annie. The old woman was sitting up in bed, wrapped in her shawl with her head tipped back in sleep. Daisy flopped back onto her stomach, shut her eyes and hoped for oblivion again. She must have dozed because the room was lighter when she next opened them and the bent old woman was moving about the room. She turned onto her side and groaned.

The old woman stopped what she was doing and came over. She had her spectacles on her nose and peered closely at her face. 'Try and sit up and I'll give you some water.'

Such nectar! The cold clear liquid slid down her rasping throat and she gulped.

'Steady,' the woman advised. 'Sip slowly.' She put a hand on her brow. 'I'll mix you another draft. The chamber pot is in that commode and there's clean water in the pitcher.'

Daisy hardly had the strength to get up from the couch but as she moved she realised that her wounds were not stinging any more and there was padding underneath her drawers. However her legs seemed to have turned to jelly and she felt cold. She shivered as she rinsed her hands and face at the washstand and was grateful to sink back on the couch and under her blanket. The old woman was busy at a small dresser full of tiny glass bottles and stoneware pots. She brought over a small thick glass full of a cloudy liquid.

'What is it?' she asked.

'It's something to help you get better.'

'Th-thank you,' she mumbled, taking the draught.

The old woman watched her swallow the bitter liquid. 'Annie Brown called you Daisy. That's a pretty name.'

Daisy managed a smile, but all she wanted to do was lie down and close her eyes . . .

She drifted in and out of sleep, aware of the old woman tending to her sore skin with ointments and mixing potions for her to drink. Sometimes Annie was there helping her to sit up and drink. She brought her soup and bread, eggs cooked in butter and fresh water. Daisy was aroused by snatches of conversation.

'How did she get here?' the old woman asked.

'Her brother brought her. He's an itinerant on Home Farm.'

'She's a vagrant, then.'

Daisy realised that she was just that. She was homeless and without a position or means. They'll send her to the work-house! Where was Boyd? She tried to sit up and mumbled, 'Is it Sunday yet? I have to get dressed for church.'

Annie came over and gave her some water. 'You'll not be going this week, ducks.'

'But I have to be – better – for – Sunday, church – on – Sunday—' Daisy drifted into fog again.

She was aware that she felt well as soon as she opened her eyes. They were sitting at the table watching her, Annie and the old lady.

'She's awake.'

'Is it Sunday yet?' Daisy asked.

Annie answered. 'Sunday's been and gone, love.'

Daisy sat up alarmed. 'I've missed church! What's happened to Boyd!'

'Calm down. Your brother came looking for you in the servants' quarters.'

'You didn't tell him I was poorly, did you? He'll only worry.'

'Aye well, he knows you're in good hands. They've sent him off with a gang to yon side of the estate so you won't be seeing him 'til the harvest is in.'

'Oh, but that's weeks away. Where is my gown? I have to go with him.'

'No, you don't. He asked us to find you summat here. Well, his overseer did. So, you've a few more days up here keeping Mrs Potter company, then I'll find out what you can do for us in the servants' hall.'

'You'll give me a position here?'

'I didn't say that.' Annie stood up and picked up an empty tray. 'Ta-ra for now.'

When Annie had left, Mrs Potter said, 'Come to the table and eat this porridge. I want you to tell me about the whippings you've had.'

Daisy hesitated. But she was hungry so she wrapped the blanket around her and staggered to the table.

Mrs Potter was bent and wizened but her mind was alert. 'You've scars and scabs as well as fresh wounds,' she said. 'What did you do to get them?'

Embarrassed, Daisy looked down into the porridge. 'I tried ever so hard to please them but the more I did, the more they found fault with me. I did work hard, I promise.' She shrugged her shoulders. 'I couldn't do anything right.'

'Where were you in service?'

'I wasn't in service. I helped my mother keep house.'

'Your mother did this to you?' Mrs Potter seemed genuinely shocked.

'Well, no. She – she – remembered every single thing that I did wrong and told Father when he came in from work. He – he did the whippings. He said it was for my own good. He said I had to learn.'

'Spare the rod and spoil the child. It's a father's task to discipline his offspring. But these were harsh beatings. You must have been a wicked child.'

'Father said I was disobedient.'

'Did you go off with lads and let them kiss you?'

'No! I wasn't allowed to go anywhere except with Boyd. He didn't know about the whippings because he's slept in the shed since he was ten. But this time Father made him watch – and – and, well, Boyd stopped him. He snatched the whip off him.' She paused and swallowed. 'We ran away after that.'

Daisy stifled a shiver of apprehension as she thought about

209

her father. She thought he had taken pleasure in whipping her and she dreaded being sent back to him. She wished Boyd were here with her now.

Daisy stayed another two nights with Mrs Potter. Mrs Potter taught her to play cards and Daisy tidied her collection of remedies. She wiped clean the containers and placed them in alphabetical order on the marble-topped dresser. She wrote new labels for some in her neat handwriting and learned something of their uses. On the second day, the under-housekeeper brought up breakfast and stayed to ask questions.

Daisy stood with her hands by her sides.

'Is she better, Mrs Potter?'

'Yes, ma'am.'

The housekeeper turned to Daisy. 'Have you any money to go home?'

Daisy tried not to show her alarm. 'I can't go back there!'

'Well, you can't stay here until your brother gets back from the harvest.'

'But Annie – I mean Mrs Brown, said I—' Daisy stopped. Annie had not actually promised her anything.

Mrs Potter came to her rescue. She lowered her voice and said, 'She had to leave home because—' The old lady crooked a finger and the housekeeper bent down closer to listen. But Daisy heard what she said right enough. 'Her father did things to her, you know. That's why her brother fetched her away.'

The housekeeper seemed overcome by this. 'Oh! Oh! Poor little lass! She's not – not – you know?'

Daisy wondered what Mrs Potter was playing at. She opened her mouth to explain but was silenced by a raised hand from the old woman who said, 'We'll all say no more about it. These things are best forgotten.'

The housekeeper had her hand held on her chest, her mouth was open and she was looking at a blank wall muttering, 'The brute. He wants stringing up.'

Daisy raised her eyebrows and received a tiny smile and a nod from Mrs Potter who was continuing, 'Aye well, just as long as you don't say nothing to nobody about it, ma'am. But the lass can read and write and she picks things up quickly.'

'Really? Brown has said she would be prepared to take her. What do you think?'

'I don't think she'll disappoint but,' Mrs Potter lowered her voice, 'you tell Annie Brown to keep a special eye on her, though, until her brother gets back.'

'Oh, I shall. She'll have to find her a uniform for a start.'

Daisy's spirits were raised and she thanked Mrs Potter and vowed to repay her somehow, someday. She clattered down the interminable wooden stairs through doors and passages, past store rooms and kitchens with steaming boilers and scurrying cooks and maids, to the outbuildings that housed the lowliest of the Abbey's servants.

The under-housekeeper found Annie pushing dirty linen into a canvas bag for the laundry.

'Higgins will be in your brigade as an under-housemaid until her brother returns. Keep a close eye on her, Brown. She has no testimonial so make sure she learns everything proper and don't let her set foot in the Abbey without my permission.'

Annie grimaced at Daisy who smiled and said, 'Thank you for helping me that night, Annie. I had a fever but I'm better now.'

'Aye, you look a bit livelier today. There's a uniform laid out on your bed in the dormitory. Then come and help me lay up the table for our dinner.'

211

Daisy hurried away feeling that her luck had changed. The grey gown gave her a sense of belonging and if she worked really hard Annie might find her a permanent position. How fortunate they would be if Boyd was taken on at Home Farm too! She laid out her own gown to brush and sponge in readiness for church and skipped off to help Annie. Daisy watched Annie carefully when she showed her what to do and determined to be the best under-housemaid Annie had ever had.

'I heard you had a hundred servants here,' Daisy commented as she helped serve up the dinner from a big iron pot. She carried the steaming plates of mutton and barley with cabbage to the table and her mouth watered.

'You heard right,' Annie answered. 'As well as the maids we have the footmen and kitchen brigade, the gardeners and gamekeepers, the grooms and stable lads, and when we have visiting parties they bring their own servants with them and I have to keep the servants' hall up to scratch for all of them.'

As Daisy became more familiar with the layout she realised that the servants' hall was not, as she had imagined, some vast chamber but a collection of rooms and buildings where the servants ate and relaxed when they had the time. She quickly learned that where you ate your dinner identified your position and whether you were employed indoors or outdoors.

Annie Brown and her brigade of under-housemaids ate together in the low stone building where Daisy had arrived. They sat around a large old kitchen table while Annie doled out ladles of stew and vegetables and carved up slices of steamed pudding on a dresser. Daisy ate hungrily and talked to the girl next to her.

'What day is it?'

'Thursday.'

Three days to Sunday, Daisy thought. Boyd wouldn't be there yet, but eventually he would return. 'Where do you go to church?' she asked.

'I go home to me mum and dad when I have my half day on a Sunday off. But most others walk to the village. There's a shortcut across the park. You can see the spire from Home Farm.'

Annie overheard and interrupted, 'You get one half day off a month, Daisy. But you won't get yours until you've worked a month and earned it.'

Daisy's face fell. If Boyd didn't get the same half day off they might never see one another!

'Don't look so miserable, lass. If there are no house guests you'll be free after four on a Sunday to go to evensong.'

'Do you have many house guests?'

'Enough to keep us busy! Lord Redfern is too old to join in too many house parties these days but he still has them. Nobody ever dreamed he would live this long. He soldiers on, though.'

'Oh.' Daisy listened as the other servants bantered about how rich his lordship was and how miserable too, with no wife and no family to speak of.

'Now then, lasses,' Annie warned. 'He has his ward, Master James.'

'Have you ever seen him?'

'He's away at school,' Annie said.

'Schools are closed for the harvest and the shooting, aren't they?'

'Well, I expect he's gone to stay with friends.'

'I might have seen him,' Daisy volunteered. 'How old is he?'

'Seventeen or eighteen, I believe,' Annie replied.

'Oh, same as me.' It could have been him, Daisy thought.

The horseman she had seen when she had arrived might have been him, but, dressed in the finery of a gentleman, he had seemed older than she was.

Daisy quickly settled into a routine under Annie's watchful eye and after a fortnight her long working day was lifted by a message from Boyd to say he was well and had heard that she had recovered from her fever. She asked Annie for paper and ink to write him a note but neither were available to her and she returned his good wishes with her own. It wasn't much but it was better than nothing and she looked forward to when the harvest was in and she would see him again.

Her weeks were full and she enjoyed being part of Annie Brown's family of servants' servants. Her hands and nails took on all sorts of colours when the Abbey gardeners brought in barrow-loads of produce and Daisy was allocated to a scullery to pick over and prepare it. Sweet sickly aromas of fruit preserves in high summer gave way to a September air filled with boiling vinegar that made her head spin. On her visits to church she met dairy maids, scullery maids, kitchen maids, house maids. So many maids, there seemed to be one for every household task. It was a very large church with grand stained-glass windows and an ancient rector. The maids sat in pews quite separate from the gardeners and stable boys.

Daisy's excitement bubbled as September wore on and evening shadows lengthened. Disappointingly, Boyd returned to Home Farm the week after her half day off but she hoped to see him at the end of the month.

'We'll get our quarter pay on Michaelmas Day,' Annie explained. 'Then there's the harvest festival. But after that it will be hard work in the Abbey because his lordship still has shooting parties and hunts when gentry from all over visit.'

* * *

The Abbey was the largest house Daisy had ever seen, bigger even than the collection of brewery buildings all put together. She saw it only from the rear but it stretched for half a mile from east to west and had underground passages for the servants to get from one end to the other.

'I don't understand why his lordship needs such a big house to live in,' she remarked.

'Royalty, me ducks,' Annie told her. 'We have dukes and duchesses to visit regular for the balls and the hunting. The chambers are huge – you'll see for yourself when you go inside.'

'Me? Go inside the Abbey? When?'

'We all go in for our quarter day pay. You won't get much but come the winter solstice you'll get more. It's right handy that quarter, coming just before the Christmas festival. I'll keep yours safe until you decide how you want to spend it.'

Annie had a strong box where she put her maids' money for safe keeping. She noted the amounts in her account book and each maid signed her name against it or put a cross if she couldn't write. Every Sunday morning, those who had a half day off lined up for coins to take with them home to their parents. Two of the older women, when it was quiet one afternoon in the week, took some of their money and walked into Redfern Village to spend on ribbons in the drapers. Daisy looked forward to coppers of her own to spend in the village shops.

Chapter 20

The day before Michaelmas, Daisy spent her free time in the afternoon brushing her gown and polishing her boots so she would look her best to collect her pay. She wished to make a good impression and had kept by a clean cap and apron to wear. On the day, Annie's maids filed past Annie who inspected the appearance of each and nodded, or made a comment and sent her back. Daisy followed the line of servants through the kitchen passages, up a flight of stone steps and through a wide swinging door into the Abbey proper. They shuffled forward slowly on stone flags down a dark wood-panelled corridor. As Daisy was the newest addition to Annie's brigade she was last, followed closely by Annie herself.

A succession of men, young and old, passed them in the opposite direction clicking the coins in their hands. One of them, a brawny fellow in riding breeches and with a spring in his step, stopped to exchange a word with a woman near the front of the queue. The girl next to Daisy turned round and said, 'Did you see that? Old bossy boots has a follower!' and the others began to whisper and giggle. Daisy didn't know the woman well and was quite scared of her because she often checked her work instead of Annie and was very strict about it being just right.

'Quiet!' Annie's strong voice came from behind Daisy's head. The brawny fellow smiled and was nudged along by the man behind him.

Daisy thought it was nice for her if she did have a follower and began to think of her differently. As she moved towards the open double doors she was fascinated by the chamber in front of her and craned her neck for a better view. There were high stone arches down one side and a vaulted decorated ceiling similar to the one in the church. The walls were covered with wooden panels and the floor – Daisy passed the sole of her shoe over the surface – the stone floor felt more like marble and was laid out in a pattern of light and dark squares. A few pieces of heavy carved furniture stood by the walls. The room was lit by large sash windows that had long velvet drapes held back by tasselled cords. From the middle of the ornate ceiling hung an enormous wrought-iron chandelier filled with candles. If she wasn't mistaken they were not tallow either, they were beeswax. She started to count them and work out how much they would cost.

'Daisy!' Suddenly there was a hand on her shoulder and she was spun round and enveloped in his arms. 'Oh Daisy, I've been so worried about you.'

'Boyd? Oh Boyd! So have I, I mean about you.'

'But you were ill, they said, with a fever.'

'I'm well now. Are you? Wait for me outside.'

'I can't. I'm one of the last from Home Farm and the cart

217

is waiting to take us back.' He continued to hug her tightly and whispered, 'I'm staying on for the ploughing. I'll help with the Shires.' Daisy heard a riffle of giggles from the line followed by a soft chant, 'Daisy's got a sweetheart, Daisy's got a sweetheart.'

'Hush, now,' Annie hissed. 'His lordship will hear you.' Her strong fingers prised Boyd and Daisy apart. 'Stop that now. Remember where you are.' A severe-looking woman in a plain black gown and lace cap loomed into view in the doorway and snapped, 'Brown. Keep your brigade in order.'

'Right away, madam.'

Daisy heard a whispered 'the housekeeper' and the group fell silent. Annie was popular with her maids and they didn't want her in trouble. Boyd let Daisy go and whispered, 'I'll see you at the harvest supper.' He looked at Annie and said, 'Beg pardon, ma'am,' then hurried away.

Annie pushed her sharply in the back to move forward but Daisy didn't mind. She was floating on a cloud of excitement. Boyd was safe and he was nearby and they would meet at the harvest supper, which was Very Soon.

The stream of men was replaced by women, all in sponged and well-brushed gowns and pristine aprons and caps. Housekeepers and parlour maids in their neat lace-trimmed uniforms and dainty aprons and caps, cooks and kitchen maids in more serviceable dress, large aprons and plain caps. As the line moved through the doorway she became interested in the table and group of gentlemen at the far end. Her boots slipped along the polished floor.

'Where are we?' Daisy whispered to Annie.

'It's the small ballroom. We have the servants' ball in here at Christmas but it's the counting house today.'

They were shuffling towards a large oblong table with a

polished wooden surface. Three gentlemen were sitting in front of open ledgers, ink pots and quill pens. There were piles of coins in front of the middle gentleman. Two other gentlemen stood around behind them.

'Who are those people?'

'The one in the middle, in the Bath chair, is his lordship. The gentlemen each side are his estate clerk and steward. When his lordship gives you your pay, sign the ledger then curtsey and say, "Thank you, my lord". Watch how the others do it.'

As she neared the table, Daisy listened. The steward called out a name and the girl moved forward to the table. The clerk stated how much pay and the girl signed the ledger, or put a cross if she couldn't write. Then the clerk counted out the coins and slid them across to his lordship who nodded. Then the steward pushed them across the table. The girl picked them up, muttered her thanks and bobbed a curtsey and backed away before turning round to walk out.

That was easy enough, Daisy thought. His lordship was old, really very old, she thought, and obviously frail. He had a woollen blanket over his knees and a similar shawl about his thin shoulders. She surveyed the gentlemen who were standing. One was old too, nearly as old as his lordship and he wore the black stockings and breeches of old-fashioned clerical dress. But it was the younger of the two gentlemen who caught her eye.

He was the rider who had passed her on the way here, when she and Boyd had peered in the high iron gates at the entrance to the Abbey. She recalled his dark eyes and air of authority. He was dressed in a smart suit of clothes: trousers not breeches and a long velvet jacket that was cutaway at the front. His dark hair was longer but he looked even more handsome than she remembered. She stared at him and as she did he turned his head towards her and raised his eyebrows.

She looked down quickly and felt herself blush. When she looked up again he was watching her with a grin on his face. Annie had warned her never to look her betters in the eye so she concentrated on the piles of coins and wondered how much his lordship needed to pay all his servants.

Her turn came and she stood to attention as her name was called, walked purposefully forwards and took the quill pen offered to her, writing her name carefully against the ledger entry. As the clerk counted out her coins, the clergyman said, 'Another servant who can write her own name. How many is that, now? They only cause trouble, you know.'

The younger gentleman frowned and added, 'They don't do that here, sir. Most learn in Sunday school before they come here to work. We ought to have Sunday school in our church, Uncle.'

The cleric widened his eyes and nudged him with his elbow.

Lord Redfern watched his steward pass across Daisy's small heap of coins. 'I am not dead yet, young James. When I am, you may speak your mind. But until then, have the grace to keep your ideas to yourself.'

'My humble apologies, sir. It was a thoughtless comment.' The young man's tone turned to one of contrition. She recognised the manner of one who had learned how to please his elders and felt sympathy.

'I trust that the education I have provided for you has not been wasted.' Daisy was surprised to hear derision in Lord Redfern's voice.

'Indeed not, sir. I should like to speak with you about my future.'

'Now is not the time, boy. I shall listen to you on the due date and not before.' Daisy thought that Lord Redfern had a very domineering tone for one who was so frail.

'Of course, sir.'

Daisy noticed that Master James did not appear to be pleased. His grin had disappeared and he was chewing at his lip. At that moment she thought she knew how he felt. You had to be perfect to please some folk. The steward waved her on. Hurriedly she scraped her coins off the table and moved away. Too late, she remembered her curtsey, dashed back and bobbed her thanks.

Lord Redfern did not seem to notice. 'Wheel me back to my library,' he ordered. 'I shall take my tea alone.' A footman came forward from the shadows behind him.

Daisy glanced at the other gentlemen whose faces, to a man, held neutral expressions, except for Master James who heaved a sigh and blew out his cheeks and caught her eye. She gave him a sympathetic smile and he responded with a resigned shrug. Then she felt Annie's strong fingers on her shoulder pulling her away.

'What do you think you are doing?' Annie propelled Daisy through the wide doorway where the others were waiting to be shepherded back down the steps to the servants' passages.

'I'm not the only one who can write her name,' Daisy protested.

'I don't mean that. You forgot to thank his lordship.'

'I went back.'

'And you – you not only looked at Master James, you smiled at him.'

'He looked at me first.'

'Never mind that! Haven't you listened to a word I've said? If you can't do as you're told, I'll not have you in my brigade.'

221

'I'm sorry, Annie. I'll know better next time. It won't happen again, I promise.'

'I should think not. When we have the harvest supper, his lordship and Master James will call in to thank us so you, young lady, had better make yourself scarce when he does.'

After the long hours and hard work of summer the approaching festival was an occasion that everyone looked forward to. It was a well-deserved celebration for the servants and killed beasts came in on a cart from Home Farm to be butchered at the Abbey. Daisy watched farm hands drag them off, hoist them over their shoulders and carry them indoors to the cold larder. She remembered when a butcher came to stick the pig at home. Mother left her to deal with the nasty job of soaking and washing the innards. It was a horrid smelly task but she liked to eat the end result when they were cooked.

'Who makes the blood puddings and chitterlings?' she asked.

'The farm lasses see to them.'

'I didn't know they had lasses at Home Farm.' She'd be nearer to Boyd if she was at the farm. 'Could I go and work over there, Annie?'

'You don't want to be out in the fields all winter cutting mangolds for the cattle. You can read and write and you learn fast. It's a pity you haven't got a father to pay for schooling. If you behave yourself you could have a position in the Abbey by the time you're one and twenty.'

'D'you think so?'

'If you behave yourself, mind. As it is I can keep you on until after the Christmas festivities as long as there are no more shenanigans like today, my lass.'

'I'm sorry.'

'Aye well, as a punishment I'm sending you to help out in the scullery where they scrub the cooking pots. The kitchens need extra hands for the harvest supper baking.'

'Can't you send me to the farm to wash chitterlings instead?'

'Do as you're told and don't answer back or I'll double your time in the scullery.'

Daisy knew when she was beaten and resigned herself to waiting until the harvest supper to see Boyd again.

The scullery was hot, wet and greasy. She spent her time stoking a boiler fire, tapping off steaming hot water and carrying it by the pailful to one of the deep wooden sinks. When the scullery maids had finished she had to drain the sinks and cart the cold smelly dregs to a cooling vat outside the washhouse where the laundry women skimmed off any fat to make soap. The washhouse was a long way away so no one had to suffer the smell from the chamber pot slops. The stronger the smell the better it was for removing stains and it made Daisy's eyes water as she walked by. She decided that laundry maid was worse than scullery maid and looked forward to returning to her housemaids' duties in the servants' hall.

Excitement grew as the harvest festival drew near. There was a shortcut across the park to the village and now Daisy had money she went there with others one afternoon to buy trimmings for her gown. She had not worn it since Annie had provided her with her servants' uniform. The draper kept a table of second-hand buttons, ribbons and lace that was popular with the younger servants. He called it 'notions' and for her few pennies she bought enough bits and pieces for a collar, cuffs and a panel down the front of her bodice. She decided not to wear her plain cap as nothing she could afford would make it look pretty. But she found a pair of horn hair combs which could be mistaken for tortoiseshell. She so much wanted to look pretty for Boyd.

'Will the farm lasses be there?' she wondered aloud on the way back, thinking how pretty they were. She remembered how she felt about Mattie. She didn't want Boyd to take up with a farm lass and have no time for her.

Every cart and dray and trap on the estate was harnessed to a horse to carry the women and girls over to the barn at Home Farm. The men walked and as they trundled past them in the afternoon light they called out in a good-natured manner to 'save them a reel' or 'take a jar with me'. They looked different out of livery in clean shirts and jaunty neckties. Some wore smart jackets and one or two of the older servants were in breeches and buckled shoes. They were blessed with a fine evening. An area of level ground between two barns had been cleared and rolled for dancing. This was the first time Daisy had attended such a large gathering and her eyes shone as she took in the scene. The fiddlers were playing a jolly tune while men set up barrels of ale and cider and unloaded boxes of crockery and baskets of food from the Abbey.

'Daisy! Over here!' Boyd was covering straw stacks with canvas for sitting on. She ran over and hugged him. 'Are you well? Did you get your pay?'

'Yes. I have to work hard for it but no more than at home.'

'It's better than home because there are no beatings.'

'And Father has not come looking for us?'

Boyd grimaced. 'I think he might have. I saw the carter who brought us in and he said a man had been asking in the village about a pair of young folk looking for work.'

A trickle of fear ran down Daisy's back. 'Did they tell him where we were?'

'They don't know us in the village so they couldn't.'

'If he does come here, will they make me go home with him?'

'He's got to find you first.'

'Well, if he does, I'll run away again.'

'If, if, if. Stop worrying, Daisy.'

'But I like it here.'

'Me too.'

'We oughtn't to have given them our real names.'

'It's best not to lie. Anyway it's too late now.' Someone called Boyd's name to help with setting up the flares. 'You go off and enjoy yourself and I'll come and find you later. I want a dance with my little sister.'

Daisy nodded enthusiastically and looked around for familiar faces. They had disappeared into the jostling groups of chattering people. Suddenly the setting sun dropped beneath the western clouds and shot rays of red across the land. A small cheer rippled around and a large florid man jumped onto a cart in front of the fiddlers and began calling for a square dance.

'Come with me, little one.' A lean grey-haired man had taken her elbow and was pushing her gently towards one of the formations. 'Do you know this one?'

'I – I think so.' Dances had been rare treats for Daisy. But she soon remembered the steps and as she joined in she noticed Annie waving at her from the next group. The man took her through another reel and then pointed out the barrels in one of the barns, where she queued for a mug of cider.

As she sipped the welcome drink she peeped into the adjacent barn where cooks and kitchen maids were setting out a supper of cold joints of meat, pies and pickled vegetables with chunks of newly baked bread and slabs of freshly churned butter. She had never seen so much food in one place. Neither had she seen so many folk gathered together like this before. Annie loomed beside her. 'Are you enjoying yourself, me ducks?'

'I am, Annie. Are you? You look lovely in that gown.'

'Ta, love. It's one from the draper's table wi' a bit of alteration here and there. I'm walking out with one of the under-gardener's, you know.'

'Oh, which one is he?'

'He's the one you danced with first, silly.'

'Oh. He was nice. That was nice of you to send him, too.'

'Aye well, if you like the dancing, you go and stand where folk can see you. You'll be safe wi' any of the lads here, else the steward will have his guts for garters.'

'Oh, is that why he's here?' Daisy had noticed the tall gentleman who had been with Lord Redfern in the counting house strolling around rather than joining in the dancing. He had a lady with him in a lovely gown who she guessed was his wife. Daisy watched her in admiration. She thought, not for the first time, that there were not enough ladies actually living in the Abbey, only Lord Redfern and his ward, Master James. Such a pity, she sighed.

But Daisy only wanted to find Boyd and dance with him. She couldn't see him anywhere in the crowds and pushed her way into the barn. She was hungry too, but no one ate until his lordship's party arrived. The flares were lit giving a lively focus on the fiddlers and callers, but casting the perimeter in gloom.

Daisy wandered around the darkness looking for Boyd. But there was no moon and the contrast with the flares made it difficult to see anything. Through the trees she glimpsed a light and quickened her step to investigate. Her boot tripped on undergrowth nearly throwing her headlong into brambles but eventually the trees gave way to a track and she saw the looming shape of a farmhouse ahead. The lights were from a carriage drawn up in front of the wooden portico. As she drew closer she saw Boyd holding the bridle of the lead horse and hurried forward.

'I've been looking for you.'

'Daisy! Go back to the dancing.'

'Not without you. What are you doing here?'

'I was called away by the stewards.'

'Is this his lordship's carriage?'

'Yes, so keep your voice down. You shouldn't be here.'

'Why shouldn't I be?' she whispered.

'His lordship was taken poorly on the way over here.'

'Is he dying?'

'I don't know. Go and wait in the trees until they've done with me.'

Satisfied with this response, Daisy wandered out of the pool of light from the coach lamps to the gloomy cover of the trees. A rider approached at a gallop followed by a second carriage. There was a commotion as some of the party changed carriages.

Liveried footmen carrying lamps were everywhere and, fascinated, she moved forward for a better view.

'Well, who have we here, I wonder?'

Daisy jumped and inhaled sharply. She had not seen the young gentleman approach. A footman was close behind him.

Chapter 21

'Are you spying on me?' the gentleman asked.

'No, sir.'

'Then what are you doing lurking in the trees?'

Daisy's eyes concentrated on the toes of her boots. 'I was looking for my—' she stopped, not wanting to implicate Boyd in her apparent misdemeanour, 'for my—' she could not think of anything she might be looking for and lapsed into silence.

'Bring me light.' The footman came forward but the young gentleman turned and wrenched the lantern from his grasp. 'Now leave me,' he ordered and the footman bowed dutifully and melted away.

He held it close to Daisy's face. She could smell the burning oil and feel the heat coming through the glass. 'I thought as much. You're the little maid who can read and write. I saw you talking to that farm worker holding the horses.'

Her eyes widened as she recognised Master James from

when she had signed the ledger on quarter day. Remembering Annie's words she looked at the ground and bobbed a curtsey. 'Beg pardon, sir.'

Daisy remained silent as he studied her in the lamplight and spoke more to himself than to her. 'You're not even pretty. But there is something about you that – that draws me . . .' Suddenly he glanced over his shoulder and added, 'He's your sweetheart, I suppose.'

Daisy's mouth turned down. She was hurt because she had tried really hard to look pretty for the dance. She concentrated on his boots. They were highly polished dancing shoes with buckles.

'Well? Is he?'

'No, sir.'

'No? He's a fine-looking fellow, don't you think? Would you like him to be?'

'Oh no, sir, he's my—' Again, her voice faded away. Then she thought that neither she nor Boyd had done anything wrong. The sounds of music and laughter could be heard in the distance. This is a feast day, she thought, and I am not anywhere I'm not supposed to be. She ignored Annie Brown's advice and raised her chin. 'He's my brother and he promised he would dance with me and now he can't because he's got to see to your horses.'

To her immense relief he seemed to find this amusing and he smiled. It was a boyish grin and she realised he wasn't any older than Boyd, it was just that he acted it with his noble airs and graces.

'What's your name?'

Oh no, she was in trouble after all. She kept her eyes down and answered, 'Higgins, sir.'

'I mean your given name.'

Only Annie and Boyd used her Christian name and she hesitated.

'Answer me,' he prompted.

'It's Daisy, sir.'

Another pair of buckled shoes appeared behind him and his footman whispered urgently, 'His lordship is asking for you, sir. He is too poorly to continue with the evening's celebrations.'

The young gentleman didn't say anything else. He handed back his lantern and followed the footman back to the carriages. Daisy watched Boyd leading the horses to turn the front carriage round for the return journey with its ailing occupant. Finally relieved from his duties he crossed to the woodland track and called her name softly.

'I'm over here,' she responded.

'What did Master James want with you?'

'Nothing.'

'Good. He will be master of Redfern Abbey one day. You oughtn't to be speaking to him.'

'I know. Annie said as much. But he spoke to me first. He asked for my name.'

'You're not in trouble, are you?'

'I don't think so. He wanted to know what I was doing talking to you.'

Boyd gave a dissatisfied groan. 'I knew they'd see you.'

But Daisy, normally so concerned about her brother, continued her own train of thought. 'He said I wasn't pretty.'

Boyd's groan turned in a guffaw. 'Well, he doesn't know what he's talking about. You're very pretty indeed.' He put his arm around her shoulders and gave them a squeeze. 'He's an aristocrat so he's used to ladies in sumptuous silks and feathers and can't see beyond your simple gown. Don't you take any notice of what he says.'

She felt better and reminded him, 'You said you'd dance with me.'

'Well, we'll have to hurry if you want a jig before the fiddlers stop for their supper.'

Daisy was breathless when they arrived at the barn just in time for an eightsome reel. As they approached Boyd pulled on her arm and said, 'Listen. Don't say anything about what you saw.'

'I don't see why not. Wouldn't folk want to know his lordship was poorly?'

'Good servants don't gossip about their masters.'

Daisy agreed and shrugged. It made no difference to her as she danced because her thoughts were distracted by her encounter with Master James dressed up in his finery. She wondered how she would have to dress so he thought she looked pretty. Like a lady aristocrat, she realised, and she hadn't ever seen one. Perhaps she might if she stayed at the Abbey.

His lordship's family did not stay long at the festivities. Master James stood on the cart that the callers used and made a short speech of thanks, explaining that his lordship's doctor had advised him to stay indoors now the autumn chill was upon us. Daisy stretched her neck to catch a glimpse of Master James and his party. But she was crowded out by others who were taller than she.

'Can you see any ladies?' she asked Boyd.

He shook his head. 'There weren't any in the carriage. Come to think of it, nobody ever mentions a Lady Redfern.'

Daisy didn't think any more about it as she joined the throng in the barn to enjoy the harvest supper laid out on

231

long tables for everyone to help themselves. After the meats there were huge plum cakes and trays of ginger parkin washed down with more ale or cider. The music started again and Daisy was taken up as a partner by three different young men she had never seen before at the Abbey. One was a footman and the other two said they were gardeners so she did not sit out for a single dance after supper. She was so tired by the finish that she fell asleep on the cart ride back to the Abbey and when nudged awake by the other maids she could not recall their names.

They laughed and teased her for a while, then went on to prod someone else. She barely remembered climbing down from the cart and dragging herself into bed. But her earlier encounter still rankled and her last waking image was of Master James in the lamplight.

Well, I don't think Master James would be quite so handsome either, she thought, without all his fancy clothes.

Daisy changed her mind at the harvest festival the following day. The church, although large, was filled with Abbey and village folk and the display of produce was a wonderful medley of autumn colours. A mixture of orchard fruit smells drifted out to the congregation. Every pew was packed apart from the front one reserved for his lordship so latecomers had to stand at the back. Daisy was squashed in next to the aisle and gave a little wave to Boyd on the other side.

When Lord Redfern was wheeled past her in his Bath chair she could have reached out and touched him. He was muffled up with woollen shawls and blankets and looked wizened and grey. His steward pushed the squeaky creaking wheeled chair, left it in the aisle by the front pew and went to sit in the second row. Master James walked behind him and took his place alone in the front pew. His lordship remained in his Bath chair throughout the service. When the rector appeared he looked grand in his vestments, though he seemed to have difficulty climbing up to the lectern to give his sermon. He started off well but his voice dropped and trembled from time to time so that Daisy couldn't hear what he said. She heard someone whisper, 'Time they put the old reverend out to pasture,' and the reply, 'Not while there's breath in his lordship.'

There weren't any ladies in the front pew which was a huge disappointment for Daisy. She had looked forward to admiring their dress and hair. Daisy hadn't thought of it before but she had not seen any pretty gowns in the front pew on the few times she had attended church. She guessed his lordship's wife had died. Perhaps Master James's mother and father had gone the same way and he did not even have a sister or aunt to grace their pew. She remembered the friendliness of the large brewery family in comparison. Rum lot, his lordship's family, she thought but was fascinated by them nonetheless.

Daisy enjoyed singing all the harvest festival hymns. It was her favourite service. She was in a cheery mood when it was over and Lord Redfern's steward wheeled him past her to the church door. Master James was cheerful too. He nodded and smiled to the left and right, gaining approving looks from his lordship's servants and tenants.

As he neared her pew, he caught sight of her and his eyes lingered. She wanted to smile at him but dared not and looked down at the worn flags as he passed. She watched his boots hesitate and concentrated on them, aware that she was blushing. It was only for a few seconds but it seemed an age before he stepped forward again and moved on. The most senior servants from the Abbey followed him and she hoped the butler or housekeeper had not noticed her discomfort.

The rest of the congregation filed out slowly and Boyd was waiting for her amongst the churchyard headstones. 'I expect you saw Master James behind Lord Redfern,' he said.

Daisy chewed on her lip and nodded.

'He took quite an interest in you as he went by,' Boyd added.

'I didn't look at him, honest, Boyd. I kept my eyes on the floor.'

'Yes, I noticed. But he did take a good long look at you.'

'I didn't ask him too,' she protested.

Boyd stared at her and heaved a sigh. 'I know. Oh Daisy, I'm worried for you. You have to be careful with his sort. They think they can take liberties with servants. Were you honest with me about when he spoke to you last night?'

'I told you! He just came over and asked about you and me. And he really did say I wasn't pretty!'

Boyd appeared to relax. 'Well, his interest may be more about me than you. Although I can't fathom why Master James has to be involved.'

'What do you mean? You don't think Father has found out where we are and wants us back.'

'No, it's nothing to do with that.' He seemed undecided about going on. Eventually he took her elbow and steered her away from the other servants. 'It's probably my fault. I had to tell the steward about us, well, about you really.'

'What did you have to tell him?' If the housekeeper asked too many questions she would get totally the wrong impression of her. She really didn't want to tell anybody else about her whippings or her fever.

'Don't be upset, Daisy. I had to tell him I was responsible for you because – because – it was to do with – oh Daisy, I haven't said anything because I don't want to raise your hopes only to have to dash them later.'

'What is it, Boyd? We ought not to have secrets from each other.' She meant this and felt a pang of guilt as she said it. She had kept her whippings a secret from him.

He gave her a wry smile. 'Mr Stanton, Lord Redfern's steward, has noticed how I handle the horses and – and, well, he wants me to move to the Abbey stables for the foaling in the New Year.'

'You mean you won't have to leave when the ploughing is finished? Oh Boyd, you are so clever!' Daisy's eyes shone. She flung her arms round him and hugged him.

He took a firm hold of her hands and pushed her away. 'Don't do that, Daisy. I had to tell him that I couldn't stay on in the New Year if you have to move on.'

'But you have to stay! You mustn't worry about me. I shall be eighteen next month. I can take care of myself.'

'You don't know what you are talking about. You can't be on your own without a position and somewhere to live. You'll be seen as a vagrant and they'll send you to the work-house. If I am to work in the stables, you have to be taken on too.'

'But Annie told me there'd be nothing for me here once the Christmas festivities are over! You have to have proper learning in a special school to gain a position in the Abbey and that costs money. Oh Boyd, what shall I do?'

'We'll move on, both of us, and find somewhere else.'

'No,' she protested. 'You can't turn down a position here because of me. I'll not let you.'

'You can't stop me,' he pointed out.

'We're not leaving,' she countered. 'I'll find something.'

'Like what?'

'I don't know,' Daisy answered and thought, I really have no idea. They parted and as Boyd moved away with other outdoor servants she wanted to call after him, 'I'll do anything. Say yes.'

She was a burden to him. If he didn't have her in tow he'd be working with fine carriage horses and hunters in the New Year, instead of labouring with the heavy horses and oxen at the farm. She couldn't be responsible for him turning down such an opportunity. She really must find a position elsewhere. Perhaps Annie would write her a testimonial and recommend her as a domestic servant in a smaller mansion? But where, how far away from Boyd would it be and dare she go there on her own?

Chapter 22

A few weeks later, Edgar felt his age when he arrived at Milo's vicarage on the far side of the Riding. He'd lived the life of a gentleman in Leeds for more than five and ten years and had grown tired of lodgings no matter how gracious they were. He'd always felt he'd deserved better and had at last achieved it with the lease on Ellis House. Not long now. A young maid took his riding coat and showed him into Milo's small study.

'Not disturbing you, am I? I thought I'd ride over myself with the news. It's seems further than before.'

Milo put down his pen. 'Come and sit down. You look quite flushed.'

'When I remember the journeys we used to do together on horseback, I can't think why I'm so exhausted.'

'Brandy?'

'Splendid.'

Milo got up to pour. 'You've got a high colour, old boy. Have you seen a physician lately?'

'I'm not ill,' Edgar replied.

'You're heavier than you used to be.'

Edgar clicked his tongue. 'Mrs Wortley's housekeeping. She's a fine woman, Mrs Wortley, exceptional I'd say.' He grinned and took the brandy glass from his friend. 'Your wife and family are well?'

'They're all in excellent health, thank you. And yours?'

'James is turning out to be a fine young man. I see him from time to time, you know.'

'I'm very pleased to hear that. Your great-uncle has relented after all.'

'Oh, he doesn't know. That's my good news. Lord Redfern has taken a turn for the worse.'

'That's hardly good news for him, my friend.'

Edgar's eyes roamed around the room. 'Don't tell me you want to stay here for ever. You want him dead as much as I do.'

'Well, this house is too small now my family is growing.'

'You see! We are all just waiting for the old man to depart this earth. Who ever dreamed he would have lasted this long? He's overdue for the pearly gates. Folk in Redfern Village are saying he'll be gone in a few months.'

Milo raised his eyebrows. 'Do you visit the estate openly?'

'Not on your life! The estate has a steward who runs the place exactly as the old tyrant decrees. He carries a shotgun and asked me to leave once! Would you credit it? Well, I shall be Lord Redfern soon and he'll be the first to go.' Edgar leaned forward and lowered his voice as though he were telling a secret. 'I'm known at the Redfern Arms, and a very good inn it is too.' He finished his brandy and held out the glass. 'And it'll all belong to me soon.'

Milo stretched for his decanter. 'What will you do about the incumbent rector? You can't turn him out.'

'Oh he's only hanging on until his lordship dies. He has some kind of loyalty to the family and all that.'

Milo refilled both their glasses. 'Well, I can't say I'm not looking forward to a better living. I want a good school for my boy.'

'Why don't you come over and stay with me for a few days? I've moved from Leeds to be nearer to Redfern Abbey and taken a lease on a country house about ten miles distant.'

Milo raised his eyebrows again but didn't ask Edgar the obvious question of how he could afford it. Nonetheless, Edgar took pleasure in telling him. 'The bank advanced the money. I can get anything I want from them.'

It was not strictly true. They gave him funds for anything that might have a resale value and a fixed quarterly sum for his living expenses. But it was never enough and he was always running out and having to go cap-in-hand for more. As if the Redfern coal field wasn't the biggest in the Riding. Edgar didn't care. Soon he would have all he could spend and more.

He raised his glass and added, 'My blood is their security.'

'We-ell,' Milo inhaled, 'I'd certainly like to show my wife and family where their future home will be.'

'Ah,' Edgar paused and then cautioned. 'Family might be a bit difficult.'

'Then your country house is really just a cottage?'

'It's big enough. I wanted something more fitting to my status.' He felt uncomfortable about this but, damn it all, he wasn't ashamed or anything, quite the opposite. 'It's your wife, you see,' Edgar groaned. 'Women folk are shocked by these things, and they gossip so much.'

'What are you talking about?' Milo pressed.

'Mrs Wortley.'

'Wasn't she your housekeeper in Leeds?'

'I've taken her with me to Ellis House.'

'But she's only your housekeeper. She does what you say, not the other way round.'

'She's – she's not exactly my housekeeper any more.'

Milo gave him a level stare which he found unnerving. 'Edgar,' he sighed. 'Please tell me she is not living with you as your mistress.'

'The house is isolated, and the servants know only what they are told, so why not.'

'You have a wife! That is why not! *I* can't visit you under those circumstances, let alone with my family.'

'Don't say that, Milo. Who's to know?'

'I'm a vicar! I can't take that risk.' Milo got to his feet irritably. 'It's not the same as when we were young. Since this young queen came to the throne everyone has to be more discreet about how they behave. Even the bishops take Her Majesty seriously.'

'Well, I'm not letting any woman, whether she's the queen or not, tell me what to do.'

'Don't be foolish, you'll cause an enormous scandal and ruin everything just as our plans are working out at last. I've waited a long time for this, Edgar, and you owe me.' There was an awkward silence until Milo added, 'How is your wife anyway?'

'I've no idea. I left that part of my life behind for Mother to handle. Mother couldn't stand my wife so she took rooms at the Golden Lion in Settle and Beth stayed at High Fell.'

'You left her to run the farm?'

'Much of the land was leased out. Only a few outbuildings and the garden remained.'

'But surely you haven't left her out there alone all these years?'

'Mrs Roberts looks after her.'

'I should imagine it's the other way round,' Milo responded. 'When did you last visit her?'

'I don't even ride over to Settle now that Mother has passed on. She used to write to me when she needed money and give me news from High Fell. Beth went quite mad, you know, but Mrs Roberts kept a lid on things.'

'I don't see how two women can make a go of a farm. How do they manage?'

'How the hell should I know?' Edgar responded. 'The bank takes care of everything.'

'Please don't blaspheme in my house. My wife might hear you.'

'I'm sorry, but you are asking me a lot of questions.'

'I'm your friend, Edgar, and concerned for your reputation. I had a visit a couple of years ago from that shepherd you dismissed. I hardly recognised him. He's made something of himself in trade.'

Edgar snorted. 'What did he want?'

'He was after an address for his daughter.'

'So he's admitted the truth at last.'

'No, not exactly. He wanted to know what had happened to both infants.'

'You didn't tell him, did you?'

'Of course I didn't! I sent him away with a flea in his ear. But I heard from the church warden he'd been asking where I was before I came here. Have you ever visited Beth at High Fell?'

Edgar shrugged and grimaced. 'I couldn't bring myself to touch her. Not after she went with that shepherd.' He noticed

241

Milo's deepening frown. 'Oh, I don't blame you for what happened. How could you have known she would turn out to be a whore?'

Milo, clearly slighted by this apparent fault, got to his feet with a stern expression on his face. He towered over Edgar and retaliated, 'I suppose Mrs Wortley isn't!'

Edgar became more agitated and stood up to challenge him. 'Now look here, old boy. Mrs Wortley is different. I love her.'

They were about the same height and eyed each other warily. Milo answered firmly. 'Well, I can't visit you while you're living with her as your mistress. You must see that.'

Edgar did and relented with a sigh. 'Very well. I don't wish to quarrel with you. I shall be living at the Abbey and you'll be installed in the rectory before much longer anyway.'

Milo seemed relieved the disagreement had passed and nodded briefly. 'Will you stay and eat dinner with us?'

'Thank you, I'm much obliged.'

'Just be careful what you say in front of my wife.'

'Of course, old boy, of course.'

Chapter 23

Late autumn of the same year

'Higgins!'

Daisy dropped a bucket of coal with a clatter and stood up straight to ease her back. She seemed to spend all day and every day carrying coal to keep the servants' fires going and her hands were permanently grimy. It was late afternoon and many of the servants had a couple of hours' rest before their evening duties. She scurried to the attention of the under-housekeeper. Two older maids from Annie's brigade were with her but there was no sign of Annie.

'Higgins, go with these two for the rest of the day.'

'Yes, ma'am. Where am I going?' Her answer was an impatient clucking from the under-housekeeper.

'Come on, Daisy. Annie's told me what to do and I've done it before. We've to help out in the main scullery. Look sharp.'

'Why us?' she asked as she trotted after the older maids.

'They're rushed off their feet with all the visitors for the shooting and there's a dozen to cater for in the hunting lodge so some of the kitchen brigade are living over there.'

The main scullery had a large deal table covered in baskets of dirty crockery and a line of wooden sinks with cooking pots in every one. The older maid took charge and handed Daisy a couple of pails. 'Draw the hot water and keep the fire going under the boiler. Once we've emptied the baskets, line them with fresh linen and stack the clean pots neatly inside them. Careful, mind, they've to go back to the Lodge and it is three miles on the provisions cart. In between time you can help Josie with the cooking pots in those sinks.'

When the last of the crockery baskets had been re-filled and taken away all three women were hot, wet and tired. Daisy's face was flushed and her fingers were red and sore from the pot soda, but her nails were the cleanest they'd been for days.

'Annie's got some stuff for your hands,' the older maid told her. 'We've just the sinks and tables to scrub now, and the floor. You can do the flags, Daisy.'

Daisy's task was nearly finished and she stood up to move to the next section of floor. The partitions between the various sections of the main kitchen were made of painted wood and glass with gaps instead of doors. She smelled the cigar smoke before she heard voices and looked through the glass in their direction. The chef in his floppy white hat had come out of his office as two gentlemen dressed for shooting hovered in the middle of the quarry-tiled kitchen.

Daisy stood quite still looking down at her hands folded across her very damp apron. She remembered Annie's instructions well. A servant becomes invisible when one of the gentry walks past her: back against the wall and quiet as a mouse until they've gone. One of the gentlemen was

Mr Stanton, Lord Redfern's steward. The other was Master James.

'Jolly decent dinner last night, Chef,' he said.

His companion was explaining to the chef, 'Master James is keen to learn how all aspects of the estate function. 'Lord Redfern has agreed to host a special celebration next month for Master James's birthday.'

'Ah,' the chef replied, 'for ze young gentleman, I prepare ze perfec' feast.'

Daisy heard a suppressed giggle from behind her and sucked in her cheeks to quell a smile.

'I want something spectacular to impress my friends.' Daisy recognised James's younger voice. 'You know the thing, ice sculptures, Russian caviar, turtle soup, pineapples.'

'Mais oui, sir. Eet will be my pleasure.' The chef sounded as though he was sighing with delight and Daisy's mouth twitched.

'I'll take a look around,' James said and his boots clicked on the tiles.

Daisy kept her head down but forced her eyelids up until she could see him under her brow. He was walking towards the glass partition and open doorway. 'What's through here?' he called.

'Only the scullery, sir,' Mr Stanton responded.

Master James came through the gap and Daisy swallowed, hoping he would not recognise her. It was bound to get back to the housekeeper if he did. She was out of luck. He stopped in front of her and said, 'Here you are. Are you a scullery maid?'

Daisy truly did not want to get into any more trouble and stayed stock still and silent hoping one of the others would answer. But he prompted, 'Well? I am speaking to you.'

She answered quickly without looking up. 'No, sir, I mean, yes, sir, for today.'

A loud whisper came from behind her. 'Curtsey!' Oh yes, she must curtsey when speaking to one of the gentry. Awkwardly, she bent one knee and lifted her chin to say, 'Beg pardon, sir.'

Mr Stanton loomed behind him. 'If you wish to learn more about the servants' duties, sir, I'll arrange for the house-keeper to inform you. I think you should return to Lord Redfern's guests now. Chef will send up menus for your approval.'

Master James turned down the corners of his mouth and rolled his eyes. Daisy pressed her lips together to stop herself laughing, but her eyes danced as he pulled a face and retreated.

Mr Stanton added, 'His lordship would not want to hear that you have been speaking directly to the lower servants, sir.'

'Then don't tell him, Stanton.'

The chef returned to his office and the kitchen was empty again.

'Get you, Daisy Higgins,' the younger of the two other maids said. 'You want to watch yourself with him. He's got his eye on you.'

'Don't be daft,' she retaliated and picked up her scrubbing brush. But as she pushed the harsh bristles backwards and forwards she wondered if there was any truth in what the maid said. Daisy thought he was the most attractive man she had seen, especially when he was dressed for riding or shooting. Each time she had seen him he seemed to notice her too. He always had a word or expression for her to share and she, in return, felt in tune with his convictions. He appeared as attracted towards her as she was to him. Were they allowed to speak to each other she was certain that they would easily find sentiments to share.

She could not deny that a thrill of excitement fizzed through her. He was a wealthy young gentleman who had shown an interest in her and for a few minutes she dreamed of herself walking out with him. She wondered what it was about him that made her so desperately want to hear his unspoken thoughts. She scrubbed away, ignoring the jibes and comments from the other maids. What a ridiculous notion! What would he want with her? Daisy pulled herself out of her daydream and wiped the suds from her arms.

A few weeks later, Boyd strolled through the village with Daisy after church and asked, 'Do you know that man over there?'

'Which one?'

'He's walking towards the inn.'

'I can't see his face.'

'He seemed to be watching you in church. I was afraid he might be someone sent by Father.'

'He won't take me away, will he?'

'I don't know,' Boyd frowned. 'Are you behaving yourself?'

'I'm trying my best.'

'What work are you doing?'

'Mainly I wait on the servants' hall and keep it clean. But I'm called all over the place to fetch and carry. They have their own butcher here with a cellar full of brining tanks, and their own brewhouse. The game larder is bigger than the cottage we used to live in, and there must be an ice house somewhere because I saw an enormous block of it carried in on a cart yesterday. Where did that come from?'

'It's from underground on the edge of the copse next to Home Farm. I helped hack out that block of ice and it was like midwinter down there, I can tell you.'

'Oh, poor you. Did you have gloves?'

'Oh aye, the steward lent them to me, and thick socks and boots. He said the ice was for the chef to make cream ices for Master James's birthday. He's going to carve a swan out of the biggest chunk to sit in the centre of the table.'

'Oooh, I'd like to see that.'

'No chance, I'm afraid. But—' he turned and beamed at her, 'I shall be working in the Abbey stables because all the young folk are riding the day after and Mr Stanton wants a dozen ponies groomed and saddled for them.'

Boyd loved working with horses. Master James's birthday party would give him a taste of what he would be giving up if he had to leave for her sake. She couldn't let that happen. She said, 'Annie says it's a big house party and we're having some village girls in to help. I've been thinking, Boyd. I'm going to ask them if there's work in the village for after Christmas.'

'Well, if there is, won't they want it for themselves?'

'Oh.' Daisy hadn't thought of that and her heart sank.

'Don't worry, little sister, as long as we stick together we'll survive well enough. I've saved some money and we'll find cheap lodgings until I get work.' His face was solemn. 'I might have to go down the pit, though.'

'Oh, you can't do that! I won't let you do that!'

'I won't have any choice if we want a roof over our heads.'

'But it's dangerous. You'll be killed or injured! I've heard about the accidents they have, roof falls, explosions and that. You're not to go down the pit, Boyd. Promise me you won't.'

'I can't, Daisy. I'd rather take that risk than see you in the workhouse.'

248

Daisy despaired. She wasn't his little sister any longer and she had to pull her weight. 'You haven't said anything about going yet, have you? You're in a good position here and you mustn't leave. Not for me. I'll find something somewhere. I promise I shall!'

Boyd shook his head. 'You are not going anywhere without me, Daisy.'

He was so serious and – and sad, she thought, that she realised he truly did not want to turn down Mr Stanton's offer of a position in the stables. She frowned. He was such a wonderful support to her, so capable, and bigger and stronger now from the labouring he had done since they had arrived. There must be some way of staying in the village. She didn't mind what it was. She felt she could tackle any task when her beloved Boyd was near.

He went on. 'Did you know Master James's birthday is in the same month as yours?'

'No! He's older than me, though.'

'He's not. Mr Stanton told me. He just acts like it because he's been brought up to be a lord. Anyway, I'm making you something special for your birthday.'

'Oooh, what is it?'

'It's a secret. You'll have to wait and see.'

She wanted to reach around his middle with her arms and hug him. But she knew he didn't like her to do that any more. So she had to be content with conversation.

She reached up and twiddled with the free ends of his necktie. 'Do you like your neckerchief?' she asked. She had bought him a bright red one with black spots from the draper's in the village and he wore it to church on Sundays so she could see him easily from a distance.

'Very much, thank you.'

'Are they new boots?' she commented.

He kicked up one of his well-shod feet. 'Mr Stanton gave them to me. My feet are the same size as his. He has two new pairs made every year for himself.'

'Two pairs? Every year?'

'Young Master James has six. He passes them on to the upper servants and some are not even worn because he grows out of them.'

Daisy let out a sigh. 'Phew, his cordwainer must be well off,' she breathed. The boot and shoe maker was not the only tradesman doing well in Redfern Village, Daisy thought. One of them must need another servant. She had to find something soon before Boyd told Mr Stanton he would not take the position.

Chapter 24

Carriages of gentry and carts of luggage and servants began to arrive a few days before the planned banquet and ball. There were young gentlemen and ladies with their families as well as Lord Redfern's political allies amongst the guests and their liveliness spread to the Abbey servants who picked up on their exuberance. When Daisy had to carry buckets of slops to the washhouse she returned the long way round to glimpse a view of the east lawn and saw a small group of young gentlemen taking the morning air.

She lingered by a wrought-iron gate in a high stone wall and peered through. She was rewarded by the appearance of three young ladies dressed in sumptuous full-skirted gowns and an older woman in black, their chaperone presumably. She held on to the iron bars of the gate and pressed her face against the cold metal. Such luxurious gowns for day wear! How beautiful they must look when dressed in their evening attire. She ran back to Annie to tell her what she had seen.

'Who are they, Annie?' she asked.

'Sons and daughters of other lords and ladies,' she answered. 'His lordship sent out the invitations. It's an honour to be asked to visit Redfern Abbey and part of a young lady or gentleman's education.' Annie leaned forward and lowered her voice. 'The servants' hall is overrun by ladies' maids and valets. We've had to get out every flat iron in the Abbey, and all the kettles, to steam the silks and feathers.'

'Oh, I wish I could see them,' Daisy breathed.

'Well, you'll get to see the ballroom because the house-keeper wants an all-round final polish. I've a village lass arriving today to do the staircase with you.'

'I'm going inside the Abbey?'

'Yes and you do exactly as I tell you or we'll both be in trouble.'

Daisy and Biddy picked up their banister brushes and polishing cloths and followed Annie through the kitchen passage.

'I didn't think you'd still be here,' Biddy commented.

'Annie said she'd keep me on until the New Year.' Daisy didn't want to be reminded of leaving. 'Do you like working at the Abbey?'

'Oh aye, but me mam doesn't because then she has to look after me dad and the little 'uns by 'erself. Mind you, the extra pay helps wi' buying our Christmas meat. Me dad likes a big joint o' beef and a collar o' bacon an' all.'

'What will you do after Christmas?'

'There's nowt much going until the weather warms up. I help me mam give our house a good fettle and hope me dad has enough work to afford us cloth for a gown.'

Daisy sympathised. She desperately wanted a new gown for Sundays.

'What do you do if he doesn't?'

'Well, there's the second-hand table in the back room at the draper's.'

Daisy searched through that every time she went into the village. It had some lovely things on it from the better-off houses in Redfern. She sighed. 'They're still too dear for me.'

'Try the market in town. One of the carters from the village'll take you for a few coppers.'

'I need to find work first, though.'

'The butcher's wife is allus looking for a maid.'

Daisy's heart lifted. 'Is she?'

'Aye, nobody sticks it at her house 'cause you 'ave to wash the chitterlings when her husband sticks a pig. Her lasses used to help her but they're all wed now. It makes me right sick, that does.'

Daisy had cleaned pigs' entrails before for Mother. 'It did me when I first had to do it. I got used to it, though. He'll have killed all the pigs by Christmas, won't he?'

'Aye, they'll be salting 'em down now afore December sets in. But he brings home beasts regular to butcher in his back yard. Cleaning the raw tripe is worse. It smells like a slurry pit.'

'I haven't done that before.'

Biddy laughed and Annie slowed her pace for them to catch up. 'You'd know if you had! Then you have the sheeps' guts to clean. She's got no shame, that butcher's wife.'

'What do you mean, "no shame"?'

Biddy grinned and raised her eyebrows at Annie. 'She doesn't know what sheep's guts are used for.'

'The same as pigs', I suppose, for sausages?' Daisy ventured.

Biddy giggled.

'What then?' Daisy pressed. 'Why are you laughing?'

'Ee, you don't know much, do you? How old are you?'

'Eighteen,' she answered proudly, lifting her head. Well, she would be soon.

Biddy lowered her voice. 'You have to get them really clean because the butcher's wife sells 'em to the apothecary and he makes – you know—'

'No, I don't.'

'You know.' Biddy cast her eyes in both directions to make sure no one else was in hearing distance. 'Things. Things for gentlemen.' She giggled again.

'What things?' Daisy said and Biddy giggled even more.

'You know,' Biddy went on. 'When they have a – *you know.*'

Daisy shook her head and Biddy added in a whisper, 'A whore.'

Daisy blushed and her mouth dropped open. What on earth would a gentleman do with washed sheeps' guts?

Biddy seemed to realise that Daisy had no idea what she was talking about and asked, 'You do know what whores are for, don't you?'

'Yes. They fornicate. They are wicked and men go to them instead of getting wed like the Bible says they should.'

Biddy rolled her eyes. 'You'd best tell her, Annie.'

Annie had been listening with a weary expression on her face. 'Ee, Biddy, does your ma know you talk about these things?'

Biddy's face fell. 'You won't tell her, will you?'

'I will if you don't shut up about it.'

'About what?' Daisy demanded.

Annie took a deep breath. 'Well, I'll tell you, but only because I don't want you chattering on when we're in the Abbey. And don't you breathe a word to anyone that I told you. I have seen one. The gentleman puts it over his – y'know

254

– before he – y'know – and it stops him catching the pox from her.'

Daisy's eyes widened with shock, partly to hear Annie speaking of such things and partly because it was about fornication! She remembered a little boy being sent home from Sunday school because he'd used the word pox, and the teacher had put the fear of God into her about the wages of sin. The following week the sermon had been about evils from the Bible she'd never heard of and most of the congregation left with reddened faces muttering to each other. Daisy knew that fornication led to hell.

'Well, it would serve him right if he did catch it,' she responded, 'because he's not supposed to do that until he's wed. That's what his wife is for.'

Annie answered her kindly. 'Ee, Daisy lass, you don't know much at all, do you? Men have these urges and some will do anything to satisfy them.'

'Well, they should get wed then, shouldn't they?'

Annie shook her head and replied briskly, 'Aye, well, they do and they still go to whore houses.'

What for, if they have a wife? Daisy thought, but didn't ask. She didn't want Biddy to make fun of her any more.

Biddy too had grown tired of the joke and said, 'Well, if you don't mind your hands in stuff that smells o' sheeps' droppings and cow pats, try the butcher's wife. She'll want a testa-, testa-whatsit, though.'

'Testimonial,' Annie said. 'Daisy hasn't got one.'

'How come she got work here, then?'

'It was a mistake at first and then they let her stay because we needed the hands. But don't you go telling nobody or else there'll be no more work here for you, my lass.'

Biddy shrugged. 'The butcher's wife won't have her

255

without one. She has some well-off customers on her books.'

Another dead end, Daisy thought. The smell from her polishing cloths was beginning to make her head ache and she held them behind her back. Annie went up some steps to a door that opened onto a plain wooden staircase. Daisy looked up and recognised it as the one that led to the indoor servants' attics. She followed her for two flights then stopped outside a simple wooden door.

'Now listen to me,' Annie said. 'Once we're through that door there's no talking unless you have to speak to me. You won't see any gentry because they are all at a reception and luncheon in the other wing. Every piece of wood and gilt on the staircase must be gleaming. I'll be following you and checking. Understood?'

Daisy was literally speechless when she went through that simple wooden door and into the majestic splendour of the Abbey proper. She was standing on a long carpeted gallery with one wall panelled in polished wood and carrying a row of ornately framed portraits. Pieces of heavy furniture lined the wall for sitting on or supporting a decorative vase or small sculpture. The opposite side was taken up by a railed banister which curved down a wide wooden staircase descending to the ballroom below her.

It was magnificent. She traced her fingers over the handrail and gazed at three glass chandeliers sparkling before her eyes.

'Stop staring, Daisy, and keep close to me.'

Daisy started on the landing, dusting and buffing until her arms ached. At one point she heard a door open and footsteps echoing on the marble floor beneath her, and the black-gowned housekeeper came into view.

'Who is up there? Announce yourself immediately.'

'Brown, madam, to finish the stairs.'

'You'd better hurry. The footmen will be here to polish the floor in an hour.'

Daisy heard the swish of silk skirts and caught sight of black lace ribbons streaming from her dainty cap. 'I wish I could be here to see the dancing,' she whispered.

Annie put her finger to her mouth. 'Me too. The parlour maids sneak in to watch.'

'Can we do that as well?'

'It's not for the likes of us. We belong t'other side of yon door. Come on, you two. Look sharp. I'll give you a hand with the staircase.'

Daisy glanced at the number of carved wooden rails stretching away and bent to her task. From time to time, a liveried footman would walk across the ballroom below carrying folded linens or a piece of furniture. She could hear their footsteps quite clearly and even heard one of them curse as a chair slipped in his grasp.

When they reached the bottom Annie sent them scuttling back upstairs while she checked every last nook and cranny of the carved gilded woodwork for a speck of dust. Daisy was sitting on the landing carpet peering through the banisters when two gentlemen entered the ballroom and lingered just inside the door. They were speaking urgently to each other and even Annie moved out of sight along the landing. But Daisy stayed to listen, putting her fingers to her lips as their conversation floated upwards. It was Master James and an older gentleman, quite portly with a florid face.

'Keep your voice down, Pater. Does Stanton know you're here?'

'I haven't seen him. Where is he?'

'He's helping the butler with the reception. I should be

257

there with my uncle. Not that he'll notice. They had to carry him downstairs in his Bath chair and he won't be at luncheon.'

'He can't hold out for much longer. When I am Lord Redfern, life here will be very different. I'm surprised Stanton doesn't realise that.'

'He follows orders, Pater. He's a good steward for the estate.'

'Well, I'll need you by me, son, not him.'

'Will you bring Mater to live here?'

'She is too sick to travel.'

'I wish you'd tell me where she is so I could visit her sometime.'

'You'll make her worse. She doesn't know you.' He gesticulated circling movements in the air around his head.

'Tell me honestly. Is she in an asylum?'

'Not yet. Forget her, James. I have asked you not to speak of her.'

'She is my mother, sir.'

'Shut up about her! I wish I'd told you she was dead. She is to me!'

'You sound like his lordship. At my quarterly interviews he does not allow me to ask questions or even speak of you or Grandmamma. The headmaster at school told me when Grandmamma died.'

'She should have had longer. She should have lived to see me installed at the Abbey. Well, her uncle will be dead and buried soon and it is your future that concerns me. I have no other sons and we must secure the bloodline as soon as possible. Your grandmamma knew how important it is and she said you ought to marry as soon as you are one and twenty.'

'But I am to do the Grand Tour as soon as I finish my

258

university education. I shall be travelling in Europe for three years. Stanton has advised it.'

His father's agitation increased. 'Damn Stanton! He is not your father. I am.'

'He is Lord Redfern's closest advisor here. He runs this estate. Do calm yourself, Pater. Remember what your physician has told you.'

There was a long silence and Daisy thought they must have left, although she had not heard footsteps. Finally, Master James said, 'I cannot be absent from the reception any longer. Where did you leave your horse?'

'He's inside that folly, the one across the park on the way to the stables. No one will notice me as there is tree cover quite near and the stables are busy with all the extra carriage horses.' The older gentleman paused before asking, 'Have you spent all your allowance yet?'

'I shouldn't think so. Lord Redfern is very generous towards me.' There was another silence, a shorter one this time. 'How much do you want, Pater?'

'Two hundred guineas would do.'

'As much as that?'

'You think a sheep farm in the Dales provides for a future lord?'

'Well, doesn't it?'

Master James's father grunted. 'Your grandmamma mortgaged it before you were born to pay for my education. The bank has owned it for years and any income it makes goes directly to them.'

'Then what did Grandmamma live on?'

'The same bank that has been funding me since Lord Redfern's lawyers acknowledged me as heir. I owe them thousands, but they know that the Redfern estate will be mine one day.' He gave a harsh laugh. 'Even they did not expect my great-uncle to live so long. Dear God, I wish he would hurry up and die.'

'Pater!'

Daisy shuffled quietly along the landing to get a better view of Master James. Her eyes were drawn to him. She didn't know why and she knew she shouldn't but she couldn't stop herself. What was it about him? He was very handsome in a formal suit of grey clothes with a high-collared white shirt and necktie, but there were plenty of other handsome fellows at the Abbey. There was something about Master James that attracted her; his voice, the way he moved, she didn't know what it was but it wasn't because he was the young master, for it was only when she remembered who he was that she pulled herself together and told herself to stop being foolish. A door opened and closed and Daisy glanced up at Annie and raised her eyebrows. Annie whispered, 'Some family feud or other. Don't you two repeat any of it. The gentry are full of them.'

No more than the lower orders, Daisy thought wistfully. Perhaps James's grandmamma had behaved wickedly. She liked the sound of the word 'grandmamma' and repeated it in her head. As Daisy made her way down the dingy back stairs she thought Master James had sounded quite sad when he spoke of his mother. She supposed he missed having a mother and felt quite sorry for him even though she wouldn't wish a mother like her own on him. Daisy chewed on her lip because she considered she was sinful for not loving her parents as the Bible said she ought. But she didn't miss her cruel mother and father one little bit and was constantly alert for Father arriving to take her home. Annie Brown had been more of a mother to her in a few short months than her own mother had been for over seventeen years.

Daisy took her dinner early so she could wait on the other servants for theirs. She was hungry and ate her boiled bacon and cabbage quickly then filled up on apple pudding. She yawned as she drank a mug of tea to finish.

'Take a nap in your hour off his afternoon because you'll be awake half the night clearing up.'

'Will I get to see any of the ladies and gentlemen?'

Annie looked stern. 'You are not to go in the Abbey under any circumstances.'

Daisy took Annie's advice and after her nap put on her best – her only – gown that wasn't Abbey uniform. She covered it well with one of Annie's huge aprons, for the main event of the day was the banquet and the ball until midnight. Dancing was followed by a cold supper and then carriages home for those not lucky enough to be staying at the Abbey. The kitchens and sculleries were a cacophony of clatter until the dining room was cleared and the music had begun.

Every servant seemed to be rushed off his or her feet but Daisy found it fun because one of the footmen brought round wine for them to taste. He even came into the scullery with proper wine glasses full of wine that was fizzing with bubbles.

'Try this,' he announced. 'It's Champagne from France.'

'Ooh la la,' Annie laughed and lifted the front of her skirt to kick her legs.

Daisy followed Annie outside to drink her wine and cool off. In the distance, flares lit up the driveway lined with waiting carriages. She heard the strains of violins and a pianoforte mingled with chattering voices and laughter through open windows in the Abbey.

'What next, Annie?'

'They'll be dancing until late. You'll hear the music stop when the chef has laid out supper and you'll be needed in the sculleries again. Cook will lay out something for us too. Put your feet up for an hour. You won't get much sleep tonight.'

'But I don't feel tired now. Could I go over to the stables and see Boyd?'

'I don't see why not if you stay with him. There'll be a late supper for the visiting coachmen, valets and ladies' maids in the servants' hall. Tell him to bring you back for that. As long as I know where you are when the work starts again.'

'Thanks, Annie.' Daisy set off in the dark to the stables.

Chapter 25

The horses were housed about half a mile away in long low buildings arranged as a square. Well, they only seemed low in comparison with the Abbey for there were two floors of rooms to house outdoor servants over the horse boxes. Daisy followed the sounds of voices until she reached an area behind the stables that was cluttered with more carriages. Visiting servants, men and women with tankards of ale or cider in their hands, stood around lanterns, talking to each other.

One of the men turned as she approached. 'Who's that?'

'Daisy Higgins, sir. I'm looking for Boyd.'

Boyd loomed out of the darkness and she darted forward, unsettling one of the nearby carriage horses and causing the carriage wheels to strain against its brakes.

'Steady on, Daisy. We don't want a stampede.'

'Sorry. Oh I'm so pleased to see you. I've been inside the Abbey today. You should see it, it's magnificent.'

'So I'm told. Mr Stanton says they haven't had a gathering as big as this for years. Some guests have travelled for more than a hundred miles.'

'Master James must be very important. Will you show me where you work?'

'If you like. It won't be for long, anyway. I'll go back to Home Farm when all the guests have departed.' Boyd picked up a lantern and they went through the carriage arch to the front of the buildings inside the huge quadrangle. Daisy followed him to one of the stable houses. There were six stalls and they strolled in front of them, admiring the horses that nosed curiously over wooden gates. Boyd stroked their noses and patted their necks fondly. 'I'm looking after these. They're ponies but they are beautiful, aren't they?'

Daisy agreed. 'Are you allowed to ride them?'

'I have to, to get the feel of them. If any of the young ladies join Master James and his friends tomorrow I shall select her mount.'

'How lucky she is. I wish I could ride.'

'You shall, one day. I shall teach you.'

'Really?'

'Yes, I promise. Here.' Boyd dug in his jacket pocket and handed her some pieces of carrot. He led her to the end stall in the corner. 'This little filly would suit you. Why don't you get to know her?'

Boyd showed her how to feed the docile animal and Daisy lingered in the quiet enjoying the appreciative snuffling of the pony as it nibbled the carrot from the palm of her hand.

'Do you mind if I take the lantern down the other end?'

Daisy shook her head and Boyd left her alone to busy himself clearing spilled straw and checking the gates were secure. Boyd was really happy working with horses, she thought. He mustn't give it up for her. She didn't mind hard work but no matter how hard she worked Annie couldn't keep her on. As it was, she was lucky to be here in the first place.

'Happy early birthday, Daisy.'

'Oh! Oh, Boyd, it's beautiful!'

Boyd had made her a wooden travelling box with a brass lock and key and rope handles on each side to carry it.

'I thought you could keep it in your dormitory and put your things in it.'

'Oh yes. Oh it's perfect. Oh Boyd, I want to kiss you. Please can I give you a hug? No one will see us.'

He placed her box on the floor and took her hand. 'It's not that, Daisy.'

'I know. We're not children any more.' She lifted his hand to her lips and kissed it. 'I do love you.'

She could not see his face in the dim light. 'I love you too, Daisy.' He sounded weary as though it was a burden to him and she wondered, again, if the responsibility for her was holding him back from the things he wanted to do. He picked up her box and added, 'I'll keep this safe until I can bring it over for you.'

She heard voices. The outdoor servants were gathering outside. 'Thank you,' she said. 'I ought to be getting back to help Annie.'

'Wait for me. I'm walking over for supper soon and then I have to help out front with the carriages.'

'Very well,' she agreed. Daisy felt secure when she was with Boyd. It didn't matter where they were, he looked after her. She brought her thoughts to a halt sharply. She could not rely on him for ever and she had to show she could take care of herself so that he would not worry about her.

265

Boyd stowed her box safely and opened the door to see who was making all the noise. Daisy stroked the pony's neck and spoke softly to her as she nuzzled her cheek. She heard raised voices and Boyd say, 'It's very late, sir. I was just locking up.'

A group of young gentlemen in evening dress crowded into the stable house. Some carried lanterns that cast weird shadows on the whitewashed stone walls, and one cried, 'I say, Redfern, haven't you any hunters for us?'

'He'd have to shorten the stirrups for you if he had.' Laughter filled the enclosed space.

Daisy shrank back into her dark corner and heard Boyd reply, 'They are settled for the night, sir. But these are some of the horses selected for tomorrow's ride.'

'Does that include the filly over there?' One of them lifted his lantern high to illuminate Daisy at the end stall and a few guffaws echoed in rafters. Embarrassed, she turned her face away from the light. She could not see Boyd but she heard him say, 'It would be better to view the horses in the morning, sir.'

More sniggers rattled around the stable and a voice quipped, 'I'll take a ride on this one, Redfern, unless she's your mount for the night?' The laughter grew louder and Daisy's embarrassment increased.

The ponies were shifting around their stalls, spooked by the unusual activity. Boyd raised his voice. 'Please take your guests outside, sir. They are disturbing my ponies.'

'Your ponies?' It was the first time Master James had spoken.

'I am responsible for them, sir, and they are becoming restless.'

'Then what are you doing cavorting with a girl in the stables? As if I don't know. What's your name, man?'

'Higgins, sir.'

'Aren't you the new fellow from Home Farm?'

'Yes, sir.'

'Then you will be aware of the penalty for having a girl in here. Stanton will hear about this. You will report to him in the morning.'

'Very good, sir.'

Daisy pressed her lips together in anger. Why were the gentry so quick to judge their servants? If only they knew how hard they worked to make sure life in the Abbey ran smoothly. She turned to face the group, stepped forward and announced sharply, 'It's not what you think. I'm his sister.'

The young gentlemen sniggered but their laughter died away as Master James snatched one of the lanterns and walked towards her, tall and unbelievably handsome in evening dress. He held the light close to her face as he had done once before, when she had encountered him at the harvest supper. She should have looked down at her feet but she was angry that he had misjudged Boyd so she held her head proudly and looked him in the eye.

'I'm Daisy Higgins.'

'So you are.' Master James examined her face in detail. His friends continued their ribald sniggering and muttering until he snapped, 'Do be quiet, gentleman, or go outside.' Then he addressed Daisy. 'Who gave you permission to enter the stables?'

Boyd pushed his way through the gentlemen and appeared behind Master James. 'I did, sir. She had an hour off duty and came to find me. I came in to check the ponies were calm for the night and Daisy was helping me.'

'He's not to blame, sir,' Daisy said, adding as an afterthought, 'I am.'

267

Boyd responded immediately, 'Do not listen to her. The fault lies with me. I invited her in here. The – the horses were quiet in her presence.'

'You're lucky to have such a devoted sister, Higgins. I apologise for my guests. They have taken too much wine and the walk over here was supposed to calm them down. You had better get your sister out of here. You wouldn't want her in any trouble, would you?'

'Daisy, go and wait outside with the others.' Boyd was tall and had broad shoulders. He elbowed a way through Master James's friends and held open the stable door for her.

Daisy curtseyed to Master James, and walked by him keeping her head high. Master James turned with his lantern to watch her. But his friends had closed their ranks again and blocked her way to the door. They were sniggering and grinning as though she had been placed in the stable for their amusement.

She kept her back straight and her face serious. They were young bloods who had been drinking and if Boyd had not been there she would have been frightened of them. But now was not the time to look at her feet. Now was the time to face it out. Eventually James snapped, 'Enough, gentlemen. Where are you manners? Let her pass.' Daisy turned her head to give James a grateful smile and murmured, 'Thank you, sir.' She was pleased to note that he responded with a kindly nod towards her, as his boisterous companions parted so that she could escape.

She hurried outside where a straggle of outdoor servants was already heading for supper at the Abbey. Boyd joined her several minutes later and she was relieved to note that he was cheerful.

'Master James said to forget about seeing Mr Stanton,' he said.

'You're not in trouble, then?'

'It seems not, nor you. I have to say I was very proud of you back there. You behaved in a dignified and graceful manner. Still, I shouldn't mention the incident to Annie Brown.'

'I thought Master James might be angry with you.'

'He asked me a few questions about where I came from. I was fairly vague but he said he wanted to know who was looking after his horses. Mr Stanton encourages him to learn as much as he can about the estate.'

'Well, his father won't know anything about it. He's never lived here.'

'So I'm told. It's due to some family feud or other. His father will be the next Lord Redfern, though.'

'You'd think, with all their wealth and luxury, they wouldn't fall out.'

'I reckon it's *because* of all the riches.'

'Well, if Master James's friends are anything to go by I'm not surprised. They have no manners.'

Boyd laughed. 'He was very civil to you, though. I thought he did rather well with them. He'll make a good Lord Redfern when his turn comes.'

Daisy agreed. There was something about Master James that warmed her heart when she thought about him. She was attracted towards him and sometimes felt he sensed the same for her. It was more than a master's interest in a servant and she did not understand it. But it was there and she could not deny it.

He would deny it, of course. It wouldn't do for the young master to be seen conversing in a friendly manner with a housemaid, not for him nor her either. And it would be worse for her because she would be blamed and dismissed and her perceived behaviour would have a detrimental effect on Boyd's prospects at the stables.

So, she reasoned, if Boyd stayed at the Abbey stables it was for everybody's good that Master James would be away for years being educated and then travelling. He would meet and marry some beautiful young lady with a title who would become his Lady Redfern of the future. How lucky that girl would be. She gave a big sigh.

Boyd heard her and asked, 'Is something wrong, Daisy?'

'I was just thinking what it would be like to be one of the ladies at the ball, dressed in silks and feathers.'

'Don't waste your time day-dreaming about what can never be.' He said it in a kindly way and he meant well. But he brought her back to reality with bump.

The dining room in the servants' hall was crowded. There was a cauldron of soup being ladled into mugs by one of the kitchen maids and the huge deal tables were covered with slices of cold pie, cheese, bread and pickled vegetables. Barrels of ale and cider were tapped and the atmosphere was jovial until the visiting servants were called away as their masters and mistresses left.

Boyd went off with the coachmen to make sure the horses were steady while their occupants climbed into their carriages and Daisy tied on her sacking apron for another stint in the scullery. By the time she was finished she was dead on her feet; she kicked off her boots, took off her gown and corset and fell onto her bed for a few hours of welcome sleep. It was still dark when Annie woke her for duty the following day.

The afternoon was quiet for the Abbey servants. Visitors were shooting, or out riding and Annie took Daisy aside with a grave expression on her face.

'There's talk about you, young lady, putting yourself in the way of the young master.'

'It's not true, Annie. Honest.'

'Did you speak to him last night at the stables?'

'I went to see Boyd. I didn't know Master James would be there.'

'Very forward, you were. One of the visiting valets heard it from his young master and he told the butler. I did warn you.'

'I was explaining—'

'So it is true?'

Daisy resigned herself to a telling off. 'Yes.'

'Well, it won't do. You'll have to go.'

Daisy knew that already. 'I'll look for something in the village after Christmas.'

'You've got to go now.'

'Now? But you said you needed help for—'

'Get your things together. There's a cart leaving for the village after tea. You've got a bit of money to come from here.'

Daisy's fear showed in her eyes. 'I've nowhere to go.'

'There's an old woman who lives on her own down by the stream. She'll let you have a bed for the night. It won't cost you much.'

'And then what?'

Annie gazed at her and shook her head. 'There'll be work at the Reddy Arms but I wouldn't recommend it for you. You're too trusting of other folk. You'll be in the family way afore the New Year.'

'Annie! I'm not like that.' Daisy knew all about keeping her virtue and not being forward with young men.

'*I* know you're not, but the men who drink at the Reddy Arms don't. They think beer-house lasses are there for the fellas and are easy targets for a bit of slap and tickle.'

271

'Then I shall tell them I am not,' Daisy explained patiently.

'See what I mean? You believe that will save you from some randy young farmhand when you've caught his fancy? You really think that others will behave as you do? Well, they won't. They'll take advantage of you. I wish I didn't have to send you away but I've had orders from the housekeeper. You've got to go today.'

'But I'll end up in the workhouse! Can I go and see Boyd before I leave?'

'No, you can't. I'll give him a message from you.'

Daisy remembered what Biddy had told her about the butcher's wife and asked, 'Would you do a testimonial for me?'

'Only the housekeeper is allowed to do that.'

'Write me a letter then? Please? Just to say how useful I've been to you.'

Daisy noticed that Annie's severe expression relaxed at this suggestion. 'Yes, I can do that for you, but it won't have the Abbey crest on the paper.'

'Oh thank you! Can you address it to the butcher's wife in the village?'

'Mrs Farrow? Aye, you might be lucky there, if she hasn't already got a lass.'

'Oh Annie!' Daisy reached forward and gave her a hug. 'How shall I be able to thank you properly?'

'Well, you haven't got the position yet. But if you do you can take me for afternoon tea in the back room of the sweet shop.' She assumed an affected position sticking out one hip, holding an imaginary teacup in her fingers and extending her little finger. 'Just like the gentry.'

PART THREE

Chapter 26

November of the same year

'Milo!

'Edgar!'

Edgar strode across to the large open fireplace in the public saloon of the Redfern Arms.

'How long is it since we last met?'

'It is too long, my friend. Is your chamber at the rectory comfortable?'

'I think the word is austere. I was greatly surprised to receive the rector's invitation. I presume I have you to thank for that?'

'I have been in correspondence with Lord's Redfern's lawyers and met with my son. They changed his name, you know, from Collins to Redfern. But he's a fine young man. He wishes to please me. So you can thank him as he is the one who can influence the estate's advisors.'

'The rector told me his lordship is very weak and rarely leaves his bedchamber. He will vacate the living soon after

– well, soon after his lordship passes on. It can't be long now. He has suggested I bring my wife when I next visit the rectory. However, I fear she will be depressed by the state it is in.'

'Tell her not to worry. When I am Lord Redfern she will live in the finest rectory in the Riding. I shall keep my promise to you, Milo.'

'Thank you, Edgar. I've waited the best part of twenty years since I learned of your plight and heard about the Blackstone girl.'

'It's a pity it didn't work out exactly as planned. Life could have been better for both of us.'

'Do you think the girl came from tainted blood?'

Edgar shrugged. 'Her madness is certainly not my doing. She was highly strung from the outset.'

'It's just as well we took her children away when we did.'

'Indeed. But dear God, his lordship was hard on me, asking me to give up my son. As I remember, you counselled me in favour of handing him over.'

'You had no choice and it was for your son's good. You were not in a position to educate him without Lord Redfern's backing and he was uncompromising in his demands,' Milo pointed out.

'We shall not argue, my friend. Not when my inheritance is so close. I am the next heir after all and I wasn't to know that his lordship would be so obstinate about Mama and me.'

'Or that he would take so long to die.'

'There is a Dower House on the estate. It's a horse-ride from the church but it would be perfect for your family until the rectory is ready for them.'

'That's very generous of you, Edgar. I was afraid you'd have Mrs Wortley there. Will you leave her at Ellis House?'

Edgar expressed surprise. 'I've already given notice on the lease. Prudence will move into the Abbey with me.'

'Edgar, you cannot do that! I thought when we spoke of the matter before, that you understood your responsibilities. Your actions will create an enormous scandal. It will jeopardise James's prospects. You must think of his future. He is well placed to marry a duke's daughter.'

Edgar rubbed the palms of his hands over his face. 'I need Prudence beside me, Milo, old boy.'

'That may be so, but you cannot have her living with you as your mistress in Redfern Abbey. Please, also, consider that I shall be your vicar. I am your friend but I cannot condone it and to ask me to do so is to compromise my position before I start!'

Edgar was shaking his head. 'I must have her with me.'

'Edgar, you have a wife! Invalid or not, society will expect to see her by your side.'

'But I've told everyone she's mad!'

'Then why have you not had her declared insane and sent to an asylum? Milo demanded. 'She could cause you a deal of trouble once she is Lady Redfern. As I recall, she had a strong will.'

'Not any more. She took to the laudanum and cares only for her next dose.'

'Is that so? Then she needs to be put away now. When did you last have news of her?'

'I used to receive reports from Mrs Roberts. But she hasn't written for any money for years so I suppose all is well.'

'Do they have income from the farm?'

'How should I know? There was enough land left with the farmhouse to provide a living.'

277

'I think you ought to find out, just in case the estate lawyers ask about her.'

Edgar thought about this and grimaced. 'I see what you mean. I don't want any trouble for Prudence.'

'Or for James, either. You really must not have Mrs Wortley living with you in the Abbey,' Milo repeated. 'It is not only our local county society who will be watching you very closely.'

'But I can't live without her now.'

'You have to. Send her back to Leeds. And take care how you speak of your wife. She may be an invalid who needs the Dales air, but she will be Lady Redfern too.'

Edgar's thoughts were greatly troubled by his conversation with Milo. He had no intention of giving up Mrs Wortley. Perhaps he ought to have Beth declared insane immediately and put away for good? Society might sympathise with his need for another woman then, or even another wife if he was able to divorce Beth. Insanity would be less scandalous than adultery before a judge.

Milo, more sensitive to his respectable position in the clergy and the future for his own children, hoped that Edgar would see sense. Nonetheless he was taken aback when he returned to his parish to find that Abel Shipton was demanding an audience with him. He had refused to go away until they had spoken. His persistence had caused much agitation for his wife and so Milo relented.

Abel wasted no time on pleasantries. 'I have been to your former parish and know where you placed Daisy. You will be good enough to sign this letter to confirm that she is Beth Collins's child.'

'I shall do no such thing, sir!'

'You knew that the couple who took her in would use

her as a servant. I am prepared to take care of her as my own.'

'So you admit it! You are her father. I knew it!'

Abel did not respond to this slur. 'Will you sign, or must I ask questions about the child in this parish? I know about Boyd, the merchant's son, too. I often wondered how you paid for your fancy carriage.'

'You wouldn't dare! I'll have the constable on you.'

'And risk being the centre of a scandal yourself? I think not, Reverend.' Abel paused and watched the clergyman's discomfort before adding, 'Sign, and I shall speak no further on the matter.'

Milo thought about this for a minute then said, 'Show me the document.'

Abel watched him read it through and handed him a pen loaded with ink from his desk. Milo scribbled his signature muttering, 'You had better keep your word, sir.'

'I shall.' Abel took the letter to the desk and shook blotting powder over the signature. 'I am pleased we understand each other, Reverend Milo. I heard that Edgar was unable to heal the rift at Redfern Abbey. But at least he has his son.'

'He does not. Lord Redfern adopted him.'

'Lord Redfern's ward is Edgar's son?' Then he was Beth's son too! Abel concealed his surprise well. He packed away his papers, satisfied with his morning's work, gave a formal bow and departed. Now he had good reason to visit Beth he could not wait to be on his way.

Abel Shipton surveyed his fields on High Fell with the new shepherd at Fellwick Hall.

'They told me this parcel of land belonged to a future lord,' the shepherd commented.

'Does he live in the farmhouse?' Abel enquired with a feigned innocence.

'Don't rightly know, sir. I don't pass that way as a rule.'

'Nonetheless, I shall call and pay my respects as I am in the neighbourhood.'

'Very well, sir. Good day to you, sir.'

Abel turned his horse's head towards the farmhouse. It was a cold overcast day but he felt a warming nervous excitement as he neared the stone-and-slate dwelling. Smoke curled from the chimney and a farmhand came out of the stable as he ambled down the track.

'Good day to you, sir. We don't get many visitors coming over the fell. Do you have business here?'

Abel gave his name, adding, 'I am acquainted with your mistress. Would you ask if I might call on her?' He had dismounted and tethered his horse when her slight figure appeared at the kitchen door. He resisted a strong urge to run towards her and embrace her. Beth too seemed to be holding on to the door, unsure of whether to step outside. She swayed and a woman appeared behind her. They waited for the farmhand to approach him. 'Would you go inside, sir?' he said.

Only then did Beth stretch out a hand to welcome him. 'Abel! Oh Abel, it is so good to see you. You are well? And your business flourishes?' She grasped his arm and tugged on it. 'Come into the hall. We have a fine fire going today.'

Her eyes shone and her skin glowed as she introduced him to her companion. She was the same nurse that Dr Brady had engaged. 'Margaret and I have become friends,' Beth explained.

'I'll make tea,' Margaret suggested and took a large tray from the kitchen dresser.

The kitchen seemed more cheerful than Abel remembered.

There were curtains at the windows and a vase of garden flowers on the table. In the hall, too, he noticed heavy drapes at the leaded casements and cushions on the heavy carved furniture. One end of the dining table was covered in pieces of fabric, paper, pins and thread.

'I have interrupted your dressmaking,' he said.

'You have interrupted nothing. Take off your coat and hat and sit by the fire.'

'You look well, Beth. Are you?'

'For the most part, yes, but I have dark times when I have to keep busy. Margaret helps, of course, and I see Dr Brady every month. We take the trap to Settle.' Her face became serious. 'But it distresses me because people stare so.'

'Have you taken the laudanum again?'

'I have not touched it since you – you saved me from it. There are times when I should like to. They are the dark times. The dark times,' she repeated sadly. Her eyes were now troubled and Abel regretted asking her how she was. Then suddenly she cheered and added, 'But you are here and it is so – so wonderful to see you. Dr Brady told me you would come back when – when you – when you had news for me.' She turned her large pleading eyes on him. 'You do have news for me, don't you, Abel?'

'I have. I have good news.'

Margaret placed a laden tray at the end of the table. 'Will the news keep a little while longer, sir?' she asked. 'Your appearance has caused some excitement.'

'I shall not apologise for my enthusiasm,' Beth protested. 'But neither shall I neglect our guest. We shall have tea before we talk further.'

'I'll bring more hot water,' Margaret suggested and returned to the kitchen.

281

Beth took his hat and coat to the cupboard by the front door then cleared her sewing notions into a commodious sewing box. Abel watched her fondly and reflected on how much he loved her.

'Come and sit at the table while I pour. We have ginger parkin today.'

Abel saw her hand shake a little as she served the tea and she noticed too. 'It's you,' she explained. 'You are making me nervous.'

'I don't mean to.'

Margaret returned with hot water and butter. 'Do you know,' she said. 'I don't feel at all hungry yet. I'll go out and see if there are any eggs.'

When they were alone, Beth cut a thick slice of parkin and slid it onto a china plate for Abel. 'Tell me before I burst,' she begged him.

'I know where they are,' he said.

'Both of them? Are they safe? Are they well?'

'I cannot say for sure. Your son has been brought up as the future Lord Redfern.'

'He has? Is he happy? And my Daisy? How has she grown? Is she pretty?'

'I – I have not made contact with her yet. But I shall, quite soon.'

'I so desperately want to see them both. Will you bring them here?' She was frowning, a deep despairing frown that marred her beauty and worried Abel. Was she being totally honest about her recovery?

'How often are you troubled by the dark times,' he asked.

She sighed. 'When I think of my children and wonder how they are growing without me.' Her eyes grew shiny with tears again. 'I try not to let my thoughts dwell on them but they are *my children* – I cannot forget them.' She lapsed into silence. A tear welled over her lower eyelid and ran down her cheek.

His heart crumbled as he grieved with her. 'I shall bring them to you, I promise. I am close but they must trust me first, otherwise I may frighten them away.' He picked up her cup and saucer. 'Drink your tea. It will calm you.'

They drank and ate in silence until Beth said quietly, 'I wish you could stay with me all the time.'

He could not deny he wanted the same. 'I dare not,' he answered. 'It would risk your freedom.'

'Edgar does not care what I do.'

'He would if he found out that I was here with you. Even this visit is dangerous for you. I must be seen in Settle by nightfall to avoid any gossip.'

'Then we have not long together. Hold me, Abel.'

They stood up and walked to the end of the table, moving as one to the shadows cast by the firelight. He clutched her tightly at first and then more gently as his lips traced the contours of her face and finally rested on her mouth. For a brief snatched second they shared a moment of bliss and then the sound of Margaret's footsteps on the flags forced them apart and they turned towards the fire again. A clock chimed the hour.

'Is that the time? I must be on my way.' Abel took Beth's hand and kissed it. 'Remember my promise,' he said.

Beth nodded and went to fetch his coat and hat. She stood at the front door and watched him ride down the track until the failing light enveloped him. 'I love you,' she whispered to the darkness.

Chapter 27

Daisy had always looked forward to visiting Redfern Village from the Abbey because it was alive with ordinary working folk. The main street had carts and carriages going backwards and forwards and groups of people talking outside the shops. She could close her eyes and know where she was on the street by the smell. However, as she approached the butcher's shop with Annie's letter in her pocket, the sickly salty bloody aroma gave her misgivings.

The butcher's, like others suppliers in this prosperous village, was housed in the downstairs of a stone-built house on the main road. On the days Mr Farrow slaughtered a beast, the pongs coming from round the back had made Daisy retch until she was well past the shop. But today an appetising aroma of baking pies wafted through an open side window onto the street and she was relieved. She walked through the open front door.

'I heard you wanted a girl to help in the tripe shed,' she ventured.

Mr Farrow was a florid-faced man with a round belly covered by a dark blood-stained apron. He stopped sawing at leg of beef and wiped the back of his hand over his brow.

'Mrs Farrow,' he called.

'What is it now?'

Mrs Farrow appeared from the back of the shop with a thick cloth in her hands and smudges of flour on her face.

'There's a lass to see you, looking for work,' her husband said and went back to his sawing.

'Well, I've plenty o' that. Who are you and where are you from?'

'I'm Daisy Higgins. I've been helping out at the Abbey. Mrs Brown wrote this for you.' She handed her the letter.

As she waited, Daisy's gaze wandered to the large pieces of animal carcass hanging from hooks in the ceiling and dripping blood that coloured the sawdust strewn across the floor. That must be from the wood mill down by the cut, she thought. The narrow canal connected to the main navigation and took away timber from estate forests as well as coal from nearby pits. The Redfern estate sat on a coal field and mining villages recognisable by their pithead winding gear were dotted across the land. Colliers' families needed food and clothing and Redfern Village was nearer than town which was five or six miles distant on the navigation.

Mrs Farrow rubbed her reddened hands down the sides of her once-white apron and unfolded the paper. 'Annie Brown, eh? Why is she letting you go?' She read to the end and then cast her eyes over the writing a second time.

'How come you fetched up at the Abbey all on your own?'

'I came with my brother. He got work at Home Farm. He's been moved to the stables now.'

285

Mrs Farrow scrutinised her appearance. 'How old are you?'

'Eighteen. I – I haven't got any other family.'

'Or any lodgings, I see. Mr Farrow would have to be responsible for you then.'

'My brother is one and twenty, ma'am.'

'Aye, but he can't take care of you or you wouldn't be here.'

Daisy chewed on her lip anxiously.

'Have you worked in a tripe shed before?'

'No, ma'am.'

Mrs Farrow gave an impatient sigh and refolded the letter.

'I used to wash the chitterlings for my – I mean before – before.' She stopped. Oh lord, she'd been caught out in a fib and went on, 'We used to keep a pig when I was little.'

'Round here?'

'No, ma'am, we hail from the other side of the Riding.'

'Well, Annie writes well of you and she knows a good worker when she sees one. Show us your boots.'

Daisy lifted her skirts. She had polished them as best she could but she would need new ones for next winter. Mrs Farrow grunted her approval. 'Are you wearing wool flannel under your skirt?'

'Yes, ma'am.'

'You'll need it for being out in the back yard. It's where my husband does his slaughtering and it can be perishing when you're standing washing the entrails at the trough. We use a lot of water here and we have our own pump. Mind you,' Mrs Farrow added with a wry smile, 'it's warm in the tripe shed when I'm boiling up.'

'I've not dressed tripe before, ma'am.'

'I'll show you. See how you do with ox innards. Is that bundle all you've got?'

286

'My brother's made me a travelling box to put them in. He – he'll bring it over when – when I find somewhere.'

Mrs Farrow had diverted her attention to her husband. 'What do you say, Mr Farrow?'

'She looks sturdy enough to me. Has she a follower?'

'No, sir,' Daisy replied.

'See how she gets on then.'

'Thank you, sir.'

'Follow me, lass.'

Mrs Farrow led the way through the back of the shop to a lobby with a staircase. 'Take your things upstairs to the small attic overlooking the yard. Then come and find me in the kitchen and I'll show you the cellar.'

Daisy's heart was thumping and it was not due to all the stairs she had to climb. Excitement bubbled through her and she could not wait to see Boyd and tell him about her good luck. Mr Farrow was respectable and had a reputation as a tripe purveyor that spread across the county. It was cheap and nourishing and those who had a taste for it travelled to Redfern for their tripe even if they had moved as far as town. The more prosperous sent their servants to buy it and word soon spread when Mr Farrow had killed a beast.

Mrs Farrow toiled as hard as her husband in the yard, kitchen and cellar, but her back and legs were feeling their age. Her children had grown. Mr Farrow's profits had purchased a farm tenancy for his elder son who reared stock for his father to slaughter. The younger had excelled at school and worked in town as a clerk while all three daughters had made good marriages and lived at some distance from the village.

Redfern was a prosperous village boasting an inn, the Redfern Arms, and an ale house. Not only did it provide for its own but it sold its reputable produce to men of commerce who had business in town and to servants of successful tradesmen who came out in dog carts to purchase for their employers. Even the poorer villagers, who could not grow enough to warrant the journey to market, sold excess fruit from their garden gates, surprised that there were folk with money in their pockets to buy it.

Daisy knew the draper's shop best. She had spent many a spare hour rummaging through his back-room table for a piece of muslin or lace. The sweetshop was run by two spinster ladies who served tea in china cups in their back room and boiled sugar in their scullery. She had had little call to go into the provisions merchant's whose wife purchased sides of cured pig meat to cut up and sell. A blacksmith and farrier's forge was situated further away, on the road to the wood mill. Next to him lived a cordwainer who kept a cobbling shop round the back where he employed a journeyman to mend the boots of the poorer people. Like the draper, he also sold castoffs from the better-off who left their old boots with him when they collected their new ones. Overlooking all this activity stood the church with its tall spire that could be seen for miles around. It sat majestically on a small hill behind the main street and, together with its nearby rectory, dominated the village.

Redfern had its share of poor folk too. They lived in small damp cottages near the cut or in terraces of small houses built by Lord Redfern for his farm labourers, wood hewers and coal miners. His lordship, of course, was the village landlord and provided the clergyman's living too. On the whole, he was considered a good landlord. He had endowed a row of almshouses for his tenants who grew old and sick so they might avoid the ultimate stigma of the workhouse.

Daisy's thrill at living in Redfern made it worth the vomiting she experienced at her first ox butchering. Carrying buckets of warm blood for Mrs Farrow to make into black puddings was not too bad. But the smell of the steaming mound of entrails that slid from the carcass was too much for her and it was worse when Mrs Farrow took away one of the ox stomachs and showed her how to clean out its contents.

When her own stomach had emptied, she drank water from the pump and tried hard to suppress any further retching. But it seemed as though the smell would not go from her nostrils and she carried it with her to bed that night along with the sight of ox innards that was imprinted under her eyelids. But she had persevered and felt proud of herself. Mrs Farrow seemed satisfied. She had watched her closely and at the end of the day given her a bitter herbal brew sweetened with honey to help her sleep. Thankfully, it worked.

The days turned into weeks and soon they were into December and Daisy's time was spent moving between a freezing cold back yard and cellar, or a warmer tripe shed and kitchen. But Mr and Mrs Farrow seemed to take well to her and treated her more as one of the family than as a servant. It was the middle of the day and she was pumping and carrying buckets of water to refill the boiler in the scullery. She heard Mr Farrow come down the creaky stairs and say, 'Watch the counter, Mrs Farrow. I'll just nip over to the Reddy Arms to slake my thirst.'

Mrs Farrow called, 'Daisy, come in here and see to the dinner. He'll be back in an hour or two with an appetite.'

'What is there to do, Mrs Farrow?'

'Well now, let me see. There's a leg o' mutton boiling over the fire so I'll need a bowl of onion sauce. Fill that pan with vegetables and set them to boil on the plate then make an apple pudding to bake in the oven. Be sure to chop the suet real fine for the crust.'

'Yes, Mrs Farrow.'

When everything was ready, Daisy set the table in the kitchen and presented herself to Mrs Farrow in the shop.

'Good lass. You take over here while I draw some ale. I've a new barrel needs tapping.' She surveyed the marble slab and worn wooden counter. 'Not much left to sell now so you can let everything go for a tanner.'

'Even that hare? He's a big fellow, Mrs Farrow.'

'Aye, only let him go to one o' the village families, mind. They'll be along soon to see what we have left. As soon as the slab's clear, wash it down and shut up shop. Oh, and give me a shout when you see Mr Farrow walking down the road.'

'Yes, Mrs Farrow.'

Daisy stood at the open door and watched Mr Farrow amble back from the Redfern Arms in conversation with another man. She'd been in the village long enough to recognise most of the inhabitants and she didn't know this one. He was wearing a tall hat, the sort she had seen on the heads of gentlemen from town. He seemed very friendly with Mr Farrow. They were talking and laughing together, occasionally swaying as they walked. Mr Farrow didn't overdo the drink like some she knew and 'a jar at the Reddy', as he called it, always put him in a good mood.

Daisy frowned. The stranger could be the man who, Boyd said, had stared at her in church a while back. Her back stiffened. Had he been sent by Father to find her and take her home? She clutched at the edge of the meat counter and prayed that Mrs Farrow would not let her go.

Mr Farrow stopped a few yards away when he saw Daisy and called to her. 'Go and tell me missus we've got company for dinner.'

Daisy hurried through to the back.

'Well, who is it, then?'

'I don't know, Mrs Farrow. He's tall with dark hair on his face and wearing a very smart hat. Don't let him take me away, will you?'

'Why should he want to do that? He's not the constable, is he?'

Daisy chewed on her lip and shook her head.

'Well, set him a place at table and give the pewter tankards on the dresser a rinse while I draw another pitcher of ale.'

Daisy set out the tankards. Mrs Farrow inspected the table and said, 'He'll be one of them commercial travelling men that stay at the Reddy Arms. Put on a clean apron and be on your best behaviour, lass.'

Mr Farrow came into the kitchen with his guest. 'Come and meet my good lady, Mr Shipton. You will take your dinner at our table?'

'That is very civil of you sir,' the stranger replied. 'I had planned to call on you later, when your working day is finished.'

'And you say you are acquainted with my wife's brother at Kimber Hill Farm?'

'I know him from my dealings at the beast market in town.'

'You are a farmer yourself, sir?'

'I own a farm in the Dales, sir, but I have found my vocation as a dealer in stock. The number of people moving to the towns is growing so fast that local farmers and butchers are hard pressed to keep pace with demand for meat.'

'Yes, my son has talked of this. But he has a ready market for his fat stock up at the Abbey.'

'I understood that the Abbey had its own farm.'

'Aye, but more folk live up there than they do in this village. They take a lot o' feeding. Talking o' feeding, we have mutton for dinner. Are you partial?'

'Indeed I am, sir.'

'Excellent! We'll take a pipe o' baccy afterwards and talk of our business then.'

Daisy placed the pitcher of ale on the table and pulled out a chair. 'Will you sit here, sir?' She avoided looking at him but he stared intently as he walked round the table.

'Is something wrong, sir?' Mrs Farrow asked.

'Not at all, madam. Forgive me, your – your daughter reminds me of – of someone I know.'

He sat down smiling, apparently to himself, and seemed to lapse into thought. Daisy froze to the spot. He had come from Father! She didn't remember him but clearly her face was familiar to him. Mrs Farrow raised her eyebrows and Daisy noticed her exchange a puzzled glance with her husband.

'This is Daisy, sir,' Mr Farrow explained. 'She is our maid but she is as good as a daughter to us. She dines with us.'

Daisy was so overcome by a warm feeling of belonging that she forgot her discomfort with the stranger for a moment. Although her tasks were gruesome at times, the Farrows were kind to her and had welcomed her as they might one of their own from the outset. But she had not realised until now that they thought so much of her. A small thrill buzzed through her and she cheered. If the stranger saw she was settled in a position he might only demand her wages for her father. That would be a small price to pay for staying

292

near to Boyd. She hoped that the Farrows would not mention Boyd in the conversation.

After dinner, Mrs Farrow helped Daisy in the scullery leaving the men to talk business over their tobacco pipes. But Mrs Farrow ear-wigged at the door as she dried the pots.

'He wants our son to raise some new stock for market,' she relayed. 'He wants a new breed that puts on more lean. I ask you! Where would we get our tallow for candles? Poor folk can't afford beeswax. And the new breed don't have horns! They won't taste the same, you mark my words.'

Daisy placed an empty bucket under the drain hole in the scullery sink to catch the dirty water. 'It's getting dark, Mrs Farrow. Won't Mr Shipton miss the carrier back to town?'

'I heard him say he's staying at the inn. Anyway, he'll be on horseback, I expect.'

Daisy was relieved that he had not quizzed her during the meal, although he did stare at her once or twice. She said, 'He didn't say who I reminded him of.'

Mrs Farrow laughed and nudged her with an elbow. 'Well, I hope it isn't one of his new breed of sheep,' she said and Daisy giggled.

Chapter 28

'Where do all the folk come from, Mrs Farrow?'

'His lordship has pit villages scattered right across this part of the Riding.'

The week before Christmas was busy. Mr Farrow shifted a whole ox, three pigs and, as well as Mrs Farrow's cured hams, a whole barrelful of brined beef from the cellar. Daisy was up in the dark at five in the morning and Mrs Farrow showed her how to cut joints to serve at an outside counter in the front of the shop. She ate her porridge standing outside in lamplight and didn't stop until ten o'clock at night except for tea and cold mutton at eleven and a hot meat pie at five. Mrs Farrow's own salt beef was the most popular choice. It was kept in a barrel of brine by the counter and Daisy had to cut, weigh and work out the price of each joint. She preferred the customers who chose a piece that looked the right size for them. But those who wanted 'about 3 pounds, me ducks', and expected just that, were the most difficult.

She had to guess how much to cut and if it wasn't right it had to go back in the barrel for another customer. Mrs Farrow didn't like waste so Daisy aimed to cut a piece under rather than over and when she gave the price they were usually satisfied. Her hands became as cold as the icy brine and she feared that she might cut off one of her own fingers by mistake and not even notice.

Poultry and game were popular choices too: hare, rabbit, all manner of fowl selected by Mr Farrow from local farmers and hung up in rows on a rack outside the shop. Buyers picked out a brace and took them inside to pay Mr Farrow.

As daylight strengthened, an intermittent loud bang rang around the village.

'What is that noise, Mrs Farrow,' Daisy asked when she came out to bring her a mug of warming broth.

'The old forge on Redfern Hill has reopened. It's been shut for years. The last time I walked that way, there were a tree growing through the roof. In the old days it had a waterwheel turned by the stream that runs into the cut. But Mr Stanton from the Abbey has put in one o' them steam engines and a great big drop hammer to beat the iron. That's the noise you can hear.'

'Oh! I thought it was from a quarry.'

'Nay, lass. Blasting doesn't sound like that. Coal and steam are our future, my youngest lad says. There'll be a railway through here before long, you mark my words. I read in the news-sheet they've even built a ship that has steam engines.'

'That sounds daft to me. Why buy coal when the wind is free?'

'Don't ask me, lass. Ask them who does it. One thing's for sure. They wouldn't do it if they couldn't turn a profit.'

Mr Farrow paid Daisy every week and she saved most of

it to buy a gift for Boyd. He was occupied for long hours at the stables and, although he was relieved she had found a position and had brought over her box, he had had little time to talk. She told him about Mr Shipton and asked if he had been to the Abbey looking for them. He had not but Boyd said he would look out for the stranger.

She would see Boyd properly at Christmas, though, and Daisy eagerly anticipated the traditional church services and hunts. She spent all her spare time at the draper's lingering over a pair of leather riding gloves for him but could not afford them and chose instead a skein of wool to knit him a neck muffler for the cold mornings.

Daylight hours were short and the nights frosty. By the evening of Christmas Eve customers were dwindling and Mrs Farrow came to the front door. 'I've not much left to sell now. Take it down the cellar, Daisy, and wash the outside counter. Mr Farrow will bring it indoors.' She raised her voice and called over her shoulder. 'What have you kept back for our Christmas dinner, Mr Farrow?'

'The biggest goose you've ever seen, with plenty o' sage and onions.'

Daisy's mouth watered at the prospect. 'Shall I pluck and draw it for you,' she volunteered.

'Not this one, lass. I don't want you losing any feathers or tearing the skin. I want him to look nice when he's cooked. I'll need to get him on early though.' She turned to address her husband again. 'Can you manage with just Daisy tomorrow morning?'

'Aye, I'll shut up well before dinner time and we can enjoy our Christmas Day together. Is the fire lit in the little parlour yet? I've got a grand Yuletide log for it this year that'll keep going through to Twelfth Night.'

'I should hope so, Mr Farrow,' his wife said. 'We don't want any bad luck in this house.'

'I have that bottle of sherry wine Mr Shipton left us an' all. Has young Daisy ever tried sherry?'

She shook her head yet the mention of his name took the sparkle of anticipated pleasure from her eyes. Mr Shipton was a very civil gentleman, she thought, but she was suspicious of him nonetheless.

'It will be nice to have another body at our Christmas table this year,' Mrs Farrow commented. 'There's hot water in the boiler, Daisy lass. Go and have a wash and put on your good gown for the late night service. We want to be early at the church to get a seat.'

Mrs Farrow had helped Daisy with a velvet ribbon trim for her best gown and bonnet and even given her some white cotton tatting that she had kept from an old bodice to make a fresh collar and cuffs. The mirror in her chamber was small and spotty but Mrs Farrow was not mean with her tallow candles and Daisy was pleased with her finished appearance.

She carried her cloak downstairs and opened the door that led to the kitchen. Mr Farrow was lighting a lantern in the back yard and she heard him call, 'Are you two women-folk ready yet?'

'Eee, Mr Farrow, come back inside a minute and take a look at this little lass.' Mrs Farrow took her cloak from her and laid it over her arm. She tweaked the velvet bonnet ribbons tied under her chin then stood back with a fond expression on her face. 'Isn't she a picture, Mr Farrow?'

Daisy was pleased to see a similar look cross his florid features. She did not want to let them down when the whole village would be there to see.

'Aye, she is that, Mrs Farrow. She's right lovely.'

'Thank you,' Daisy beamed and turned to let her old cloak, now also trimmed with velvet ribbon, drop over her shoulders.

She followed Mrs Farrow and her husband out into the chilly night air, through the backyard gate and down the side of the house to join clusters of other well-wrapped folk hurrying towards the church path. Mr and Mrs Farrow slowed as the incline increased. Daisy had once reflected to Boyd that churches were built on hills so that worshippers would be nice and warm when they had reached them and their feet wouldn't grow cold as they listened to the sermon. He had laughed and said that it made them too hot in summer. Ah yes, she had replied, but churches were always chilly so you soon cooled off, and he had laughed again.

Daisy was thinking fondly of this past exchange as she climbed the track through the churchyard. Lanterns ducked and bobbed in front of her. Normally she wouldn't have dared cross the graveyard at night but tonight it wasn't ghostly at all. The hushed murmurings she heard were from village folk that she knew by name, whose breathing turned to steam in the frosty air. A warm feeling spread through her veins as some regular customers greeted her with obvious pleasure and complimented her on her pretty bonnet. They clustered around the church door waiting their turn to shuffle into the high ceilinged, cavernous interior.

In fact, Daisy was surprised to see the church so well lit with extra lamps and candles, as well as the villagers' lanterns which were placed on any convenient surface. Her eyes darted backwards and forwards over old and young faces with nose tips and cheeks reddened by the cold until she spotted Boyd quite near the front. He raised his arm and beckoned her.

298

'May I sit with my brother for the service, Mrs Farrow?'

'I don't see why not. What do you say, Mr Farrow?'

Mr Farrow nodded. 'He's that Higgins fellow from the Abbey stables, isn't he? Where is he? Oh yes, I see him. Off you go then but don't keep us waiting to go home when the service is over.'

'No, I won't, Mr Farrow. Thank you ever so much.' Daisy hurried forward, only to be held up by folk in the aisle looking for a pew space to squeeze into. As she hovered impatiently behind them she heard Mr Farrow say, 'He's a fine grown fellow, isn't he. D'you think the lass'd like him to come over for tea one Sunday?'

'Oh how kind of you, Mr Farrow. I am sure she would.'

'In the New Year, then. Is there enough room in this pew, Mrs Farrow?'

'Plenty, my dear. Oh look, there's the rector now. His lordship must be outside.'

Redfern's ageing rector had acquired his living through his late mother who had been a cousin of his lordship's late mother. He stood in front of his congregation as they shuffled and crushed together in the pews, or resigned themselves to standing next to the walls.

Boyd was indicating a space next to him and Daisy stood at the end of his wooden pew smiling expectantly at the row of masculine faces beside him. She wondered if they would behave in the same way as the young gentleman had in the stables and her smile faltered. But they were Abbey servants and they were in church, so three of them filed out into the aisle and she gathered her cloak closely to sit by Boyd.

'You look very pretty tonight, Daisy,' he said.

She wanted to take his hands and lean over to kiss him but did not wish to embarrass him. 'Do you think so?' she responded.

'I know so. Have you settled well at the butcher's house?'

She nodded. 'I've got used to the blood and guts and smells and Mr and Mrs Farrow are very kind. They treat me like one of their own.'

'Can you get away tomorrow afternoon?'

'They are taking the trap to visit their son's farm after dinner.'

'Come to the stables and I'll give you a riding lesson.'

She nodded excitedly.

'Hush now, his lordship's here.'

The congregation stood quietly as Lord Redfern was pushed in his Bath chair by a liveried servant down the central aisle. The wheels squeaked and rattled as they bumped over the uneven flags. Daisy stretched her neck to catch a glimpse of him and was shocked to see a tiny wrinkled old gentleman wrapped in fur, apart from his head which was thinly covered in wisps of white hair over a scalp splashed with liver spots. He seemed barely alive and she considered he really should not have left his bedchamber. Another servant followed carrying his fur hat and Daisy thought that God wouldn't have minded if he'd kept it on his head just this once. Dear heaven, she thought, he had not been well since the harvest supper and ought not to be out of doors in this cold weather!

However, her attention was quickly diverted as she recognised the younger figure of Master James following the servants. His handsome features and thick dark hair contrasted sharply with Lord Redfern's ageing presence. Daisy held her breath as he walked past. She was three in from the aisle, but Master James knew the outdoor servants she had joined because they were from the stables where he spent much of his time when he was home. He was smiling and nodded to either side as he progressed slowly towards the front pew. When he saw her his steady pace faltered and his eyes widened as he stared at her.

Mr Stanton was directly behind James and Daisy saw him nudge Master James in the back and glance along the aisle. Daisy sat back in her pew sharply and stared straight ahead, aware that her heart was thudding in her breast. She felt herself blushing and concentrated hard on the backs of the necks of the people in front of her. But she could feel Boyd's eyes on her heightened colour and hoped Mr Stanton had not noticed her. How foolish, she thought. He was the estate steward and did not miss anything. Of course he had seen her!

'I'm sorry,' she whispered to her brother. 'Will I get you into trouble?'

'It's not your fault! It's not mine either and Mr Stanton knows that. Just keep well away from Master James, Daisy. *He* is trouble where you are concerned.'

Lord Redfern remained in his Bath chair in the aisle and Master James took the adjacent seat in the otherwise empty pew, whilst his most senior servants filed into the pew behind them. The rector greeted his congregation and as his opening words finished and the church organ thundered into life, they stood up to sing. Daisy adored all the Christmas hymns and knew them by heart. She was soon taken up by the joy of the service and only occasionally did her eyes stray to the front pew across the aisle.

But on one such dalliance, Master James noticed. He was turning towards Lord Redfern presumably to check his comfort when he twisted his head fully and looked for her. Daisy pressed her lips together anxiously but, even so, returned his steady stare. She could not stop herself. There was

301

something about him that made her want to look at him. He was handsome and dashing and when she thought about him, an unsettling thrill of excitement rippled through her. She truly believed that she might have fallen in love with him and she began to breathe faster.

There was absolutely no future in loving a man so far removed from her in status. He would never love her in return and she had learned enough about fornication in her time at Redfern Abbey to know that any interest in her would be for that alone. Boyd had advised her well. She must beware of Master James. But she didn't want to beware of him. She wanted to be held in his arms and be loved by him. Dear Lord, forgive her for these wicked thoughts in church!

'Daisy,' Boyd whispered urgently and tugged her skirt. 'Kneel down.'

'Oh, yes. Yes.' She pulled herself together and slid off the polished pew to kneel on the hassock, resting her confused head on the cold hard wood in front of her. She didn't hear any of the prayers and if she was honest she sang the remaining Christmas hymns mindlessly, not thinking of the words that she normally enjoyed.

When the service ended the congregation stood as his lordship's party made their slow progress back down the aisle, followed by estate and village dignitaries from the pews in front of her. Daisy kept her eyes firmly on her feet and thought about how cold her toes had become until she was aware of a general surge as less important village folk prepared to take their leave.

Boyd took hold of her arm. 'Sit down, Daisy. We'll wait for the throng to ease.'

And for Master James to be on his way back to the

Abbey, she thought. It was the right thing to do, she realised, but she still yearned to rush after him. Daisy tried to respond to cheery greetings and lively wall shadows caused by jostling lanterns as the crowd thinned. But dismay set in when she noticed Mr Stanton waiting in the church porch with his lamp. Surely he would have left with his lordship?

'Higgins. A word with you now, if you please.'

'Of course, sir' Boyd replied. 'May I see my sister safely to the care of her employer first?'

'I've spoken with Mr Farrow. He has taken his wife home and I have assured him I shall deliver your sister safely to his door within the half hour. Bring her with you. We shall speak in the Lady chapel.'

Boyd exchanged a troubled frown with Daisy and a whispered, 'Don't say anything,' as they followed the bobbing lantern through an ornate iron gate into a private corner of the church.

'Your sister is eighteen, is she not,' Mr Stanton began. Boyd nodded wordlessly and stood silently as the older man went on. 'It is difficult for you, having no parents to guide you, so I shall take that role upon myself.'

'There is no need to trouble yourself, sir. Daisy is housed and has a position now.'

'Do not interrupt me. I have noticed how much you care for her and also how attractive she is growing. So you will not disagree when I say that I must find her a husband.'

Chapter 29

'I most certainly shall!' Boyd protested. 'She is not yet ready for marriage, and she does not have a follower.'

'It is not up to you, Higgins. She is not of age so it is her employer's permission I shall seek. I shall inform him that she must marry soon.'

Daisy's eyes had become wider with each exchange. She ignored Boyd's advice and interrupted, 'I do not wish to marry!'

'Be quiet, Miss Higgins.'

Daisy was ready to continue her protest but she was thrown off guard by the steward's manner of address. He called her 'Miss Higgins' as though she were a person of some consequence and she really, really liked the sound of it. 'Miss Higgins' implied she was grown up and – well, ready for marriage. Yet she had never imagined herself wed to anyone, except of course her beloved Boyd and she could not marry him. She had toyed with her fantasies of Master James. Her girlish dreams had wandered in that direction in spite of her self reproach.

'Why must she marry, sir?' Boyd demanded. Daisy picked up a simmering anger in his tone and stance.

'Do I have to explain? She is attracting the wrong kind of attention.'

'You insult her, sir. What you speak of is in the mind of others. She does not seek it for herself.'

Boyd was not quite right about this, she thought. She had not sought male attention in the way she had seen some of the female servants act at the Abbey. But, if she were being totally honest with herself, she had sought – did seek – the attention of Master James. She couldn't help herself and she reckoned he felt the same whatever their differences in status were.

Mr Stanton appeared irritated by Boyd's last remark. 'Yes, yes, Higgins, I know your sister's character is unblemished. You have mistaken my meaning. I am concerned only for the attention she receives from one particular direction. Do not deny that you have noticed it too.'

Daisy knew he could not and neither could she. Boyd blew out his cheeks. 'You mean from Master James?' he said.

'I do indeed and I cannot knowingly allow any breath of scandal to affect his reputation. The Riding looks to the Abbey for example and there are too many past misdemeanours in his lordship's family waiting to be resurrected.'

'It is not her doing, sir. She has moved out of the Abbey.'

'But not very far.'

'She has to be near to me, sir. I am her only kin.'

'Precisely, Higgins! That is the reason she must marry. She will no longer be a temptation and out of harm's way. You must see the sense of it.' Mr Stanton gave a satisfied nod. 'I have one or two servants who are suitable. I shall approach them tomorrow.'

Daisy had listened quietly for long enough, and whilst Boyd had valiantly defended her position, she knew he could not go against the steward's declared intentions. But she could. She stepped forward and said, 'Truly, sir, you need not be concerned. I have no improper notions and I have no wish to marry anyone.'

'Do not be ridiculous! You are a young woman. Of course you wish to marry.'

'But I should like to choose my husband for myself!' She saw the impatience on Mr Stanton's face and pleaded, 'Boyd, don't let him do this to me!'

Her brother moved closer and took hold of her hand. 'I believe I must take my sister's side in this, sir.'

'You won't if you know what's good for you, Higgins,' the steward warned. 'The sooner I have her settled with a brood of infants to occupy her, the more secure your position at the Abbey will be. Without a husband, she will be a constant source of temptation.'

Daisy knew that Boyd did not like to be pressured in any way and she held her breath. His grip on her hand tightened and his stance told her he was angry. 'Then so be it,' he replied. 'I shall not see my sister wed to a man who does not love her simply because Master James, who should know better, cannot control his carnal instincts!'

Alarmed that this outburst would anger the steward further and seriously threaten his position, Daisy tugged at his hand anxiously. 'Hush, Boyd.' She appealed to the steward. 'He does not mean that, sir. He is simply concerned for my happiness.'

This time Mr Stanton did not tell her to be quiet, or

ignore her response. 'Then you should understand why you must marry,' he replied.

'But I do not wish to wed anyone *yet*, sir. And I believe that Mrs Farrow would not wish me to leave her employ.'

'Stubborn girl!' the steward responded irritably. 'What has Mrs Farrow to do with it? Mr Farrow is an Abbey tenant and he will do as he is told. He will give his permission for you to be courted and you, Higgins, will not object.'

Daisy stared at Boyd in the lamplight. He must do as the steward demanded. If he didn't, he would lose his position. 'I don't want to wed a stranger, Boyd,' she whispered.

'Don't worry, Daisy, I'll not let you.' He squared up to the steward. 'My sister has grown into a striking young woman, sir, but there are many pretty girls employed at the Abbey so why would any Abbey servant choose to wed her, a penniless servant whom he does not love?'

'Love? Love has nothing to do with it! I shall allocate an estate cottage to her suitor upon his marriage and he will welcome his good fortune. She will have a husband and a secure home, Higgins. Would you deny your sister that?'

'I won't see her wed to a man who does not love her and will not care for her as much as I do.'

The steward lost his patience. 'Now you are being ridiculous. This interview is at an end. As soon as I have found her a willing suitor she will be wed.' He picked up his lamp. 'I shall wait for your sister in the churchyard. Do not keep Mr Farrow waiting up.' He walked out, leaving Daisy and Boyd in the darkness.

Daisy turned her face into her brother's broad chest and flung her arms around him. 'You must not go against him, Boyd! What shall I do? Tell me what to do.'

'I don't know, Daisy.' He sounded desperate and his arms

tightened around her. He hugged her body against his, as though he did not want to let her go.

Nor did she wish him to, for he had always been there for her and if she had to wed someone else she would lose him. 'Don't let this happen to me, Boyd. We should be separated, and then you would get wed too and we should be parted for ever,' she whispered. 'I don't want to lose you.'

The edge of her bonnet pressed into his cheeks and he pushed it back with his nose to drop a soft kiss on her hair. 'You won't ever lose me, dearest Daisy. I love you too much to let you go.' His lips trailed across her brow and he wanted to hold her very close. Dear Lord, no! He shoved her away from him abruptly. What was happening to him? Daisy was his sister and he loved her but not as a sweetheart, for heaven's sake! He could not, *should not,* feel like this about *his sister.*

She resisted his rejection. 'Don't push me away, Boyd! I'm fearful of the future and need you. Will you not hold me for just a little longer?' She reached out tentatively with a gloved hand.

He knocked her hand away brusquely. 'No! I – I – Mr Stanton will be waiting for you. You – you must not test his patience.'

For a moment Daisy's lower lip trembled and she felt a tear threaten. Boyd was angry with her because she had jeopardised his position. And she wasn't even sure what she had done wrong, only that it always seemed to be she who was the root cause of the trouble. Maybe the steward was right. 'I'm truly sorry. I didn't mean any harm,' she whispered.

In spite of the cold dank air in the church, Boyd's head was hot and confused. He took Daisy's elbow roughly and shoved her after the steward. 'Hurry, before you lose sight of his lantern.' But Daisy could not leave Boyd if he felt ill of her. She turned, stretched her neck and gave him a kiss on his cheek before scurrying after the steward.

Boyd stood in the blackness, rubbing his face where her lips had been and realised with horror that the feelings she stirred in him were not those of brotherly love. He stumbled out of the tiny Lady chapel and staggered along a pew until he reached the central aisle. Two candle stubs still burned dimly, one each side of the large brass cross that adorned the altar. Lord Jesus Christ, forgive me, he begged silently. His heart was thumping and his head was burning. He collapsed to his knees and then spread himself, prostrate, on the cold stone floor. Forgive me, Lord. Forgive me.

He could not say how long he prayed, only that his eyes were damp and his flesh was cold when he heard the church door open and he scrambled to his feet.

'Who's there?' It was the rector, carrying a burning candle.

'Higgins, sir, from the Abbey stables.' He slid onto a pew and bowed his head.

'You are praying alone? Does something trouble you, my son?'

'It does, sir.'

'Will you talk of it?'

'I – I cannot, sir.'

'Move along the pew and I shall pray with you.'

Boyd obeyed and the vicar settled on the wooden seat beside him.

'Have you asked God for forgiveness?'

Boyd nodded, tried to speak and choked on the words.

'You can tell me, son,' the rector went on. 'It will help you to overcome your sin.'

'I – I have had impure thoughts, sir, about – about—' He couldn't say it.

'Are your impure thoughts of a carnal nature?'

Boyd nodded.

'Have you acted upon these thoughts?'

'Oh no, sir, she is – she is – I mean—' He rubbed the palm of his hand over his face.

The rector seemed relieved. 'You are praying for forgiveness because you have had carnal thoughts about your sweetheart?'

'She is not my sweetheart, sir.'

'She belongs to another?'

'No, sir! Yes, sir. I mean she is – she is –' He couldn't say it because he knew he should not have these feelings. Incest was a heinous sin and the church would not forgive him for such wicked thoughts, not ever. 'She is young sir,' he finished lamely.

'I trust that the maid in question is old enough to wed?' The vicar sounded so censorious that Boyd protested, 'Oh yes, sir.'

'Then God has given you his answer. If you desire her so strongly you must woo her and wed her, my son. Marriage is an institution endowed by God to prevent fornication.'

Marriage? Yes, of course, the rector was right, just as the steward was right. Boyd must remove temptation. But he was her only kin so he could not send her away, or indeed leave himself. Daisy's sisterly love for him must be diverted to romantic love for another. He would never neglect his responsibilities for her welfare. He would always look out for her, but if she were wed, he would be distanced from her.

He saw now the errors of their upbringing. The cruelty of their parents had driven them together more closely than a brother and sister should be. Running away from home had thrown them into an even closer alliance. He shut his eyes in shame as he remembered their night at the gamekeeper's hut.

He had been aware of his weakness for her then. He, too, would have to remove himself from temptation. He must heed the vicar's words and find himself a sweetheart. But not until his beloved Daisy was secure in the devotion of another. In the darkness, he frowned at the pain these thoughts aroused. A knife was twisting in his heart and he suppressed a strangled sob.

'You are distressed, my son?'

'I fear my weakness will be the better of me, sir.'

'Then pray to our Lord for strength. I, too, shall pray for you and your loved one.'

'Th-thank you, sir.'

The rector stifled a yawn and rose awkwardly to his feet.

Boyd noticed his gait and asked, 'Are you quite well, sir?'

'My bones are weary. But I do not complain for they are not as weary as Lord Redfern's. Good night, my son.'

'Good night, sir.'

Boyd went out into the crisp night air. Moonlight picked up a keen frost on shrubs and grass and a black sky sparkled with stars. It was Christmas Day, a time for joy and celebration but his heart was heavy as he contemplated a life without his beloved sister and then choked back a strangled groan that this love he had for her was an evil sin. He hurried along the track to the Abbey stables, his anxiety and shame overcoming any sense of the forgiveness he had prayed for. What kind of man was he to harbour such wicked desires? He broke into a run, felt his breath rasping in his chest and wished he had a horse to ride away his sins. In spite of the cold, sweat trickled down his spine and his hair became damp under his cap.

311

As he approached the stables he heard singing from his fellow servants. It was not the normal drunken revelry, but the Christmas hymns that everyone knew by heart. He slowed his pace and breathed deeply to quieten his thumping heart. He had a task to complete. If his darling Daisy had to marry, he must make sure her husband would be a good and sober man, with a position and prospects.

He must do his best to ensure her marriage was a happy one. Yes, he would do that first and then . . . and then he must look to his own future, take the rector's advice and woo a wife for himself. Perhaps if he directed his urges towards another woman, he might fall in love with her and his love for Daisy would fade. Yes. That was his answer from God. Both he and Daisy must find sweethearts to marry. His breathing subsided as he pondered this solution.

The outdoor servants were sitting on felled tree trunks around a crackling fire to sing their Christmas hymns. A few held lanterns but most warmed their frozen fingers around tankards of mulled ale, served to them by Mr Stanton. It was the custom at the Abbey for his lordship's family to wait on the servants at their Christmas celebration. As family was in short supply at Redfern Abbey, the senior servants honoured this tradition and were proud to do so. The steward had arranged for hot chestnuts from the kitchens and a wooden tray of pastries made savoury with cheese or spice passed from hand to hand. Boyd sat on the end of a log and joined in the singing. He knew what he must do, but the knowledge did not quell his confusion and uneasiness.

Chapter 30

Daisy's shiny eyes were put down to the cold weather when she reached the butcher's shop with Mr Stanton. He had not uttered a word to her until he bid her goodnight and a Happy Christmas as he handed her over to Mr Farrow. How could Boyd side with him about marrying when she said she didn't want it? She thought Boyd loved her. But clearly he loved his position at the stables more. She sighed. She was being unfair. That was not true and she understood why he had to agree.

It's just that she had not, since her silly childhood proposal to Boyd, given marriage a thought. She didn't want to marry and she didn't need to while she had Boyd. He was all she wanted for a husband and, yes, she knew she could not marry him, he had told her so quite firmly when she was eight. However, that didn't stop her thinking that she would rather be a spinster and live with him than be married to someone she did not love.

She was so used to Boyd being there for her that she hadn't given their future much thought until now. But the notion that they would be separated if she were forced to marry someone else alarmed her. Who would love her as much as Boyd did? He would lay down his life for her, not that she would ever let him for she felt the same about him. Boyd must know this for how could he not? She had to make the steward understand this and then, surely, he would not insist on a marriage for her.

But it was not love for anyone that was on the steward's mind, she realised. It was lust. It was Master James's attraction towards her that had driven him to his decision. She had done her best to keep away from him but as soon as she saw him in church, that familiar thrill had coursed through her. She wanted to return his attentions, get to know him more and to let him woo her. She wanted to explore the unknown territory that was this desire connecting them and – and yes, she knew what he would want from her and it made no difference because she was sure it would be a proper love between them. True love, married love that lasted a lifetime, a love that her young body craved and when she thought of that her common sense deserted her.

She had to trot to keep up with the steward. Mr Farrow was stamping his cold feet and blowing into his cupped hands as he waited outside the shop door for her, but he knew better than to complain to the steward. He said, 'I trust everything is in order, Mr Stanton.'

'I need to speak with you about your maid,' the steward replied. 'Call into my office at the stables after his lordship's Boxing Day hunt.'

'Of course, sir.' He pushed open the shop door as the

steward went off to collect his horse from the churchyard. 'What have you been doing, my lass?'

'Nothing, Mr Farrow. Honest, I haven't.'

'Well, something must have gone on for him to want to see me. Whatever it was, don't you go saying nothing to Mrs Farrow. I don't want her upset until I know what this is about.' He looked down at her with a pitying expression on his face. 'Dear me, lass, you've been such a boon to us so far, I hope you've not gone and done summat daft. You'd best not venture out without Mrs Farrow until I've listened to what Mr Stanton has to say. I'll not have a scandal linked with my shop.'

'Boyd promised me a riding lesson tomorrow.'

'You heard what I said. If you've been up to something with one of them stable lads – ee, lass, I thought you knew better.'

Daisy gave up her protest. She knew what people thought when young girls got wed all of a sudden, especially if it was to somebody they hadn't walked out with. Mr Farrow was going to think the worst when he found out the steward's plans for her. Mrs Farrow might believe the truth though, Daisy thought wearily as she lit a candle and climbed the creaking stairs to her attic. She would be sorry to leave the butcher's house. Mrs Farrow had put a wrapped hot brick on top of her nightgown in her bed and Daisy undressed quickly, snuggling down into the warmth. It was Christmas Day already and she dreamed of catching a glimpse of Master James at the Boxing Day hunt.

Mr Farrow, his bulging tummy wrapped in a clean blue apron, stood in front of his shop with a broad smile on his face and wished the compliments of the season to all who passed whether they were buying from him or not. It was

315

a busy Christmas morning in Redfern Village and the Farrow household was no exception.

Daisy carried the Christmas pudding, well wrapped in a greased cloth, to the pan of water simmering on the range. She had helped Mrs Farrow make it weeks ago and had never seen so many dried fruits go into one pudding. Mrs Farrow had put just as much in the fruit cake that stood in the small parlour beside a slab of crumbly Wensleydale cheese for Christmas tea by the log fire. Daisy thought that the butcher's wife was justly proud of her pudding for she used a recipe that had come from the Abbey kitchen. She looked forward to tasting it and resolved not to eat too much Yorkshire pudding to begin with so she would have room.

Mrs Farrow was fully occupied cooking Christmas dinner while Daisy fetched and carried for her as well as helping at the shop counter. Beef was still the most popular choice for Christmas dinner in the village, although Mr Farrow told her about the turkeys that the chef cooked at the Abbey. 'Much bigger than a goose,' he commented, adding, 'Too much for the three of us, but I might buy in one or two for the shop next Christmas.' As the morning wore on she became intoxicated by the mingling smells of burning Yule log and roasting goose that reached every corner of the house. At mid-morning Mr Farrow poured glasses of sherry for all of them and within minutes Daisy's cheeks were glowing.

Mrs Farrow was more excited than her usual cheerful self as they took their seats to eat a meal that was large compared to their regular Sunday feast. She was to see her son and grandchildren this afternoon and Daisy knew that nothing pleased her more. She had helped Mrs Farrow wrap new toys as presents for the children.

'You are quiet this morning, Mr Farrow,' his wife commented. 'I do hope you're not coming down with anything.'

''Tis nothing, my love,' he responded. 'Did the gypsy lad polish up the trap?'

'He did that. He's not a gypsy, dearest, he just looks like one. He buffed up the tack and rubbed down the pony, too, and his pa was right pleased with their rib trimmings and suet when he called to collect him.'

'Have you plenty to keep young Daisy busy while we're out visiting?' Mr Farrow asked.

'She is going over to the stables to see her brother.'

Her employer turned on his serious expression. 'She saw him last night at church. Didn't you, lass?'

'He said he would give me a riding lesson,' Daisy explained.

'Oh I don't think that's a good idea, do you, lass.' Mr Farrow stared hard at her until she replied, 'No sir. The ground is too frosty.'

'When our own lass were at home,' he went on, 'on a Christmas afternoon she made pies to take out to hunt followers on Boxing Day and turned in a tidy penny or two. It stood her in good stead for when she asked for a new gown.'

'Indeed it did, sir,' his own wife echoed. 'And Daisy will be wanting new boots before this winter is out. That is a splendid notion, husband. She will be too busy to be lonely while we are out. Will you leave her a few coppers for the Lucky Birds?'

'Aye, they'll be round after dinner as sure as God made little apples.'

This cheered Daisy for she liked children and they sang a Christmas hymn before knocking on the door and adding, 'We wish you a Merry Christmas and a Happy New Year. Please may we be the Lucky Birds here!'

317

Mrs Farrow smiled at her. 'We'll be back before you know we've gone and we'll bring Spanish chestnuts to roast around the Yule log.'

Daisy managed a smile in return. She didn't mind not having a riding lesson, but she was desperate to see Boyd and talk about last night. She was sure he had been as upset as she by the steward's plans. Mr Farrow's insistent stare at her had not been about the riding. It concerned her staying away from the stables until he had spoken with the steward about her apparent misdemeanour.

Mr Farrow continued his paternal control. 'We shall all go over to the Abbey for the hunt tomorrow. What do you say, Mrs Farrow?'

This seemed to settle the matter and Daisy spent a pleasant enough Christmas afternoon and evening giving her plenty of time to reflect on her reasons for not wedding some estate worker chosen for her by the steward.

Mr Farrow drove his wife and Daisy in the trap with her baskets of pies. It was another sharp day and the grass was crisp underfoot. The sun was out but it never climbed high in the sky at this time of year and there was no warmth in its weak rays. The trap overtook a constant straggle of village folk, shoulders hunched against the cold, walking in the same direction, anxious not to miss the opening spectacle, and already folk were buying her pies.

It really was a very grand occasion, one of the few where servants and villagers were allowed on the parkland in front of the Abbey. Gentry from across the Riding paraded astride beautifully groomed horses with plaited manes and tails and steam pushing from their nostrils, and they champed at their bits impatient to begin their gallop. Incredibly, Daisy thought,

318

his lordship surveyed the gathering from his Bath chair at the top of the stone steps outside the Abbey entrance.

Master James was there, splendid in hunting pink. He was so dashing and handsome on a fine chestnut horse that Daisy was distracted enough to drop a pie so that it broke apart in her basket. She was too far away for him to notice her and there were hunting ladies in neatly tailored jackets and matching skirts spread attractively over their side saddles to catch his attention.

Indeed the ladies' headgear fascinated Daisy too. They wore high hats with veils that covered their faces and underneath their long hair was caught up in velvet snoods. She watched one elegant lady lean down to take a glass of stirrup cup from a servant with a silver tray. The rider carefully lifted the edge of her veil to tip the warming drink down her throat.

Hungry hunt followers crowded around the trap.

'What pies have you, miss?'

'Bacon or mutton,' Daisy answered automatically and handed the coppers to Mrs Farrow.

More riders walked their mounts from the stables to join the group and then the dogs arrived, snapping and yapping and wagging their erect tails, anxious to be away and pick up a scent. It seemed, to Daisy's inexperienced eye, a scene of total chaos.

Then she heard the horn and the atmosphere became charged as riders marshalled their horses into order. Barking reached a crescendo, the pack broke away, the horn called again and the horses followed, their hooves thundering across the cold hard ground.

'Redfern Moor!' someone yelled. 'He's drawing across the moor!' and an excited band of followers chased after them, some riding, others running and the rest walking.

'Old reynard'll lead them a merry dance over yonder and if he's fast they'll lose him. He'll go to ground in the woods.' Mr Farrow picked up the reins and turned the pony's head. 'They'll end up in Redfern woods and walk back down the drover track. We'll pick up the followers there.'

'Oh, Mr Farrow,' his wife exclaimed, 'that track is very rocky. It'll jolt me to pieces.'

'You're right. It won't do my trap any good either.'

'But what about the pies I have left, Mr Farrow?' Daisy added.

'We've sold the best of them,' Mrs Farrow commented. 'Shall we set Daisy down with her basket? She can walk back to the village when they've all gone.'

Daisy was ready to agree, but Mr Farrow was not. 'She stays with us,' he said.

'Well, take the trap round to the stables. She can sell what's left there.'

'Aye. I have an interview with the steward.'

'You have, Mr Farrow? What does he want with you?'

'It's business, my dear. You'll find out soon enough.'

Daisy kept her eyes on the pie hamper on the trap floor as Mr Farrow walked the pony down the tradesmen's track to the stables at the back of the Abbey. If Mrs Farrow knew that she knew, she wouldn't stop pressing her until she had the truth. Anyway, she might see Boyd so Daisy cheered at the prospect. Boyd was on her side and he would have thought of a way out for her.

Mr Farrow drove the trap through the archway under the clock tower and tethered his pony while he went in search of the steward. Several coaches with monogrammed doors were lined up without their horses in the middle of the square. Outside the servants' housing, coachmen and footmen in liveries that Daisy had not seen before talked and laughed, huddled in small groups.

Mrs Farrow stood up suddenly. 'I cannot sit in here any more. My toes are chilled to the bone. That's the Fitzkeppel coat of arms on that coach over there. Surely they haven't come back from Italy? I'm off to find out. Daisy, you run along to the stalls with your basket and find a few hungry stable lads. Half price for what's left.'

'Mr Farrow said I had to stay with you.'

'Do as I say, dear. There's a good girl.'

Effectively dismissed, Daisy did as she was told and went to look for Boyd only to find that he had been sent out early on horseback to flush out the fox. Disappointed, she left her basket on a mounting stone and wandered into the stable where Boyd kept his ponies. The doors were wide open, the stalls empty and swept. Daisy sighed. She was tired from yesterday's baking and today's early start. She climbed the ladder to the hayloft, which was actually full of straw, to wait for him. She took off her bonnet, lay back, closed her eyes and let her mind drift . . .

First of all she was aware of the straw rustling and then a soft voice.

'Daisy?'

Where was she? For a second she could not think. She blinked. It was daylight. A piece of straw scratched at her neck and she shifted awkwardly. A pair of riding boots crossed her line of vision. Expensive boots, new boots, barely scuffed at all.

'Daisy?'

She sat up straight. 'Master James?'

'I saw your pie basket on the mounting stone.'

'What are you doing here, in that jacket?' It was a plain dark one, the kind worn by the stable lads for church.

'I borrowed it so I wouldn't be noticed.'

'But shouldn't you be with the hunt?'

'They won't miss me for a while. I saw you in a trap earlier and doubled back to find you.'

Her heart leapt but her eyes were troubled. 'You mustn't! I'm not allowed to talk to you.'

'Who says?' He sounded genuinely surprised.

She looked up and saw a face that was hurt and puzzled at the same time. 'It was Mr Stanton—'

'Oh him? He thinks he can behave as my guardian does.' He sounded more resigned than angry about this.

'He doesn't want us to be together.'

Master James sat down on the straw beside her. '*I* want us to be together. Since I first saw you on the track by the gates I've wanted to find out about you. Every time I have seen you I have wanted to know more about you.'

Daisy stared at him. She felt the same but dared not say so. 'I shouldn't talk to you. You're the master and I'm a servant.'

'It doesn't make a difference to us, though. Does it?' Daisy became wary and wondered what he meant. He went on, 'I've tried to work out what it is that attracts me so. It's you, just you. I want to be with you.'

'And I you,' she murmured.

'Do you feel it, too?'

Daisy chewed her lip, regretting her admission, and asked, 'What is it you want from me, Master James?'

'I want to know who you are and why I am so drawn to you and—' he stopped and lifted her chin gently to look directly in her eyes. 'Why should you think I must want something from you? Because one day I shall be the master, you believe I shall demand my *droit de seigneur* from you?'

She blushed at his directness and he shook his head slowly.

'You do not know me, Daisy, and I wish to rectify that. We must meet and talk so that we may learn about each other properly.'

'We can't. Mr Stanton won't allow it.'

'He cannot stop us. His job is to show me how the estate is run so that I'll do the same when his lordship – when my real father inherits.'

Daisy wasn't sure if she was supposed to know about his real father. But she did, so she asked, 'Won't he – your real father – want to do that for himself?'

'He's not interested in running the estate. It's the only thing he and my guardian agree on, though they haven't the least notion of it because they have never spoken to each other.'

'Never?'

'Apparently not,' Master James shrugged. 'Lawyers write letters instead.'

Daisy thought he sounded sad and could think of nothing helpful to say. Suddenly, he picked up her hand and traced the lines on her palm with his index finger. 'I was cheered no end to see you in church and you looked so lovely in your bonnet. I wanted to stay behind and talk to you then but it was difficult to get away. Lord Redfern insists that I am beside him for most of his waking time. Are you living in the village?'

'I have a position and lodgings at the butcher's.'

'You do? That is excellent news. We shall be able to meet when I'm home from the university.'

Daisy gave a slight shake of her head. 'Mr Stanton won't allow it.'

'I've told you. He cannot dictate what I do.'

But he can order my life as he sees fit, she thought. She

323

pressed her lips together in a personal gesture of defiance. If Master James took her side he might persuade the steward to see reason. Yet even as the notion flitted across her mind she dismissed it. It would make the situation worse in Mr Stanton's view. Besides, she daren't ask Boyd to risk his position and she was already disregarding the steward's wishes.

Master James bent his head and kissed the palm of her hand making her skin tingle. 'You do like me, don't you?' he asked.

I love you, she thought. It was strange to feel this way about someone she hardly knew so she kept her silence as he turned back her cloak and pushed up her sleeve. He bent his head and very gently trailed his lips along her arm. She didn't stop him so she supposed he had his answer.

She was finding it really difficult to resist him and made no attempt to move away. No one had so much as kissed her hand before and she became lightheaded as though she were sickening for something. As his mouth explored the crook of her elbow, the tingling spread to more private areas of her body and she wanted to kiss the luxuriant dark hair on the back of his head.

The sound of voices drifted up through the open stable door and brought her sharply back to reality.

'I left her in the trap with my good wife, sir, but her basket is here.'

'Well, she isn't in here with her brother. I cannot spend any more time on this. You understand what you have to say to her?'

'Yes, sir.'

'Good man. You can be sure the Abbey chef will order mutton from the new breed on your son's farm.'

'Thank you, sir. Good day to you, sir.'

The voices drifted away.

'Stanton.' Master James sat up. 'He mustn't find me here.'

'He's with Mr Farrow, my employer. I'll go down and show myself.'

'Very well.' He kissed her palm again as she scrambled to her feet and picked straw off her gown. 'Wait.' He tugged at some persistent stalks from the back of her skirts. 'I'll come and find you in the village.'

He clambered after her to kiss her forehead as she climbed down the ladder but it only served to make her frown and she hoped he hadn't noticed. She wasn't stupid. Would anyone believe that she had not encouraged him? Reluctantly, she realised that no one would and why would they when it wasn't true? In spite of James's reassurance, she remembered Boyd's warning about the gentry and the way they treated their maids.

This could come to no good at all and she would be the one to suffer. But she was unable to stop herself wondering when she would see him again and a thrill ran through her every time she thought about being with him. She couldn't explain it; nor could she quell it for she knew he felt the same. It was as though they were meant for each other and being close to him only reinforced the attraction she – they – had felt before. She didn't care what the steward thought, or what he said he was going to do. All she cared about was the next time she could be with Master James and she walked out into the weak winter sun certain in the knowledge that she would be with him again.

'Well, Mr Farrow, are you going to tell me what your meeting was about?' Mrs Farrow demanded.

Daisy was in the scullery and aware that Mr Farrow was

whispering about her to his wife. They had eaten cold goose for Boxing Day dinner. Daisy was wiping out the sink after washing the pots when she heard Mr Farrow raise his voice. 'When you've finished in there, lass, come back and join us at the table. These matters concern you.'

She dried her hands quickly, took off her apron and went into the kitchen.

Mrs Farrow looked curious but beamed at her. 'Come and sit down, lass.'

'Well, now,' Mr Farrow began, 'you are indeed a lucky young woman. There's no doubt that we shall miss you, won't we, Mrs Farrow, but we shall not stand in your way.'

'Just think, Daisy. You'll be in your own cottage by next Christmas with a husband and – eee, lass, maybe even a babby. Oh I'm so pleased for you.'

A baby? She might have a baby within the year? She had no idea how to care for a baby! She protested, 'But I don't want to leave you. Truly, I am happy here and you need me in the tripe shed—'

'Now then, lass. It's true that you are the best help we've ever had, but we'll find usselves another. We shall have to, for Mr Stanton is determined you will be wed early in the New Year.'

That soon! 'But I don't have a sweetheart,' she explained.

'You will have. You're presentable and can look after a home as well as any of the village girls. With the promise of an estate cottage, you'll have the lads queuing up for your hand.'

Mrs Farrow continued where her husband had left off. 'When we have his name, we'll ask him over for tea so he can court you proper.' She gave her a conspiratorial wink.

'But I don't want a sweetheart yet.'

326

'Don't be silly. Of course you do. We have received an invitation to Mr Stanton's home to let in the New Year.'

Mr Farrow added, 'Your brother will be there and Mr Stanton will bring your suitor to ask my permission first. You're honoured, my girl. Mr Stanton is doing this proper.'

'New Year? But that's next week!' She resolved to talk to Boyd before then. Surely he could do *something* to stop this?

'Indeed it is. I shall have you wed afore Lady Day. The steward wished for a speedy conclusion.'

'I don't have to say yes,' Daisy pointed out stubbornly.

Mr Farrow's voice took on a sterner note. 'You do if you know what's good for you and that brother of yours. This is not just about you, you know.'

Mrs Farrow echoed her husband's concern. 'I won't have you being difficult about this. None of my girls made a fuss about the husbands we chose for them and neither will you.'

Daisy was unaware of how disgruntled and grumpy she appeared until Mrs Farrow's tone softened and she added, 'You'll have new things, you know. Mr Stanton has given us, well, it's a kind of dowry I suppose, to buy cloth for what you'll need. The draper generally has a clear-out of his old stock come January. We'll go there together.' Mrs Farrow smiled brightly but Daisy did not feel at all cheerful. How was she going to get over to the stables to see Boyd before next week?

Chapter 31

Daisy considered running away. The last time had been with Boyd and she learned from him how to survive on the road. But it had been early summer then and now they were in the depths of winter. Even gamekeepers' huts were freezing at night and if she lit a fire the smoke would give her away. Besides, Mr and Mrs Farrow kept her too busy to get away.

There was little trade after Christmas and her employers took their ease. It was Daisy who had to watch the shop and sell the occasional pieces of salt beef or pickled tripe. They even invited her with them to his son's farm where the new sheep would be raised. She took his six children for a walk while his wife's housemaid stayed with their parents and grandparents in the warm farmhouse to serve them food and drink. They were all very merry when she returned, cold and frazzled from their children's unruly antics, and she was sent to the kitchen to make their tea from the leftovers.

Daisy's bad humour did not lift. She wouldn't have a maid to look after her children when she was wed, she reflected irritably as she boiled up soup and sawed at bread. Then the children didn't want the soup because they had eaten cake from the pantry while they waited for it. As a child, she would have been whipped for such a misdemeanour!

However, she was cheered when she woke to snowfall on the eve of New Year. Surely Mr Farrow would not take out his pony and trap in this weather? But Mr and Mrs Farrow had no wish to miss a celebration on the estate especially at the behest of its most important servant. They were honoured to be invited to the steward's own home, and excited about seeing inside the square detached house set well apart from the stables and domestic buildings behind the Abbey. It had been built especially for him and his growing family in the villa style that was popular in the towns. So, Daisy piled up rugs and wrappings in the trap and Mr Farrow put a horse blanket on his pony. They travelled so slowly that Daisy's feet were frozen solid by the time they arrived.

Mrs Farrow had lent her a woven woollen shawl with a paisley pattern and fringe. Daisy had seen them in the draper's and they were very dear to buy. She liked it too. It was soft and very warm and the colouring suited her. When the maid took her cloak and bonnet she realised how nice it was to be waited on and smiled gratefully. As she straightened her gown she caught a glimpse of herself in a looking-glass. Mrs Farrow came up behind her and adjusted one of the combs holding up her thick light-brown hair. Daisy's eyes glistened at her reflection and her skin glowed from the cold.

In spite of her misgivings about the evening's proceedings, she felt confident as a – she hesitated and looked at her image again – as a woman. She had grown a little in height over the recent months and had filled out significantly, no doubt due to regular meals of butcher's meat.

Boyd was here tonight and he always lifted her spirits. He understood that she didn't wish to marry someone chosen for her and that no one could make her. Dearest Boyd. How would she get by without him? He would be on her side she was sure. Mrs Farrow was still standing behind and she whispered in her ear, 'You'll do very nicely, my dear. Come along now.'

Boyd was the first person she noticed standing by the fireplace when she was shown into the Stanton's downstairs drawing room, and a wide smile lit up her face. His response was a serious nod and a sip from the tiny glass he was holding. Daisy followed his lead and calmed her instinct to rush over and hug him. The room was spacious but filled with furniture and people and a good coal fire burned in the grate. Even so, the wintry air was chilly and Daisy welcomed the tot of spirit offered to warm her.

There were murmurings and moving around the room to allow Daisy and the Farrows to sit nearest the fire. When they were settled, Daisy was presented to Mr and Mrs Gardner and their son Joseph. This is him, she realised. This is who Mr Stanton has chosen for my husband. He was, she was forced to admit, very presentable, of a good height with regular features and neatly trimmed hair. He held himself upright and was politeness itself in his manners. He sat between his parents at one side of the fire and Daisy was between Mr Stanton and Boyd at the other.

'Mr Gardner, as his name suggests, is responsible for his lordship's walled garden. He has been a part of the estate since he was born. His father was a gardener here before him.'

Mr Gardner sat bolt upright proudly. His prim little wife smiled pleasantly at Daisy. 'Boyd has told us how he has looked after you since you lost your parents and how well he is progressing at Redfern. You are indeed lucky to have such a clever brother. Mr Stanton assures us that all reports of you are positive. We wish for nothing less for our dear son.'

'She's been such a help since she's been with us,' Mrs Farrow replied. 'I really don't know how I shall manage without her.'

Mr Farrow continued quickly, 'But of course we are pleased to let her go, especially to a respectable estate family.'

Boyd added, 'Joseph has worked as an indoor servant at the Abbey since he was twelve, Daisy, and has risen to the position of footman.'

Daisy gave her brother a questioning look. Why was he singing Joseph's praises? And why couldn't Joseph tell her himself? However, she had expected a farm labourer rather than a footman and realised why he held himself well. All footmen had to look like sentries when they were standing to attention in their livery. I bet he looks very handsome in it too, Daisy thought, for he had the height to carry it off. She was annoyed with herself for being impressed by Mr Stanton's choice of a footman for her. Either the steward thought very highly of Boyd, or he was more anxious to keep her away from Master James than she realised.

There was an awkward silence. Boyd was staring at Daisy and was moving his head slightly and nudging her. He seemed to be urging her to speak. Why didn't Joseph say something? Perhaps he didn't want to marry her any more than she wanted him. But when she took a closer look at his even features she detected a widening of his eyes and a relaxing of his lips. He liked what he saw! He approved of her! She'd rather he didn't but now was not the time to put him off her. There would be time enough for that in the future. Boyd would be furious with her if she embarrassed him tonight. Anyway, Boyd was on her side so, confident that he would argue later on her behalf, she heaved a sigh and smiled.

'Do you enjoy being a footman, Joseph?' she asked.

'I have a good position,' he said.

That isn't what I asked you, she thought and hoped he would ask her something next. He didn't so she said, 'You must look very handsome in your livery.'

This was obviously the right thing to say to Joseph because his smiled widened. He looked very satisfied with himself as he replied, 'Indeed I do, miss. Did you not notice me when you worked at the Abbey?'

'I can't honestly say that I did, sir.' Dear heaven, his expression told her that she had slighted him and she added hastily, 'Mrs Brown trained me not to stare when inside the Abbey.'

'What about when I partnered you at the barn dance?'

She kept her features still. She couldn't remember him but responded for appearances' sake, 'Oh, yes, sir. It was fun, wasn't it?'

Now he was even more self-satisfied. They lapsed into silence again until Mrs Farrow ventured, 'Would you like to come to tea with us after the New Year hunt, Joseph?'

'Thank you, Mrs Farrow,' he said immediately.

They all heard the clock over the stables striking and Mr Stanton rose to his feet. 'Is that the midnight hour?' But it wasn't. It was only the third quarter. 'Let me charge your glasses,' he added and poured out more tots of brandy. His parlour maid brought in cheese straws that were warm from the bake oven. Mrs Stanton, a serene, rather regal woman, offered them round and the atmosphere in the room relaxed.

Daisy backed Boyd into a corner and whispered, 'What's going on?'

'He's respectable and a good match for you, Daisy. You like him, don't you?'

'No.'

'You have implied that you do.'

'Well, I don't. I was being polite. How can I like him when I don't even know him?'

'That's why he has formally asked to court you.'

'He has?'

'What do you think tonight is about, Daisy?'

'But you said I didn't have to marry if I didn't want to!'

'Don't be awkward about this.'

'You said you were on my side, that I didn't have to do anything I didn't want to. Well, I don't want to marry him.'

'You don't know him yet,' he flung back at her.

'Boyd!'

They were interrupted by Mrs Stanton. 'What are you two huddled together for? Come over to the window. It's snowing again and it will be midnight soon.'

'We'd best be on our way as soon as the clock has chimed,' Mr Farrow warned. 'It wouldn't do to get stuck on Redfern Hill.'

Mrs Stanton protested, 'Oh, not until someone has let in the New Year proper. Joseph has arranged for one of his lordship's black-a-moors to bring us good luck.'

Her husband added, 'There'll be plenty of strong lads out and about the estate and village tonight, Mr Farrow. They'll see you home safely.'

'Do stay a while, dearest,' Mrs Farrow urged, nudging her husband's elbow.

'I'll go with you, sir,' Boyd volunteered, 'just to be sure.'

The chimes began again, four quarters and then a stroke for each hour. They counted them out loud until twelve when Mr Stanton raised his glass and cried, 'Happy New Year, one and all!' They all stood to raise their glasses in a toast.

Across the small group Daisy noticed Joseph watching her intently. He was looking at her furtively, up and down, taking in her gown and shawl, her features and hair. The pleased expression on his face turned to smugness and, as she met his eyes she was shocked to see him give her a distinct wink, a self-satisfied and suggestive wink that Daisy found – found – dear heaven, she was offended by his forwardness and looked away immediately.

She really did not want this self-important footman to court her and she must make Boyd understand. She must talk to Boyd, and became anxious to leave the small gathering as soon as she could. She heard the fall of the heavy wrought-iron door knocker on the front door. Thank goodness, the black-a-moor had arrived to let in the New Year. Daisy hadn't seen either of his lordship's two black-a-moors close to. They were big muscular footmen with black skins and very dark eyes. If she were honest, they frightened her. But not when Boyd was with her.

Mr Stanton excused himself to open the front door and Daisy, along with the others present, heard the greeting and then the low voices of a hurried conversation. There was a pause before the drawing-room door opened.

'A healthy and prosperous New Year to all!'

It was not one of his lordship's black-a-moors. It was

– Daisy frowned. He appeared from his livery to be one of the footmen. He had dark hair and had blackened his face in keeping with the tradition. To ensure good luck, the first person in the New Year to cross the threshold had to be a dark man. He carried a large piece of shiny black coal and strode over to the fire to place it on the flames. The small gathering clapped as the cold wet fuel hissed in the heat. Daisy recognised him straightaway but it was not until he turned round that Mrs Stanton cried, 'Master James!'

Master James grinned broadly showing a good set of teeth in his black face. 'I am discovered,' he laughed.

Daisy wanted to laugh with him, but dared not. He swept his dark eyes over the small gathering, lingering with surprise on her. He really had not expected to see her here. But his eyes were teasing, bringing hers alive too. She had to press her lips together firmly to prevent them breaking into a grin. She was tempted to wink at him as Joseph had at her. Master James would have thought it forward and suggestive of her, as she did of Joseph, yet he would have winked back, she was sure. *And she would not have been offended.*

Better not, she decided. But at that moment she resolved to reject Joseph's courtship. She would make it quite plain to him that she – she what? That she loved another. As her eyes twinkled in the lamplight, Daisy basked in the warm feeling this gave her and could not prevent a smile as it spread to all her features.

Mr Stanton had followed Master James into the room. He was agitated and said, 'My wife was not expecting you, sir.'

Master James bowed to the lady of the house. 'Please accept my humblest apologies, madam. I had not the slightest notion that you had company, otherwise I should not have persuaded Granger to change places with me.'

'Nonsense, sir,' Mrs Stanton replied. 'We are honoured and delighted to welcome you. His lordship is quite well this night?'

'There is no change in him, ma'am. He has not left his bed this day, but his physician tells me he is comfortable.'

'Oh.' An uneasy silence settled on the group until James added brightly, 'He insists that Redfern carries on as normal and my good wishes tonight are his, too.'

This cheered everyone except Mr Stanton and Boyd who seemed determined to be cross with him. When Daisy glanced at Mr and Mrs Gardner she understood where Joseph got his smug expression from. She guessed that none of the other estate gardeners would have had Master James to bring in their New Year, even if it wasn't exactly at their own more humble cottage.

'Daisy, it is time to leave,' Boyd whispered in her ear.

'Not yet,' she responded.

'Mr Farrow is worried about his pony on the ice.'

'Very well.' She saw her employer talking to Mr Stanton.

'And who will bring in your New Year, Miss Daisy?' It was Master James who made this enquiry and the buzz of conversation quietened.

'Mr Farrow will, sir.'

'But he is grey-haired!'

'He used to be as dark as you, sir,' Mrs Farrow protested.

'I shall go with them,' Boyd added.

'You are as fair as your sister, Higgins,' the young master argued. 'Besides, you live here in the stable block and the Abbey is much nearer to the village. Will you allow me to let in your New Year, Mr Farrow?'

'Oh, Mr Farrow,' his wife breathed with a glance at the Gardners. 'Do say yes.'

'My trap is very small, my dear,' her husband cautioned.

'I was not thinking of riding in it in this icy weather,' James responded. 'The snow is not deep. I shall lead your pony most carefully and make sure you reach home safely.'

'I must protest, sir,' Mr Stanton said. 'It is too dangerous. You will be walking back to the Abbey alone.'

'I think not. Many of the Abbey servants will still be at the Redfern Arms and I shall have plenty of company.'

'Even so, sir,' Mr Stanton began.

'I am no longer a youngster,' James interrupted firmly.

'No, sir,' the steward agreed with a sigh.

'Then it is settled. Mrs Stanton, bring in the ladies' cloaks and bonnets to warm by the fire.'

Master James did not even glance in her direction while she wrapped herself against the night air and said her good-nights. Joseph was not at all happy for some reason but his parents assured Daisy that he would present himself for tea the following Sunday.

'Come and see me at the shop,' she whispered to Boyd.

'I'll try,' he answered. But he did not sound hopeful and she desperately wanted to speak with him about putting off Joseph.

Mr Stanton brought the trap round and held the pony's head while James helped Mr and Mrs Farrow aboard. Daisy waited patiently at the back while Master James put his lump of coal safely inside on the trap floor. Then he placed a thick blanket on the backward facing rear seat and as he did so, stooped to kiss her forehead.

'Don't,' she breathed. 'You'll be seen.'

His head stayed close to hers and he trailed his lips down to her ears. 'There is another meeting of the Redfern Hunt next week. I'll come to the pony stable loft as before.' He hoisted her easily onto the seat.

She inhaled with excitement. An assignation with him and only a few days away! 'I'll wait for you,' she whispered.

He smiled, and wrapped the blanket securely around her legs. The next thing she knew he was leading the pony away and she was gazing at the watching figure of Mr Stanton standing outside his front portico. He stayed there for a long time until the night closed in on him and he disappeared from her view.

The trap bumped and jolted along the frozen track that skirted the park, the one that had first brought her to the Abbey, and eventually they passed the entrance gates, where she heard Mr Farrow suggest that he get down and lead the pony now if Master James wished to cut along to the Abbey. She didn't quite catch James's reply but nothing changed as they rumbled down the hill.

He helped Mr Farrow stable the pony and trap, then brought in the coal and good wishes. He accepted a tot of warming spirit and said his goodnights. 'I trust I shall see you at the hunt next Saturday, sir,' he said as he took his leave. 'The hunt followers relish your pies.'

'Such a charming gentleman,' Mrs Farrow sighed. 'Oh, it will be a welcome change when he is lord of the Abbey.'

'Well, it's his father's turn next,' Mr Farrow reminded her as he came in with the key from the front door. 'But at least he will be younger than the present crusty old incumbent. Off to bed with you, Daisy. Shop'll be open first thing.'

It was a busy week. There were the pies to make and Mr Farrow insisted that Daisy bake bread, scones and a cake for Joseph when he visited on Sunday. On top of that, Mr Shipton, the stock dealer, turned up at the inn and Mr Farrow invited him to take dinner with them one day after he had closed the shop.

Mrs Farrow seemed delighted that he had accepted and became quite excited at planning what they would eat. Daisy tried to be enthusiastic but she was apprehensive about his visit. He was well dressed and very civil but that only made her more wary of him. Better-off folk had more power than poorer ones.

'Leek soup followed by roasted mutton chops,' Mr Farrow decreed.

'Do you think mutton is wise, my dear. He will have tasted meat from the new breeds and may think ours inferior.'

'Pork, then. Yes, we shall eat pork. I have a loin on the bone that will do splendidly. Have we apples in the larder to roast with it?'

'Indeed we have, sir.'

'Excellent. And for pudding?'

As they were arguing over this, a caller rapped at the front door.

'Shop's closed,' Mr Farrow called.

'I have a package from the Abbey.'

Three people raised their eyebrows and Daisy hurried to the door. She vaguely recognised the young man who handed her a box-shaped package wrapped in fabric and tied with ribbon. Ribbon? Daisy took it back to the table. 'He said it was for the lady of the house with Mrs Stanton's compliments.'

'Oooh, a gift.' Mrs Farrow smiled and tugged at the ribbon bow. The fabric fell away to reveal a box of sweetmeats bearing the label of a Leeds store. 'Oh look, Mr Farrow. I have seen these in the catalogue at the provisions merchant. They are ever so dear.'

A small card fell from the folds of fabric.

'Oh. Oh, I'm all a-flutter,' Mrs Farrow fussed. 'Oh, Mr

Farrow, she is at home to me. Look! Here are the days. How exciting! She is asking me to call on her!'

'Well now, that is an honour. You must have made a good impression on her.'

'Eee, I think it's our Daisy who's done that. Although there's no reason to send a gift, is there?'

'It'll be a thank you for what you'll have to do for the lass, her not having a mam, like. They'll want to make sure one of their footmen gets a proper wedding.'

'Well, I've seen three of me own lasses wed so I'm sure we can give this one as good a send off. What do you say, Mr Farrow?'

'I say go and see what Mrs Stanton has in mind.'

'Aye. I won't open these now. I'll save them for when Abel Shipton calls.'

Daisy retrieved the ribbon and wound it around her fingers to straighten out the creases. She wasn't comfortable with the way everyone was talking as though she had already agreed to marry Joseph Gardner. She had no desire to go against her or Boyd's employers' wishes but nobody had asked her what she wanted and she did not want to wed Joseph. Sooner or later she must tell them.

Chapter 32

'I must compliment you on the excellence of your table, ma'am.'

Mrs Farrow smiled. 'Thank you, sir, but I cannot take all the credit. Daisy has a sure hand in the kitchen.'

Abel's keen eyes lingered on Daisy and she looked away.

'Shall I make coffee now, Mrs Farrow?'

'Yes, dear, and bring in the sweetmeats. Do you have a taste for coffee, Mr Shipton?'

'I do indeed.'

'Mr Farrow has a liking for it too and we are lucky with our provisions merchant in Redfern. He is not afraid to buy in special goods from Leeds, even when it is not ordered.'

'I am heartened to see the prosperity that the Redfern estate brings to its tenants.'

'It's the coal, sir,' Mr Farrow added. 'Folk have money in their pockets, and since the manufactories have spread along the valley, we have a lot more folk in the Riding.

His lordship has built a whole row of houses for his colliers and he's planning a new village at yon side of his land.'

And they all need feeding, Daisy thought as she cleared away the pudding plates. It is not just the mines and manufactories that gain. Farmers and shopkeepers prospered too. She ground the roasted coffee beans in a little machine Mrs Farrow had bought especially for the purpose and laid up a tray with tiny porcelain coffee cups and saucers, also purchased from the provisions merchant's catalogue. She had buffed the pewter coffee pot, retrieved from the dusty top shelf of a cupboard, and warmed it with hot water. When the coffee was brewed she poured it carefully from the saucepan through muslin into the pot. To her the aroma was intoxicating but she remembered servants at the Abbey who had felt sick at the same smell. In the small dining room, Mrs Farrow served it to her guest from the dresser and offered him her coveted sugared-fruit sweetmeats.

Mr Farrow appeared to be really enjoying himself. 'Now, ladies, Mr Shipton and myself will smoke a cigar so why don't you take the box of sweeties to enjoy in the kitchen?'

Abel responded quickly. 'Perhaps they may stay a little while longer, sir. I have not had a chance to converse with Daisy.'

Daisy looked up sharply. Why should he wish to speak with her? Mrs Farrow also looked surprised.

Mr Farrow laughed. 'Now then, my good fellow, I'll not let you poach the best maid my good lady has ever had.'

Abel joined in the good humour. 'No, sir, I should not be so cruel.'

'Then why are you interested, sir?' Mr Farrow went on.

'I understand that she is more of a daughter to you than a servant.'

342

Suddenly the laughter died and Mrs Farrow's eyes rounded. Daisy saw her exchange a glance with her husband. She spoke carefully. 'Yes, we do think of her as such, sir, and I feel I must tell you that she is spoken for and soon to be betrothed.'

Now it was Abel's turn to be surprised. 'I assure you, sir – and madam – that, truly, I have no such intentions towards her. I am old enough to be her father!'

'That wouldn't stop a fellow,' Mr Farrow said. 'She's lovely enough to land herself a lord.' He grunted. 'Well, the heir, anyway.'

'Mr Farrow! You have said too much!'

Daisy was embarrassed that they were speaking of her in this way. Mr Stanton must have told Mr Farrow why he wished her to be wed so hastily. She blushed to the roots of her hair. For a moment, she concentrated on her hands neatly folded in her lap then thought that they – all of them – should know the truth about *her* feelings and now was the time to tell them. She raised her chin defiantly and surveyed the faces at the table.

Mr Shipton's face was so grave that she faltered. He was shocked! His eyes were – were – almost fearful. He hadn't talked much during the meal. Mr and Mrs Farrow had kept up a lively banter of entertaining conversation. But Daisy reckoned that Abel Shipton absorbed everything. He remembered things and he mulled them over.

'Do I understand correctly?' he queried. 'Daisy is to be betrothed to his lordship's heir?'

'Good God, no!' Mr Farrow spluttered. 'But she will—'

'Mr Farrow! Your language!' Mrs Farrow interrupted.

'—she will be wed within the month,' her husband finished.

343

Within a month! They had decided when she would marry Joseph before he had even been to court her! 'No, I shan't!' Daisy cried. 'I shan't marry him. I don't like him.'

Abel Shipton's eyes darted from one face to another taking in the surprise of Daisy's outburst.

Mrs Farrow became fidgety and hastened to explain. 'Daisy! That is uncalled for!' She smiled weakly at Abel. 'Mr Farrow has taken too much ale and he is confused,' she said. 'What he means is that Daisy has a follower from the Abbey. He is a footman so his lordship must approve of the match and his — his ward is involved in such estate duties. Of course, I do not want to lose Daisy but I shall not stand in the way of his lordship's wishes.'

'Mr Stanton's wishes you mean,' Daisy muttered.

'So just exactly who is it you don't like, Daisy?' Mr Shipton asked, looking directly at her.

'Joseph, the footman,' she replied, holding his gaze.

Mrs Farrow gave a nervous laugh. 'Nonsense. Come along, Daisy, away with you to the scullery now.'

Daisy scraped back her chair, anxious to be excused from further awkwardness. At least she had said it, whether they believed her or not.

Mrs Farrow had to go outside to the privy and Daisy returned briefly to the dining salon with port and glasses. She heard the end of a conversation between the two gentlemen.

'—a relation of a friend of mine.' Abel stopped speaking as soon as she appeared on the threshold.

'Do you want anything else, sir?' Daisy asked and stood quietly waiting for an answer.

Mr Farrow grunted and waved her away, but Mr Shipton said, 'If I have caused you any embarrassment, Daisy, then I apologise.' He raised his eyebrows as though he expected her to respond.

It was not he but her employers who had embarrassed her but she replied graciously, 'Thank you, sir. I am sorry I raised my voice.' She wanted to ask if her father and mother had sent him but no one here knew about them so she bobbed a polite curtsey adding, 'Goodnight, sir. Goodnight, Mr Farrow,' and retreated thankfully to the kitchen.

'By heaven, it's chilly out there tonight.' Mrs Farrow came in with a blast of cold night air and went to stand by the scullery boiler. 'I'll not say any more about your behaviour in front of our guest,' she said to Daisy, adding, 'Not tonight, I shan't anyway. Finish up in here and take yourself off to bed. There's a brick for you in the oven.' She went back to her dining table without another word.

'How can you say you don't like Joseph? You've hardly met him yet.'

A few days later, Mrs Farrow was standing at her kitchen range, beating flour into hot water and lard to make pie crusts. Daisy was preparing wooden moulds and lining them up on the kitchen table. She worked on in silence.

'You see how Saturday goes first, after the hunt. He'll be charm itself. Him being a footman, he knows how to carry on. He has a secure position at the Abbey. And he'll get a cottage! You don't know how lucky you are, my lass.'

'Well, I didn't like the way he looked at me.'

'What do you mean?'

'He was scary, as though – as though, somehow, he thought I wanted – you know – what married people do.' Daisy knew she was blushing and felt uncomfortable.

345

'And don't you want that?'

'Not with him, not even if I am wed to him.'

Mrs Farrow took her pan off the range and set it down on the table with a thump. 'I think you and me will have to have a little talk before your wedding day.' She frowned and tipped out the hot mix on to a board where she began working it with vigour. 'Joseph is a grown man and he'll have his needs,' she added, passing over lumps of paste for Daisy to roll out and shape over the moulds. 'Now leave these to cool while I get on with the filling. I want you to nip down to the provisions shop for a nutmeg.'

Daisy was glad to escape and even more pleased when she saw Boyd riding a pony down the middle of the road. She waved and he dismounted.

'Boyd! What are you doing in the village?'

'I've come to see you.' He stroked the pony's nose. 'And this one needed an outing.'

'I'm on an errand. Meet me in the churchyard in a few minutes.'

They separated and Daisy ran on to the provisions merchant. Boyd was waiting under the trees for her and she hurried towards him, throwing her arms around his neck. He pulled them free and stepped back from her.

'You'll frighten the pony,' he said with a half laugh. 'I've come to talk about Joseph.'

'What for?'

'Well, what do you think of him?'

'I don't like him.'

'Why not? Mr Stanton thinks well of him. Apparently, a lot of the Abbey housemaids would change places with you.'

'Well, why doesn't he marry one of them instead of me?'

346

'Come on, Daisy. You'll have your own little house on the estate and enough money to live on.'

'You said I didn't have to wed if I didn't want to!' she cried. 'Why are you trying to persuade me otherwise?'

'Don't shout at me. I'm trying to do what's best.'

'But it's not what's best for us, is it? It's what's best for Master James.'

'Believe me, Daisy, it'll be better for all of us!'

'Now who's shouting? Why have you changed your mind?'

'We have to let each other go. Don't you understand? My duty is to see you safely wed and – and you have to let me—'

He did not finish his sentence but she understood perfectly. She realised what this was all about. 'I'm a burden to you, aren't I? You want me off your hands.'

'No, of course I don't.'

She didn't believe him. She knew her brother. She was watching his eyes and he didn't mean it. 'Then why—' she began. '—Oh yes, I see now.' All of a sudden her world tumbled around her. Boyd had met someone he cared for. He needed to see his sister safely settled before he declared his own love. 'You have a sweetheart,' she said. Daisy wondered who she was.

'I don't, I don't,' he anguished. 'I wish I did, truly I do.' He took a deep breath and recovered his composure. 'Daisy, you are very attractive but you have a strong will that gets you into trouble and I worry for you. I have tried to do my best by you, but I cannot be mother and father to you. You must marry.'

Daisy didn't understand the whole of what he was saying to her and pleaded, 'Why must I?'

'Because I say you must! Daisy, my precious Daisy, the

Abbey owns this village. It owns the shop where you work and it owns me. I have a good position in the stables. Will you at least make an effort to like Joseph? For me?'

She hadn't realised Boyd was quite so concerned. It wasn't just about her. The Farrows had said as much. It was about both of them, his future, her future, their future. She sighed. There wasn't going to be a future with just her and Boyd. That was what he was trying to say to her. They had to make lives separate from each other. The realisation depressed her and her mood became gloomy. But she would be letting Boyd down if she refused to go along with his wishes. 'Very well,' she replied. 'For you, I'll try. He is coming for tea after the hunt next week.'

The church clock chimed the hour.

'I have to get back before dark,' Boyd said and secured one foot in a stirrup. He swung up onto the pony's back. 'Remember I shall always love you, little sister.'

She nodded wordlessly. There were tears in her eyes but she blinked them back and she waved him away. As she hurried home to Mrs Farrow with nutmeg for the pork pie fillings she realised that she must be practical about her future. She had been fanciful to ever imagine a romantic liaison with Master James. Boyd had advised her from the beginning to be wary of the young master. He was an aristocrat and they did things differently.

The pie cases were waiting, lined up on the kitchen table. The larger ones had a strip of strong brown paper tied round with string to stop the sides sagging in the oven. Bowls of filling stood waiting on the dresser and the smell of bones boiling for the jelly filled her nostrils. Mr Farrow had gone to the inn and Mrs Farrow was upstairs having a lie down, so Daisy was left alone with her thoughts to finish the pies.

Aristocrats didn't wed servants. They used them for – for – the word tightened around her heart – fornication. But Master James did not want her for that. He had said so to her face and she believed him because – because she loved him. The steward might be trying to prevent a scandal, but Boyd, dearest Boyd, was trying to protect her from making a fool of herself with Master James. Had she already done that by their brief exchanges and – and by agreeing to meet him in the hayloft tomorrow? Even now, after all Boyd had told her, she was excited by the prospect. Master James wanted to see her!

James had said he didn't care what others thought and he would do as he wished. He wished to become more acquainted with her. He was attracted to her as much as she was to him. She had to see him tomorrow. She had to. When she dreamed of this, all rational thought fled from her head, all sensible caution was carried away. There was something wholly irresistible about Master James that fired her in a stirring and passionate manner. And that of course, she realised miserably, was the danger.

But she was strong. Did not folk say that to her? Well, strong-willed anyway. But was she strong-willed enough to turn away from Master James when every fibre of her being was urging her to welcome his advances? Perhaps he would not be there, in the hayloft, tomorrow? Perhaps Mr Stanton had spoken with him as firmly as he had done with her? And perhaps Master James had ignored his advice as she did?

The first meeting of the New Year was one of the biggest, drawing in villagers and townsfolk alike. Anyone with a connection to Redfern, if they owned or could hire a suitable mount, was invited to hunt. Mr Farrow's son from the farm was there and, to Daisy's surprise, so was Mr Shipton, smartly turned out on a fine black hunter. He cantered over to say good day to Mr and Mrs Farrow who were hovering on the perimeter in their trap.

'You ride to hounds, sir,' Mr Farrow boomed.

'I was a farmer before I became a stock dealer and your son secured me an introduction. Are you enjoying the spectacle, Mrs Farrow, Daisy?'

'We are, sir,' Mrs Farrow replied.

Daisy avoided his eye but was forced to look at him when he addressed her. 'Mr Farrow was telling me about your brother last night. I hope I shall meet him later.'

Why would he be interested in Boyd? Daisy felt uneasy. He must know who they were and where they came from! He was from Father after all and, no doubt, after Boyd's wages too. Her desolation deepened and she was pleased to be occupied selling pies from the back of the trap. But as the morning wore on and the cacophony of hunting horn, calling and barking receded into the distance her mood began to lift. Every minute took her nearer to James.

'I'll take the rest of the pies to the stables as before, shall I?' she suggested.

'I suppose you may. We don't want them going to waste. Don't be late for tea.'

'My brother will make sure of that, ma'am.'

'Well, Joseph is expected at five and you want to look your best.'

'I have laundered my lace collar and cuffs ready.'

'That's the spirit, my girl,' Mr Farrow responded. He held the reins steady while she climbed down with her basket. 'All the pennies you make today will go towards your bottom drawer.'

350

'Oh, you are so generous, Mr Farrow,' his wife gushed.

The stables were quiet as many of the servants were following the hunt. She left her basket on the mounting stone by the pony stables. The horses were out and she wandered from empty stall to empty stall then went outside to wait for Master James. She noticed him on the edge of the woods taking off his riding hat and swapping jackets with one of the stable lads who was holding his horse. She slipped inside the pony stable door out of sight and was lingering in the dark interior when he arrived. He stood at the foot of the hayloft ladder with the jacket hooked casually over his shoulder and called, 'Daisy, are you up there?'

'Over here.'

'What are you doing hiding in the shadows?' He flung the jacket on a pile of clean straw, crossed the swept floor and put his arms around her, dropping kisses on her hair. 'I thought you might not be here.'

'I haven't long.' Any further conversation was lost in an embrace that squashed the breath out of her, along with all her resolutions to reject his aristocratic advances.

He lifted his head and tipped her chin so she was looking directly into his eyes. 'What's wrong?' He had undone his waistcoat and now he unwound his necktie and opened the top buttons of his shirt. She noticed a spring of dark hair curling at his throat. He took out a small package wrapped in white silk and tied with a narrow red ribbon. 'You're not happy,' he stated, taking hold of her hand. 'Come and sit with me on the straw. Perhaps this will cheer you.'

He handed her the small soft package.

'For me?' She untied her gift carefully. Inside, neatly folded, lay three laced-edged handkerchiefs with beautifully embroidered corners. 'Oh,' she breathed. 'They're daisies, how thoughtful.' She looked up at him with tears in her eyes. 'They are very pretty. Thank you.' How would she explain them to Mrs Farrow? They would have to be her secret. She rewrapped them carefully in the silk and stowed them safely in her skirt pocket.

He sat on the straw stack and tugged at her hand to join him. She resisted an overwhelming urge to throw herself into his waiting arms. Oh, how she would have loved to feel his arms around her. But she replied, 'I cannot.'

'What has happened, Daisy? Why are you unhappy?'

'I shall not be able to meet you after today.'

'I don't understand. Are you going away?'

'No,' she groaned with a choking sob. 'I wish I were. I am to be married.'

'Married? It cannot be. I shall not allow it.'

'Oh, James, even you cannot stop this. You and I can never be together.'

'Don't say that!'

'But it's true! All this – this clandestine meeting is fanciful and – and – has no – no future.'

'It is only secret from my guardian and soon he will be in a higher place. Truly, he does not have much longer. His physicians have advised me so and his lawyers have already written to my real father.'

'And what will your real father say when he hears of our trysts?'

'He has his own secrets and he will understand.'

'It will all be too late,' she cried. 'I have a suitor. My brother approves and Mr Farrow has given his permission. Your steward's wife is already planning the ceremony.'

'Mrs Stanton is involved?'

'My suitor is one of your footmen. He – he is to take tea with me after the hunt today.'

'So this is Stanton's meddling. I see that now. Well, I shall just have to put a stop to it, shan't I?'

'No!' she cried. 'You mustn't!' Her outburst caused him to frown irritably but she went on before he could protest. 'Please don't interfere. Mr Stanton has made my situation clear. If I do not marry I shall have to leave Redfern and Boyd will not let me go alone. He will lose his position and we shall both be homeless.

'Mr Stanton? Mr Stanton? He is not Lord Redfern!'

'But he is in charge of the servants. James, I beg of you, do not approach him. He will lay the blame at my door and Boyd will suffer. Hush! That might be him.' She heard voices from outside and scurried to the door.

'There you are, Boyd,' Daisy said and stepped outside in the bright sunshine. 'I've been looking for you in the stable.'

'Thank goodness you're here. Master James is about some-where. One of the stable lads said his mare went lame. I've had a look at her but she seems fine to me. Still, it was sensible of him not to risk the hunt.' He bit into one of her pies. 'These are good. It was the last one, but you've got quite a few coins in your basket. Come on, I'll walk part of the way to the village with you. I have something to ask you.'

Chapter 33

Daisy glanced back at the closed stable door once and it remained firmly shut. It was most likely to be the last time she would see James alone and her heart felt heavy. It was a silly fantasy of hers but, nonetheless, it was strange how they had both recognised a kindred spirit the moment they had set eyes on each other.

She wondered if she could forget him just as quickly. She thought not. He was under her skin. She did not understand how she could believe that she loved him when she hardly knew him. But she did. It was as though he were already part of her although they had not even kissed. And now she had to forget him.

She heaved a great sigh and said, 'What is it you want to ask me, Boyd?'

'Oh yes. What do you know about Abel Shipton? They say he's a friend of Mr Farrow's farming son.'

Daisy told him what she knew about his occupation and connections. 'I think Father has sent him.'

'Me too. He's been asking me a lot of questions. He actually came looking for me during the hunt.'

'He's been to dinner with the Farrows a couple of times. He said I reminded him of someone.'

They walked for several yards in silence before Boyd went on. 'He was questioning me about you, Daisy. He wanted to know personal things, like he – he might want to court you.'

'Oh it's definitely not that. He's not interested in me in that way. He said so to Mr Farrow. Ask him, he'll tell you.'

'I don't need to. I believe you. I asked him straight why he wanted to know. He wouldn't say until he had spoken again with you, but he hinted that we might have relations in the Dales.'

A cold hand clutched to her heart. 'Relations! He has been sent by Mother and Father, hasn't he? You're almost of age but I'm not.' Daisy suddenly thought of a really good reason to marry Joseph.

'I asked him the same question and he was vague. I didn't know what to make of him. He seems a trustworthy sort of fellow most of the time. But I tell you, Daisy, he was quite secretive. I don't like secrets as well you know. He wanted to know if we knew a vicar called Milo.'

Daisy shook her head at first and then remembered. 'Wasn't he the vicar when we were little and went to Sunday school? He upset Mother by moving to Leeds.'

'Oh yes. I remember. Reverend Miles Milo. Mother said he married for money and secured a better living.'

'She never mentioned any relations in the Dales. She would have done if we had any, wouldn't she?'

'Not if they weren't the religious sort, or she thought they were common,' Boyd answered.

Daisy lapsed into silence at the memory of her own parents. Eventually she said, 'They must still be looking for us.'

'Abel said he met up with them. The church folk put him in touch.'

'He visited the cottage?'

'He said they went funny after we left. Y'know – loony. Anyway they were taken into an almshouse.'

Daisy stared into the distance. 'Perhaps they were always a bit like that.'

Boyd shrugged. 'Who can tell? But they were lucky it was an almshouse and not a workhouse.'

'At least they'll be looked after. We did do the right thing by running away, didn't we, Boyd?'

'Of course we did.' He put his arm around her shoulders and squeezed them. Then seemed to think better of the gesture and moved away from her.

Daisy was getting used this hot and cold behaviour from Boyd. She understood. He was trying to make her more independent of him for both their sakes and she tried her best to struggle with her own beleaguered feelings. Boyd pushed her away in the same manner that she had had to push James away. She felt so alone that she would have welcomed the discovery of new relations anywhere. But she had had enough of fanciful dreams and declared, 'Well, I think Abel Shipton is mistaken.'

'I'm not so sure.'

They walked on in reflective silence and parted on the edge of the village.

'Give Joseph a fair hearing, Daisy,' Boyd said.

'I shall. But I have to be able to care for him a little, don't I?' She hurried down the main street past the inn and the shops until she came to the butcher's. Mrs Farrow was watching for her from the window of her upstairs chamber, and waved excitedly when she saw her. Daisy suppressed a sigh. Everyone seemed to want this marriage; everyone except the prospective bride.

She lay awake for ages that night re-living Joseph's visit. Her first impressions of him were reinforced. He was pompous and patronising, believing himself to be a desirable match for her and the instrument of closer connections between the Farrows and the Abbey. When Mrs Farrow suggested they would be forever in his debt, he readily agreed.

Daisy tried to give him the benefit of the doubt. He was loquacious and cheerful. Her 'dowry' of an estate cottage was generous and tempting bait, and one that few men would refuse. But his behaviour towards her in the scullery set her mind against him for ever.

He had gone out to the privy and she was stacking the tea pots ready to wash later, when a left-over piece of scone fell on the floor and she bent to retrieve it. Then she felt his hand run up the back of her leg and squeeze the flesh of her behind and she would have squealed if he had not stifled her mouth with his other hand. He pulled her upright and breathed, 'Don't make a sound. You wouldn't want to upset Mrs Farrow if I have to tell her of your lewd ways.'

'Yours, you mean,' she tried to say.

He turned her round and pinned her against the rough stone wall, still pressing a hand over her mouth. The hand under her skirts moved around to the front and began stroking her lower abdomen, trailing down between her legs, his probing fingers finding her flesh through the opening in her drawers.

'Stop it,' she mumbled.

357

'Not on your life. It's what married folk do and we're as good as.'

'We are not,' she muttered through his fingers.

He ignored her, pressed the full length of his body hard against hers and plonked his open mouth over her lips. She flailed around with her hands and managed to knock a plate to the floor so that it shattered noisily on the flags. She heard a door open and, thankfully, he released her as Mrs Farrow called, 'Daisy!'

'Coming, Mrs Farrow,' she answered.

'Better get back in there.' Joseph shoved her in the middle of the back. 'I'll follow in five minutes.'

Daisy fled from the scullery. The incident troubled her and disturbed her sleep that night so she was awake when the church clock chimed the hour. But it wasn't the clock. It was the Big Bell, and the deep sonorous bong continued, one note, one repetitive note. She heard Mrs and Mrs Farrow climb out of bed and raise a window. There were voices, shouting, coming from the street. Something was amiss! A flood? A fire? Daisy scrambled out of bed, pulled on her cloak and went on to the small landing. The single bell from the church tower continued to ring.

'What is it?' she called. 'What's happening?'

The door to the front bedchamber opened and Mrs Farrow appeared with a lighted candle.

'He's gone,' she said vacantly. 'After all these years, he's gone.'

Daisy's lack of sleep had made her irritable and she demanded, 'Who?'

'Lord Redfern, of course. Who else? He slipped away in the early hours.'

Mr Farrow appeared beside her. 'Best get yourself dressed

and the range going, lass. The whole village will be up and about soon.'

'Over here, Boyd.' Daisy jumped up and down to see over the heads of folk lining the main street in Redfern Village. The sash window above her head slid open and Mrs Farrow leaned out.

'Come inside quickly, before you are both crushed to your de—' Her head disappeared inside abruptly as Mr Farrow yanked her back.

Daisy took hold of Boyd's hand and dragged him down the side of the shop to the backyard, into the house and up the stairs to Mr and Mrs Farrow's front bedchamber.

'Come along in, lad,' Mr Farrow said. 'You two young 'uns kneel in the front then we can see over you.'

'How long can you be away from the stables?' Daisy asked.

'I have to be back before the carriages arrive from church. I've never seen so many lined up along the driveways. Every grand family in the country must be here.'

'It'll take 'em an hour to fill the church and just as long to empty. We've been told there's no room for us villagers. Most have taken up positions on Church Rise for a view of the churchyard.'

'Who are these people out here, then?'

'They've come from all over the county to pay their last respects. There's not many folk that don't benefit from Redfern Abbey one way or another.'

'Here they come!'

Daisy watched in silence as a procession of grand carriages, many with ornate coats of arms painted on the doors and black leatherwork on their horses, rolled slowly down the main street. Drivers and liveried footmen wore dark coats and sombre expressions. The coffin rumbled past covered by the Redfern standard and resting on a black bier drawn by two black horses with black plumes on the heads. An open carriage followed carrying Master James accompanied by a thick-set older man with a swarthy ruddy face who was vaguely familiar to Daisy.

Daisy stared at James. He was dressed in black and wore a tall hat. His countenance, as Daisy expected, was serious. But he appeared so very sad that she wanted to rush out and comfort him with hugs and kisses. Her sentiment was so strong that she had to blink back tears. Onlookers were standing on boxes and even chairs brought along for the purpose of securing a good view of the visiting gentry that followed the chief mourners.

'Who is the gentleman with Master James, sir? I saw him arrive at the Abbey on horseback,' Boyd asked Mr Farrow.

'That's his real father. He's stayed at the Reddy Arms recently.'

'I didn't know he had a father.'

'I did,' Daisy said. 'Why doesn't he live at the Abbey?'

'Ooh, there was a scandal to do with his mother and grandmother,' Mrs Farrow replied. 'I heard his lordship – his late lordship, that is – tried to cut them out of any inheritance, but he couldn't break the entail.'

Her husband added, 'It's the same with all big estates. It all goes to the nearest male heir. Keeps it together for future generations, you see.'

'Yes, I do see,' Boyd said. 'Wouldn't his father have had to run things for James anyway, as he is not yet one and twenty?'

'Eighteen's old enough to inherit a title. Queen Victoria ruled from the start without a regent.' Mr Farrow chuckled.

'I heard that old King William hung on until she was eighteen just to spite her mother who was desperate to be regent.'

Mrs Farrow was peering at James and his father as their coach moved forward. 'He's the new Lord Redfern, then. The one that wasn't allowed anywhere near the Abbey.'

'Can't stop him now, can he?' Boyd commented. 'I wonder if he'll make a lot of changes.'

Daisy was thinking about James. How awful for him to lose the only family he had known, even though his lordship was reputed to be a bitter old man. James had no brothers or sisters to turn to and now he had to mourn in a most public manner with a father who was all but a stranger to him. She wanted to be with him, to be by his side as he grieved. 'Shall we go and see the burial?' Daisy asked. 'We can try round the back of the churchyard?'

'Your best bet is the big cedar tree,' Mr Farrow suggested. 'I climbed it reg'lar when I was a lad. It'll give you a fine view of the Redfern vault.'

'I don't think so for Daisy.' Mrs Farrow sounded shocked. 'You'll rip your gown.'

'Oh please, Mrs Farrow. I'll be careful. Boyd will see to that.'

Mr Farrow came to her rescue. 'Let her go, dear. There'll not be another spectacle like this for a generation. Hurry along though. I won't be the only one who's remembered the cedar.'

He was right and the highest of the thick spreading branches was taken. Boyd made a back and Daisy took hold of a hand offered from above. Someone came after Boyd and made a stirrup for him to climb after her. Before long the ancient tree was laden with young folk sitting and standing amongst the strong branches. They were near enough to hear the singing inside the packed church, and the silence when it stopped.

The bell tolled again and two clergymen came out slowly. Daisy heard snatches of a conversation from beneath her. 'The old rector is to retire.' 'This new fellow is tekking over.' 'Oh yes, he has a wife and family.' 'Aye, there'll be a bit of life in the rectory now.'

The single repetitive ring continued as the coffin came out on the shoulders of six tall men. Mr Stanton was one of the front coffin bearers and, Daisy inhaled sharply, Joseph was there too. He really must be an honoured and trusted servant. She grimaced and thought, I bet his butler has no idea how he can behave towards ladies.

Master James and his father followed the coffin. A procession of grand gentlemen in regal or military uniforms wearing black arm bands came after them and stood around the Redfern vault. It was a large stone-built mausoleum with steps to the crypt below ground. The coffin disappeared first. The clergy continued their prayers as mourners filed one by one into the crypt and emerged from the other side. A significant group, however, stayed above ground and bowed their heads.

'Boyd?' Daisy gave him a nudge. 'Isn't that Abel Shipton? He's that tall fellow at the back?'

'I do believe it is. How come he got a seat in the church?'

'I don't know.' But Daisy watched as James detached himself from his father's side and moved amongst the mourners. Daisy couldn't see his face but he was standing quite straight and she thought he was being very brave. The clergymen came to speak with him but the old rector moved away after a moment. Then she was surprised to see James's father approach the new vicar and embrace him in a way that suggested they were well acquainted. The other mourners began to disperse as their carriages appeared at the churchyard gate to take them to the Abbey.

The villagers crowding the churchyard perimeter started to move away and someone in the cedar tree announced free ale and a good spread at the Reddy Arms.

'I'd better be getting back to the stables,' Boyd said. He dropped easily from the branch and held out his arms to catch Daisy as she pushed herself off her temporary perch. She fell onto him heavily but he didn't budge an inch. Strong, steady Boyd, he was her rock and she clutched at him. He hugged her back for the briefest second then stepped away. 'I've not had a chance to ask you how you got on with Joseph.'

'I don't like him,' she said.

'Why not?' He sounded surprised.

She looked at the ground and didn't answer.

'You ought to tell me, Daisy.'

She lifted her shoulders in a shrug.

'Look, everywhere is shut for the day so why don't you come back to the stables with me? There's a spread in one of the barns for the outdoor servants.'

'Will Joseph be there?'

'He'll be waiting on the gentry today.' He gazed at her for a moment. 'You really don't like him, do you?'

She shook her head.

Boyd blew out his cheeks. 'What am I going to do with you, eh? Run and tell Mrs Farrow where you're going and we'll cut across the park to the stables.'

Daisy's eyes roved around the churchyard hoping for one last glimpse of James. He was talking to his father.

* * *

'The carriage is waiting to take us back to the Abbey, Pater.'

'I'm not going.' Edgar had already had more than enough of this celebration for the life of a man he hated.

'The mourners will expect you, sir.'

'And have all the South Riding gentry staring at me and asking questions?'

'You are Lord Redfern now, Pater.'

'I can't do it alone. I've not lived among them as you have and I need – look, son, why don't you do it for me. You are acquainted with them.'

'Certainly, if that is what you wish. The villagers will want you to put in an appearance at the Redfern Arms as well.'

'I've told you, I can't do it.' He moved from side to side, hesitating over how much to say. 'I have to talk to you, James, to explain things.'

'What things?'

'I'll ride over to the Abbey tomorrow when they're gone.'

'You said your home was ten miles distant. It will be too much for you, especially in this cold weather. I'll come to you.'

But Edgar was firm. He wanted to find out how much James knew about Prudence before his son met her. 'No,' he said. 'I mean it. I do not invite you.'

'Then at least let me send my carriage.'

'*My* carriage.'

'Sorry, Pater.'

Edgar's shoulders sagged. 'You've been schooled well for the role of lord. Send my horse to the rectory as soon as you can.'

'I shall instruct Stanton to see to it personally. You will – I mean, you can be a proper father now, if – if you wish it.'

'Of course I wish it! I had no desire to give you up to that – that tyrant in the first place.'

'Then why do you not stay with me now, at the Abbey?'

James was pleading with him and Edgar grimaced. He muttered, 'You don't understand.'

'What shall I say to your waiting guests?'

'Tell them – tell them I am speaking with my tenants and giving surety about their futures.'

Edgar was aware that he should have returned to the Abbey with James, but he hadn't expected this day to be so difficult. He didn't know the mourners and they didn't know him. If only Mrs Wortley were by his side instead of this boy. His boy, he corrected himself. But he was no longer a boy so maybe he would understand, if he could talk to him about her first. Milo understood, even if he didn't approve. Edgar needed to speak with James and Milo before he visited the lawyers again. But here, today, was not the place or the time.

Daisy did not take her eyes off James until he disappeared from view. Then she watched his father talking to the new vicar and, to her surprise, Abel Shipton walked over to join them.

'Did you see that, Boyd?' she said.

He grasped her wrist and responded, 'Do come on, Daisy. I'm needed at the stables.'

Reluctantly, Daisy stumbled after her brother.

Chapter 34

Edgar refused to acknowledge the man who had cuckolded him all those years ago and moved away, leaving his friend Milo to get rid of him. He blamed Abel Shipton for ruining his mother's plans. But in reality, Edgar knew it was the despot he had just buried that had done that by insisting he give up his son. He had never stopped hating him for that. Still, his mother had died knowing her grandson was living the life she wanted for him, and she had never known the truth about how Edgar had funded her last few years on earth. She would have enjoyed living in the Redfern Dower House marshalling a brigade of servants, he reflected.

The housekeeper at the rectory was busy preparing roast venison for the old rector's final dinner with the new vicar after the wake. She made no comment when Edgar arrived to wait for his horse and when she offered him her meat-and-potato pie luncheon, he accepted and asked for a bottle of claret to go with it. Clergymen always kept a good cellar. He was not disappointed and finished the bottle with slices of stilton and plum cake. He considered opening another, but was anxious to be on his way.

As soon as his horse appeared, he left and spent a couple of hours riding the vast tracts of land that were now his. *His*. Yet he didn't want any of it if he couldn't share it with Prudence. They could have enjoyed life here for years if it hadn't been for his great-uncle's intransigence. Everyone had danced to his lordship's tune. Well, he was his lordship now and he was giving the orders.

He could do what he liked and if that meant bringing his mistress to live with him in the Abbey, then so be it. Dear God, the stories of revelry and fornication that he'd heard of Abbey life in the old Regent's day were nothing compared with his comparatively quiet life now. He needed Prudence by his side and to hell with protocol and these new Victorian virtues the preachers preached of. Why should the morals of some Germanic princess with a French name dictate his future?

But even his friend Milo had changed as he'd married and grown older and he didn't want to risk Prudence being shunned by church or gentry. He had to be firmly established as the new Lord Redfern before he introduced her. The farmers' wives and villagers might gossip to begin with, but not the servants. They knew better.

He was Lord Redfern now and he could do as he wished. In spite of feeling cold he was cheered by this thought – and by the last of the brandy from his pocket flask. He spurred his horse to a gallop to tell Prudence of his decision.

His body ached from the ride and he was hungry when he arrived at Ellis House. But he was in good spirits. Damn his ageing limbs! His left arm in particular always suffered from holding the reins.

Prudence was dressing for dinner as he arrived. His butler and cook were busy preparing for the meal. 'I'll be another hour,' he told them, took a slice of cold pie from the larder and climbed the stairs two at a time. But he had to stop and catch his breath on the landing. He swallowed the rest of the pie in chunks, wiped his mouth with the back of his hand and tried to square his shoulders. His chest was hurting from the cold but no matter. He was Lord Redfern. He ruled the biggest estate in the Riding. It had been a long time coming but no one – *no one* – could take it away from him now.

Prudence was holding on to the bedpost while her maid heaved on the laces in her corset. She saw him in the doorway through her long cheval glass and told her maid to leave them. He came up behind her, placed his purple face on her shoulder beside her white one and began loosening the laces.

'It's almost time for dinner,' she murmured.

'I told them to delay.' The corset dropped away and he covered her large soft breasts with his hands. Then he stroked her belly and rump, his fingers squeezing her flesh, before they reached between her legs. 'How would you like to be Lady Redfern and live at the Abbey?'

He watched her face in the mirror and her eyes widened. 'Is it possible? What about your wife?'

'She's been mad for years. I'll put her in an asylum and then divorce her.'

'Divorce? Won't that cost a fortune?'

'I'm a wealthy man now.'

Prudence looked away so he would not see her triumphant smile in the glass. She'd have a title, the grandest home in the Riding and as much money as she needed! It was well worth the humiliations she had suffered over the years as Edgar's mistress.

'Will it not cause an enormous scandal, dearest one?'

'Not if she's declared insane. The judge will understand. Besides, I'm rich and I can have anything I want.' His fingers stroked back and forth between her legs, his way of telling her what he wanted from her.

Her hands crept behind her body to fondle him. She didn't need to arouse him. His blood was up already. She knew what he expected. 'Oooh,' she protested mildly. 'Oooh, Lord Redfern is awake and arisen! Does he want his way with me now?' She wiggled her bottom from side to side and held onto the bed post, hoping he would do it standing up and get it over with quickly.

Edgar relished the way she gave in to him at any time he wanted her, no matter where. It gave him a sense of power, something he craved over any woman he met. He might have driven into her there and then if he had not been fully clothed. But he needed to feel his skin on hers, be on top of her, in control, dominating her. The anticipation made his breathing more laboured. 'Get these things off me,' he ordered hoarsely, 'and mind my left arm.'

It was not only his arm that ached. His chest hurt too. The long ride in the cold air had not done him any favours. But a rut with Prudence would soon heat him up and, afterwards, another bottle of claret would keep him warm.

Prudence Wortley removed his clothing with practised ease and marvelled just as readily at the disgusting sight of his grossly distended offering poking out from under his lardy belly. He gave her the familiar jerk of his head which meant 'on the bed'. She slid off her chemise and drawers and lay

369

face down lifting her round white rear for his pleasure. He hoisted himself over her and jabbed around until he pushed into her and he was away, heaving and grunting, causing rucks and wrinkles on the silken bedcovers.

She had taught herself not to think of him when he did it to her. He was a noisy animal of a man who seemed to have learned his technique from the farmyard, so she closed her eyes and counted her gowns and pairs of shoes and – and – this time she dreamed of jewels. He was very generous to her when he was in funds, although sometimes she had to wait far too long for him to replenish her allowance. As he pumped away growling like a bear, she took her gratification from the fact that she was now the mistress of a very rich lord who was, actually, rather dependent on her.

She had begun as his housekeeper, having grown too old to earn a living in Leeds as a provincial courtesan for travelling gentry. But she retained the skills of her former occupation and offered him more than a well-run home. Everything a wife might offer in fact.

He said often that he adored her. Now, he'd told her he was going to move heaven and earth to make her his wife. She never imagined that. Ageing mistresses don't expect marriage as a rule and she was no different. But when the stakes are high and there's a title involved, it was not a situation to be denied. She was to be Lady Redfern! She wondered if she'd have a tiara. He'd be sure to give her jewels and a proper carriage of her own with a pair of matching horses to draw it.

Dear God, he was making more noise than usual, but then he always sounded like a stuck pig and he yelled out obscenities when he shed his seed. What a pity it was too late for her to become with child. She'd stopped using a sponge when she stopped her bleeding so there was no chance for that. Edgar wasn't bothered. He told her he'd once had a son and that was enough for him. She winced. He was slavering over her and she could feel the dribble on the back of her neck. Now he was groaning and – and slowing. Slowing? He didn't normally slow down. Generally he hammered her at full tilt until he'd finished. He was gibbering away at something. His title must have gone to his head for he wasn't making sense. Oh well, he'd finish soon and collapse on top of her and go to sleep as usual. She would have to wait for his snoring before she tried to move.

James had ridden alone in his father's carriage to the Abbey, where Mr Stanton was waiting anxiously.

'Where is his lordship?'

'He – he is meeting with his villagers to – to reassure them about their futures.'

'His guests are gathering in the long drawing room. They have wine and biscuits but they wish to pay their respects.'

'I shall receive them on his behalf.'

'Very well. You are more of a lord than he will ever be.'

'You speak of my father, sir.'

'I beg your pardon. It was meant as praise for you and not—'

'Yes, yes,' James interrupted. 'Make sure my father's horse is taken to the rectory stable immediately.'

'I shall attend to it personally, sir.'

James straightened his shoulders, took a deep breath and nodded. A footman opened the doors to the long drawing room.

* * *

In a large barn near to the stables, the outdoor servants were tapping a barrel of ale sent over for the wake, along with cold meats and smoked fish laid out on a board. Boyd had been called upon to saddle and ride a horse to the rectory and Daisy had walked outside to watch for his return. The gravity of the occasion had little effect on the younger servants who were glad of a day off their routine grind, whilst the older ones were talking in groups and speculating on how the new Lord Redfern would change things. Boyd was out of breath from running when he returned.

'I called in to see Mr and Mrs Farrow and asked if you could stay late so that you could see Joseph.'

'But you know I don't like him!' she protested.

'He may not have time to come over to the stables anyway. But it means that we can have a proper talk at last, about what you really want.'

'Why can't I be just as I am?'

'Because we both want to stay here,' he answered.

They lapsed into silence.

Eventually, Daisy suggested, 'I know! Show me the ponies, Boyd.'

'Very well.' They changed direction away from the noisy barn and Boyd continued, 'Do you remember the tall fellow talking to the new lord and his vicar in the churchyard.'

'Abel Shipton?'

'I saw him outside the Reddy Arms. He's got something to say to you and he wanted me to be with you when he said it. He's riding over later. Are you sure he hasn't made advances on you?'

'I think I'd know if he had. I don't want to speak to him. I think he's from Father.'

'Don't take on so. Father can't touch us now.'

Boyd opened the pony stables and checked on each of the occupants while Daisy stroked the noses of her favourites and fed them morsels of chopped carrot. The pony stable reminded her of James and she felt a cosy warmth inside her when she thought of him. But he'd looked so sad at the funeral that she worried about him and stood gazing at the whitewashed walls wondering if – no, hoping that he was well.

'There's a footman looking for you two.' An under-gardener and his wife had strolled by and saw the stable door open. 'He's in the barn.' They wandered on.

'It'll be Joseph. Go and tell him you can't find me. Oh please, Boyd. He's horrid! Truly! When we were alone in the scullery he tried to—' She stopped, unable to find the words.

'Tried to what?'

'You know.' She hunched her shoulders. 'Kiss me and – and that.'

'And what?' Boyd demanded.

'He said we were as good as married and it wasn't wrong.'

'What did he do to you, Daisy?'

'He – he wouldn't let me go even when I asked him.'

'What did he do, Daisy?' Boyd insisted.

'He put his hand under my skirts and – and touched me where he shouldn't.

'I'll kill him! So help me God, I'll kill him.'

'I wish you would but you mustn't because they'll hang you and then I'll have nobody.'

'I can give him a thumping he won't forget.'

'Well, don't. You'll be in trouble and I'd rather you just sent him away. I never asked for him to court me.'

'I'll see what I can do. Stay here with the ponies.'

Daylight was beginning to fail already and the noise from

the barn was getting louder. It didn't seem right to Daisy to be celebrating a death with such revelry. But she supposed they were drinking to the old lord's life and welcoming the new one. She wondered how James was feeling about his loss.

Boyd was gone a long time so she closed up the stables and went for a walk to warm her feet. Away from the barn she heard the sounds of carriages from across the park and the glimmer of flares to light up the driveways. There was a folly to one side of the expanse of grass and trees and Daisy headed in that direction. A brisk walk there and back would revive her flagging spirits. As she neared the dome-shaped building fronted by four stone pillars she became fascinated by its purpose. She probably wasn't allowed inside but no one would see her in the dark and she quickened her step.

Inside, the folly was small, round and very high. But there were signs of use. An old chair, a horse blanket, even an oil lamp. She wished she had means to light it for it was getting dark. But as her eyes got used to the gloom she saw that it was clean, with a covering of dry brown leaves on the floor, blown in during the autumn. It must be dry too, for they rustled as she moved them around with her boot. She wrapped herself in the blanket and sat on the rickety chair. From the doorway she could see the last of the carriages rattling down the driveway before they disappeared into the trees towards the lodge gates.

She must have dozed for the next thing she knew she was aware of a dull thumping and opened her eyes. It was a few moments before her eyes got used to the darkness, by which time the runner whose feet were pounding on the grass was upon her. She stood up, her mind racing with excuses for her trespass.

Chapter 35

He was panting heavily and he leaned his back against the outside stonework. He was – she hurried to the doorway – he was sobbing in a strangled, desperate way. It was James and he was distressed. 'Why?' he cried. 'Why?'

'James?'

'Who's there?' He inhaled raggedly. 'Show yourself.'

'It's me, Daisy.'

He whirled around to get a full view of her. 'Daisy? What are you doing here?'

'I – I was walking—'

'Daisy. My dearest Daisy. God has sent you to comfort me, Hold me, will you? Please.'

She placed her arms around him and he bent his head to rest on her shoulder. 'What's wrong, James? Tell me.'

His voice was muffled by her clothing and it took him a few moments to compose himself. 'A letter arrived, from my father's house, written not an hour since.' He took a deep shuddering breath. 'He's dead, Daisy. My father, my real father, is dead.'

'But – but – but – surely it cannot be so? Was he not with you at the burial today?'

He shook his head in the crook of her neck and shoulder. 'He's gone. Just when we had a chance to get to know each other, he's gone.'

James seemed to have lost his strength as he leaned on her and Daisy staggered under his weight. She held him for a few moments longer, not wanting to let him go but fearing she might collapse beneath him. She turned her head to kiss his ear and his hair and whispered, 'Why don't you sit down, my love.' The endearment slipped out without thinking.

'My love,' he repeated and his lips brushed her cheek as he moved. He sat in the chair with his elbows on his knees and his head in his hands until his ragged inhaling had eased.

It was such a cruel blow for him. Daisy hated to see him so distressed and was hurting with him. Tears were welling in her eyes. She stroked the back of his head, gently smoothing his thick dark hair with her fingers. Weeping helped with grieving and she felt his grief as though it were her own. She had no idea of the time, of how long she stood there, or when the weeping ceased, or of how her arms came to be locked around his body, hugging him tightly. Her cloak fell from her back to the floor.

He kissed her gently at first, then more insistently, exploring the contours of her features and murmuring her name. Dear heaven, how she had longed for him to do that! The only sound in the surrounding silence was their hushed breathing and the rustle of clothing as his hands moved over her curves, tightly corseted in her best gown. The desire to throw off that gown and restricting corset to enjoy a more intimate

376

closeness with him was overwhelming. There was an urgency about his lips and fingers as though he wanted the same, to be nearer, nearer, as near as a man could be to the woman he loved. He needed her and wanted and – and excitement rippled through her – she was unable to stop him because she did not wish to.

He discarded his jacket and pulled her to the ground. She did not resist because she could not. I truly love him, she realised, and he must love me. It had been inevitable since the first day she had seen him, queuing for her quarterly pay in the Abbey. There was something intangible between them that was strong enough for others to notice. They may not approve but they could not stop it and her heart pounded in her ears.

He was nuzzling her hair and kissing her ears. 'Daisy, this cannot be. You are betrothed to Joseph.'

'I am not. Oh please don't stop. I don't love Joseph. I love you.'

'And I love you.' His lips moved to her chin and cheeks and whispered, 'But this is – this is dangerous madness. I do not want to hurt you.'

She was aware that if she allowed him to continue the outcome would be shame and degradation for her. Her reputation would be lost for ever. Joseph most certainly would not want her if he knew she had been taken by another. But to be loved by James – the thought chased away any consideration of propriety on her part.

'You can never hurt me, James,' she breathed.

He groaned weakly. 'You are so beautiful,' he whispered. 'I have been drawn towards you since I first set eyes on you.'

Daisy was in heaven. James loved her and was making love to her, proper love, real love. She shifted her head so that her

377

lips brushed his. As she did a glimmer of light crossed her vision. She was mesmerised by the dancing lamp as it came closer to the doorway. Then she heard the voice.

'Master James! Are you in there?'

James went rigid and his eyes locked on hers. 'Stanton! Good God, he is searching for me.' He rolled to one side and sat up, waiting to be discovered.

'Master James! I thank God I have found you.' He stood in the doorway and held the lamp high. 'Miss Higgins?' Then he added more strongly, 'Miss Higgins! What are you doing in here?'

'Don't speak to her in that tone. She is not one of your servants.'

'She is betrothed to one. What do you think you are doing?'

'You forget, sir, that I am no longer your charge.'

'I do not, *my lord*. But I expect better from you than to find you cavorting with a village wench.'

Daisy sat up sharply and retrieved her cloak, dragging it about her shoulders. 'I am no village *wench,* sir!'

'Indeed you are! You and Joseph are well matched. Master James needs protection from your wily ways and my housemaids need protection from him.'

My God, she thought. That is the reason he was chosen for her. She snapped, 'Yes I can well believe that. He is not to be trusted with anyone wearing skirts! How dare you use me so.'

James stood up and confronted his steward. 'What is this mischievous game you play, Stanton?'

The older man calmed and his shoulders sagged. 'Come away from her, my lord. Everything is different now.'

Daisy watched her beloved James crumple in the lamplight.

He covered his face with his hands and sank into the creaking chair. 'For a few brief moments with Daisy my life was tolerable. Now it is shattered again.'

Daisy scrambled towards him and held his head against her body. 'Leave him be, Mr Stanton. Can't you see how much he is grieving?'

Mr Stanton stepped across the threshold to retrieve James's jacket from the floor. She heard more voices outside. Dear heaven, how many does it take to escort his lordship home? The space became crowded as two more figures both carrying lanterns appeared in the open doorway.

'We heard raised voices.'

'Daisy! I have been searching for you. Do you know the hour?'

'Boyd?' Her voice was weak and tearful.

He stood in front of her taking in the picture of her crumpled cloak and dishevelled hair, and of the way she was cradling James against her. Daisy tightened her grip on James. She was unhappy and confused. She wanted to be alone with James, to comfort him as only she could. Yet, as Boyd stared at her, she reached out searching for his hand. If she grasped it he would give her the strength she needed for James.

Boyd straightened her cloak around her shoulders but he did not touch her and her arm dropped to her side. He said, 'I'll take you home, Daisy.'

James slowly turned his head. His words were muffled by Daisy's body close to his mouth. 'She is coming with me to the Abbey.'

'She is not, sir. She is my sister and I shall guard her reputation even if you will not.'

Another stronger voice interceded. 'Please, do as Boyd suggests, Miss Higgins.'

Daisy recognised Abel Shipton. He had been standing silently in the doorway. Now, he lifted his lantern and stepped forward. In the pool of yellow light his bearded face was grim. 'I should have spoken sooner. This must stop.'

'And who are you, my good man?' Mr Stanton demanded.

'Abel Shipton, sir. I am the owner of High Fell Farm in the Dales.'

James gave Daisy a small push so that he could see Abel more clearly and responded sharply. 'You are a liar, sir, High Fell is my – my father's farm.'

Daisy felt isolated as James stood up to challenge the stranger. She was distressed and confused, but above all, concerned for James in his grief and moved forward towards him. Abel must have noticed because he handed his lantern to Boyd and quickly placed himself between James and her. He spoke softly. 'You have to let him go, Miss Higgins.'

'Who are you to tell me what to do?' She attempted unsuccessfully to push Abel aside.

Boyd tried to separate them and a scuffle developed until Boyd cried, 'Stop this, Abel. You say you are a friend but can you not see my sister is upset?'

Daisy turned and flung her arms around her brother. She had not forgotten that he had asked her not to behave towards him in this way. But at this moment he was the only person she could rely on to have her best interests at heart and she needed him. 'Who is he, Boyd?' she pleaded. 'Who is Abel Shipton?'

For a few brief and precious moments, he held her as he used to and she felt safe. And then he gently kissed the top of her head and stood back from her. 'He has something to tell us both. He says it is important.'

James stood up, his clothes were awry but he spoke with

the authority of his status. 'Whatever irks you may be dealt with at some other time, sir. You will be good enough to leave now.'

Abel stood firm. 'I shall not go until these young people know the truth.'

Mr Stanton weighed in on James's side. 'You will, sir. The Abbey is in mourning.'

'This truth should be known now.'

James was younger and smaller than Abel but he faced him and responded, 'The truth? None of you know the truth! The truth is that on the day of my guardian's funeral, the day when I may meet freely and speak with my own—' His voice cracked and Daisy took a hasty step in his direction only to be restrained by Boyd and Abel. James continued, 'My own true father.' His head and body sagged. 'My father died today.'

'What?' The cry came from Abel, who was clearly stunned by this news. He directed his query at Mr Stanton. 'Is this true?'

His reply was a brief nod and, 'A rider came with a letter not an hour ago. We are all deeply upset.'

Abel repeated his question. 'Edgar Collins is dead?'

James responded, 'Did you know him?'

'I leased the fields at High Fell before – before you were born. I have not lied to you, sir.'

'Then you must have been acquainted with my mother?' James asked.

Abel glanced at Daisy and she noticed an uneasiness, a wariness even, in his eyes. He said, 'Forgive me. I was not aware of Edgar's passing. This is, indeed, too much grief for everyone. But my business does concern you, sir, and it is of an urgent nature. Perhaps we may speak in the morning?'

381

'Thank you, sir,' James answered. 'Come to the Abbey at ten.'

Abel addressed Stanton. 'I wonder, sir, if you would take Miss Higgins into the care of your good lady wife for the night.'

'That isn't necessary,' Boyd said. 'I shall see her safely home.'

Daisy glanced at Abel. She thought he had a handsome, if lined, face underneath his dark beard. But his features were totally expressionless as he responded to her brother, 'The hour is late and Mr Stanton's house is nearer than the village. I'll return with you to the stables for my horse.'

Boyd seemed satisfied and said to Daisy, 'Mrs Stanton is a kindly lady. She will look after you.'

Daisy remembered her last visit to Mrs Stanton to meet the awful Joseph. 'James?' she murmured. In the yellow lantern light he looked exhausted and his eyes were sad. But he smiled at her, took her hand and kissed it softly. 'Until tomorrow, Daisy.' She was desperate to take him in her arms and hold him and all she could do was watch him set off, alone, with a lantern to cross the park to the Abbey.

Chapter 36

Mrs Stanton was indeed a very kindly lady. Her own children were long since grown and wed and Daisy spent a comfortable if restless night in a charmingly furnished chamber. She found it difficult to comprehend that James was now Lord Redfern. She had felt so comfortable in his presence that he never seemed much different from her in spite of their diverse backgrounds. But, on reflection, it was Boyd who had seemed more concerned for her and she was glad that he had been there to support her last night. Abel, too, had seemed to have her best interests at heart and she felt less alone as watched the dawn break.

A neatly presented maid brought her hot water to wash and she breakfasted with her temporary guardians in their dining room. Boyd and Abel Shipton were waiting outside for them as they donned warm cloaks and all five of them set off to walk to the Abbey.

Boyd was quiet. He linked arms as they walked and he

smiled at her. But his eyes were troubled. The three older people followed them silently.

'Will Joseph be there?' she asked him anxiously.

'You do not have to marry him,' he answered and squeezed her arm gently. 'Don't fret, Daisy. Abel said that no one will demand it after today.'

'Will I have to go back to Mother and Father?'

'Abel has assured me that he really, truly, has no connection with our father.'

'Then what is it that must be known?'

'He will tell us when we are all together.'

'But why has it anything to do with James?'

'He is Lord Redfern now. Everything that happens on his estates is his business.' She clutched his arm more tightly and he went on, 'Do not fear. I shall be with you.'

Daisy's heart swelled. She seemed to have her old brother back. The one she trusted, who always had her welfare at heart and who made her feel safe. She had missed him dreadfully when he had distanced himself from her.

James was waiting for them in a small drawing room overlooking the park. The morning room, his butler called it. Daisy was relieved that there was no sign of Joseph. James appeared to have grown in stature overnight. The butler addressed him as 'my lord' and his expression was grave. Abel Shipton waited until the ladies were seated. The gentlemen chose to remain standing.

'My lord,' Abel began, 'you were correct in your assumption that I knew your mother. I had planned to enlighten all concerned last evening, but events for which we are deeply sorry overtook me. I must not keep silent any longer and I sincerely hope that what I have to say will not cause prolonged distress. I have been anxious to be relieved from the burden of my knowledge and yesterday at the folly my anxiety escalated.'

He paused to exchange a querying glance at the assembled party.

'Your information concerns my mother?' James prompted.

'And Miss Higgins.'

Daisy wished she was sitting next to Boyd on the couch instead of Mrs Stanton. Nonetheless she reached across her full skirts and took hold of the older woman's hand resting on her lap. Mrs Stanton gave her fingers a reassuring squeeze.

James responded, 'I understand why Stanton might wish to separate us. But you, sir, have no such allegiance.'

Mr Stanton went to stand beside James as though he were his protector. Daisy could not see Boyd. He had moved to the rear of the chamber.

'I have, my lord,' Abel replied. 'I have made a promise to your mother. She is well and resides at High Fell Farm.'

'You are acquainted with my mother? She is not mad?' James was visibly shaken and took the chair offered by Mr Stanton.

'She has been very ill, so ill that for a time all hope of a normal life was lost. But she has received the best medical attention and is blessed with a sound constitution.'

'My father did not speak of a physician for her.'

'No, sir.' Abel hesitated. 'I believe he did not know of her treatment for he never visited.'

James turned to his steward. 'Stanton, did you know of this?'

'I did not, sir.'

'You must have! My father did not ask me to pay for her physician and who else would foot the bills?'

'High Fell Farm has income, my Lord,' Abel answered. 'The land is leased to Fellwick Hall.'

385

'But you have said the farm is yours,' James stated and demanded, 'Who are you, sir, and what are you to my mother?'

Daisy noticed that, underneath his beard, Abel's features were pale and strained. She knew him from his acquaintance with the Farrows and at the hunt as a man who was self-assured in all levels of company. But he was finding this interview difficult and his response was sharp.

'I am her friend, my lord, and nothing more. Without any support from your father, the restoration of your mother's strength has been a long and painful process.'

'Guard your words, sir. My father is not yet buried.'

Abel closed his eyes briefly. 'Please accept my apologies, your lordship. I wish only to emphasise your mother's resilience. She is recovering well and I believe she will benefit all the more by seeing you, my lord. Indeed, I promised that I would find you for her.'

'And so you have. I shall bring her here. We have a Dower House empty and waiting.'

'She may not wish for that, sir. You must give her time to adjust.' Abel inhaled deeply. 'Were you aware, from your late father, that you had a sister, my lord?'

'A sister? No, I have no sister.'

'You have, sir.'

'Then I do not know about her. Does she live with my mother?'

Unusually, Daisy thought, Abel was at a loss for words. She was beginning to feel very uneasy about sitting here listening to an exposure of the Redfern's private lives and wished again that Boyd was next to her instead of hovering somewhere at the back of the chamber.

'Your mother was obliged to give her up when she was born.'

386

James began to frown. 'There are not many reasons for that. Was she sickly or was she—' The furrows on his brow deepened. 'Dear God, no! Is that why father would not have her in his house? She took a lover.' He stood up and stepped towards Abel. 'So that is your interest in Redfern Abbey. You are saying that my sister – my half-sister, that is – is –'

James could barely say the words but Daisy knew what he meant. She stared at Abel and finished James's sentence in a whisper. 'Yours?'

'No, ma'am, I am not. My lord, I am most definitely not saying that.' It was the first time Abel had raised his voice. 'But your father believed she was my child and would not be persuaded otherwise.'

'You will have the grace to answer me truthfully, sir! Was he correct?' James retaliated.

Abel looked angry and took a moment to compose himself. Daisy wondered warily who James's sister might be and if Abel wasn't her father, why he appeared to be so involved with her.

Abel continued. 'It has taken me a long time to trace your sister. The Reverend Milo was instrumental in placing her as a newborn and if you do not believe me he will verify my searches.' He reached for a pocket inside his coat and withdrew a letter. 'This is a sworn statement of his actions at the time.'

Stanton came forward to take the folded paper and moved to the window to read it.

'So where is she, this half-sister of mine?' James insisted.

The silence in the room lengthened and grew heavy. Stanton appeared satisfied with the contents of the letter but his wife had not lessened her grip on Daisy's hand and was as curious as she to know the answer to James's question. 'Well, sir?' James pressed.

Abel took a breath and said, 'She is not your half-sister, my lord. She is your full blood sister.'

'You must be mistaken. Father never spoke of her.'

'He did not believe the truth when it was presented to him! The truth is—' Abel inhaled again. 'The truth is that Miss Higgins is your sister.'

'No, Mr Shipton! I cannot be!'The strangled cry of disbelief came from Daisy. 'You are incorrect, sir!'

Abel turned to her. 'Why do you say that, ma'am?'

'I cannot be James's sister. It is not possible for we are the same age.'

James added to this denial. 'That much is true. Daisy was born in the same year as I, *in the same month, even.* We cannot be brother and sister.'

'My lord, please sit down and calm yourself.' Mr Stanton gave his shoulder a gentle push and James retreated to his chair.

'You are, my lord,' Abel insisted. 'I have collected papers and affidavits that prove it; that the Reverend Milo has read and verified. Miss Higgins is your twin, sir. By some fate of nature she was born more than a week later than you and – and that caused the doubt in your father's mind.'

Daisy was stunned. She gazed at James whose face was distorted with distress. Her instinct was to rush across the room to him and she started to rise but Mrs Stanton kept a firm hold on her hand and tugged her back saying, 'Stay where you are, Daisy.'

'But we love each other,' she anguished.

James gazed at her with an unspoken agony in his eyes. 'It's true,' he murmured. 'I love her.'

Mr Stanton broke in. 'I believe you do, my lord. I noticed that there was an attraction between you from the very first day I saw you together and I remember my unease.'

388

'Then you knew about her? You knew she was my sister?' James cried.

'Never! My concern was due to the difference in status alone.'

James covered his face with his hands and croaked, 'I feel ill.'

As Daisy realised what they were on the point of doing last night, she felt a nausea rise in her throat and choked, 'James is my *brother?*' A turmoil of emotion swirled around her. She had fallen in love with her own *brother*. 'I want – *wanted* – him,' she whispered.

A glass of water appeared in front of her. 'You didn't know.' Mrs Stanton was speaking softly. 'How could you? You are not to blame and neither is his lordship.'

'I love him. I do,' Daisy whispered.

'Of course you love him. He is your brother,' Mrs Stanton continued. 'Had you been brought up as brother and sister you would love each other just as much, but in a different way.' She exchanged a glance with her husband who appeared as shocked as she and went on quickly, 'We have found out in time and we must thank God for his mercy.'

Daisy gulped at the water, spluttering it over her gown. She could have – they could have – Her stomach churned and she swallowed to quell the acid in her throat. Dear Lord, if this was true Abel had found her only minutes before – before – A horrified shudder ran down her back. Abel had not known of her secret liaisons with James and, surely, he had not suspected it? So why had he come to Redfern Village in search of her? What was she to him?

'Daisy?' James whispered. He was distraught. Daisy tried to get up to go and comfort him but Mrs Stanton restrained her. He cleared his throat and addressed Abel. 'You did not answer my question, sir. Was my father correct about your relationship with my mother?'

Daisy held her breath as she waited for his reply. Was it possible that Abel was her father? Certainly he had always behaved in a civil manner towards her. He seemed to be a good man and she would, she realised, welcome him as a parent. She watched his face contort as he wrestled with his answer and could bear it no longer. 'Are you my father, sir?' she cried.

'I wish I were.' It took him a few moments to compose himself. 'It would be so easy for me to say that I could be and I should like nothing more than to claim you as my daughter. But it would be a lie and it would defame your mother's reputation. She was a faithful wife to Edgar Collins and he is − was − your father.'

The small drawing room fell silent again as this devastating revelation was absorbed. Finally James stood up and announced, 'I shall visit my mother immediately. Mr Shipton, is she well enough to see me?'

'I believe she will be greatly improved when she is reunited with you and your sister, my lord.'

Mr Stanton too sprang into action. 'I shall have a carriage and four ready after luncheon.'

But James was impatient. 'A carriage will take too long. I should prefer to ride and arrive before nightfall. Will you be my guide, Mr Shipton?'

'Of course, my lord.'

Daisy looked around for Boyd. His face was impassive as though he had no reactions to this devastating news. But she knew her Boyd. He had stifled his feelings for the present to deal with at another time. She must speak with him soon and asked, 'Boyd, will you come with me in the carriage?'

Mrs Stanton answered, 'My husband and I shall travel with you. There will be an overnight stop at an inn, my lady.'

'My lady?' she repeated in a whisper.

'Yes, my lady. We shall take footmen to attend to your comforts on the journey.'

Her husband added, 'Boyd has duties in the stables, my lady.'

Daisy appealed directly to Boyd who had moved closer to the couch. 'Please come with me.'

Abel interceded to support her. 'Boyd has been a part Lady Daisy's life as Miss Higgins. She cannot sever all ties immediately.'

'Or ever, ma'am!' Daisy protested. 'Nor should I wish to.' She appealed to Mr Stanton. 'The stables can spare him, surely?'

'If that is your wish, my lady.'

'It is.'

'Then it is settled,' James stated. 'We have much to prepare.'

Boyd spoke directly to James. 'I'll take one of the hunters if I may, sir, and ride with the carriage.'

Daisy recognised a firm tone in Boyd's request. A nod and wave of James's hand was enough to silence the Stantons. She believed that Boyd would have taken the horse anyway with or without permission. He would not have let her travel without *his* protection. She was lucky to have such a brother. Except that, dear heaven, if she was James's sister she could not be Boyd's sister too, could she? Maybe she was his half-sister? That didn't make sense either, for he would be half-brother to James and, surely, Abel would have told them that too? Daisy's confusion returned. If James was a full brother to her, then Boyd – Boyd couldn't be.

Boyd had said little during Abel's speech and had

returned to the grave, distanced man she was becoming accustomed to, until this morning when he had supported and cheered her during the walk to the Abbey. She drew him aside as the others discussed the journey.

'Are you not happy with this news,' she asked. 'You seemed more cheerful earlier.'

'Abel had given me reason to be. He had told me that neither of us was a true child of the parents who had raised us. That alone cheered me as they were such awful people. I asked him about you but he would not be drawn except to say that you were not my true sister.'

'And that gave you joy?'

Boyd took a breath and opened his mouth to speak but no words came out.

'Well, your joy has certainly disappeared now. You are frowning at me,' Daisy commented.

'I don't mean to, but I fear our lives will be so very different now that you are a lady.'

Daisy was astounded. 'Abel said it and I echo it now. We cannot ignore our past. You will continue to be a part of my life, and I a part of yours.'

'That may not be possible.'

'Boyd, you are talking nonsense. Nothing will change.'

'Don't be naive, Daisy. Of course your life will change. You are the sister of a lord and I am a stable hand.'

'Now you are being ridiculous.'

She would have carried on the argument with him if Mrs Stanton had not tugged insistently on her arm, urging her to return to her home and prepare for the journey. She glanced longingly and ruefully at James in conversation with Abel and as she did James moved away. 'I should like to speak with Daisy before I leave.'

His steward replied, 'Come, gentlemen, we shall make ready the horses. My wife will chaperone her ladyship.' He gave a formal bow, added, 'My lord,' and left the room.

Abel and Boyd followed, leaving Daisy with James and Mrs Stanton who went to stand by the window. James held out his hands uncertainly but Daisy stood still and shook her head. She dared not even touch him until her head was clearer about her feelings for him and — and for Boyd.

'I don't want to believe this, but I must,' he said. He sounded weary. 'I feel so alone, so isolated.'

'So do I and I am finding it too much to take in. But at least I have Boyd to support me.'

'And we both have our mother. We must thank God for her.'

Daisy agreed. 'It will be easier to think of you as my brother when we are with her.'

'We can still be together,' James suggested. 'But not as we were before.'

'I don't think it will be that easy, James. I am in a turmoil about what we meant to each other. How did it happen?'

'I don't know. It just did and it was real for me. There was something about you that drew me towards you, Daisy,' James said. 'I knew it from the day I set eyes on you outside the park gates. Do you remember?'

'Oh yes. I think I fell a little in love with you then and a little more when I saw you in the counting house on quarter day.'

He managed a laugh. 'You were the lowliest maid in the Abbey and you were able to sign your name in the steward's pay book.'

'I was warned about you several times and sent away from the Abbey in the end.'

'But they could not keep us apart.'

They gazed at each other. 'I should like to embrace you, Daisy,' James said eventually. 'A brother may do that, surely?'

Daisy shook her head. 'Please don't. I think we should keep away from each other for a while; until I am accustomed to who I am.'

'I don't want to do that,' James replied.

'*You must, my lord*' Mrs Stanton interrupted them. 'Your sister has more to come to terms with than you, sir.'

James frowned. 'Are you saying goodbye to me, Daisy?'

'No, James. We shall meet again at High Fell when I have had time to think and clear my head.'

Mrs Stanton added, 'You will arrive first, my lord. You must prepare your mother to receive her daughter.'

'Very well, ladies.' James bowed formally and went after the others.

Daisy lapsed into her own thoughtful silence as she travelled. Although bewildered by recent events, it was a new and exciting experience for her. She had a mother, a true mother who wished to see her! It was also a time of grief. She had gained and lost a father in the space of a morning. She had never met him so her loss was not as great as James's. Her separation from James was a much greater hurt. She didn't need to have it explained to her that it would be difficult for them to live in close proximity for the foreseeable future and her spirits were low.

She spent much of the journey staring out of the carriage window catching glimpses of Boyd as he rode. She wished she was riding out there with him, with the wind and the rain in her face. He must have noticed her watching him but stubbornly refused to return her waves, or even acknowledge her.

Did he believe she would spurn him because they had discovered a difference in their births? As she reflected on this she realised that he did. He was a proud man. He was his own man, not given to following the lead of others without good reason. He had believed that marriage to Joseph was in her best interests yet had taken her side when she had complained of his lewd behaviour. She loved Boyd for that.

He could not avoid her at the inn where they stayed for the night. The West Riding was prosperous, punctuated by the tall stone chimneys of mills from spreading townships, and the inn proved to be well appointed and comfortable. They were shown upstairs to private rooms for sitting and dining. The maid who attended Daisy's chamber offered her services to dress for supper.

She was embarrassed at first by her close attention but the maid appeared to enjoy her task and Daisy wished to present herself well. She was grateful for the loan of a soft woollen gown in a gentle shade of green from Mrs Stanton's wardrobe. It had belonged to her daughter who had gone as a lady's maid to a duchess and received much grander castoffs now. The maid pressed white lace collar and cuffs, pulled her corset laces tight and dressed her hair with borrowed combs and feathers. In spite of her fatigue, Daisy was in better spirits when she entered the dining room.

The furniture was dark oak and the heavy chairs scraped noisily on the floorboards as Mr Stanton and Boyd rose to their feet. Boyd had on a new jacket, fashionably long, a shirt with a high white collar and silk tie. She smiled at him but he nodded formally, avoiding her eyes. Daisy was cross but did not wish to argue with him in front of others. A footman came forward and pulled out her chair at the dining table.

395

'You look very well in that gown, my lady,' Mrs Stanton said.

'Thank you ma'am,' Daisy replied.

The hot food was carried in and they ate in silence as they were all hungry from the journey. But when the wine was drunk and the pudding presented, Daisy's dining companions relaxed and they talked. Well, she realised, Boyd conversed with Mr Stanton about coaches, highways and the value of railways while his wife occupied her discussing boots and bonnets. Finally, Mrs Stanton suggested they go to bed as they had to be on their way at first light. Boyd stood up and bowed formally as she left. She pursed her lips, flared her nostrils and returned his formality with a steady gaze. Her message was clear and he chose to remain expressionless so that her crossness turned to anger. A title and some pretty clothes did not make her any different from the girl he had known all his life!

The maid helped her get ready for bed, removed the warming pan and tended the fire. As Daisy climbed onto the huge four poster furnished with heavy drapes to keep out the cold, she made herself a promise.

'No,' she said to herself. 'This is not how it is going to be between us.' As she drifted into sleep she remembered a promise he had made to her and murmured, 'He can teach me to ride for a start.'

Chapter 37

The large Redfern carriage laboured up the track to High Fell and the party were obliged to get out and walk over the stone bridge while Boyd and the driver led the horses across. Daisy's anxiety at meeting a mother she had never known became acute. How would they be with each other? Her mother had been ill and Daisy hoped the shock of seeing her son and daughter would not be too much for her constitution. What if she refused to be reunited after so many years? Daisy tried not to dwell on that but she became increasingly apprehensive as they climbed the fell and was glad that Boyd was with her.

'It can't be much further. I'll ride ahead,' Boyd suggested.

The farm was in view when he returned. 'All is well,' he called. 'Lord Redfern and Abel have arrived. We are expected and welcome.'

Daisy's relief brought a smile to her face. Her companions in the carriage were reassured also and they arrived hopefully at a farmhouse that was grander than Daisy had imagined. She stood in a cavernous hall with a wide wooden staircase and a huge fireplace crackling with logs. A large rectangular table was set in front of it. James walked towards her with an older woman on his arm. She is pretty, Daisy thought. Her hair was greying and as she neared, Daisy noticed her features were lined with the weariness of past troubles. But it gave her a fragile ethereal appearance that was appealing. As she stared at both of them, she realised where James's handsome features came from. Her own face, she knew, was less beautiful.

Daisy's nervousness intensified as they neared and she was grateful to James for opening the conversation.

'My dearest Daisy,' he said gently. 'This is our mother.'

'Are you? Are you truly?' she whispered.

Her mother nodded. She seemed unable to speak. Tears were welling in her eyes and spilling over onto her soft cheeks. But she held out her arms and Daisy fell forward into them as her own tears ran down her face. Her mother clung to her tightly. 'I knew Abel would find you for me, my darling, darling child.'

Eventually her mother released her and stood back to take in all of her appearance and added. 'But you are no longer a child. You are a woman – and a very gracious lady.'

Daisy found her voice at last. 'Are you well, Mother?'

'I am. I have been restored to health with the help of friends and you, my children, have given me back my happiness.' She opened her arms again, putting one around James and the other around Daisy. 'We have much to talk about. Shall we dine first?'

There was a delicious aroma of roasting mutton seeping through from the kitchen and the party was hungry. James sat on one side of his mother. As Daisy was about to sit down at the other side, she looked around the table.

'Where is Boyd?' she asked.

Mr Stanton answered her. 'He is helping Abel with the horses.'

'He will be joining us, won't he?'

Her mother replied, 'I have set places for both of them, dear.'

'Oh. Oh yes, I see.'

For the next two days, between eating and sleeping, James, Daisy and Beth walked and talked on the fell, always accompanied by the watchful and protective Stantons. Boyd and Abel occupied themselves with surveying the farm and fell on horseback.

At breakfast on the third day Mr Stanton reminded James of his duties. 'We must return to the Abbey for your father's funeral, my lord,' he explained

'Of course,' James agreed.

'I do not wish to leave my mother yet,' Daisy said anxiously.

'Then stay,' James suggested. 'You will not be expected to attend the graveside and I shall make your excuses at the wake.'

'I should like Boyd to stay too.'

'Of course,' James repeated.

The carriage set off the following morning. Before James mounted his horse he announced, 'I have decided to complete my education at Cambridge and then travel. I shall do the Grand Tour. This will keep me away from the Abbey for several years. I may even find myself a wife.'

'You will be sure to visit when you are in Yorkshire?' Beth queried lightly.

'Oh yes. I shall look forward to returning here. Always.'

'Will you write?' Daisy asked.

'I'll send letters to Mother. You will take good care of her, won't you, Daisy?'

'I shall.'

'Then this is goodbye for the present.' James stretched out his arms towards Daisy, offering his hands. She chewed her lip nervously but took both his hands in hers, clutching at them firmly and giving them a small shake. 'And Mother will look after you,' he added. 'She is a wise lady.' He did not release his grip.

'Who will watch out for you, James?'

'Stanton will engage a learned professor and his wife to accompany me on my travels.' His horse snorted as he waited.

'Goodbye then.' Daisy didn't smile but she felt more comfortable with him as her brother now.

'Goodbye, Daisy.'

Their fingers slid apart and James reached up for the reins and placed his foot in the stirrup. He hopped a couple of times then heaved himself into the saddle. 'Goodbye, Mother,' he added and turned his horse's head in the direction of the carriage.

As the party rumbled away, Beth said, 'He is very mature for one so young.'

Abel commented, 'He's an aristocrat. He's been trained for it all his life.'

'I suppose so. He has a lot of power, hasn't he?' He says I can go and live in the Dower House; Daisy too, or in the Abbey if she wishes. We should all be near to your business concerns in the South Riding.'

'What do you want to do, Daisy?' Abel asked.

'I don't know.' She meant it. She wanted to be with her

mother, but she wanted to be with Boyd as well, and wandered away to find him. She did not wish to reside at the Abbey, she thought. She felt no strong compulsion to return.

'Well,' Abel remarked as he and Beth went indoors. 'I have decided to turn over High Fell to Boyd. He has been asking me about ladies' saddles. Daisy would like him to teach her to ride as well as her mother can.'

'Really?' Beth commented and looked at Abel. 'Let us leave them to their lesson.'

Abel drew two of the large carver chairs near to the fire. 'Sit down, Beth.' He covered his face with his hands for a second then looked directly at her. 'I have never felt so drained of energy. Since I learnt of Edgar's death I have had so much to deal with, when all I have ever wanted was to be here with you.'

'Then why did you not stay with me when I needed you most?'

'When you were a married woman, you mean?' he argued. 'We were both acutely aware of the dangers.' He ran his fingers through his greying hair. 'I knew that I couldn't forget you but I tried really hard to build another life. It's just that there was never anyone who came close to filling your shoes. Ever since our first meeting on the Fell you have been the only woman in my thoughts.'

Beth stretched out her hand to grasp his and they sat, side by side, watching the flames.

'You saved my life, Abel. I did not deserve it because, although I have loved you since that day, I had to push you away to do my duty by my husband, albeit a husband who disrespected and abused me.'

'And I dared not stay. I should have given into my desires and ruined you.'

401

'I – I wish you had,' Beth added wistfully. 'I ruined myself instead. But it is over now and I shall not waste another day in remorse. I often wanted Edgar dead and I pray to God to forgive me for that. I shall not grieve for him.'

'Nor I. You are a free woman and I love you.'

He slid forward to kneel on the floorboards. 'Dearest Beth, will you marry me?'

'Oh Abel, do you have to ask me? Of course I will. But we ought to wait awhile before we have the ceremony.'

'You mean allow for mourning? Dear heaven, I have waited for you for too many years already. I am not going to wait six months or more before we can be together as man and wife.'

'I am not going to ask you. I do not wish to waste any more time either. It is still possible for me to become with child, but the years are slipping away.'

Abel's heart did a somersault and his loins stirred. 'You mean we can – you will –'

'Take you to my bed,' she finished softly.

He stood up and tugged at her hand. 'Come on, then.'

She rose to her feet with a hitherto unknown girlish excitement bubbling through her.

'Come *on*,' he repeated, pulling her towards the stairs.

'What are your feelings for James now, my dear?'

Daisy shrugged. 'I shall always love him because he is my brother. But we must live separate lives. I understand that. James does too. It is very odd, Mother. My attraction for James was immediate and flared quickly. It was out of control and I was confused. When Abel told me who he really was I felt quite ill. Now – now my feelings for him are, well, sort of unclear. I mean I love him but not in the same way. I do not think we shall share our lives. His world is so very far removed from mine.'

'It need not be.'

Daisy shuddered. 'He has been schooled to be a lord. I have had no such preparation to be a lady. It will difficult for me.'

'Take your time to decide, my dear.' She paused before adding, 'You are very fond of Boyd, aren't you?'

'I have not known a life without him. Neither do I want to.'

'That is understandable. You thought *he* was your brother,' her mother stated.

Daisy was silent for a moment. 'I believe it was my feelings for Boyd that confused me in the first place. My regard for him runs deep and always has. It is different from the way I felt about James before – before, well you know. You see I *believe* in Boyd. I trust him. It's as though our hearts are in step with each other and, I admit, I have clung to him at times.' Daisy gave a rueful half-laugh. 'I asked him to marry me when I was about eight. He put me right of course and as we grew up he set me apart from him whilst still caring for me.'

'Were you hurt by that?'

'Yes I was. He said I should marry and I thought it was because he wished to find a wife himself and wanted me settled first. He tried to separate our lives but I truly believe that he found it as difficult as I did.'

'Well, my darling, it is clear to me that he no longer wishes to be separated from you.'

'Do you think so, Mother? Since Abel told us about my birth he has avoided me even more. He spends his time with the horses and talking to Abel about sheep farming!'

'He sees you as the daughter of a lord now and not his little sister who was brought up in a cottage.'

'Yes, that's it, Mother! He thinks that he is beneath me! How can that be when we were brought up together? He has expected me to change but I think it is he who has changed, not me.'

'He does not know that, does he?'

'But I am the same person and so is he! I cannot let him walk away from me now.' She lowered her voice and added, 'I shall not.'

'Why do you say that, my dear?'

'Because I love him, of course!' Daisy cried, and repeated it softly to herself. 'I love him.' She looked up with tears in her eyes. 'I love him, Mother, and he constantly puts this distance between us. He behaves as though he is afraid to be close to me.'

'Oh I don't think he is afraid, do you?'

Daisy shook her head. 'Boyd does not flinch from fear. He faces it. Then why does he avoid me?'

'He is allowing you to choose the life you want. He is thinking only of your welfare.'

'Really?' Daisy blinked away her tears.

Beth smiled and nodded. 'You can't see it but I can because he is like Abel in that respect.'

'But Abel loves you as – well, as a husband loves his wife.'

'Dearest Daisy, open your eyes to Boyd as a man. He is a fine young fellow and he is not your brother. Do not treat him as such.'

Daisy stared into the distance. Might Boyd love her in the same way as Abel loved her mother?

Beth added, 'How is your riding coming along?'

'Very well,' Daisy answered slowly and thoughtfully.

*　*　*

Boyd lifted her down from the saddle and they tethered their horses to a gate. The day was bright and sharp with white clouds hurrying across a blue sky.

Daisy surveyed the desolate moorland and commented, 'The wind is wilful today but it adds to the beauty of the fell.'

Boyd climbed the gate and shaded his eyes against the sun. 'There's a lake in the distance.'

'It's a tarn. It's called a tarn.'

'We'll ride there one day. As soon as you feel confident enough, we'll take a picnic and make a day of it.'

'I'd like that.'

He sat on top of the gate and offered his hand. 'Come and sit beside me and share the view.'

She clambered up beside him. 'Do you like the Dales, Boyd?'

'Very much. Being here is the first time I have felt truly free.'

A lock of hair escaped from underneath her riding hat and whipped across her face. 'I feel as though I belong here.'

'So you should. You were born here.'

'Thank you for teaching me to ride. Are we kindred spirits again, just as we were before Redfern?'

'We can never go back to how we were when we were brother and sister.'

'Was I such a nuisance to you?'

'What makes you say that? You were never a burden to me.'

'I thought so at the Abbey, when you pushed me away and tried to marry me off to that horrible Joseph.'

'I had my reasons.'

'I was so hurt. I felt I was losing you. Perhaps that was why I was so vulnerable to James. Why did you do it?'

He stared into the distance and did not answer.

'I don't want any more secrets between us, Boyd.'

'I had to do it. I was in love with you and you were my sister.'

'But I have known that I loved you since I was eight years old.'

'I was *in love* with you! It was different. It was desire, passion, a love I had not experienced before. I prayed to God for the strength to overcome it.'

Daisy had felt those urges too, more so since he had been teaching her to ride and she wished to tell him so. 'During the time we have been at High Fell I have been praying for us to regain the nearness we used to have.'

'It has not been lost. I have tried to resist it and have failed. When Abel told me the truth about your birth I was overjoyed, until I realised that you would be destined for the higher levels of society.'

'But you were mistaken. Abbey life is not for me. I am not prepared for it, nor do I wish to live it.'

'What do you wish for, Daisy?'

'I want a life here in the Dales, on a farm like this one.'

'Well I suppose you can have it. You are a wealthy woman.'

'I am not. My brother James is a wealthy man. All of Redfern belongs to him and anything I have is by his grace and favour. Anyway, I do not want a life in the Dales if I cannot have you with it.' She inhaled sharply and went on, 'I love you, Boyd. I admire and respect you and – and I want you as a lover not a brother.' There, she had said it. Her heart was on her sleeve for him to see. She held her breath as she waited for his response.

'Do you mean that, Daisy? Do not say it if you do not truly mean it because I really do love you.'

Daisy let out a ragged sigh that quickly turned into a smile. 'I mean it, Boyd. I cannot imagine my life without you.'

He jumped down from the gate and placed his hands around her waist to lift her to the ground. 'I want to kiss you like your lover not your brother.'

She raised her face to the sun and closed her eyes. His lips discovered hers with a gentle exploration at first that quickly developed into a searching hunger and then a passionate desire that she returned wholeheartedly. Boyd was all she wanted in a husband. She had known that since she was eight years old.

When they paused for breath he whispered, 'Shall we marry soon?'

'Oh I think so, don't you?' she murmured. 'There is so much more I want to find out about you. Kiss me again, Boyd.'

They parted eventually and went back to their horses. He helped her into the saddle, mounted his own horse and they set off side by side to return to High Fell and their future together.